D0861285

Bison Frontiers of Imagination

MILES J. BREUER

The Man with the Strange Head

and Other Early
Science Fiction Stories

Edited and with an introduction
by Michael R. Page

UNIVERSITY OF NEBRASKA PRESS

LINCOLN AND LONDON

Library of Congress
Cataloging-in-Publication Data
Breuer, Miles John, 1889–1945.
The man with the strange head
and other early science fiction stories /
Miles J. Breuer ;
edited and with an
introduction by
Michael R. Page.
p.   cm. —
(Bison frontiers of imagination)
Includes
bibliographical references.
ISBN 978-0-8032-1587-0
(pbk. : alk. paper)
1. Breuer, Miles John,
1889–1945—Correspondence.
I. Page, Michael R., 1967–
II. Title.
PS3503.R494M36 2008
813'.52—dc22
2008008625
Set in Scala by Bob Reitz.
Designed by R.W. Boeche.

Contents

Acknowledgments

Preparation of this volume was made possible by a Maude Hammond Fling Fellowship from the Graduate College at the University of Nebraska–Lincoln (UNL) and from grants from the UNL English Department and the Center for Great Plains Studies. I'd like to thank the following faculty members at UNL for their encouragement and suggestions: Stephen Behrendt, Robert Stock, Laura White, Guy Reynolds, Franz Blaha, Stephen Hilliard, and department chair Joy Ritchie. I thank the English Department's office staff for valuable assistance with paperwork, copying, and all those other intangibles. Grateful acknowledgment for research and technical assistance also goes out to the following librarians: Gene Bundy from the Jack Williamson Science Fiction Library at Eastern New Mexico University; Kathie Johnson, Kate Cain, Paul Myers, and Carmella Orosco from UNL; the staff at the Nebraska State Historical Society; the Spencer and Watson Libraries at the University of Kansas; and Kim Jorgenson at Lincoln City Libraries for her diligent work in uncovering facts relating to Breuer's biography. Further thanks to my editor, Elisabeth Chretien, for answering questions along the way and for her enthusiasm for this project. I'd also like to thank the science fiction greats: the late Jack Williamson for an encouraging e-mail as this project got underway, and James Gunn for the hours he spent visiting with me at his office and over lunch (and the numerous e-mails since) at the University of Kansas where he shared his editorial insights. I'd like to recognize my father, Monte, and my brother, Kevin, who have always served as sounding-boards for my ideas and projects. Finally, to my wife, Susan, who has to listen—and listens well.

Miles J. Breuer

Science Fiction Pioneer of the Nebraska Plains

MICHAEL R. PAGE

In March 1926 a new magazine appeared on newsstands with a wondrous cover that showed skaters gliding on a sheet of ice with a Saturn-like planet looming in the background, and it featured classic stories by H. G. Wells, Jules Verne, Edgar Allan Poe, and others. This was the April 1926 issue of *Amazing Stories*, and with its appearance a new literary genre, science fiction, was born. Well . . . not quite. Science fiction had been around since the early nineteenth century when Mary Shelley published her classic novel *Frankenstein* in 1818 and had been a recognizable, but still largely undefined, genre when Verne penned his *Voyages extraordinaires* from 1864 to the end of the nineteenth century and Wells produced his scientific romances and stories in the 1890s. The selection of reprinted stories that Hugo Gernsback included in *Amazing*'s first issue, and those he published over the course of the rest of 1926, bear this out. Still, Gernsback's *Amazing Stories* was the first magazine devoted exclusively to science fiction (called "scientifiction" in the early years), and in its pages the genre, particularly in its American idiom, was formed and defined.

Gernsback was an innovative publisher, with a special interest in radio and electronics, who had published several technological magazines since the first decade of the new century, starting with *Modern Electrics* in 1908. When *Modern Electrics* ended its run in 1913, Gernsback started a new magazine called *Electrical Experimenter*, which eventually morphed into *Science and Invention* in 1920. In these magazines Gernsback often included fiction and even published his own novel, *Ralph 124C 41+*, which also appears in the Bison Frontiers of Imagination (BFI) series. It dramatized the ideals of the scientific philosophy and the wonders of science and technology that were fast becoming part of everyday life. In the introduction to the Bison Books edition of *Ralph 124C 41+*, Jack Williamson notes that "the book was written to dazzle and enchant the reader with the wonders of coming technology."[1] And that it certainly does, despite its stylistic limitations. *Ralph 124C 41+* was the first of many significant science fiction stories published in the teens that led to the development of the specialized category in the 1920s.

Science fiction had been developing in the pulps — the early American popular fiction magazines — and in the more literary fiction magazines in Britain since the late nineteenth century. The pulp era began when Frank Munsey's boys' paper *Golden Argosy* evolved into the adult all-fiction magazine *Argosy* in 1896. The success of *Argosy* at the turn of the century led to many competing all-fiction magazines, and Munsey expanded his publication list with *All-Story* in 1905, where the scientific romances of Edgar Rice Burroughs and A. Merritt were later featured in the 1910s. Science fiction, mostly of a high romance-adventure vein, was regularly featured in the fiction pulps of the early twentieth century, and by the end of the second decade other genre categories were emerging and specialty pulps began to appear. The first specialty pulp, *The Railroad Man's Magazine*, appeared as early as 1906, but the now-familiar major genre categories did not fully materialize until later: *Detective Story Monthly* appeared in 1915, *Western Story* in 1919, and *Love Story* in 1921. The short-lived *Thrill Book*, which appeared in 1919, anticipated the development of the weird fantasy and science fiction categories in the '20s. The success of both Burroughs and Merritt was instrumental in the future development of science fiction, despite the fact that their stories emphasized the romance rather than the science of the scientific romance. The "sense of wonder" that still awes readers, even in the most sober hard science fiction of today such as the planetary explorations of Gregory Benford or Arthur C. Clarke, derives from Burroughs's and Merritt's fantasies of forgotten worlds. Burroughs remains widely popular today, as is evident from the success of his editions in the BFI series, and he must be counted among the central figures in the history of science fiction. As James Gunn notes in his genre history, *Alternate Worlds*, "Burroughs demonstrated once again the popular appeal of science fiction . . . [he] carried the pulps through a difficult time—if not alone at least in significant part. Now the field was ready for the specialized magazines, and a young publisher of radio and invention publications was dreaming about a magazine that would predict in detail the delightful, thrilling future in store for us through scientific progress."[2]

In the '20s Gernsback began devoting more space to fiction in his popular science magazines. As magazine historian Mike Ashley notes, Gernsback regularly published one scientific story per issue of *Science and Invention*, and in 1923 he published a special all-fiction issue with great success, the same year that another landmark pulp magazine, *Weird Tales*, was introduced.[3] Undoubtedly aware of the success that the scientific romances of Burroughs and Merritt were enjoying in the Munsey adventure pulps, Gernsback recognized a market for a new genre of fiction compatible with the new electrical technologies and the growing engineering paradigm that his magazines addressed. Historian Leon Stover has argued that science fiction emerged during what he calls the "research revolution" that took place in the closing decades of the nineteenth century when American industrialism and invention blossomed. Stover concludes: "Magazine science fiction, then, is a response to the research revolution, to the romance of industrial research. The romance is a bit faded now, but in the early days, when research was a new gospel to be missionized, its spirit was quite literally electrifying."[4] The obvious symbolic figure for this research revolution was Thomas Edison, and it is worth noting that Gernsback's associate editor, T. O'Connor Sloane, was Edison's son-in-law. Soon Gernsback was to launch a magazine wholly devoted to science fiction in direct response to this budding "romance of industrial research."

Gernsback launched *Amazing Stories* with the April 1926 issue, and science fiction as a recognizable genre of popular fiction was born. The magazine soon became widely popular and influential among science and radio enthusiasts, first reprinting classics of scientific fiction and then launching the careers of many new writers. In the 1930s *Amazing* was joined by Clayton Magazines' *Astounding Stories of Super-Science* (which began in 1930 and is still published today as *Analog*), *Wonder Stories* (Gernsback's immediate follow-up after he lost control of *Amazing*), and many others as the years went on. *Amazing Stories* weathered many ups and downs, changes of publishers, editors, and formats, and only recently ceased publication in 2005 after a run of over six hundred issues—though one expects that it will eventually reemerge.

In the early issues of *Amazing*, Gernsback relied on reprints of works by Poe, Verne, and Wells among others, as well as works by writers he had published in his radio magazines, since he had to build a readership for the new fiction out of which new writers could emerge. This happened quickly, and many new writers of note began contributing regularly to the magazine in its second year. However, in 1926 only eleven new stories appeared in the first nine issues of the magazine, and almost all of these were either from one-shot authors (perhaps pseudonyms of Gernsback and his staff) or from writers who had regularly appeared in *Science and Invention*. Late in 1926 a two-part serial, *Beyond the Pole*, appeared by a new author, A. Hyatt Verrill. Verrill, who would go on to become one of the most prolific writers of the early magazine era, could arguably be called the first new science fiction writer of consequence in Gernsback's magazine. But Verrill had already been writing juvenile novels (in his *Boy Adventurers* and *Radio Detectives* sequences) and other fiction since the middle teens, which were nominally science fiction, in addition to numerous exaggerated accounts of his real-life adventures into the South American interior. By the time Verrill appeared in *Amazing* he was fifty-six years old and had a substantial writing résumé.

Instead, the first new writer of consequence who can be said to have started his fiction-writing career in the science fiction magazines was Dr. Miles J. Breuer, a prominent physician and community leader from Lincoln, Nebraska. His first story, "The Man with the Strange Head," appeared in the January 1927 issue of *Amazing*, and from that beginning he went on to publish thirty-six stories, two novels, three poems, two editorials, and numerous letters in *Amazing* and its various competitors through 1942. It is not a stretch to suggest that Breuer *is* the first original writer to come out of the science fiction magazine market. Some of his contemporaries who also appeared in the next few years in *Amazing* had published science fiction earlier in *Weird Tales*, including Edmond Hamilton and Clare Winger Harris, but Breuer was the first of the new writers to get his start in *Amazing*. He would go on to be one of the most popular and influential writers in these pioneering years. Breuer's work was, in general, more representative of the genre ideals that Gernsback claimed he was looking for in his editorials and advertisements, even though much of what appeared in *Amazing* did not actually fit those ideals. Thus, Breuer is also, perhaps, the consummate writer of the early *Amazing*. Through careful devotion to the ideals of the genre, and by using Wells as a model, Breuer led the way toward the mature science fiction that emerged in the next generation during John W. Campbell's Golden Age.

Miles J. Breuer was born in Chicago on January 3, 1889, to Charles and Barbara Breuer, both immigrants from Czechoslovakia. The Breuers moved to Nebraska in 1893 while Charles pursued his medical studies at Creighton University in Omaha, where he received his MD in 1897. Charles Breuer became a prominent physician in southeastern Nebraska and an active member of the Czech community, publishing many popular medical articles in local and national Czechoslovak publications. Miles Breuer grew up in the Czech community of Crete, Nebraska, and graduated from Crete High School in 1906. He earned his bachelor's and master's degrees from the University of Texas in 1911 and his medical degree from Rush Medical College at the University of Chicago in 1915. He began practicing medicine in partnership with his father in Lincoln in June 1915 and was married to Julia Strejic in 1916. (They had three children: Rosalie, Stanley, and Mildred. The two girls became successful physicians in their own right, but Stanley was tragically killed in a 1939 hiking accident.)

Not long after his marriage, Breuer's fledgling medical practice was interrupted by World War I, and he served for twenty months in France as a first lieutenant in the medical corps, where he worked to combat disease; indeed, his experiences as a frontline medical doctor sometimes inform his writing. A small collection of Breuer's war photographs is housed at the Nebraska State Historical Society. After the war, Breuer was extremely active in the local medical community and in other civic organizations, holding memberships and leadership roles in several medical associations, the Optimist's Club, the American Legion, the Elks, the Masons, the Chamber of Commerce, and the local schools, running for the board in 1928. He organized the junior Boy Scout movement, the Wolf-Cub Scouts, in Lincoln and is said to have been an avid hiker and nature photographer.[5]

Before beginning his career as a fiction writer, Breuer, like his father, frequently contributed medical articles to Czechoslovak newspapers, including a health column in the largest Czech agricultural monthly in America; he also frequently published medical papers and articles in both professional journals and popular periodicals from the late teens through the '30s. One article on menopause, "Change of Life" (*Hygeia*, May 1931), was recently cited in Judith Houck's *Hot and Bothered: Women, Medicine, and Menopause in Modern America* (2006), and another, "The Construction of Chemical Laboratory Equipment" (*Journal of Laboratory and Clinical Medicine* 2 [1916–17]), in Joel D. Howell's *Technology in the Hospital: Transforming Patient Care in the Early Twentieth Century* (1996). In both cases, Breuer's articles are cited as representative samples of medical practice in the early twentieth century. Other articles appeared in *Hygeia* in the years that Breuer produced his major fiction: "Something I Ate" (February 1930), "Tonics" (August 1930), and "Value Received for Doctors' Bills" (February 1931). In 1925 he was appointed to the editorial board of *Social Science*, the publication of the honorary social science fraternity Phi Gamma Mu in recognition of his work with college students suffering from psychological and social problems while at the University of Nebraska, where Breuer served as consulting physician. Breuer's interest in psychology and social dynamics would later figure into much of his science fiction. In later years, his interest in photography led to articles in photography magazines. Toward the end of his career, Breuer also published a brief how-to article in *The Writer*, which gives some insight into his writing process and is rather poignant considering that by that point Breuer's own fiction writing had virtually stopped. Here Breuer instructs beginning writers to "nail down the vague germ-idea so it does not escape" and then systematically build the story from there.[6] As involved as Breuer was, it is a wonder that he had time for science fiction at all. Yet he managed to be one of the most prolific writers in the early years of magazine science fiction.

The high point of Breuer's early medical writing is his handbook *Index of Physiotherapeutic Technic*, where he catalogs a variety of methods for physical therapy, using both tried and true traditional methods (i.e., the human touch) and new advances in understanding and technology that facilitate patient recovery. The handbook purports to be one of the first such books on the topic of physical therapy and is meant as a quick ready-reference for practicing physicians. In the introduction to the book Breuer writes, "The widespread interest of the medical profession in the use of physical agents in treating the sick prompted this book. It seemed to the author that an index of technique proven valuable in the treatment of various diseases amenable to physical therapy might help to standardize technique and give a better method of comparing results."[7] This is reflective of the basic attitude toward technology, science, and human psychology that Breuer was to endorse in his science fiction. More than most of Gernsback's early writers, Breuer followed the ideals that Gernsback called for in his initial editorial for the field where he insisted that *Amazing Stories* was an entirely *new* sort of fiction magazine. As Gernsback famously wrote: " . . . a magazine of 'Scientifiction' is a pioneer in its field in America. By 'scientifiction' I mean the Jules Verne, H. G. Wells, and Edgar Allan Poe type of story—a charming romance intermingled with scientific fact and prophetic vision."[8] A few paragraphs later Gernsback voiced the general thesis behind science fiction (probably derived from Wells) that has been repeated in its essentials by most historians of the field ever since:

It must be remembered that we live in an entirely new world. Two-hundred years ago, stories of this kind were not possible. Science, through its various branches of mechanics, electricity, astronomy, etc., enters so intimately into all our lives today, and we are so much immersed in this science, that we have become rather prone to take new inventions and discoveries for granted. Our entire mode of living has changed with the present progress, and it is little wonder, therefore, that many fantastic situations—impossible 100 years ago—are brought about today. It is in these situations that the new romancers find their great inspiration.[9]

Of course, further on in this editorial and in later ones Gernsback advocated scientifiction as a vehicle for what Bleiler calls "sugar-coated education into science; inspiration toward a scientific career; and prophecy of future technology."[10] And though Breuer is notable for being one of the writers who actively refined Gernsback's initial definition to insist on literary values of style, character, and psychologically nuanced themes—not dull stories of scientific pedagogy—he was at the same time writing the kind of Wellsian stories that Gernsback distinguished as scientifiction, as opposed to the science-fantasy romances of Burroughs and Merritt (though some of these were reprinted in the pages of *Amazing*, too) and the super-scientific space opera that would later emerge and come to dominate the magazine.

Indeed, Breuer contributed a significant editorial essay of his own, "The Future of Scientifiction" (see appendix 1 in this volume), which further defined the fledgling genre. Reiterating Gernsback's point that everyday life was becoming increasingly oriented to the technological and the scientific, Breuer argued that as scientifiction progressed it would develop a more refined literary technique and take its place as a significant category of world literature. Recognizing the literary limitations of its early form of discourse, Breuer nonetheless predicted that scientific fiction would "take its seat at the banquet" with other literary forms because it examined the technological present and future and the real consequences of change on human beings and, therefore, could not be dismissed.

While Gernsback's inaugural editorial is rightfully famous in the history of science fiction, Breuer's needs greater attention. It is an encouraging and anticipatory essay that voices many of the central attitudes of the genre's later critical discourse. These significant editorials can be grouped with another fairly well-known essay published in the Fall 1928 issue of *Amazing Stories Quarterly* by a young reader named Jack Williamson, who became one of the major writers in the field. In "Scientifiction, Searchlight of Science," his first appearance in a science fiction magazine, Williamson reaffirmed Gernsback's wondrous vision of the genre and claimed that "the chief function of scientifiction is the creation of real pictures of new things, new ideas, and new dreams."[11] Though he echoes Gernsback in this prize-winning essay, Williamson had, in part, developed his position through a thoughtful reading of Breuer's fiction and letters that had appeared in *Amazing*, since Breuer was the writer whom Williamson most admired from the early years of the magazine. While Williamson's essay has become a landmark in the discussion of the attitudes of early science fiction, due to his position as a major figure in the field for nearly eighty years, Breuer's essay is just as significant in articulating and defining the genre in its early days. These essays and the letters that appeared in the "Discussions" column are, despite their crudeness, the foundation of science fiction criticism.

Breuer's thoughts on what the fledgling genre should be did not wholly come from his encounter with *Amazing Stories*; he was also an avid book collector. His collection was reported to consist of over eight thousand volumes, some of which are now housed in the stacks at the University of Nebraska–Lincoln. Most intriguing is Breuer's H. G. Wells collection, which includes such novels as *Meanwhile, Joan and Peter, The Wheels of Chance, The Bulpington of Blup,* a French edition of *The First Men in the Moon,* and *Mr. Blettsworthy on Rampole Island.* The books appear to have been sold to the library shortly after Breuer's death, but sadly there is no clear record of other volumes that were Breuer's. Unfortunately, it doesn't appear that his copies of Wells's scientific romances made it into the library collection, but some of those books with Breuer's bookplate contain marginalia that indicate he was a careful reader of Wells. His deep interest in Wells also suggests how Breuer might have discovered Gernsback's magazine, which was filled with Wells reprints, and how he subsequently became one of its most frequent contributors. Indeed, the impact of Wells in *Amazing Stories* is worth recounting.

Because Gernsback had to fill the early issues of *Amazing* with reprints until he developed a readership that would produce new writers, it took nearly a year before Gernsback was able to publish new fiction regularly. The most prominent author to appear in the first few years of *Amazing* was H. G. Wells, whose works provided the model for the kind of fiction that Gernsback was looking for. Wells appeared in every issue of *Amazing* from April 1926 to August 1928, by which time Gernsback had nearly exhausted his stories and novels. All told, nineteen of Wells's most significant short stories and all of his major scientific romances—*The Island of Dr. Moreau, The First Men in the Moon, The Time Machine, The War of the Worlds, The Invisible Man,* and *When the Sleeper Wakes*—appeared in *Amazing* and *Amazing Stories Quarterly.*

Wells's importance to the development of early magazine science fiction was enormous. In *H. G. Wells: Critic of Progress*, Jack Williamson argues that "Wells formed the *genre*. He invented the methods of projecting possible futures, defined and explained its narrative techniques, created many of its most imitated examples. His tales are the first and often the best of most of its popular types."[12] According to Williamson, by reprinting Wells in his magazines, Gernsback's "greatest service, perhaps, was the rediscovery of H. G. Wells for a new generation of readers."[13] Like Williamson, many of the major writers of the next generation (Heinlein, Asimov, Del Rey, etc.) discovered Wells in the pages of the early *Amazing*. In those early issues, the Wells reprints were coupled with works by such luminaries as Poe and Verne. In fact, Gernsback advertised in his inaugural editorial that he would secure the rights to all of Verne's stories, though it turned out that Wells was to be the dominant figure in the early issues. Other important reprint authors included Garrett Serviss, Austin Hall, Murray Leinster (who continued as a major science fiction figure into the 1960s), Abraham Merritt, Edgar Rice Burroughs, Otis Adelbert Kline, and Gernsback himself. Not all illustrated the kind of fiction Gernsback was calling for, but Gernsback hoped that the scientific romances of Merritt, Burroughs, and Kline would still stimulate scientific creativity (as, despite their fanciful drawbacks, they have done). But it was H. G. Wells with his vision of the future, which was shaped by a Darwinian view of the universe and his superior literary sensibilities, who pointed the way for the genre's future development.

Appropriately (and ironically), the April 1928 issue in which Wells's last story appeared also featured the first Buck Rogers story by Philip Francis Nowlan, "Armageddon—2419," and the first installment of E. E. "Doc" Smith's *The Skylark of Space*, and certainly stands as one of the touchstone issues in the history of science fiction magazines. Nowlan's Buck Rogers and Smith's Richard Seaton, and their super-science space adventures, shifted the center of the genre from the thoughtful scientific and philosophical fiction associated with Wells to juvenile super-science stories of widescreen cosmic vision—what has come to be called space opera. As Mike Ashley notes in a recent article:

> Readers of *Amazing Stories* responded to the "super science" and it was soon selling around 150,000 copies a month. However, it was evident that the gaudy covers by Frank R. Paul and the gosh-wow adventures were attracting a younger and less discerning readership. Gernsback was all for encouraging the young reader, but not at the expense of bastardizing science fiction, but this is what was happening. Having launched a science fiction magazine upon the world Gernsback very rapidly lost control of its contents.[14]

Science fiction was not to fully recover until John W. Campbell (ironically one of the most prominent offenders of juvenile space opera) took over the editorial duties at *Astounding* in late 1937. Nonetheless, some writers were still writing stories within the Wellsian paradigm, Breuer the foremost among them.

As *Amazing* moved into its second year, the classic reprints began to give way to original stories from new writers. As noted, Breuer followed Verrill as the first new writer of significance in the January 1927 issue of *Amazing* with his story "The Man with the Strange Head." Soon, several other new writers appeared. Clare Winger Harris, the first female writer in the magazine who would collaborate with Breuer on "A Baby on Neptune," appeared in June 1927 with "The Fate of Poseidonia"; she would go on to publish several more stories that were collected in *Away from the Here and Now* in 1947. Frequent contributor Bob Olsen also appeared for the first time in June 1927 with "The Four-Dimensional Roller-Press." The September 1927 issue saw the publication of H. P. Lovecraft's "The Colour Out of Space," arguably the best original story ever published in the early *Amazing*. Lovecraft had already established himself in *Weird Tales* and has since been recognized as one of America's great gothic writers. Francis Flagg first appeared in November 1927 with the still interesting "The Machine Man of Ardathia," an early exploration of the cyborg. Edmond Hamilton, who got his start in *Weird Tales*, appeared with "The Comet Doom" in January 1928. David H. Keller with his famous "The Revolt of the Pedestrians" appeared in February 1928. The list goes on: Fletcher Pratt (May 1928), Harl Vincent (June 1928), Stanton Coblentz and R. F. Starzl (both in the Summer 1928 *Amazing Stories Quarterly*), and the previously mentioned Philip Francis Nowlan and E. E. "Doc" Smith (August 1928). Finally, and perhaps most significantly, twenty-year-old Jack Williamson's first story, "The Metal Man," appeared in the December 1928 issue (the same issue featuring Breuer's "The Appendix and the Spectacles," included in this volume). These writers would dominate the magazines over the next several years, and they were soon joined by a young John W. Campbell Jr., whose first story appeared in 1930; Raymond Z. Gallun (1929); S. P. Meek (1929); P. Schuyler Miller (1930); and Nat Schachner (1930). Williamson survived them all and continued to contribute new stories and fresh ideas to the genre into the twenty-first century. His history intersects significantly with Breuer's.

Jack Williamson was just twenty years old when "The Metal Man" appeared. A shy young man from the wind-blown plains of eastern New Mexico, Williamson had discovered *Amazing Stories* in the fall of 1926 when a friend loaned him the November issue. He sent for a free copy and received the March 1927 issue featuring T. S. Stribling's "The Green Splotches"—from then on he was hooked. He began writing stories to send to the magazine and soon began corresponding with Breuer and with Edmond Hamilton. Hamilton and Williamson became good friends and later would adventure down the Mississippi together; Williamson saw the older Breuer as a man of science and an experienced writer from whom he could learn. After noticing Breuer's name in the Science Correspondence Club, Williamson wrote to him and they soon forged a teacher-student relationship. This quickly turned into a collaboration on the story "The Girl from Mars," which was published by Gernsback as a chapbook after he lost control of *Amazing* and before he started *Wonder Stories*—it might be considered the first book published as science fiction. Their collaboration also produced the novel *The Birth of a New Republic* (*Amazing Stories Quarterly*, Winter 1931, now available in volume 1 of Williamson's *Collected Stories*), later imitated and admired by Robert A. Heinlein. Williamson credits Breuer with moving his own writing away from the florid prose and weird romanticism of Merritt to the realistic mode of H. G. Wells.[15] He was later to write a worthwhile critical study on Wells, *H. G. Wells: Critic of Progress*, when he took a PhD in English later in life, which can arguably be traced back to his early discussions with Breuer. In *The Early Williamson*, Williamson describes how their collaboration worked: they would discuss ideas in letters, and Williamson would then do most of the writing; when finished, he would send it to Breuer for editing and criticism, and Breuer would then send it to his agent for publication.[16] Williamson has often expressed his appreciation for the early mentorship that Breuer gave him, perhaps best in his autobiography *Wonder's Child*:

> Miles J. Breuer. He had fans then, and his name on magazine covers. . . . The long decades since then have almost

erased his reputation, but he was among the first and best of the amateurs whose work Gernsback began to print. ... Breuer drilled me in the values of character and theme and believability, people the reader can know and love or hate or both, plots that somehow reflect the reader's actual hopes and fears. .... I owe him a considerable debt for sympathetic and intelligent help when I needed it, and I'm sorry to see him so completely forgotten. He was one of our pioneers, his vision nobler than anything he did.[17]

Breuer's influence extended beyond Williamson, as witnessed in the "Discussions" column in *Amazing*. Breuer's own letters feature prominently, as do letters written in response to his work—the discussion surrounding "The Gostak and the Doshes" went on for months. Several of Breuer's letters are included at the back of this volume (see appendix 2), and in them we see how Breuer worked to shape the discussion of science fiction, first by offering a definition and insisting that it have literary quality, and then by praising other writers whom he saw as successfully following through on these demands, such as G. Peyton Wertenbaker, Stanton Coblentz, and Jack Williamson. A slight controversy surrounds Breuer from an editorial comment in the June 1927 issue of *Amazing*. As Bleiler points out in his monumental *Science-Fiction, The Gernsback Years*, the editorial comment attached to Breuer's letter in that issue refers to Breuer as "well-known to our readers from the interesting story entitled 'New Stomachs for Old.'"[18] At this point, Breuer had only published his first story, "The Man with the Strange Head." "New Stomachs for Old" was a story by one W. Alexander that had appeared in the February 1927 issue. Noting that Breuer did not disavow credit for the story and had attacked a later Alexander story involving organ transplants, Bleiler makes the point that sometimes such editorial comments reveal the true identities of authors, but they also may show the considerable carelessness in pulp editing. In any case, Alexander's stories (there are six of them) do not compare well with Breuer's, and Bleiler's conclusion that "the attribution is best left unresolved" is probably the wisest course. In the letter column and in the story blurbs, Breuer was always presented by the editors of *Amazing* with respect and as an authority in both literature and science; Breuer and his ideas and opinions mattered. But like many of his contemporaries, Breuer soon faded from view as the genre evolved during the depression years of the '30s. His peak years were 1929, when six of his stories were published, and 1930, which saw the publication of eight stories, the novels *Paradise and Iron* and *The Birth of a New Republic*, and two poems. After 1935 Breuer averaged only one story per year until his last in 1942. Nonetheless, the editorial blurb on a late guest editorial in *Startling Stories* (May 1940) designates him as a "famous scientifiction writer," showing that the memory of his impact on the field was still on the minds of the new generation.

After receiving a letter complimenting him on *The Birth of a New Republic* from his good friend Robert A. Heinlein at Christmas 1949, Williamson began inquiring about book publication for this early collaborative novel he'd written with Breuer and possibly for Breuer's solo work. After a long delay, he finally contacted J. L. Mc-Master, Breuer's estate agent in Lincoln, and suggested that in addition to finding a publisher for *The Birth of a New Republic*, he might be able to interest someone in Breuer's *Paradise and Iron*, perhaps as "a memorial volume containing that and several of his short stories, perhaps an essay on him and his contributions to science fiction."[19] Fifty-eight years after Williamson's suggestion, I am happy to present just such a collection of Breuer's stories and his long-neglected novel, *Paradise and Iron*. I had the good fortune to exchange e-mails about this project with Williamson just months before his death in November 2006 at the age of ninety-eight. He wrote, "I'm happy to see Breuer rediscovered. He was a pioneer of American Science Fiction, one of the new writers Gernsback began publishing when the reprintable classics were gone. A busy physician, he had limited time for writing, but he was intelligent and very deeply interested in the craft. The fan letters in magazine columns showed his popularity. I admired him and learned from him."[20] Sadly, Williamson will not see this book, but I hope it would have cheered him to see his old mentor back in print.

This volume contains some of Breuer's best and most interesting work. Like those of all writers of the period, Breuer's stories are at times uneven (as are those of most later writers), and the situations often no longer equate with the real future in which we live. Yet they are full of intriguing ideas and explore important science fiction themes that have continued to develop in the stories of later writers. In his anthology, *Science Fiction of the 30s*, Damon Knight admits that many of the forgotten stories of the early magazine era "contain ideas usually thought to have appeared much later; some of them now seem startlingly modern, even prophetic."[21] Knight's anthology is itself now over thirty years old, and the older stories are even more forgotten. But now that the Golden Age paradigm of Asimov, Campbell, Knight, and others is itself gathering dust, we can look back at the early magazine era with a new perspective and appreciate these stories for what they were: the pioneering work in a genre that has become a significant part of our cultural discourse. The BFI series has significantly contributed to the reassessment of early science fiction by reprinting over forty classics of the genre, but with a few exceptions, the fiction of the early magazine era has not been reprinted in this series or elsewhere. Hopefully, this volume will foster a reexamination not only of Breuer, but also of some of the other significant writers of the period who have remained virtually inaccessible and who deserve reassessment.

Breuer's first published story, "The Man with the Strange Head" (*Amazing*, January 1927), shows him in the process of learning how to write fiction by putting his own experiences into a science fiction setting and imitating the Wellsian story model. Set in downtown Lincoln, Nebraska, the story evokes the local environment and also exhibits Breuer's medical knowledge. Its presentation is very much in the Wellsian mode, recalling such stories as "The Flowering of the Strange Orchid" and "In the Avu Observatory," where a man of science or letters is presented with a strange occurrence and goes on to uncover the circumstances. In this case, a doctor has been called to the Cornhusker Hotel where he meets a magazine writer who has been hearing odd noises coming from the apartment below his own. Interestingly, Breuer puts himself into the story as the narrator, Dr. B., which gives it an extra sense of verisimilitude.

"The Appendix and the Spectacles," Breuer's fifth story, appeared in the December 1928 *Amazing*. Another medical story, it explores another of Breuer's favorite themes, the fourth dimension. The story also reveals Breuer's distaste for self-righteous power mongers—a characterization he would use frequently in later stories—as portrayed by the curmudgeonly Cladgett, president of the First National Bank of Collegeburg (a veiled evocation of downtown Lincoln and the university), who seeks treatment for appendicitis and gets more than he bargained for when he becomes the subject of a fourth-dimensional experiment. The presentation of the story is greatly indebted to Wells, recalling such stories as "The Remarkable Case of Davidson's Eyes" and "The Truth About Pyecraft."

"The Gostak and the Doshes" (*Amazing* 1930) is certainly Breuer's best and most famous story. Relying again on the device of the fourth dimension, Breuer sends his protagonist to an alternate Earth, where he is caught up in the chaos and anarchy brought about by the misuse and subsequent misapprehension of the phrase "the gostak distims the doshes," which sparks open warfare between nations. It is a story of mass psychology, totalitarianism, and the misprision of language, and, like Orwell's *1984*, still holds considerable relevance. Published in 1930 it eerily anticipated the rise of European fascism, but it can also be placed among those literary works of the '20s that reflected upon the senselessness of World War I (Breuer, after all, spent almost two years as a medic in France). In some ways, "The Gostak and the Doshes" fits with the exploration of Korzybski's general semantics in Golden Age science fiction, particularly that of Van Vogt, and it further anticipates the postmodern critique of language by such critics as Derrida, McLuhan, Foucault, and Chomsky. The story generated many comments in the Discussions column, where it was praised for its keen observations on mass thinking and totalitarianism.

Breuer's neglected solo novel, *Paradise and Iron*, appeared in the

Summer 1930 issue of *Amazing Stories Quarterly*. The novel is set on a utopian island where humans passively pursue the arts in the "City of Beauty," while all their material needs are fulfilled by the machines of the "City of Smoke." But paradise has a price that might ultimately be the enslavement of the human race. Paul Carter has argued that *Paradise and Iron* is an allegory about the possible ramifications of human creativity in a future increasingly dominated by machines, and Brian Stableford has cited it as "a particularly early example of mechanization-anxiety," which is a major theme of science fiction, most notably in Williamson's *The Humanoids* and Philip K. Dick's "Autofac" and "Second Variety," among others.[22] Until now *Paradise and Iron* has remained out of print, though references to it can occasionally be found in criticism. It is a pleasure to bring this major science fiction novel back into print.

In 1930 Breuer's work began appearing in some of the new magazines such as Gernsback's *Science Wonder Stories* ("The Fitzgerald Contraction," not included here) and in the newly launched *Astounding Stories of Super-Science*, with the excellent "A Problem in Communication" (September 1930). "A Problem in Communication" is another dystopian vision that involves a cultish science community in Virginia that threatens the sovereignty of the United States. The Science Community has had numerous parallels in the contemporary world from Jonestown to various UFO cults, and even to the benign "campuses" of computer and pharmaceutical firms. One sees further parallels with L. Ron Hubbard's Scientology, which itself emerged out of the science fiction magazines in the early '50s, in the depiction of a religion devoted to modern science.

"On Board the Martian Liner" (*Amazing*, March 1931) is notable for being a murder-mystery story set in space. Here the science fictional background and setting serve merely as a backdrop for a traditional mystery story. But it is the *assumed* science fiction background that makes the story intriguing. In the Golden Age *Astounding*, John W. Campbell wanted his writers to write stories that could be published in a twenty-fifth century magazine. In other words, Campbell insisted on realism—a *future* realism. As in some of his other stories, Breuer successfully anticipates the Campbellian idiom. It is one of Breuer's few stories to involve any interplanetary setting, and he effectively conveys the themes of planetary exploration and colonization, even though they primarily serve as a backdrop to the murder mystery.

"Mechanocracy" (*Amazing*, April 1932) continues the dystopian themes from *Paradise and Iron* and "A Problem in Communication." Like Nat Schachner, who also regularly explored such dystopian themes, Breuer presents a world in which the machine-systems have taken over, and humans have become more machine-like in their passive adherence to the dictates of the machine.[23] The story recalls E. M. Forster's classic "The Machine Stops" (1909) and Fritz Lang's stunning film *Metropolis* (1927). We see the theme of an all-controlling machine intelligence used frequently in later science fiction, as in Poul Anderson's cold war parable, "Sam Hall," Thomas N. Scortia's fine novella "The Shores of Night," John Brunner's important novel *The Shockwave Rider*, and most famously in Harlan Ellison's "Repent Harlequin, Said the Ticktockman." Democratia's location in the Himalayas, the last enclave of free people outside the global Mechanocracy, also recalls James Hilton's utopian novel *Lost Horizon*, which appeared in the following year. Though somewhat more clumsy in execution than these later stories on the theme, "Mechanocracy" remains of interest for its meditations on the problems of mechanization and totalitarianism in the context of the early 1930s and the rise of the totalitarian states in Europe that led to another world war and genocide.

"The Finger of the Past" (*Amazing*, November 1932) shows the range of Breuer's fiction by moving away from the gloomy anxieties of his dystopias to a lighter satire on the consequences that new technologies might have for human beings in their personal and professional lives. It anticipates much of the amusing satire that was prominent in *Galaxy* in the 1950s—by writers like Frederik Pohl, C. M. Kornbluth, and Robert Sheckley—with its jesting critique of corporate managerial values and conceits. The gadget that allows glimpses into the past recalls such classics as T. L. Sherred's "E for Effort" and Robert A. Heinlein's first story, "Life-Line" (which, in effect, looks into the future), and countless other science fiction stories that explore time and its consequences.

Bleiler has noted that "Millions for Defense" (*Amazing*, March 1935) is one of the few stories to evoke the depression-era landscape in early science fiction magazines,[24] but he otherwise dismisses the story and does not consider it science fiction. But his restrictive definition of science fiction misses the point: "Millions for Defense" is an early example of the engineering problem-solving story that was so prominently a part of Campbell's *Astounding/Analog*. It also interestingly fictionalizes the very real outbreak of bank heists that occurred throughout the Midwest during the period when Pretty Boy Floyd, John Dillinger, and Bonnie and Clyde were robbing small-town banks from Indiana to Texas (in fact, two million dollars was stolen from a Lincoln bank in 1930).

"Mars Colonizes" first appeared in the Summer 1935 issue of William C. Crawford's semipro-zine, *Marvel Tales*. Here Breuer combines the mood of the depression era with his dystopian concerns and his deep interest in H. G. Wells. Unlike Wells's Martians, Breuer's Martians arrive on earth in a peaceful manner and soon begin to buy up real estate, stock, commodities, and other valuables. Within a few generations they dominate Earth's economy and segregate its inhabitants, which leads to an underground movement to rid the Earth of its Martian usurpers. Like Wells's, Breuer's Martians die suddenly and mysteriously, conveniently wrapping up the story and solving the invasion problem. The story evokes issues of the Great Depression, especially immigration in the United States, both external and internal. The fears expressed by the Earth's inhabitants for the "whiter" Martians might be a thinly veiled metaphor for the migration of southern blacks into northern cities. At the same time, however, Breuer may have simply been innocently using the current headlines to create a science fiction story. If he is in fact exhibiting the fears and prejudices of many of his contemporaries in this story, he is far less bigoted than some of his contemporaries, most notably David H. Keller. In any case, the story is ripe for critical interpretation and is one of Breuer's most interesting. When read as an amusing satire on the follies of

American culture, it anticipates Fredric Brown's uproarious *Martians Go Home!* (1955), where the Martians also abruptly depart after wreaking havoc on their terran victims and exposing the follies of Cold War America.

Finally, one of Breuer's last stories, "The Oversight" (*Comet Stories*, December 1940), fittingly shows Breuer's long obsession with Wells's fiction. Roman legions mysteriously appear along the Missouri River outside of Omaha and begin to launch an attack on the local inhabitants. Unbeknownst to the human population, the Roman legions are products of a genetic-engineering experiment by a disembodied Martian brain that has come to conquer earth. Breuer's use of the advanced, bodiless evolutionary brain is reflective of a common trope in early science fiction, examples being Joe Kleier's "The Head" (1928), David H. Keller's "The Cerebral Library" (1931), Curt Siodmak's *Donovan's Brain* (1942), Rog Phillips's "The Cyberiad" (1953), and the cult classic film, "The Brain that Wouldn't Die" (1963). The story also nicely evokes the regional setting of Nebraska, as anyone who occasionally drives the Omaha-Lincoln corridor can appreciate.

In these stories and the others in Breuer's oeuvre, certain themes stand out; for example, medicine and laboratory experiments are prominent in the early stories. To Breuer's credit, he expands his thematic range in later stories even though the "scientist in the lab" theme is so suitable to his own personal circumstances. Breuer also interestingly evoked his local environment, particularly in many of the early stories. His descriptions of Lincoln and other areas of Nebraska make his work appealing to Nebraska readers, but he also effectively captures the atmosphere of a typical state university in many of his stories, making the interesting and vital link between university research and education and science fiction. In "The Raid from Mars" (*Amazing*, March 1939—the same issue in which Isaac Asimov's first story "Marooned Off Vesta" was published), Breuer's brief description of the local neighborhoods in Lincoln is both accurate and familiar. In "The Perfect Planet" (1932), Breuer nicely uses the Nebraska Sandhills as the setting for a story of extraterrestrial contact. His use of the landscape south of the Omaha metropolitan area as the battleground in "The Oversight" has already been noted. University settings are featured in "The Appendix and the Spectacles," "The Captured Cross-Section" (1929), "Rays and Men" (1929), "The Hungry Guinea Pig" (1930), "The Inferiority Complex" (1930), "The Gostak and the Doshes," and others. "Rays and Men" (a slow-moving but still interesting dystopia that might be considered a first attempt at the themes of his later, more successful dystopias) depicts a future Lincoln where life is highly regimented, mechanized, and dull. The narrator's escape into the cornfields outside the city is a recognizable Nebraska image.

Breuer also had a great deal of interest in then-current scientific movements. His interest in psychology can be seen in such stories as "The Gostak and the Doshes" and "The Inferiority Complex." Sam Moskowitz has pointed out that Breuer was—along with Keller who was a practicing psychiatrist—one of the few writers who tackled psychological themes in the early magazines.[25] This interest is further revealed by his marginalia in some of the Wells books in the University of Nebraska collection, in his popular medical writings, and in his editorial duties with *Social Science*. He was also clearly interested in Einstein's theory of relativity and the fourth dimension both of which appear in numerous stories from "The Appendix and the Spectacles" to "The Einstein See-Saw" (1932). This probably derived from his interest in Wells, as many of his stories use variations on the mechanism of extra-dimensional travel used in *The Time Machine*, the best example being "The Gostak and the Doshes." In "Rays and Men," Breuer used Wells's device of a sleeper in suspended animation from *When the Sleeper Wakes*.

Like many writers and artists of the period for whom the mistakes of World War I appeared to be repeating themselves, Breuer explored the problems of mechanization and totalitarianism in stories like "The Gostak and the Doshes," *Paradise and Iron*, "A Problem in Communication," and "Mechanocracy." All of these stories parallel more famous contemporary explorations of the theme, such as Aldous Huxley's *Brave New World* (1932) and Fritz Lang's film *Me-*

tropolis, and parallels can also be found with contemporary mundane fictions, such as John Dos Passos's modernist masterpieces *Manhattan Transfer* (1925) and *U.S.A.* (1930–36), as well as Charlie Chaplin's cinematic comic masterpiece *Modern Times* (1936). Breuer might well have been familiar with Lang's film, which certainly owes a debt to Wells, though it is also likely that he was familiar with the writings of Franz Kafka and Karel Capek, given his Czech heritage, and such influences might help account for his dystopian impulses. But, again, many of these thematic concerns are straight out of H. G. Wells. The hectic megalopolis of Wells's *When the Sleeper Wakes* and "A Story of the Days to Come" is evoked by the vast, mechanical city of "Mechanocracy," the City of Smoke in *Paradise and Iron*, and in the mad mass hysteria of "The Gostak and the Doshes."

The Wells influence is seen even more clearly in Breuer's Mars stories. "Mars Colonizes," "The Oversight," and "The Raid from Mars" show how much of Breuer's thinking was occupied by a considered reading of Wells. Breuer had already borrowed heavily from Wells's short fiction and from such novels as *The Time Machine, When the Sleeper Wakes,* and *The Invisible Man,* but in these last stories, it is clear that *The War of the Worlds* increasingly occupied him. "The Oversight" and "The Raid from Mars" both appeared after Orson Welles's famous Halloween radio broadcast of *The War of the Worlds* that caused panic in some of America's cities in 1938, and the stories may owe as much to the sensation caused by that broadcast as they do to Wells's original novel. Though these late Mars stories remain interesting, probably because they are in conversation with Wells and Welles, it is clear from the evidence that Breuer had lost steam as a writer and was no longer able to match the caliber of his earlier stories.

Indeed, in late December 1938 Breuer wrote to Williamson to suggest that they try another collaboration for *Amazing Stories,* now edited by young Raymond J. Palmer, who had contacted Breuer about doing another collaboration with Williamson for his magazine. Williamson had developed into one of the most successful science fiction and fantasy writers of the '30s and most of his science fiction was appearing in *Amazing*'s rival magazine, *Astounding Stories. Astound-*

ing's editorial chair had recently been handed over to John W. Campbell, and Palmer clearly wanted to get Williamson back into his own magazine. Williamson responded enthusiastically and sent Breuer a long story synopsis for a sequel to *The Birth of a New Republic*. Williamson's correspondence file at Eastern New Mexico University does not contain Breuer's response to this proposal, but Williamson's subsequent letters indicate that Breuer wanted the collaboration to work the way it had in the past; in other words, Williamson would do most of the work and Breuer would act as consulting editor with equal author credit. The now-established Williamson balked at this, but he generously made suggestions for less time-consuming collaborative projects. Breuer, though, admitted to being unable to get his creative engine running: "my mind refuses to get a good idea at the present time."[26] In the end nothing came of the collaboration, and Breuer soon disappeared from science fiction, though his final story (and certainly his worst), "The Sheriff of Thorium Gulch" (1942), seems to be a poor lifting of some of the ideas that Williamson sent to Breuer for *The Birth of a New Republic* sequel. Williamson himself would rework these ideas to produce his seminal *Seetee* stories for Campbell's *Astounding* in the '40s.

There are several reasons for Breuer's disappearance from science fiction so soon after his attempt to reestablish his writing relationship with Williamson in 1939. At some point his marriage to Julia dissolved, and he was quickly remarried in Chicago in early 1939. The demands of his practice were increasing, and the amount of energy he once expended as a younger man now left him haggard. He had little time for his writing though he still wished to belong to the science fiction field, which continued to grow as the 1940s approached, as is attested to by his self-portrait in the "Meet the Authors" section of the March 1939 *Amazing* and his guest editorial in the May 1940 *Startling Stories*. In September 1939 his family life met with great tragedy when his son, Stanley, just ready to embark on his sophomore year at the University of Nebraska, died in a fall off a glacier while hiking in Colorado with a friend. The circumstances were not pleasant—a sudden storm forced a recovery party to leave his body on the glacier overnight—and this must have been a great blow to Breuer, who had himself been an avid hiker, a Boy Scout leader, and a university health consultant over the years. Sixteen-year-old radio enthusiast Ronald Worth, the lead protagonist in "The Raid from Mars," was certainly modeled on Stanley, and the father-son relationship in the story is given greater poignancy as Stanley's death occurred just months after the story's publication. In his introduction to the facsimile reprint edition of *The Birth of a New Republic*, Williamson expressed his impression of a deep conflict in Breuer, particularly in those last letters, noting that "reread today, the letter suggests to me that his own life had turned tragic."[27] It does not appear that Williamson was aware of Stanley's fatal fall, but his insights suggest that Breuer's troubles extended beyond the loss of his son. Williamson concludes: "Though I never knew him really well, I got the impression of some deep conflict, perhaps between the demands of his medical practice and his artistic aspirations, that left him less than satisfied with his whole career."[28]

Late in 1942 these personal troubles culminated when Breuer suffered a nervous breakdown, as indicated by notes scrawled in the back of his copy of Wells's *Mr. Blettsworthy on Rampole Island*. In response to the novel, he writes, "Appropriate, 12/27/42, because I am now in a hospital for nervous & mental diseases, getting over a severe breakdown. I crowded as much material into 2 wks as Blettsworthy did into 5 years." Soon after, Breuer left Lincoln for Los Angeles where he died on October 14, 1945, though all science fiction resources up to this point have mistakenly recorded his date of death as 1947. His obituary in the *Lincoln Evening Journal* for October 16, 1945, reads, "Dr. Miles John Breuer, 57, former Lincoln physician, died Sunday in Los Angeles after a short illness. He had moved to Los Angeles, where he continued his medical practice, after practicing in Lincoln for 28 years."

Miles J. Breuer's legacy as one of the early pioneers of magazine science fiction has gone under-noticed. In general, Breuer has been assessed with some admiration for his accomplishments in the early magazines but seldom with any depth to the analysis. For example, John Clute remarks that Breuer was "an intelligent though somewhat crude writer" and "was particularly strong in his articulation of fresh ideas."[29] Walter Gillings considers Breuer as having written "some of the most intriguing tales that appeared in the early volumes of *Amazing Stories*" and that "he wrote with a conviction that was rare in those days."[30] Moskowitz notes that "for off-beat ideas handled with a degree of depth and maturity he ranked high."[31] In a recent article on the magazines, Ashley credits Breuer, along with Keller, as being "the best in the early years,"[32] but surprisingly he failed to include a Breuer story in his important 1974 anthology *The History of the Science Fiction Magazines*. Despite these observations and those of other critics and historians who list him as a leading writer of the early period, Breuer has remained largely out of print, as have many of his pioneering colleagues—Nat Schachner in particular—who are often mentioned in histories and criticism of the field but whose works are virtually inaccessible. Until now, with the exception of *The Girl from Mars* chapbook and a facsimile reprint of *The Birth of a New Republic* in 1981, no book bearing Breuer's name has been published, and his stories have only occasionally been reprinted (see the list of Breuer's works at the end of this volume). This may in part be because of the clumsy handling of Breuer's literary estate by his lawyer J. L. McMaster when Williamson was trying to interest publishers in *The Birth of a New Republic* and Breuer's other stories, but it is also because Breuer died before the advent of the paperback era and the science fiction boom of the 1950s. Had he lived and remained at least partly active in the field, it is quite possible that *Paradise and Iron* or a collection of his stories might have interested a publisher. Instead, most of Breuer's work has only been available to those who are fortunate enough to have access to the crumbling original magazines or the patience and diligence to seek them out in microfilm. This volume should rectify the oversight.

Breuer's place as an early mentor to Jack Williamson stands as a testament to his importance to the science fiction genre, and with the revived interest among scholars in reassessing Williamson since his death in 2006, this edition of Breuer's stories comes at a ripe moment. As an early pioneer of magazine science fiction—one of the few that Nebraska can call its own—and as a prominent Lincoln physician with ties to the University of Nebraska, there is no better place to reintroduce Breuer's' fiction to a new audience than through the University of Nebraska Press and its Bison Frontiers of Imagination series.

Notes

1. Williamson, introduction to *Ralph 124C 41+*, viii.
2. Gunn, *Alternate Worlds*, 116.
3. Ashley, "Science Fiction Magazines," 61–62.
4. Stover, "Science Fiction and the Research Revolution," 35–36.
5. Baldwin and Baldwin, *Nebraskana*, 156; Baldwin, *Who's Who in Lincoln*, 43–44; *Who's Who in Nebraska*, 668–69.
6. Breuer, "The Assembly-Line for Writers," 275.
7. Breuer, *Index of Physiotherapeutic Technic*, n.p.
8. Quoted in Bleiler, *Science-Fiction*, 544.
9. Quoted in Bleiler, *Science-Fiction*, 544.
10. Bleiler, *Science-Fiction*, 545.
11. Williamson, "Scientifiction, Searchlight of Science," 1.
12. Williamson, *H. G. Wells*, 8.
13. Williamson, *H. G. Wells*, 7.
14. Ashley, "Science Fiction Magazines," 62.
15. McCaffrey, "An Interview with Jack Williamson," 237.
16. Williamson, *The Early Williamson*, 14.
17. Williamson, *Wonder's Child*, 61–62.
18. Bleiler, *Science-Fiction*, 2–3.
19. Williamson to McMaster, April 2, 1949, Jack Williamson Science Fiction Library Archive.
20. Williamson, e-mail message to the editor, July 5, 2006.
21. Knight, *Science Fiction of the 30s*, 1.
22. Carter, *The Creation of Tomorrow*, 208; Stableford, "Man-Made Catastrophes," 116.
23. Carter, *The Creation of Tomorrow*, 210.
24. Bleiler, *Science-Fiction*, 35.

25. Moskowitz, *Strange Horizons*, 111–12.
26. Breuer to Williamson, January 7, 1939, Jack Williamson Science Fiction Library Archive.
27. Williamson, introduction to *Birth of a New Republic*, 5.
28. Williamson, introduction to *Birth of a New Republic*, 5.
29. Clute, "Breuer, Miles J.," 157.
30. Gillings, "Miles J. Breuer," 78–79.
31. Moskowitz, *Seekers of Tomorrow*, 91.
32. Ashley, "Science Fiction Magazines," 62.

Bibliography

Ashley, Mike. *The History of the Science Fiction Magazines, Volume 1: 1926–1935*. London: New English, 1974. Rpt. Chicago: Henry Regnery, 1976.

———. "Science Fiction Magazines: The Crucibles of Change." In *A Companion to Science Fiction*, edited by David Seed, 60–76. Oxford: Blackwell, 2005.

Baldwin, Sara Mullin, ed. *Who's Who in Lincoln: Biographical Sketches of Men and Women of Achievement*. Lincoln: Robert M. Baldwin, 1928.

Baldwin, Sara Mullin, and Robert Morton Baldwin, eds. *Nebraskana: Biographical Sketches of Nebraska Men and Women of Achievement Who Have Been Awarded Life Membership in The Nebraska Society*. Hebron: The Baldwin Company, 1932.

Bleiler, Everett F. *Science-Fiction: The Gernsback Years*. Kent: Kent State University Press, 1998.

Breuer, Miles J. "The Assembly-Line for Writers." *The Writer*, September 1942. 273–75.

———. *Index of Physiotherapeutic Technic*. Omaha: American College of Radiology and Physiotherapy, 1925.

———. "Meet the Authors: Miles J. Breuer." *Amazing Stories*, March 1939. 125.

———. "The New Frontier." *Startling Stories*, May 1940. 111.

Carter, Paul. *The Creation of Tomorrow: Fifty Years of Magazine Science Fiction*. New York: Columbia University Press, 1977.

Clute, John. "Breuer, Miles J." In *The Encyclopedia of Science Fiction*, edited by John Clute and Peter Nicholls, 157. New York: St. Martin's Press, 1993.

Gillings, Walter. "Miles J. Breuer." In *Twentieth-Century Science Fiction Writers*, 2nd ed., edited by Curtis C. Smith, 78–79. Chicago: St. James Press, 1986.

Gunn, James. *Alternate Worlds: The Illustrated History of Science Fiction*. Englewood Cliffs: Prentice-Hall, 1975.

Harris, Clare Winger, *Away from the Here and Now: Stories in Pseudo-Science*. Philadelphia: Dorrance, 1947.

Knight, Damon, ed. *Science Fiction of the 30s*. Indianapolis: Bobbs-Merrill, 1975.

McCaffrey, Larry. "An Interview with Jack Williamson." *Science Fiction Studies* 18, no. 2 (July 1991): 230–52.

Moskowitz, Sam. *Seekers of Tomorrow*. Cleveland: World Publishing, 1966.

———. *Strange Horizons: The Spectrum of Science Fiction*. New York: Scribner's, 1976.

Murray, Terry A. *Science Fiction Magazine Story Index, 1926–1995*. Jefferson: McFarland, 1999.

Stableford, Brian. "Man-Made Catastrophes." In *The End of the World*, edited by Eric S. Rabkin, Martin H. Greenberg, and Joseph D. Olander, 97-138. Carbondale: Southern Illinois University Press, 1983.

Stover, Leon. "Science Fiction and the Research Revolution." In *Teaching Science Fiction: Education for Tomorrow*, edited by Jack Williamson, 33-37. Philadelphia: Owlswick Press, 1980.

Who's Who in Nebraska. Lincoln: Nebraska Press Association, 1940.

Williamson, Jack. *The Early Williamson*. Garden City: Doubleday, 1975.

———. *H. G. Wells: Critic of Progress*. Baltimore: Mirage Press, 1973.

———. Introduction. In *The Birth of a New Republic*, by Miles J. Breuer and Jack Williamson, n.p. New Orleans: PDA Enterprises, 1981.

———. Introduction. In *Ralph 124C 41+: A Romance of the Year 2660*, by Hugo Gernsback, vii–xi. Lincoln: University of Nebraska Press, 2000.

———. Letter to J. L. McMaster, April 2, 1949. Jack Williamson Science Fiction Library Archive, Eastern New Mexico University.

———. "Scientifiction, Searchlight of Science." *Amazing Stories Quarterly*, Fall 1928. Rpt. in *The Metal Man and Others: The Collected Stories of Jack Williamson, Volume One*, 1–2. Royal Oak: Haffner Press, 1999.

———. *Wonder's Child: My Life in Science Fiction*, 2nd ed. Dallas: BenBella Books, 2005.

The Man with the Strange Head

A man in a gray hat stood halfway down the corridor, smoking a cigar and apparently interested in my knocking and waiting. I rapped again on the door of Number 216 and waited some more, but all remained silent. Finally my observer approached me.

"I don't believe it will do any good," he said. "I've just been trying it. I would like to talk to someone who is connected with Anstruther. Are you?"

"Only this." I handed him a letter out of my pocket without comment, as one is apt to do with a thing that has caused one no little wonderment:

> "Dear Doctor": it said succinctly. "I have been under the care of Dr. Faubourg who has recently died. I would like to have you take charge of me on a contract basis, and keep me well, instead of waiting till I get sick. I can pay you enough to make you independent, but in return for that, you will have to accept an astonishing revelation concerning me, and keep it to yourself. If this seems acceptable to you, call on me at 9 o'clock, Wednesday evening. Josiah Anstruther, Room 216, Cornhusker Hotel."

"If you have time," said the man in the gray hat, handing me back the letter, "come with me. My name is Jerry Stoner, and I make a sort of living writing for magazines. I live in 316, just above here."

"By some curious architectural accident," he continued, as we reached his room, "that ventilator there enables me to hear minutely everything that goes on in the room below. I haven't ever said anything about it during the several months that I've lived here, partly

I

because it does not disturb me, and partly because it has begun to pique my curiosity—a writer can confess to that, can he not? The man below is quiet and orderly, but seems to work a good deal on some sort of clockwork; I can hear it whirring and clicking quite often. But listen now!"

Standing within a couple of feet of the opening which was covered with an iron grill, I could hear footsteps. They were regular, and would decrease in intensity as the person walked away from the ventilator opening below, and increase again as he approached it; were interrupted for a moment as he probably stepped on a rug, and were shorter for two or three counts, no doubt as he turned at the end of the room. This was repeated in a regular rhythm as long as I listened.

"Well?" I said.

"You perceive nothing strange about that, I suppose," said Jerry Stoner. "But if you had listened all day long to just exactly that you would begin to wonder. That is the way he was going on when I awoke this morning; I was out from 10 to 11 this forenoon. The rest of the time I have been writing steadily, with an occasional stretch at the window, and all of the time I have heard steadily what you hear now, without interruption or change. It's getting on my nerves.

"I have called him on the phone, and have rung it on and off for twenty minutes; I could hear his bell through the ventilator, but he pays no attention to it. So, a while ago I tried to call on him. Do you know him?"

"I know who he is," I replied, "but do not remember ever having met him."

"If you had ever met him you would remember. He has a queer head. I made my curiosity concerning the sounds from his room an excuse to cultivate his acquaintance. The cultivation was difficult. He is courteous, but seemed afraid of me."

We agreed that there was not much that we could do about it. I gave up trying to keep my appointment, told Stoner that I was glad I had met him, and went home. The next morning at seven he had me on the telephone.

"Are you still interested?" he asked, and his voice was nervous.

"That bird's been at it all night. Come and help me talk to the hotel management." I needed no urging.

I found Beesley, the hotel manager, with Stoner; he was from St. Louis, and looked French.

"He can do it if he wants to," he said, shrugging his shoulders comically; "unless you complain of it as a disturbance."

"It isn't that," said Stoner; "there must be something wrong with the man."

"Some form of insanity—" I suggested; "or a compulsion neurosis."

"That's what I'll be pretty soon," Stoner said. "He is a queer gink anyway. As far as I have been able to find out, he has no close friends. There is something about his appearance that makes me shiver, his face is so wrinkled and droopy, and yet he sails about the streets with an unusually graceful and vigorous step. Loan me your pass key; I think I'm as close a friend of his as anyone."

Beesley lent the key, but Stoner was back in a few minutes, shaking his head. Beesley was expecting that; he told us that when the hotel was built, Anstruther had the doors made of steel with special bars, at his own expense, and the windows shuttered, as though he were afraid for his life.

"His rooms would be as hard to break into as a fort," Beesley said as he left us; "and thus far we do not have sufficient reason for wrecking the hotel."

"Look here!" I said to Stoner; "it will take me a couple of hours to hunt up the stuff and string up a periscope; it's an old trick I learned as a Boy Scout."

Between us we had it up in about that time; a radio aerial mast clamped on the window sill with mirrors at the top and bottom, and a telescope at our end of it, gave us a good view of the room below us. It was a sort of living room made by throwing together two of the regular-sized hotel rooms. Anstruther was walking across it diagonally, disappearing from our field of view at the further end, and coming back again. His head hung forward on his chest with a ghastly limpness. He was a big, well-built man, with a vigorous stride. Always it was the same path. He avoided the small table in the middle each time with exactly the same sort of side step and swing. His head bumped limply as he turned near the window and started back across the room. For two hours we watched him in shivering fascination, during which he walked with the same hideous uniformity.

"That makes thirty hours of this," said Stoner. "Wouldn't you say that there was something wrong?"

We tried another consultation with the hotel manager. As a physician, I advised that something be done; that he be put in a hospital or something. I was met with another shrug.

"How will you get him? I still do not see sufficient cause for destroying the hotel company's property. It will take dynamite to get at him."

He agreed, however, to a consultation with the police, and in response to our telephone call, the great, genial Chief Peter John Smith was soon sitting with us. He advised us against breaking in.

"A man has a right to walk that way if he wants to," he said. "Here's this fellow in the papers who played the piano for 49 hours, and the police didn't stop him; and in Germany they practice making public speeches for 18 hours at a stretch. And there was this Olympic dancing fad some months ago, where a couple danced for 57 hours."

"It doesn't look right to me," I said, shaking my head. "There seems to be something wrong with the man's appearance; some uncanny disease of the nervous system—Lord knows I've never heard of anything that resembles it!"

We decided to keep a constant watch. I had to spend a little time on my patients, but Stoner and the Chief stayed, and agreed to call me if occasion arose. I peeped through the periscope at the walking man several times during the next twenty-four hours; and it was always exactly the same, the hanging, bumping head, the uniformity of his course, the uncanny, machine-like exactitude of his movements. I spent an hour at a time with my eye at the telescope studying his movements for some variation, but was unable to be certain of any. That afternoon I looked up my neurology texts, but found no clues. The next day at four o'clock in the afternoon, after not less than 55

4

hours of it, I was there with Stoner to see the end of it; Chief Peter John Smith was out.

As we watched, we saw that he moved more and more slowly, but with otherwise identical motions. It had the effect of the slowed motion pictures of dancers or athletes; or it seemed like some curious dream; for as we watched, the sound of the steps through the ventilator also slowed and weakened. Then we saw him sway a little, and totter, as though his balance were imperfect. He swayed a few times and fell sidewise on the floor, we could see one leg in the field of our periscope moving slowly with the same movements as in walking, a slow, dizzy sort of motion. In five more minutes he was quite still.

The Chief was up in a few moments in response to our telephone call.

"Now we've got to break in," he said. Beesley shrugged his shoulders and said nothing. Stoner came to the rescue of the hotel property.

"A small man could go down this ventilator. This grill can be unscrewed, and the lower one can be knocked out with a hammer; it is cast-iron."

Beesley was gone like a flash, and soon returned with one of his window-washers, who was small and wiry, and also a rope and hammer. We took off the grill and held the rope as the man crawled in. He shouted to us as he hit the bottom. The air drew strongly downwards, but the blows of his hammer on the grill came up to us. We hurried downstairs. Not a sound came through the door of 216, and we waited for some minutes. Then there was a rattle of bars and the door opened, and a gust of cold wind struck us, with a putrid odor that made us gulp. The man had evidently run to open a window before coming to the door.

Anstruther lay on his side, with one leg straight and the other extended forward as in a stride; his face was livid, sunken, hideous. Stoner gave him a glance, and then scouted around the room—looking for the machinery he had been hearing, but finding none. The Chief and I also went over the rooms, but they were just conventional rooms, rather colorless and lacking in personality. The Chief called an undertaker and also the coroner, and arranged for a post-mortem examination. I received permission to notify a number of professional colleagues; I wanted some of them to share in the investigation of this unusual case with me. As I was leaving, I could not help noting the astonished gasps of the undertaker's assistants as they lifted the body; but they were apparently too well trained to say anything.

That evening, a dozen physicians gathered around the figure covered with a white sheet on the table in the center of the undertaker's workroom. Stoner was there; a writer may be anywhere he chooses. The coroner was preparing to draw back the sheet.

"The usual medical history is lacking in this case," he said. "Perhaps an account by Dr. B. or his author friend, of the curious circumstances connected with the death of this man, may take its place."

"I can tell a good deal," said Stoner, "and I think it will bear directly on what you find when you open him up, even though it is not technical medical stuff. Do you care to hear it?"

"Tell it! Go on! Let's have it!"

"I have lived above him in the hotel for several months," Stoner began. "He struck me as a curious person, and as I do some writing, all mankind is my legitimate field for study. I tried to find out all I could about him.

"He has an office in the Little Building, and did a rather curious business. He dealt in vases and statuary, bookends and chimes, and things you put around in rooms to make them look artistic. He had men out buying the stuff, and others selling it, all by personal contact and on a very exclusive basis. He kept the stock in a warehouse near the Rock Island tracks where they pass the Ball Park; I do not believe that he ever saw any of it. He just sat in the office and signed papers, and the other fellows made the money; and apparently they made a lot of it, for he has swung some big financial deals in this town.

"I often met him in the lobby or the elevator. He was a big, vigorous man and walked with an unusually graceful step and an appearance of strength and vitality. His eyes seemed to light up with recognition when he saw me, but in my company he was always formal and reserved. For such a vigorous-looking man, his voice was singularly cracked and feeble, and his head gave an impression of being rather small for him, and his face old and wrinkled.

"He seemed fairly well known about the city. At the Eastridge Club they told me that he plays golf occasionally and excellently, and is a graceful dancer, though somehow not a popular partner. He was seen frequently at the Y.M.C.A. bowling alleys and played with an uncanny skill. Men loved to see him bowl for his cleverness with the balls, but wished he were not so formally courteous, and did not wear such an expression of complete happiness over his victories. Bridley, manager of Rudge & Guenzel's book department, was the oldest friend of his that I could find, and he gave me some interesting information. They went to school together, and Anstruther was poor in health as well as in finances. Twenty-five years ago, during the hungry and miserable years after his graduation from the University, Bridley remembered him as saying:

"'My brain needs a body to work with. If I had physical strength, I could do anything. If I find a fellow who can give it to me, I'll make him rich!'

"Bridley also remembers that he was sensitive because girls did not like his debilitated physique. He seems to have found health later, though I can find no one who remembers how or when. About ten years ago he came back from Europe where he had been for several years, in Paris, Bridley thinks; and for several years after this, a Frenchman lived with him. The city directory of that time has him living in the big stone house at 13th and 'G' streets. I went up there to look around, and found it a double house, Dr. Faubourg having occupied the other half. The present caretaker has been there ever since Anstruther lived in the house, and she says that his French companion must have been some sort of an engineer, and that the two must have been working on an invention, from the sounds she heard and the materials they had about. Some three or four years ago the Frenchman and the machinery vanished, and Anstruther moved to the Cornhusker Hotel. Also at about this time, Dr. Faubourg retired from the practice of medicine. He must have been about 50 years old, and too healthy and vigorous to be retiring on account of old age or ill health.

"Apparently Anstruther never married. His private life was quite obscure, but he appeared much in public. He was always very courtly and polite to the ladies. Outside his business he took a great interest in Y.M.C.A. and Boy Scout camps, in the National Guard, and in fact in everything that stood for an outdoor, physical life, and promoted health. In spite of his oddity he was quite a hero with the small boys, especially since the time of his radium hold-up. This is intimately connected with the story of his radium speculation that caused such a sensation in financial circles a couple of years ago.

"About that time, the announcement appeared of the discovery of new uses for radium; a way had been found to accelerate its splitting and to derive power from it. Its price went up, and it promised to become a scarce article on the market. Anstruther had never been known to speculate, nor to tamper with sensational things like oil and helium; but on this occasion he seemed to go into a panic. He cashed in on a lot of securities and caused a small panic in the city, as he was quite wealthy and had especially large amounts of money in the building-loan business. The newspapers told of how he had bought a hundred thousand dollars worth of radium, which was to be delivered right here in Lincoln—a curious method of speculating, the editors volunteered.

"It arrived by express one day, and Anstruther rode the express wagon with the driver to the station. I found the driver and he told the story of the hold-up at 8th and 'P' streets at eleven o'clock at night. A Ford car drove up beside them, from which a man pointed a pistol at them and ordered them to stop. The driver stopped.

"'Come across with the radium!' shouted the big black bulk in the Ford, climbing upon the express wagon. Anstruther's fist shot out like a flash of lightning and struck the arm holding the pistol; and the driver states that he heard the pistol crash through the window on the second floor of the Lincoln Hotel. Anstruther pushed the express driver, who was in his way, backwards over the seat among the packages and leaped upon the hold-up man; the driver said he heard

Anstruther's muscles crunch savagely, as with little apparent effort he flung the man over the Ford; he fell with a thud on the asphalt and stayed there. Anstruther then launched a kick at the man at the wheel of the Ford, who crumpled up and fell out of the opposite side of the car.

"The police found the pistol inside a room on the second floor of the Lincoln Hotel. The steering post of the Ford car was torn from its fastenings. Both of the hold-up men had ribs and collar-bones broken, and the gunman's forearm was bent double in the middle with both bones broken. These two men agreed later with the express driver that Anstruther's attack, for suddenness, swiftness, and terrific strength was beyond anything they had dreamed possible; he was like a thunderbolt; like some furious demon. When the two men were huddled in black heaps on the pavement, Anstruther said to the driver, quite impersonally: 'Drive to the police station. Come on! Wake up! I've got to get this stuff locked up!'

"One of the hold-up men had lost all his money and the home he was building when Anstruther had foreclosed a loan in his desperate scramble for radium. He was a Greek named Poulos, and has been in prison for two years; just last week he was released—"

Chief Peter John Smith interrupted.

"I've been putting two and two together, and I can shed a little light on this problem. Three days ago, the day before I was called to watch Anstruther pacing his room, we picked up this man Poulos in the alleyway between Rudge & Guenzel's and Miller & Paine's. He was unconscious, and must have received a terrible licking at somebody's hands; his face was almost unrecognizable; several ribs and several fingers on his right hand were broken. He clutched a pistol fitted with a silencer, and we found that two shots had been fired from it. Here he is—"

A limp, bandaged, plastered man was pushed in between two policemen. He was sullen and apathetic, until he caught sight of Anstruther's face from which the Chief had drawn a corner of the sheet. Terror and joy seemed to mingle in his face and in his voice. He raised his bandaged hand with an ineffectual gesture, and started off on some Greek religious expression, and then turned dazedly to us, speaking painfully through his swollen face.

"Glad he dead. I try to kill him. Shoot him two time. No kill. So close—" indicating the distance of a foot from his chest; "then he lick me. He is not man. He is devil. I not kill him, but I glad he dead!"

The Chief hurried him out, and came in with a small, dapper man with a black chin whisker. He apologized to the coroner.

"This is not a frame-up. I am just following out a hunch that I got a few minutes ago while Stoner was talking. This is Mr. Fournier. I found his address in Anstruther's room, and dug him up. I think he will be more important to you doctors than he will in a court. Tell 'em what you told me!"

While the little Frenchman talked, the undertaker's assistant jerked off the sheet. The undertaker's work had had its effect in getting rid of the frightful odor, and in making Anstruther's face presentable. The body, however, looked for all the world as though it were alive, plump, powerful, pink. In the chest, over the heart, were two bullet holes, not bloody, but clean-cut and black. The Frenchman turned to the body and worked on it with a little screw-driver as he talked.

"Mr. Anstruther came to me ten years ago, when I was a poor mechanic. He had heard of my automatic chess-player, and my famous animated show-window models; and he offered me time and money to find him a mechanical relief for his infirmity. I was an assistant at a Paris laboratory, where they had just learned to split radium and get a hundred horse-power from a pinch of powder. Anstruther was weak and thin, but ambitious."

The Frenchman lifted off two plates from the chest and abdomen of the body, and the flanks swung outward as though on hinges. He removed a number of packages that seemed to fit carefully within, and which were on the ends of cables and chains.

"Now—" he said to the assistants, who held the feet. He put his hands into the chest cavity, and as the assistants pulled the feet away, he lifted out of the shell a small, wrinkled emaciated body; the body of an old man, which now looked quite in keeping with the well-known Anstruther head. Its chest was covered with dried blood, and there were two bullet holes over the heart. The undertaker's assistants carried it away while we crowded around to inspect the mechanism within the arms and legs of the pink and live-looking shell, headless, gaping at the chest and abdomen, but uncannily like a healthy, powerful man.

The Appendix and the Spectacles

Old Cladgett, President of the First National Bank of Collegeburg, scowled across the mahogany table at the miserable young man. He was all hunched up into great rolls and hanging pouches, and he scowled till the room grew gloomy and the ceiling seemed to lower.

"I'm running a bank, not a charity club," he growled, planting his fist on the table.

Bookstrom winced, and then controlled himself with a little shiver.

"But sir," he protested, "all I ask for is an extension of time on this note. I could easily pay it out in three or four years. If you force me to pay it now, I shall have to give up my medical course."

Harsh, inchoate, guttural noises issued from Cladgett's throat.

"This bank isn't looking after little boys and their dreams," he snarled. "This note is due and you pay it. You're able-bodied and can work."

Mechanically, as in a daze, Bookstrom took out a wallet and counted out the money. When the sum was complete, he had ten dollars left. The hope that had spurred him on through several years of hardship and difficulty, the hope of graduating as a physician and having a practice of his own, now was gone. He was at the end of his resources. Once the medical course was interrupted, he knew there was no hope of getting back to it. Nowadays the study of medicine is too strenuous; there is no dallying on the path to an M.D. degree.

He went straight over to the University to apply for an instructorship in Applied Mathematics that had recently been offered to him.

In the movies and in the novels, an ogre like Cladgett usually meets with some kind of retribution before long. The Black Hand gets him or a wronged debtor poisons him, or a brick house collapses on his head. But Cladgett lived along in Collegeburg, growing more and more prosperous. He was bound to grow wealthy, because he took all he could get from everybody and never gave anybody anything. He kept growing a little grayer and a little fatter, and seemed to derive more and more pleasure and happiness from preying financially on his fellow-beings. And he seemed as safe as the Rock of Gibraltar.

Then, after fifteen years, a sudden attack of acute appendicitis got him. That morning he had sat at his desk and dictated letters to his directors commanding them to be present at a meeting four days hence without fail. The bank was taking over a big estate as trustee, and unless each director signed the contract personally, the deal was lost and with it a fat fee. In the afternoon he was in bed groaning with pain and cursing the doctor for not curing him at once.

"Appendicitis!" he shrieked. "Impossible!"

Dr. Banza bowed and said nothing. With delicate fingertips he felt of the muscles in the right lower quadrant of the abdomen. He shook his head over the thermometer that he took out of the sick man's mouth. He withdrew a drop of blood from the patient's finger-tip into a tiny pipette and took it away with him.

He was back in an hour, and Cladgett read the verdict in his face.

"Operation!" he yowled like a whipped boy. "I can't have an operation! I'll die!"

He seemed to consider it the doctor's fault that he had appendicitis and would have to have an operation. "Say," he said more rationally, as an idea occurred to him. "Do you realize that I've got an important directors' meeting in three days? I can't miss that for any operation. Now listen; be sensible. I'll give you a thousand dollars if you get me to that meeting in good shape."

Dr. Banza shrugged his shoulders.

"I'm going to dinner now," he said in the voice that one uses to a peevish child. "You have two or three hours in which to think it over. By that time I'm afraid you will be an emergency."

Dr. Banza sauntered thoughtfully over to the College Tavern, and walking in, looked around for a table at which to eat his dinner. He felt his shoulder touched.

"Sit down and eat with me," invited his unnoticed friend.

"Why, hello Bookstrom!" he cried warmly, as he perceived who it was.

"Hello yourself," returned Bookstrom, now portly and cheerful enough, with a little twinkle in each eye.

"But what's the matter? You look dark and discouraged."

So, over the dinner, Banza told his friend about the annoying dilemma with the obdurate and irascible Cladgett, who threatened certain ruin to his career.

"I feel like telling him to go to hell," Dr. Banza concluded.

Bookstrom sat a long time in silent thought, his elbows leaned on the table, sizzling a little tune through his cupped hands.

"Just the thing I've been looking for," he said at last slowly, as though he had come to a difficult decision. "Do you want to listen to a little lecture, Banza? Then you can decide whether I can help you or not?"

"If you can help me, you're some medicine-man. Shoot the lecture, though." Dr. Banza leaned back and waited, with much outward show of patience.

"You remember," opened Bookstrom, "that I had a couple of years of medical college work, and had to quit. That accounts for my having gotten this idea so suddenly just now.

"My present title of Professor of Applied Mathematics is not an empty one. I've applied some mathematics this time, I'll tell the world.

"You hear a lot about the Fourth Dimension nowadays. Most people snort when you mention it. Some point a finger at you or grab your coat lapel, and ask you what it is. *I don't know* what it is! Don't get to imagining that I've discovered what the fourth dimension is. But, I don't know what light is, or what gravitation is, except in a 'pure-mathematics' sense. Yet, I utilize light and gravitation in a practical way every day, do I not?

"Well, I've learned how to utilize the fourth dimension without knowing what it is. And here's how we can apply it to your Cladgett. Only, I've got an ancient grudge against that bird, and he's got to pay me back in real money for it, right now. You take your thousand and get a thousand for me—.

"Now, how can we use the fourth dimension to help him? In order to explain it, I'll have to illustrate with an example from a two-dimensional plane of existence. Suppose you and Cladgett were two-dimensional beings confined to the plane of this sheet of paper. You could move about in any direction upon the paper, but you could not get upwards off of it. Here is Cladgett. You can go all around him, but you can't jump over him, any more than you can turn yourself inside out.

"The only way that you, a two-dimensional surgeon can remove an appendix from this two-dimensional wretch, is to make a hole somewhere in his circumference, reach in, separate the doojigger from its attachments and pull it out, all limited to the surface of the paper. Is that plain so far?"

Banza nodded without interrupting.

"But, suppose some Professor of Applied Mathematics arranges it so that you can rise slightly, infinitely slightly above the plane of the paper. Then you can get Cladgett's appendix out without making any break in his circumference. All you do is to get up above him, locate your appendix, and reach down or lower yourself down to the original plane, and whisk out the appendix.

"He, being confined to the two-dimensional plane of the paper, cannot see how you do it, or comprehend how. But here you are, back down to the plane of the paper again beside Cladgett, with the appendix in your hand, and he marvels how you did it."

"Brilliant reasoning," Dr. Banza admitted. "But unfortunately for its value in this emergency, Cladgett is a three-dimensional old hulk and so am I."

"To proceed," Bookstrom made a show of ignoring the interruption, "suppose I had constructed an elevator that could lift you a little, ever so little along the fourth dimension, at right angles to the other three. Then you could reach over and hook out Cladgett's appendix without making any abdominal wound."

15

Bookstrom stopped and smiled. Banza jumped to his feet.

"Well, dammit, have you?" he demanded. People in the Tavern were turning around and looking at them.

"Come and see!"

They hooked arms and went up to Bookstrom's laboratory. Apparently Banza was satisfied with what he saw, for in five minutes he came racing out of the door, and called a taxi and had himself whirled to Cladgett's house.

There he had some trouble about the two thousand dollars in advance. It was an unethical thing to demand, but he was a clever enough psychologist to sense and respect Bookstrom's reasons.

"I've found a specialist," he announced, "and am personally convinced that he can do what you want. With the next two days quiet in bed and subsequent care in diet, you can get to the meeting."

"Go ahead then," moaned Cladgett.

"But this man wants a thousand dollars, and insists that his thousand and mine must both be paid in advance," said Banza meekly.

Cladgett rose up in bed.

"Oh, you doctors are a bunch of robbers!" he shouted. Then he groaned and fell back again. The appendicitis was too much for him. A pain as sustained and long-enduring as that of an acute appendicitis will compel anyone to do anything. Soon Cladgett and a nurse were in an ambulance speeding toward the University, and Banza had two checks in his pocket.

Bookstrom was all ready. A half dozen simple surgical instruments to suffice for actually detaching the appendix, were sterilized and covered. He put Cladgett on a long wooden table and asked the nurse to sit at his head with a chloroform mask, with orders to use it if he complained. He directed Banza to scrub his hands. Beside Cladgett was the "elevator."

There wasn't much to the machine. All great things are simple, I suppose. There were three trussed beams of aluminum at right angles to each other, each with a cylinder and plunger, and from them, toggles coming together at a point where there was a sort of "universal joint" topped by a mat of thick rubber. That was all.

16

"You mean for me to get on that thing and be shoved somewhere into nowhere—?" Banza looked worried.

"I won't insist," Bookstrom smiled.

"No thanks," Banza backed away with alacrity. "I'll give him whatever anesthetic he needs." Banza was no doubt uncomfortable with responsibility, for the patient was seriously ill.

"Fine!" Bookstrom seemed to be enjoying the situation thoroughly. "I still know how to whack off an appendix. That's elementary surgery, amateur stuff."

A storm of protest broke from Cladgett.

"I don't want to be operated. You promised—"; he wrung his hands and beat his heels upon the table.

"We promised," said Bookstrom sweetly, "that we would not open you up. You'll never find a scratch on yourself."

Cladgett quieted down. Bookstrom scrubbed his hands, and wrapped his right one in a sterile towel in order to manipulate the machine. He stepped on the rubber mat, and in a moment, Dr. Banza and the nurse were amazed to see him click suddenly out of sight. Click! and he was not there! Before they recovered from their astonishment, Cladgett began to complain. Dr. Banza had to start giving chloroform. He gave it slowly and cautiously, while Cladgett groaned and cursed and threshed himself about.

"Lie still, you fool!" shouted Bookstrom's voice in a preoccupied way, just beside them. It made their flesh creep, for he was not there.

Gradually the patient quieted down and breathed deeply and the doctor and the nurse took a breath of relief, and had time to wonder about everything. There was another click! and there stood Bookstrom with a tray of bloody instruments in his hand.

"Pippin!" he exclaimed enthusiastically, pointing to the appendix. It was swollen to the size of a thumb, with purple blotches of congestion, black areas of gangrene, and yellow patches of fibrin. "You're not such a bad diagnostician, Banza!"

"Put it in formalin—to show him how sick he was," suggested Banza.

"You'll have a fat time proving to anybody that that was taken out of *him*. Forget it, and deposit your check. Some day when you get up your nerve, let me show you how it feels to see the inside of a man, all at once, everything working."

Cladgett was much better the next day. His pain was all gone and he did not feel the terrible, prostrating sickness of the day before.

As soon as he awoke he felt himself all over for an operation wound, and finding none, mumbled to himself surlily for a while. The second day his fever was gone and he was ravenously hungry. On the third day he was merely tired. On the fourth day he went to the directors' meeting in his own car, grumbling that he had never had any appendicitis anyhow, and that the doctors had defrauded him of two thousand dollars.

"Got a notion to sue you for damages. May do it yet!" he snarled at Dr. Banza. "I'll include the value of my spectacles. You smashed them for me somewhere. Damn carelessness."

Dr. Banza bowed himself out.

"The next time he needs a doctor," he said to himself, "he can call one from Madagascar before I'll go to see him."

But Dr. Banza was no different from any other good physician. It wasn't two weeks before Cladgett called him, and again he was "fool enough to go," as he himself expressed it.

This time Cladgett was not in bed. He was nursing his hemispherical abdomen in an arm-chair.

"Thought you said you'd cure me of this appendicitis!" he wheezed antagonistically.

"Aha, so you did have appendicitis?" thought the doctor to himself. Aloud, he asked Cladgett to describe his symptoms, which Cladgett did in the popular way.

"I think it's adhesions!" he snapped.

"Adhesions exist chiefly in the brains of the laity, and in the conversation of doctors too lazy to make a diagnosis." Dr. Banza's courteous patience was deserting him.

He temperatured and pulsed his patient, gently palpated the abdominal muscles, and counted the leucocytes in a drop of blood.

18

"You do have a tender spot," he mused; "and possibly a slight palpable mass. But no signs of any infectious process. No muscle rigidity. Is it getting worse?"

"Getting worse every day!" he groaned histrionically. "What is it, doc?"

Dr. Banza resisted heroically the temptation to tell him that he had carcinoma of the ovary, and said instead with studied care:

"I can't be quite sure till we have an X-ray. Can you come down to the office?"

With much grunting and wheezing, Cladgett got up to the office and up on the radiographic table. Dr. Banza made a trial exposure and then several other films. He remained in the developing room for an interminable length of time, and then came out with a red face.

"Well! What?" yapped Cladgett.

"Oh, just a trifling matter of no importance. Come, get into the car with me. We'll drive over to Professor Bookstrom's laboratory, and in a moment we'll have you permanently relieved and feeling good."

"I'll not go to that charlatan again!" roared Cladgett. "And you doctors are always trying to talk all around the bush and refusing to tell people the truth. You can't work that gag on me! I want to know exactly!" He shook both arms at Banza.

"Why, really!" Dr. Banza acted very much embarrassed. "It's nothing that cannot be corrected in a few seconds—"

"Dammit!" shrieked Cladgett. "Gimme that X-ray picture, or I'll smash up your place!"

Dr. Banza went in and got the wet film clipped in its frame. He led the way to the outside door. Cladgett angrily followed him thither and there received the film. Banza backed away, while Cladgett held the negative up to the light. There, very plainly visible in the right lower quadrant of the abdomen was a pair of old-fashioned *pince-nez* spectacles!

Strange heavings and tremors seemed to traverse Cladgett's bulk, showing through his clothes. He shook and undulated and heaved suddenly in spots. His face turned alternately white and purple; his jaw worked up and down, and his mouth opened and shut convulsively, though no sound came forth. Suddenly he turned and stamped out of the building, carrying the wet film with him.

The old man was a pretty good judge of character, or he never would have made the money he did. In some subconscious way he had realized that Bookstrom must be the man to see about this thing.

Banza telephoned Bookstrom at once and told him the details.

"How unfortunate!" Bookstrom exclaimed. There was a suspicious note in his voice. That solicitude for Cladgett could hardly have been genuine.

"He's coming over there!" warned Banza.

"I shall be proud to receive such a distinguished guest."

That was all Banza was able to accomplish. He was sick with consternation and anxiety.

Bookstrom could hear Cladgett's thunderous approach down the hall. Then the door burst open and a chair went down, followed by a rack of charts and a tall case full of models. Cladgett seemed to derive some satisfaction from the havoc, this time little dreaming that Bookstrom was quite capable of setting the stage for just such a show. "You—you—" sputtered Cladgett, still unable to speak coherently.

"Too bad; too bad," consoled Bookstrom kindly. "Let's see your roentgenogram."

"Ah, how interesting!" Bookstrom could put vast enthusiasm into his voice. "The question is, I suppose, how they got in there?" He looked back and forth from Cladgett's protruding hemisphere to the spectacles on the X-ray film, as if to imply that in such an immense vault there surely ought to be room for such a trifling thing as a pair of spectacles.

"You put them there, you crook, you scoundrel, you robber, you dirty thief!" The "dirty thief" came out in a high falsetto shriek.

"You do me much honor," Bookstrom bowed. "That would be a 'stunt' I might say, to be proud of."

"You don't deny it, do you?" Cladgett suddenly calmed down and spoke in acidly triumphant tones.

"It strikes me," Bookstrom mused, "that this is something that would be difficult either to prove or to deny."

"I've got the goods on you." Cladgett spoke coldly, just as he had on that occasion fifteen years before. "You either pay me fifty thousand dollars damages, or this goes to court at once."

"My dear *Sir!*" Bookstrom bowed gravely. "You or anyone else have a standing invitation to go through my effects, and if you find more than a hundred dollars, you are welcome to half of it, if you give me the other half."

Cladgett did not know how to reply to this.

"I'm suing you for damages at once!" His words came like blows from a pile-driver.

Bookstrom bowed him out with a smile.

The damage suit created considerable flare in the headlines. A pair of spectacles left in a patient's abdomen at operation! That was a morsel such as the public had not had to scandalize over for some time! Newspapers dug up the details, even to the history of the forced payment on the note fifteen years before and the disappointed medical student; and the fact that the operation had been performed in secret and at night, in the laboratory of a man who was not a licensed medical practitioner, for Bookstrom's title of "doctor" was a philosophical, not a medical one. The public gloated and licked its chops in anticipation of more morsels at the trial.

But no such treat ever came off. Immediately after the suit was filed Bookstrom's counsel requested permission to examine thoroughly the person of the plaintiff. This was granted. The counsel then quietly and privately called the judge's attention to the fact that the plaintiff's body contained no scars or marks of operation of any kind; therefore, it was evident that he had never been operated upon and, therefore, nothing could have been left in his abdomen. The judge held an informal preliminary hearing and threw the case out of court. He admitted that there were curious phases to it, but he was busy and tired, and his docket was so full that it made him nervous; he was glad to forget anything that was technically settled.

Cladgett continued to grow sicker. The pain and the lump in his side increased. In another two weeks he was a miserable man. He still managed to be up and about a little, but his face was drawn from suffering (and rage), and pains racked him constantly. He had lost twenty-five pounds in weight, and looked like a wretched shadow of his former self.

One day he thrust himself into Bookstrom's office. Bookstrom dismissed the stenographer and the two student-assistants, and faced Cladgett blandly.

"Banza says you can fix this up somehow," he said, and it sounded like "gr-r-rump, gr-r-r-ump, r-r-rump!" "I've decided to *let* you go ahead."

"Very kind of you," Bookstrom purred. "I ought to feel humbly grateful for as big a favor as that. As a matter of fact, I've decided to let the Sultan of Sulu go jump in the lake. But I've a lurking suspicion that he isn't going to do it."

Cladgett sat and stared at him awhile, and then picked himself up and stumped out, grumbling and groaning.

The next day Dr. Banza brought him into Dr. Bookstrom's laboratory. He eased himself down into a chair before saying anything.

"I'm convinced that Banza's right and that you can help me. Now what's your robber's price?"

"It's a highway robber's price, with the accent on the high," murmured Bookstrom deprecatingly.

"Well, out with it, you—" there Cladgett wisely checked himself.

"I ask nothing whatever for myself," said Bookstrom, suddenly becoming serious. "But if you want me to get those spectacles out of you, right here and now you settle a sum to found a Students' Fund to loan money to worthy and needy scientific students, which they may pay back when they are established and earning money. I think when you spoke to me about a damage suit you mentioned the sum of fifty thousand dollars. Let's call it that."

"Fifty thousand dollars!" screamed Cladgett in a high falsetto. He was weak and unstable. "That's preposterous! That's criminal extortion."

"This transaction is not of my seeking," Bookstrom suggested.

"You've fixed it all up on me," Cladgett wailed, but his voice sank toward the end.

"Tell that to the judge. Or, go to a surgeon and have him open you up and take them out. That would come cheaper."

"Operation!" shrieked Cladgett. "I can't stand an operation."

He looked desperately at Banza, but there was no hope there.

"This seems to me a wonderful opportunity," Banza said, "for you to do a public service and distinguish yourself in the community. I'm sure that amount of money will not affect you seriously."

Cladgett started for the door, and then groaned and fell back heavily into his chair. He sat groaning for awhile, his suffering being mental as well as physical; finally he reached into his pocket for his pen and his checkbook. He kept on groaning as he wrote out a check and flung it on the table.

"Now, damn you, help me!" he yelped.

They put him on the table.

"Banza, you scrub. You deserve to see this," directed Bookstrom.

So Banza stepped on the rubber mat and Bookstrom instructed him.

"Move this switch one button at a time. That will always raise you a notch. Look around each time until you get it just right."

With the first click Banza disappeared, just as people vanish suddenly in the movies. Cladgett groaned and squirmed and then was quiet. With another click Banza appeared, and in his hand was a pair of old-fashioned *pince-nez* spectacles, moist and covered with a grayish film. He held them toward Cladgett, who grabbed them and mumbled something.

"Can you imagine!" breathed Banza, "standing in the center of a sphere and seeing all the abdominal organs around you at once? Something like that, it seemed; not exactly either. There above my head were the coils of the small intestine. To the right was the cecum with the spectacles beside it; to my left the sigmoid and the muscles; attached to the ilium, and beneath my feet the peritoneum of the anterior abdominal wall. But, I was terribly dizzy for some reason; I could not stand it very long, much as I should have liked to remain inside of him for awhile—"

"But, you weren't inside of him," corrected Bookstrom.

23

Banza stared blankly.

"But, I've just told you. There I was inside of him, with his viscera all around me, stomach and diaphragm in front, bladder behind—I *was* inside of him."

"Yes, it looked that way to you," nodded Bookstrom. "That is the way your brain, accustomed to three-dimensional space, interpreted it. But look. If I draw a circle on this sheet of paper, I can see all points on the inside of it, can I not? Yet, if you were a two-dimensional being, I would have a hard time convincing you that I am not inside the circle."

The Gostak and the Doshes

Let the reader suppose that somebody states: "*The gostak distims the doshes.*" You do not know what this means, nor do I. But if we assume that it is English, we know that the *doshes* are *distimmed* by the *gostak*. We know that one *distimmer* of the *doshes* is a *gostak*. If, moreover, doshes are galloons, we know that some galloons are distimmed by the gostak. And so we may go on, and so we often do go on.

—Unknown writer quoted by Ogden and Richards, in *The Meaning of Meaning*, Harcourt Brace & Co., 1923; also by Walter N. Polakov in *Man and His Affairs*, Williams & Wilkins, 1925.

"Why! That is lifting yourself by your own bootstraps!" I exclaimed in amazed incredulity. "It's absurd."

Woleshensky smiled indulgently. He towered in his chair as though in the infinite kindness of his vast mind there were room to understand and overlook all the foolish little foibles of all the weak little beings that called themselves men. A mathematical physicist lives in vast spaces where a light-year is a footstep, where universes are being born and blotted out, where space unrolls along a fourth dimension on a surface distended from a fifth. To him, human beings and their affairs do not loom very important.

"Relativity," he explained. In his voice there was a patient forbearance for my slowness of comprehension. "Merely relativity. It doesn't take much physical effort to make the moon move through the treetops, does it? Just enough to walk down the garden path."

I stared at him, and he continued: "If you had been born and raised on a moving train, no one could convince you that the landscape was not in rapid motion. Well, our conception of the universe is quite as relative as that. Sir Isaac Newton tried in his mathematics to express a universe as though beheld by an infinitely removed and perfectly fixed observer. Mathematicians since his time, realizing the futility of such an effort, have taken into consideration that what things 'are' depends upon the person who is looking at them. They have tried to express common knowledge, such as the law of gravitation, in terms that would hold good for all observers. Yet their leader and culminating genius, Einstein, has been unable to express knowledge in terms of pure relativity; he has had to accept the velocity of light as an arbitrarily fixed constant. Why should the velocity of light be any more fixed and constant than any other quantity in the universe?"

"But what's that got to do with going into the fourth dimension?" I broke in impatiently.

He continued as though I hadn't spoken.

"The thing that interests us now, and that mystifies modern mathematicians, is the question of movement, or, more accurately, translation. Is there such a thing as *absolute translation?* Can there be movement—translation—except in *relation* to something else than the thing that moves? All movement we know of is movement in relation to other objects, whether it be a walk down the street or the movement of the earth in its orbit around the sun. A change of *relative* position. But the mere translation of an isolated object existing alone in space is mathematically inconceivable, for there is no such thing as space in that sense."

"I thought you said something about going into another universe—" I interrupted again.

You can't argue with Woleshensky. His train of thought went on without a break.

"By translation we understand getting from one place to another. 'Going somewhere' originally meant a movement of our bodies. Yet, as a matter of fact, when we drive in an automobile we 'go somewhere' without moving our bodies at all. The scene is changed around us; we are somewhere else; and yet we haven't *moved* at all.

"Or suppose you could cast off gravitational attraction for a mo-

26

ment and let the earth rotate under you; you would be going somewhere and yet not moving—"

"But that is theory; you can't tinker with gravitation—"

"Every day you tinker with gravitation. When you start upward in
an elevator, your pressure, not your weight, against the floor of it is
increased; apparent gravitation between you and the floor of the elevator is greater than before—and that's like gravitation is anyway:
inertia and acceleration. But we are talking about translation. The
position of everything in the universe must be referred to some sort
of coordinates. Suppose we change the angle or direction of the coordinates: then you have 'gone somewhere' and yet you haven't moved,
nor has anything else moved."

I looked at him, holding my head in my hands.

"I couldn't swear that I understand that," I said slowly. "And I repeat that it looks like lifting yourself by your own bootstraps."

The homely simile did not dismay him. He pointed a finger at me
as he spoke. "You've seen a chip of wood bobbing on the ripples of a
pond. Now you think the chip is moving, now the water. Yet neither is
moving; the only motion is of an abstract thing called a wave.

"You've seen those 'illusion' diagrams—for instance, this one of a
group of cubes. Make up your mind that you are looking down upon
their upper surfaces, and indeed they seem below you. Now change
your mind and imagine that you are down below, looking up. Behold,
you see their lower surfaces; you are indeed below them. You have
'gone somewhere,' yet there has been no translation of anything. You
have merely changed coordinates."

"Which do you think will drive me insane more quickly—if you
show me what you mean, or if you keep on talking without showing
me?"

"I'll try to show you. There are some types of mind, you know, that
cannot grasp the idea of relativity. It isn't the mathematics involved
that matters; it's just the inability of some types of mental organization to grasp the fact that the mind of the observer endows his environment with certain properties which have no absolute existence.
Thus, when you walk through the garden at night the moon floats

27

from one treetop to another. Is your mind good enough to invert this: make the moon stand still and let the trees move backward? Can you do that? If so, you can 'go somewhere' into another dimension."

Woleshensky rose and walked to the window. His office was an appropriate setting for such a modern discussion as was ours—situated in a new, ultramodern building on the university campus, the varnish glossy, the walls clean, the books neatly arranged behind clean glass, the desk in most orderly array; the office was just as precise and modern and wonderful as the mind of its occupant.

"When do you want to go?" he asked.

"Now!"

"Then I have two more things to explain to you. The fourth dimension is just as much *here* as anywhere else. Right here around you and me things exist and go forward in the fourth dimension; but we do not see them and are not conscious of them because we are confined to our own three. Secondly: If we name the four coordinates as Einstein does, x, y, z, and t, then we exist in x, y, and z and move freely about in them, but are powerless to move in t: Why? Because t is the time dimension; and the time dimension is a difficult one for biological structures that depend on irreversible chemical reactions for their existence. But biochemical reactions can take place along any one of the other dimensions as well as along t.

"Therefore, let us transform coordinates. Rotate the property of chemical irreversibility from t to z. Since we are organically able to exist (or at least to perceive) in only three dimensions at once, our new time dimension will be z. We shall be unconscious of z and cannot travel in it. Our activities and consciousness will take place along x, y, and t.

"According to fiction writers, to switch into the t dimension, some sort of apparatus with an electrical field ought to be necessary. It is not. You need nothing more to rotate into the t dimension than you do to stop the moon and make the trees move as you ride down the road; or than you do to turn the cubes upside down. It is a matter of *relativity*."

28

I had ceased trying to wonder or to understand.

"Show me!" was all I could gasp.

"The success of this experiment in changing from the z to the t co-ordinate has depended largely upon my lucky discovery of a favorable location. It is just as, when you want the moon to ride the treetops successfully, there have to be favorable features in the topography or it won't work. The edge of this building and that little walk between the two rows of Norway poplars seems to be an angle between planes in the z and t dimensions. It seems to slope downward, does it not?—Now walk from here to the end and imagine yourself going upward. That is all. Instead of feeling this building behind and *above* you, conceive it as behind and *below*. Just as on your ride by moonlight, you must tell yourself that the moon is not moving while the trees ride by.—Can you do that? Go ahead, then." He spoke in a confident tone, as though he knew exactly what would happen.

Half credulous, half wondering, I walked slowly out of the door. I noticed that Woleshensky settled himself down to the table with a pad and a pencil to some kind of study, and forgot me before I had finished turning around. I looked curiously at the familiar wall of the building and the still more familiar poplar walk, expecting to see some strange scenery, some unknown view from another world. But there were the same old bricks and trees that I had known so long, though my disturbed and wondering frame of mind endowed them with a sudden strangeness and unwontedness. Things I had known for some years, they were, yet so powerfully had Woleshensky's arguments impressed me that I already fancied myself in a different universe. According to the conception of relativity, objects of the x, y, z universe ought to look different when viewed from the x, y, t universe.

Strange to say, I had no difficulty at all in imagining myself as going *upward* on my stroll along the slope. I told myself that the building was behind and below me, and indeed it seemed real that it was that way. I walked some distance along the little avenue of poplars, which seemed familiar enough in all its details, though after a few minutes it struck me that the avenue seemed rather long. In fact, it was much longer than I had ever known it to be before.

With a queer Alice-in-Wonderland feeling I noted it stretching way on ahead of me. Then I looked back.

I gasped in astonishment. The building was indeed *below* me. I looked down upon it from the top of an elevation. The astonishment of that realization had barely broken over me when I admitted that there was a building down there; but what building? Not the new Morton Hall, at any rate. It was a long, three-story brick building, quite resembling Morton Hall, but it was not the same. And on beyond there were trees with buildings among them; but it was not the campus that I knew.

I paused in a kind of panic. What was I to do now? Here I was in a strange place. How I had gotten there I had no idea. What ought I do about it? Where should I go? How was I to get back? Odd that I had neglected the precaution of how to get back. I surmised that I must be on the *t* dimension. Stupid blunder on my part, neglecting to find out how to get back.

I walked rapidly down the slope toward the building. Any hopes that I might have had about its being Morton Hall were thoroughly dispelled in a moment. It was a totally strange building, old, and old-fashioned looking. I had never seen it before in my life. Yet it looked perfectly ordinary and natural and was obviously a university classroom building.

I cannot tell whether it was an hour or a dozen that I spent walking frantically this way and that, trying to decide to go into this building or another, and at the last moment backing out in a sweat of hesitation. It seemed like a year but was probably only a few minutes. Then I noticed the people. They were mostly young people, of both sexes. Students, of course. Obviously I was on a university campus. Perfectly natural, normal young people, they were. If I were really on the *t* dimension, it certainly resembled the *z* dimension very closely.

Finally I came to a decision. I could stand this no longer. I selected a solitary, quiet-looking man and stopped him.

"Where am I?" I demanded.

He looked at me in astonishment. I waited for a reply, and he continued to gaze at me speechlessly. Finally it occurred to me that he didn't understand English.

"Do you speak English?" I asked hopelessly.

"Of course!" he said vehemently. "What's wrong with you?"

"Something's wrong with something," I exclaimed. "I haven't any idea where I am or how I got here."

"Synthetic wine?" he asked sympathetically.

"Oh, hell! Think I'm a fool? Say, do you have a good man in mathematical physics on the faculty? Take me to him."

"Psychology, I should think," he said, studying me. "Or psychiatry. But I'm a law student and know nothing of either."

"Then make it mathematical physics, and I'll be grateful to you."

So I was conducted to the mathematical physicist. The student led me into the very building that corresponded to Morton Hall, and into an office the position of which quite corresponded to that of Woleshensky's office. However, the office was older and dustier; it had a Victorian look about it and was not as modern as Woleshensky's room. Professor Vibens was a rather small, bald-headed man with a keen-looking face. As I thanked the law student and started on my story, he looked rather bored, as though wondering why I had picked on him with my tale of wonder. Before I had gotten very far he straightened up a little; and farther along he pricked up another notch; and before many minutes he was tense in his chair as he listened to me. When I finished, his comment was terse, like that of a man accustomed to thinking accurately and to the point.

"Obviously you come into this world from another set of coordinates. As we are on the z dimension, you must have come to us from the t dimension —"

He disregarded my attempts to protest at this point.

"Your man Woleshensky has evidently developed the conception of relativity further than we have; although Monpeters's theory comes close enough to it. Since I have no idea how to get you back, you must be my guest. I shall enjoy hearing all about your world."

"That is very kind of you," I said gratefully. "I'm accepting because I can't see what else to do. At least until the time when I can find myself a place in your world or get back to my own. Fortunately," I added as an afterthought, "no one will miss me there, unless it be a few classes of students who will welcome the little vacation that must elapse, before my successor is found."

Breathlessly eager to find out what sort of world I had gotten into, I walked with him to his home. And I may state at the outset that if I had found everything upside down and outlandishly bizarre, I should have been far less amazed and astonished than I was. For, from the walk that first evening from Professor Vibens's office along several blocks of residence street to his solid and respectable home, through all of my goings about the town and country during the years that I remained in the *t*-dimensional world, I found people and things thoroughly ordinary and familiar. They looked and acted as we do, and their homes and goods looked like ours. I cannot possibly imagine a world and a people that could be more similar to ours without actually being the same. It was months before I got over the idea that I had merely wandered into an unfamiliar part of my own city. Only the actual experience of wide travel and much sight-seeing, and the knowledge that there was no such extensive English-speaking country in the world that I knew, convinced me that I must be on some other world, doubtless in the *t* dimension.

"A gentleman who has found his way here from another universe," the professor introduced me to a strapping young fellow who was mowing the lawn.

The professor's son was named John! Could anything be more commonplace?

"I'll have to take you around and show you things tomorrow," John said cordially, accepting the account of my arrival without surprise.

A redheaded servant girl, roast pork and rhubarb sauce for dinner, and checkers afterward, a hot bath at bedtime, the ringing of a telephone somewhere else in the house—is it any wonder that it was months before I would believe that I had actually come into a different universe? What slight differences there were in the people and the world merely served to emphasize the similarity. For instance, I think they were just a little more hospitable and "old-fashioned" than we are. Making due allowances for the fact that I was a rather remarkable phenomenon, I think I was welcomed more heartily in this home and in others later, people spared me more of their time and interest from their daily business, than would have happened under similar circumstances in a correspondingly busy city in America.

Again, John found a lot of time to take me about the city and show me banks and stores and offices. He drove a little squat car with tall wheels, run by a spluttering gasoline motor. (The car was not as perfect as our modern cars, and horses were quite numerous in the streets. Yet John was a busy businessman, the district superintendent of a life-insurance agency.) Think of it! Life insurance in Einstein's t dimension.

"You're young to be holding such an important position," I suggested.

"Got started early," John replied. "Dad is disappointed because I didn't see fit to waste time in college. Disgrace to the family, I am."

What in particular shall I say about the city? It might have been any one of a couple of hundred American cities. Only it wasn't. The electric streetcars, except for their bright green color, were perfect; they might have been brought over bodily from Oshkosh or Tulsa. The ten-cent stores with gold letters on their signs; drugstores with soft drinks; a mad, scrambling stock exchange; the blaring sign of an advertising dentist; brilliant entrances to motion-picture theaters were all there. The beauty shops did wonders to the women's heads, excelling our own by a good deal, if I am any judge; and at that time I had nothing more important on my mind than to speculate on that question. Newsboys bawled the *Evening Sun* and the *Morning Gale*, in whose curious, flat type I could read accounts of legislative doings, murders, and divorces quite as fluently as I could in my own *Tribune* at home. Strangeness and unfamiliarity had bothered me a good deal on a trip to Quebec a couple of years before; but they were not noticeable here in the t dimension.

For three or four weeks the novelty of going around, looking at things, meeting people, visiting concerts, theaters, and department stores was sufficient to absorb my interest. Professor Vibens's hospitality was so sincerely extended that I did not hesitate to accept, though I assured him that I would repay it as soon as I got established in this world. In a few days I was thoroughly convinced that there was no way back home. Here I must stay, at least until I learned as much as Woleshensky knew about crossing dimensions. Professor Vibens eventually secured for me a position at the university.

It was shortly after I had accepted the position as instructor in experimental physics and had begun to get broken into my work that I noticed a strange commotion among the people of the city. I have always been a studious recluse, observing people as phenomena rather than participating in their activities. So for some time I noted only in a subconscious way the excited gathering in groups, the gesticulations and blazing eyes, the wild sale of extra editions of papers, the general air of disturbance. I even failed to take an active interest in these things when I made a railroad journey of three hundred miles and spent a week in another city; so thoroughly at home did I feel in this world that when the advisability arose of my studying laboratory methods in another university, I made the trip alone. So absorbed was I in my laboratory problems that I only noted with half an eye the commotion and excitement everywhere, and merely recollected it later. One night it suddenly popped into my head that the country was aroused over something.

That night I was with the Vibens family in their living room. John tuned in the radio. I wasn't listening to the thing very much; I had troubles of my own. $F = g \frac{m_1 m_2}{r^2}$ was familiar enough to me. It meant the same and held as rigidly here as in my old world. But what was the name of the bird who had formulated that law? Back home it was Newton. Tomorrow in class I would have to be thoroughly familiar with his name. Pasvieux, that's what it was. What messy surnames. It struck me that it was lucky that they expressed the laws of physics in the same form and even in the same algebraic letters, or I might have had a time getting them confused—when all of a sudden the radio blatantly bawled: "THE GOSTAK DISTIMS THE DOSHES!"

John jumped to his feet.

"Damn right!" he shouted, slamming the table with his fist.

Both his father and mother annihilated him with withering glances, and he slunk from the room. I gazed stupefied. My stupefaction con-

tinued while the professor shut off the radio and both of them ex-
cused themselves from my presence. Then suddenly I was alert.

I grabbed a bunch of newspapers, having seen none for several
days. Great sprawling headlines covered the front pages:

"THE GOSTAK DISTIMS THE DOSHES."

For a moment I stopped, trying to recollect where I had heard those
words before. They recalled something to me. Ah, yes! That very afternoon there had been a commotion beneath my window on the
university campus. I had been busy checking over an experiment so
that I might be sure of its success at tomorrow's class, and looked out
rather absently to see what was going on. A group of young men from
a dismissed class was passing and had stopped for a moment.

"I say, the gostak distims the doshes!" said a fine-looking young
fellow. His face was pale and strained.

The young man facing him sneered derisively, "Aw, your grandmother! Don't be a feeble—"

He never finished. The first fellow's fist caught him in the cheek.
Several books dropped to the ground. In a moment the two had
clinched and were rolling on the ground, fists flying up and down,
smears of blood appearing here and there. The others surrounded
them and for a moment appeared to enjoy the spectacle, but suddenly
recollected that it looked rather disgraceful on a university campus,
and after a lively tussle separated the combatants. Twenty of them,
pulling in two directions, tugged them apart.

The first boy strained in the grasp of his captors; his white face was
flecked with blood and he panted for breath.

"Insult!" he shouted, giving another mighty heave to get free. He
looked contemptuously around. "The whole bunch of you ought to
learn to stand up for your honor. The gostak distims the doshes!"

That was the astonishing incident that these words called to my
mind. I turned back to my newspapers.

"Slogan Sweeps the Country," proclaimed the subheads. "Ringing Expression of National Spirit! Enthusiasm Spreads Like Wildfire!
The new patriotic slogan is gaining ground rapidly," the leading article went on. "The fact that it has covered the country almost in-

stantaneously seems to indicate that it fills a deep and long-felt want in the hearts of the people. It was first uttered during a speech in Walkingdon by that majestic figure in modern statesmanship, Senator Harob. The beautiful sentiment, the wonderful emotion of this sublime thought, are epoch-making. It is a great conception, doing credit to a great man, and worthy of being the guiding light of a great people—"

That was the gist of everything I could find in the papers. I fell asleep still puzzled about the thing. I was puzzled because—as I see now and didn't see then—I was trained in the analytical methods of physical science and knew little or nothing about the ways and emotions of the masses of the people.

In the morning the senseless expression popped into my head as soon as I awoke. I determined to waylay the first member of the Vibens family who showed up, and demand the meaning of the thing. It happened to be John.

"John, what's a gostak?"

John's face lighted up with pleasure. He threw out his chest and a look of pride replaced the pleasure. His eyes blazed, and with a consuming enthusiasm he shook hands with me, as deacons shake hands with a new convert—a sort of glad welcome.

"The gostak!" he exclaimed. "Hurray for the gostak!"

"But what is a gostak?"

"Not *a* gostak! *The* gostak. The gostak is—the distimmer of the doshes—see! He distims 'em, see?"

"Yes, yes. But what is distimming? How do you distim?"

"No, no! Only the gostak can distim. The gostak distims the doshes. See?"

"Ah, I see!" I exclaimed. Indeed, I pride myself on my quick wit. "What are doshes? Why, they are the stuff distimmed by the gostak. Very simple!"

"Good for you!" John slapped my back in huge enthusiasm. "I think it wonderful for you to understand us so well after being here only a short time. You are very patriotic."

I gritted my teeth tightly to keep myself from speaking.

"Professor Vibens, what's a gostak?" I asked in the solitude of his office an hour later.

He looked pained.

He leaned back in his chair and looked me over elaborately, and waited some time before answering.

"Hush!" he finally whispered. "A scientific man may think what he pleases, but if he says too much, people in general may misjudge him. As a matter of fact, a good many scientific men are taking this so-called patriotism seriously. But a mathematician cannot use words loosely; it has become second nature with him to inquire closely into the meaning of every term he uses."

"Well, doesn't that jargon mean anything at all?" I was beginning to be puzzled in earnest.

"To me it does not. But it seems to mean a great deal to the public in general. It's making people do things, is it not?"

I stood a while in stupefied silence. That an entire great nation should become fired up over a meaningless piece of nonsense! Yet the astonishing thing was that I had to admit there was plenty of precedent for it in the history of my own z-dimensional world. A nation exterminating itself in civil wars to decide which of two profligate royal families should be privileged to waste the people's substance from the throne; a hundred thousand crusaders marching to death for an idea that to me means nothing; a meaningless, untrue advertising slogan that sells millions of dollars' worth of cigarettes to a nation, to the latter's own detriment—haven't we seen it over and over again?

"There's a public lecture on this stuff tonight at the First Church of the Salvation," Professor Vibens suggested.

"I'll be there," I said. "I want to look into the thing."

That afternoon there was another flurry of "extras" over the street; people gathered in knots and gesticulated with open newspapers.

"War! Let 'em have it!" I heard men shout.

"Is our national honor a rag to be muddied and trampled on?" the editorials asked.

As far as I could gather from reading the papers, there was a group

37

of nations across an ocean that was not taking the gostak seriously. A ship whose pennant bore the slogan had been refused entrance to an Engtalian harbor because it flew no national ensign. The Executive had dispatched a diplomatic note. An evangelist who had attempted to preach the gospel of the distimmed doshes at a public gathering in Itland had been ridden on a rail and otherwise abused. The Executive was dispatching a diplomatic note.

Public indignation waxed high. Derogatory remarks about "wops" were flung about. Shouts of "Holy war!" were heard. I could feel the tension in the atmosphere as I took my seat in the crowded church in the evening. I had been assured that the message of the gostak and the doshes would be thoroughly expounded so that even the most simpleminded and uneducated people could understand it fully. Although I had my hands full at the university, I was so puzzled and amazed at the course events were taking that I determined to give the evening to finding out what the slogan meant.

There was a good deal of singing before the lecture began. Mimeographed copies of the words were passed about, but I neglected to preserve them and do not remember them. I know there was one solemn hymn that reverberated harmoniously through the great church, a chanting repetition of "The Gostak Distims the Doshes." There was another stirring martial air that began: "Oh, the Gostak! Oh, the Gostak!"—and ended with a swift cadence on "The Gostak Distims the Doshes!" The speaker had a rich, eloquent voice and a commanding figure. He stepped out and bowed solemnly.

"The gostak distims the doshes," he pronounced impressively. "Is it not comforting to know that there is a gostak; do we not glow with pride because the doshes are distimmed? In the entire universe there is no more profoundly significant fact: the gostak distims the doshes. Could anything be more complete yet more tersely emphatic! The gostak distims the doshes!" Applause. "This thrilling truth affects our innermost lives. What would we do if the gostak did not distim the doshes? Without the gostak, without doshes, what would we do? What would we think? How would we feel?" Applause again.

At first I thought this was some kind of introduction. I was inexperienced in listening to popular speeches, lectures, and sermons. I had spent most of my life in the study of physics and its accessory sciences. I could not help trying to figure out the meaning of whatever I heard. When I found none, I began to get impatient. I waited some more, thinking that soon he would begin on the real explanation. After thirty minutes of the same sort of stuff as I have just quoted, I gave up trying to listen. I just sat and hoped he would soon be through. The people applauded and grew more excited. After an hour I stirred restlessly; I slouched down in my seat and sat up by turns. After two hours I grew desperate; I got up and walked out. Most of the people were too excited to notice me. Only a few of them cast hostile glances at my retreat.

The next day the mad nightmare began for me. First there was a snowstorm of extras over the city, announcing the sinking of a merchantman by an Engtalian cruiser. A dispute had arisen between the officers of the merchantman and the port officials, because the latter had jeered disrespectfully at the gostak. The merchantman picked up and started out without having fulfilled all the customs requirements. A cruiser followed it and ordered it to return. The captain of the merchantman told them that the gostak distims the doshes, whereupon the cruiser fired twice and sank the merchantman. In the afternoon came the extras announcing the Executive's declaration of war.

Recruiting offices opened; the university was depleted of its young men; uniformed troops marched through the city, and railway trains full of them went in and out. Campaigns for raising war loans; home-guards, women's auxiliaries, ladies' aid societies making bandages, young women enlisting as ambulance drivers—it was indeed war; all of it to the constantly repeated slogan: "The gostak distims the doshes."

I could hardly believe that it was really true. There seemed to be no adequate cause for a war. The huge and powerful nation had dreamed a silly slogan and flung it in the world's face. A group of nations across the water had united into an alliance, claiming they had to defend themselves against having forced upon them a principle they did not desire. The whole thing at the bottom had no meaning. It did not seem possible that there would actually be a war; it seemed more like going through a lot of elaborate play-acting.

Only when the news came of a vast naval battle of doubtful issue, in which ships had been sunk and thousands of lives lost, did it come to me that they meant business. Black bands of mourning appeared on sleeves and in windows. One of the allied countries was invaded and a front line set up. Reports of a division wiped out by an airplane attack; of forty thousand dead in a five-day battle; of more men and more money needed, began to make things look real. Haggard men with bandaged heads and arms in slings appeared on the streets, a church and an auditorium were converted into hospitals, and trainloads of wounded were brought in. To convince myself that this thing was so, I visited these wards and saw with my own eyes the rows of cots, the surgeons working on ghastly wounds, the men with a leg missing or with a hideously disfigured face.

Food became restricted; there was no white bread, and sugar was rationed. Clothing was of poor quality; coal and oil were obtainable only on government permit. Businesses were shut down. John was gone; his parents received news that he was missing in action.

Real it was; there could be no more doubt of it. The thing that made it seem most real was the picture of a mangled, hopeless wreck of humanity sent back from the guns, a living protest against the horror of war. Suddenly someone would say, "The gostak distims the doshes!" and the poor wounded fragment would straighten up and put out his chest with pride, and an unquenchable fire would blaze in his eyes. He did not regret having given his all for that. How could I understand it?

And real it was when the draft was announced. More men were needed; volunteers were insufficient. Along with the rest, I complied with the order to register, doing so in a mechanical fashion, thinking little of it. Suddenly the coldest realization of the reality of it was flung at me when I was informed that my name had been drawn and that I would have to go!

All this time I had looked upon this mess as something outside of me, something belonging to a different world, of which I was not a part. Now here was a card summoning me to training camp. With all this death and mangled humanity in the background, I wasn't even interested in this world. I didn't belong here. To be called upon to undergo all the horrors of military life, the risk of a horrible death, for no reason at all! For a silly jumble of meaningless sounds.

I spent a sleepless night in maddened shock from the thing. In the morning a wild and haggard caricature of myself looked back at me from the mirror. But I had revolted. I intended to refuse service. If the words "conscientious objector" ever meant anything, I certainly was one. Even if they shot me for treason at once, that would be a fate less hard to bear than going out and giving my strength and my life for—for nothing at all.

My apprehensions were quite correct. With my usual success at self-control over a seething interior, I coolly walked to the draft office and informed them that I did not believe in their cause and could not see my way to fight for it. Evidently they had suspected something of the sort already, for they had the irons on my wrists before I had hardly done with my speech.

"Period of emergency," said a beefy tyrant at the desk. "No time for stringing out a civil trial. Court-martial!"

He said it to me vindictively, and the guards jostled me roughly down the corridor; even they resented my attitude. The court-martial was already waiting for me. From the time I walked out of the lecture at the church I had been under secret surveillance, and they knew my attitude thoroughly. That is the first thing the president of the court informed me.

My trial was short. I was informed that I had no valid reason for objecting. Objectors because of religion, because of nationality and similar reasons, were readily understood; a jail sentence to the end of the war was their usual fate. But I admitted that I had no intrinsic objection to fighting; I merely jeered at their holy cause. That was treason unpardonable.

"Sentenced to be shot at sunrise!" the president of the court announced.

The world spun around with me. But only for a second. My self-

41

control came to my aid. With the curious detachment that comes to us in such emergencies, I noted that the court-martial was being held in Professor Vibens's office—that dingy little Victorian room where I had first told my story of traveling by relativity and had first realized that I had come to the t-dimensional world. Apparently it was also to be the last room I was to see in this same world. I had no false hopes that the execution would help me back to my own world, as such things sometimes do in stories. When life is gone, it is gone, whether in one dimension or another. I would be just as dead in the z dimension as in the t dimension.

"Now, Einstein, or never!" I thought. "Come to my aid, O Riemann! O Lobachevski! If anything will save me it will have to be a tensor or a geodesic."

I said it to myself rather ironically. Relativity had brought me here. Could it get me out of this?

Well! Why not?

If the form of a natural law, yea, if a natural object varies with the observer who expresses it, might not the truth and the meaning of the gostak slogan also be a matter of relativity? It was like making the moon ride the treetops again. If I could be a better relativist and put myself in these people's places, perhaps I could understand the gostak. Perhaps I would even be willing to fight for him or it.

The idea struck me suddenly. I must have straightened up and some bright change must have passed over my features, for the guards who led me looked at me curiously and took a firmer grip on me. We had just descended the steps of the building and had started down the walk.

Making the moon ride the treetops! That was what I needed now. And that sounded as silly to me as the gostak. And the gostak did not seem so silly. I drew a deep breath and felt very much encouraged. The viewpoint of relativity was somehow coming back to me. Necessity manages much. I could understand how one might fight for the idea of a gostak distimming the doshes. I felt almost like telling these men. Relativity is a wonderful thing. They led me up the slope, between the rows of poplars.

Then it all suddenly popped into my head: how I had gotten here by changing my coordinates, insisting to myself that I was going upward. Just like making the moon stop and making the trees ride when you are out riding at night. Now I was going upward. In my own world, in the z dimension, this same poplar was *down* the slope.

"It's downward!" I insisted to myself. I shut my eyes and imagined the building behind and *above* me. With my eyes shut, it did seem downward. I walked for a long time before opening them. Then I opened them and looked around.

I was at the end of the avenue of poplars. I was surprised. The avenue seemed short. Somehow it had become shortened; I had not expected to reach the end so soon. And where were the guards in olive uniforms? There were none.

I turned around and looked back. The slope extended on backward above me. I had indeed walked downward. There were no guards, and the fresh, new building was on the hill behind me.

Woleshensky stood on the steps.

"Now what do you think of a *t* dimension?" he called out to me.

Woleshensky!

And a *new* building, modern! Vibens's office was in an old Victorian building. What was there in common between Vibens and Woleshensky? I drew a deep breath. The comforting realization spread gratefully over me that I was back in my native dimension. The gostak and the war were somewhere else. Here were peace and Woleshensky.

I hastened to pour out the story to him.

"What does it all mean?" I asked when I was through. "Somehow—vaguely—it seems that it ought to mean something."

"Perhaps," he said in his kind, sage way, "we really exist in four dimensions. A part of us and our world that we cannot see and are not conscious of projects on into another dimension, just like the front edges of the books in the bookcase, turned away from us. You know that the section of a conic cut by the *y* plane looks different from the section of the same conic cut by the *z* plane? Perhaps what you saw was our own world and our own selves intersected by a different set of coordinates. *Relativity*, as I told you in the beginning."

Paradise and Iron

Chapter I. A New Kind of Ship

Why anyone so old as Daniel Breckenridge, my grandfather's brother, should keep on working as hard as he did, was a mystery to me. He was about eighty-four; and a million little crinkles crisscrossed on the dry, parchment-like skin of his face where it was not covered by his snow-white beard. But he still went briskly about his duties as shipping manager of a great ship chandler's establishment at Galveston.

Just now he whispered sharply to me, and drew me by the arm behind some bales of canvas in the depths of the vast shipping-room.

"Look! There he is!"

He seemed to be trembling with intense excitement as he pointed toward the great sliding doors.

There, watching the men loading up a truck with a pile of goods consigned to some ship, was an old man, just as old and snowy and crinkled, and just as firm and active as my grand-uncle himself. I looked at him blankly for a moment. He was an interesting-looking old man, but I saw nothing to set me off a-tremble with excitement. But my old grand-uncle clutched my arm.

"Old John Kaspar, the Mystery Man!" he whispered again.

That suddenly galvanized me into action. I took one more good look at him, and got into motion at once.

"Do you think you could hold him here somehow until I get my outfit?" I asked. "I'll be back in ten minutes." It was now my turn to be tense and thrilled.

"It will take them longer than that to load up the truck," he said; "but hurry."

I shook hands with him hastily but fervently, knowing that I might have no further opportunity to do so, and then dashed out after a taxi. While my taxi is rushing me off to my room, I can explain all I know about John Kaspar, the mysterious octogenarian.

Forty years ago, back in the days when the gasoline industry was just being opened up, John Kaspar was the richest man in the world. His father had been a manufacturer of automobiles in Ohio and, foreseeing the importance of gasoline, he had bought up half a county of the most promising oil lands in East Texas. Before his death, oil was found on every acre of it. The son John, the old man at whom we have just been looking, was not interested in becoming a financier; he was working out some original ideas in automobile design. There were some wildly headlined newspaper clippings in my grand-uncle's collection, about John Kaspar's having thrown a reporter bodily into the ash-can because the poor fellow had made his way into Kaspar's shop and was looking too closely at some marvelous new invention on an automobile.

Then all of a sudden, John Kaspar disappeared! One morning the world woke up to the fact that he had been gone for two or three weeks. Investigation showed that he had converted all his properties into liquid securities, and it constituted the greatest single fortune the world had ever seen. With it in his hands, this young man, not yet twenty-five years old, was more powerful than the old Kings of France. This entire fortune had vanished with him. There was a tremendous lot of excitement about it in the papers and magazines; it furnished much conversation; running about and investigating, puzzling and wonderment; alarm that he might have met with foul play, and apprehension that he might have some sinister designs on civilization.

But no trace was ever found of him.

John Kaspar's closest friend was my grandfather, just recently died at the age of eighty-seven, having kept up his practice as a country doctor to the day of his death. The two had been roommates at college, and had been together a great deal in the years following their graduation. My grandfather, at the time, had been very much distressed about his friend's disappearance. To the day of his death he had lived in hopes that he would hear from Kaspar again.

The world forgot about John Kaspar and his vanished fortune long before I was born. I first learned of the story something over four years ago, when I was just beginning my work in Galveston at the State University Medical School. My aged grand-uncle had pointed out the mysterious old man to me, standing by the loading-door of the shipping room at Martin & Myrtle's.

"It's Kaspar!" he had said in a vehement whisper. "I can swear it is!"

Then he told me the story of the millionaire inventor's disappearance, back in the early years of the century.

"He first came in here several years ago," he concluded. "I could take an oath that it is John Kaspar. Your grandfather and I knew him more intimately than did anyone else."

He had studied him awhile—this was four years ago—and then shook his head.

"I wonder what has happened to him? He looks worried and sad, though he still seems to have his old iron constitution. There must be something strange going on somewhere—" My aged relative's voice trailed off reminiscently. After a moment he continued:

"When he first came in here, I hurried up to him with outstretched hand, joyful to see him again. He stared coldly at me, shook his head with an apologetic smile. He insisted that he did not know me, and I could not possibly know him. He was very courteous and very apologetic, but absolutely firm in the matter. Why does he hide his identity?

"He has been here twice since then. I followed his loaded truck both times in a taxi when he rode away. He comes to Galveston in a black yacht, black as ink. He has our truckmen unload the goods on his deck, and the instant the last package has touched the ship, he leaves the dock, with the things piled up on the deck.

"Where does he go? Where does he come from? What can he be up to, and where? And I can't forget that gloomy, worried look on his face."

My grand-uncle's account, and the sight of the wrinkled, but upright old man, with white hair and white beard, aroused my interest. And his pitiful eagerness to know more of his old friend aroused my sympathy.

I decided to go. I got together an outfit of clothes, weapons, preserved rations, first-aid kit, and money; and packed it, ready to seize and run at an instant's notice. My two years of service in the Texas Rangers gave me an excellent background for an adventure such as this promised to be.

I was in my Sophomore year at the Medical College at Galveston when we last saw the aged Kaspar come into the ship chandlers' firm for his boatload of supplies. Then for two years my emergency outfit lay packed and ready, inspected at intervals. I had graduated, received my doctor's degree, and was loafing around, resting and trying to decide what to do next.

Then one day my grand-uncle drew me behind the bales of canvas and pointed out our visitor. I did not recognize him at once. As soon as I did, I jumped into a taxi, dashed to my room, seized my kit, which was packed in a suitcase, and hurried back.

My grand-uncle stood there watching for me.

"Follow that truck!" he said to the taxi-driver, which the latter promptly did, nearly turning me on my ear.

The truck led us to a dock at the eastern extremity of Galveston Island.

The black yacht lay there right alongside the dock, just as she had been described to me. She was a trim, swift-looking craft, about a hundred feet long; but her black color gave her a sinister appearance among the bright white ships around her. And there also was the white-bearded old man walking up the gangplank. He ascended to the somber deck, and without looking around disappeared down a hatchway.

Knowing that my time was short, I quickly paid off my taxi-driver and hurried up on the dock. Catching hold of the swinging board with my hands, I scrambled up over the edge of it and rolled down on the deck.

"Now I'm aboard the old hearse whether I'm wanted or not," I said to myself. "If it continues the way it has started, this is going to be a lively trip."

Then the astonishing fact came home to me that there was no one anywhere on deck. Ordinarily the deck of a ship leaving dock is a busy scene, with sailors scurrying about, officers giving orders, and passengers at the rail taking a last look back. This deck might as well have been a graveyard; in fact it had somewhat that effect on me with its somber black everywhere.

A big searchlight in the bows rotated slowly on its pivot until its lens was turned squarely on me, and I caught a distorted reflection of myself in its depths; and then it turned back into its original position. It gave me a creepy, momentary impression of a huge eye that had looked at me, stared for a moment, and then looked away again.

In a few moments the ship was slipping along at considerable speed between the jetties, and Galveston was only a serrated purple skyline astern. The small machinery on deck had become quiet; and there remained only the deep and steady vibration of the engines. No one had as yet shown himself anywhere on board. I picked up my suitcase and walked around the deck, up one side and down the other, from bow to stern. At first I walked hesitatingly, and then, as I continued to find no one, I stepped out boldly.

It was a queer ship. Even though my knowledge of ships was limited to what I had acquired during a few years' residence in a seaport city, I could see that it was an uncommonly built and arranged vessel.

There was no wheel, and no steersman! The usual site of the wheel and binnacle was occupied by a cabin with some instruments in it; nor could I find anywhere any signs of anything resembling steering-gear. How was the ship piloted? Who was watching the course? There wasn't a lookout to be seen anywhere! Yet the ship had picked a tortuous course from its dock down the harbor and between the jetties.

A big, wide hatch in the waist led to the engine-room, if I might judge from the hot, oily smelling draft and the hum of machinery that came up through it. So I explored down there and looked the engines over. They were huge, heavy things, apparently of the Diesel type, but with a good deal of complicated apparatus on them that I had never seen on any Diesel engine and of which I could not guess

48

the purpose. Every moment I expected to see a greasy engineer come around a corner or from behind a motor. My curiosity overcame my hesitation, and I gathered up the courage to search all the niches and corners down there, but found no one. Was I to conclude that the engines were running themselves, without care?

The fore-hatch apparently led into the hold, whose gloomy depths were piled with bales and boxes. Obviously, there was no forecastle. No quarters for a crew! Well, all the crew I had seen so far would not require much space for quarters. The captain's cabin was where it belonged, but there was no one in it; only tables covered with apparatus. Gradually my exploration of the ship changed into a frantic search for some human being.

When I paused in my search, it was dusk. The ship was tearing along through the water at an unusual speed. From the high bow-wave and the churning wake, I would have guessed it at thirty knots. Galveston was but a faint glow on the horizon astern.

There was one place that I had not yet searched, and that was the cabin just ahead of the middle of the vessel. This was the space usually reserved for passengers on ships of this size. Down there it was that the mysterious old Kaspar had gone. Unless I was to conclude that he was the only living soul aboard, that is where the officers and crew must be. If all the officers and men were shut up together in the passengers' cabin, even a landlubber like myself was compelled to pronounce it a strange proceeding.

I opened the hatchway and looked down. My flashlight showed several steps leading to a passageway several feet below. There were three doors on each side and one at the end; and the latter had a line of yellow light under it coming through a crack. That is where Kaspar was at any rate! I went down quickly, threw open one of the doors, and pointed a flashlight into the room. It was empty. The others were the same. I knocked loudly on the door at the end of the passage.

A chair scraped on the floor and the door swung swiftly open. There stood the strange old man, erect as a warrior, but pale with surprise.

"For God's sake, man!" he gasped. "What do you want here? How did you get here? You unfortunate man!"

49

He clasped his hands together nervously. For the first time it occurred to me that I probably looked dirty and disheveled, from my scramble up the gangplank.

"For the love of Pete!" I exclaimed. "Who is running this ship?"

"If you only knew," the old man said in a melancholy voice, peering at me closely, "the powers that control this ship, you would implore me to take you back. But I am afraid I cannot take you back. I have some influence, but not enough to do that."

"But I'm not asking you to take me back," I protested. "Don't worry yourself about that end of it"

"You *must* go back before it is too late."

His voice quivered with earnestness.

"Your only hope," he continued, "lies in meeting some ship and putting you across on a boat."

"I'm not going back," I said shortly. "It was hard enough to get here the first time."

He studied me another moment in silence, and then stepped backwards into the room, motioning me in. I looked about eagerly, but my theories fell helpless. He certainly was not controlling the ship from this room. It had four bare walls, ceiling, and floor; a porthole, a bunk, and a washstand. A traveling bag stood in a corner; a few Galveston newspapers were piled on the bunk. That is all!

"Who are you?" he said patiently.

I related to him briefly who I was and why I had come.

"Then you're not a newspaper reporter nor an oil or copper prospector?" He regarded me eagerly.

I merely laughed in reply, for I could see that he was now convinced.

"But that does not alter the danger for you," he went on earnestly. "If we do not get you on a ship before it is too late, you will never see Galveston again."

"Sounds bad!" I remarked, not very seriously impressed. "Tell me about it. What will happen to me?"

He sat and thought a while.

"If it were possible to tell you in a few words," he said abstractedly, "I should do so."

He looked out of the porthole awhile, lost in thought. I studied his profile. Certainly the tall forehead and prominent occiput denoted brain power. Through the circular window I could see the waves rushing backwards between the ship and the rising moon. He finally turned to me again.

"So Kit Breckenridge is dead?" he said softly. "And Dan wanted you to come and find out about me? Good old Dan."

"My great-uncle Dan was very much puzzled as to why you denied your identity to him."

"It hurt me to do that. I was hungry for a talk with him. Can't you imagine how I should like to ask him about people and places? But how can I ever talk to my old friends again? I've often thought of trying it. But there would be endless complications."

"I'll respect your secret, sir!" I argued eagerly. "And I shall behave myself on your island, and keep out of trouble."

"No!" he exclaimed. His voice was troubled, and there was a pained look in his kind old face. "I cannot permit you to go to an almost certain doom."

"I've gone to 'em before," I said cheerfully, "and my skin is still all here. I've been in the Texas Rangers, and can take care of myself."

He shook his head. He had been straight and tall when he marched up the gangplank. Now he was bent, and looked very old.

"Now you have seen me and talked with me," he finally said. "You can be content to go back and tell Dan Breckenridge and your father that you have seen me, and that I am well and happy."

"Mr. Kaspar," I said, striving to conceal the impatience and excitement in my tones; "wouldn't I look foolish coming back with a story like that? They know that much already. Besides: you may be well, but you don't look happy to me. You're under some shadow or in some difficulty. I shouldn't be surprised if I could find some way of helping you."

"You cannot!" he groaned. "You are lost! I know the courage of youth. I am glad that it still exists in the world. But that will not avail you. It is not danger from men that you need fear. There are forces far more subtle and more terrible than you can imagine."

There was such an expression of worried anxiety on his face, and he seemed so genuinely concerned for me, that I regretted to be the cause of such distress. He sighed as I shook my head in reply to his last protest.

"I don't mind admitting to you," I added, "that if I were really anxious to go back to Galveston, waiting to meet a ship would not be my way of doing it. You must indeed have been lost to the world for forty years if it does not occur to you that I might call an airplane by radio to take me back."

"Well, I'll have to find you a bed then, as it is getting on into the night," he said resignedly, and beckoned to me to follow him. He led the way down the passage and opened one of the doors. As I entered with my suitcase, he bade me good-night.

I found myself in a small cabin with the usual furniture, a bunk, a chair, a washstand. The bunk was made up with a blanket, and I hopped into it at once, taking only the precaution to take with me to bed my service pistol, a Colt .45 automatic. The ship was quiet; the hum and vibration of the machinery were not disturbing; there was only the splashing of the water outside my room. For a long time I could not go to sleep. It was hot, and I was a little seasick.

I tossed around and pondered. The swift, lifeless ship terrified me, now that I was alone in the dark.

Finally the motion of the ship rocked me into a sound sleep. I awoke suddenly and at first was surprised to find the sun shining on me through a round window, and myself fully, though untidily dressed.

Then, recollecting myself, I jumped out of my bunk, extracted a toilet kit from my suitcase, and washed and shaved. I replaced my white collar and creased trousers with a flannel shirt, whipcord breeches and a pair of heavy, laced boots. I put the big service pistol back into the suitcase, but slipped a little .25 caliber automatic into my pocket.

By the time I got myself into shape, I was hungry, and went in search of food. I stole softly to the old man's door, and listened. Sounds of deep breathing indicated that he must still be asleep; my search would have to be made alone. Again I hunted thoroughly through the entire ship, the deck and its structures, the hold, the engine-room, and several cabins like the one in which I had slept. There was no dining room and no galley, and not a sign of food. Of course, if there were no people on the ship, it was quite logical that there should be no food.

For a moment, the after deck engaged my attention and made me forget my hunger. The space ordinarily occupied by officers' quarters was filled by masses of apparatus. Through the windows and doors I could see great stacks of delicate and complicated mechanisms, such as I had never dreamed of before in connection with a ship. There were clicking relays and fluttering vanes and delicate gears; little lights would go on and off, little levers would jerk, here and there, in twos and threes and dozens, and then all would be silent and motionless for an instant.

Before I had regarded it very long, hunger drove me to a further search of the ship. Everything was clean and orderly. A peculiarity of the black paint on everything struck me; it had the appearance of the japanning or enameling that is usually found on metal machine parts; it was more like the finish on an automobile than like the paint job on a ship; it gave the suggestion of being machine-processed, perhaps by air brush. And all over the ship there were various bits of mechanical activity: here water running from a hose; there a rotating anemometer; yonder a pump sliding and clicking back and forth. It looked for all the world as though an efficient and well-disciplined crew had left but a moment ago.

The venerable old man appeared about eleven o'clock.

"I must ask your pardon for having kept you hungry so long. It is a long, long time since I have entertained guests, and I forgot. I could not go to sleep till nearly morning, and now I have overslept. Come, you must be hungry; though I have not much to give you."

He led the way to his cabin. I looked it over again carefully, thinking that perhaps on the previous evening, during the excitement of the conversation, I might have overlooked the mechanism by which he controlled the ship from his cabin. But there was nothing there.

The most surprising thing about it all is for me to think back now, and realize how far even my imaginative and astonishing explanation fell short of the actual truth.

He opened the suitcase and set out some preserved fruit, meat, and bread for me; and a bottle of carbonated fruity beverage. In the absence of other evidence, the few little jars of food that he had were eloquent enough testimony that he was the only man on the ship besides myself.

When we came out on deck again, it was nearly noon.

Kaspar put his hand on my shoulder.

"Last night I urged you to go back," he began. "I was tired after a strenuous day, and I allowed you to dissuade me from my purpose. Here is your opportunity. We can signal the ship over there, to take you."

"I'm not going back," I said calmly. "I know it is rude of me to force myself on you, and I apologize; but—"

"My dear boy, that is foolish. You know that my only concern is for your own welfare. Personally, I like your company. You remind me of my young days in Texas. For other reasons, that you could never guess, I should like to take you along. But, for your own good, your career, your friends and loved ones—"

"You speak as though this were my funeral," I interrupted.

"It is certain that you will never get back. Knowing what I know—not even many of my own island people know it—I can see clearly that you, of all people, will be in serious danger upon the island."

"Why can't I come back to Galveston with you on your next trip?" I urged.

"Who knows where you or I shall be by that time? I may never live to take another; and you—inside of a week, a young fellow of your type would be a marked man on the island."

"What *is* the danger?"

"I am not even sure myself. I only know that many brave and brilliant people have disappeared forever. Your world needs you; it needs brains, courage, and skill, and you seem well gifted with all of these. Our island does not need these qualities."

His argument did not sound convincing to me; it looked too fantastic to be real. For that matter, has anyone ever been convinced by spoken warnings of a vague danger? Has any old man's warning ever stopped a young man's headlong rush?

"Listen!" I exclaimed. "You have said that you do not mind my company personally. I am therefore going to stick to you."

"But, Davy! I cannot have it on my conscience that I was the cause of you—the cause of a horrible end for you. I am troubled enough about the others, for whose doom I do feel responsible. Come—"

On the previous night, all alone in my bunk in the darkness, I had felt some misgivings and some fear. Even an hour before, what with solitude and hunger, I might have taken advantage of an opportunity to flee. But this old man's face and bearing showed that he was carrying some heavy burden of trouble. A first glance showed that there was wisdom, intelligence, and ingenuity there; and the most careful scrutiny could show naught but kindness, benevolence, and sympathy. The mere sight of his face strengthened my resolve to see this adventure through.

Kaspar sighed, as though he were glad that he had done his part and that it had come out this way.

"You're a good boy," he said. It sounded very affectionate and quite old-fashioned. Then, after a few moments' silence:

"You do not have a wife and children at home?"

"Nobody!" I shook my head vigorously at the strange sound of it.

"I suppose it is all right," he murmured, mostly to himself; "One person more or less on the island—what does it matter?"

We met no more ships, though several times we saw smoke in the distance. A number of times we sighted land; now high and rocky, and again flat and sandy with tropical vegetation. From the direction in which we went and the tremendous speed that the boat was making, I concluded that we would soon be in the Caribbean Sea. After I had given up hope of making the old man talk, I sat and watched him staring out over the water. No question about it: he was totally oblivious of any responsibility for navigating the ship.

Toward six o'clock in the evening of the strangest day I ever spent, I saw a light blue line of haze, straight over the bows. This grew darker and more solid as the minutes went by; slowly it broadened and darkened and spread out on both sides of us. So great was the speed of the ship, that it was still twilight when we drew close enough for me to see a row of pinkish granite cliffs in front of us, extending as far as I could see on either side, with a haze of black smoke high in the sky behind them. A volcano? I wondered. The tropical night was closing swiftly down as the ship tore through the water at unabated speed.

Nervously I stood on the deck and searched for some sign of a harbor or a landing-place. Every moment I expected the ship to swerve to one side or another. I began to get worried—for the ship plunged straight on toward the wall of cliffs.

Chapter II. An Island and a Girl

As the darkness rapidly gathered, three searchlights in the bow blazed out, lighting up the rocky wall ahead into an intense relief of brightly lighted cliffs and inky black shadows. Straight ahead of us there was a cleft in the rocks, an irregularly vertical band of Stygian blackness, extending from the water up as high as the rays of our searchlight fell. Then, I suddenly grasped the remarkable fact that though the breakers roared on both sides of us, we were in comparatively quiet water; and on ahead was a quiet strip extending right into the darkness of the fissure in the rocks, whereas on either side of it were the foamy white rollers beating against the rocks.

There was, in fact, a huge cleft in the granite structure of the island—for I assumed that it was an island—extending down below the level of the water as well as upwards; and as the rocky bottom sloped away from the shore, this cleft furnished a safe and excellent channel through a dangerous area. In another moment we had slipped into the depths of the gorge.

It occurred to me that to a watcher from out on the sea, it would have seemed that our ship had disappeared suddenly, as though it had been swallowed up. The appearance of the island to anyone approaching as we had done, was bleak, desert, and inhospitable, the last place in the world to invite a landing. And now we were slipping down a secret passage, and were quite hidden from the outside. The whole procedure had the appearance of having been cleverly arranged to conceal whatever the island contained. My temples throbbed with excited anticipation.

Kaspar stood erect and motionless, just forward of the deckhouse, gazing ahead. I judged from his attitude that he was expecting to land soon; so I ran down into the cabin and brought up my suitcase and found as I did so, that my hands and knees were shaky from the sudden and severe strain on my nerves of the previous quarter of an hour. The sudden fright and equally sudden relief left me weak and perspiring.

The luminous rift of the sky above us began to widen; within twenty minutes, the tops of the rocky walls at the sides were low enough to be visible in the illumination of the searchlights; and the channel had widened considerably. The noise had sensibly diminished, and the speed of the ship continued to decrease. Soon the walls became irregular, interrupted by black clefts, then gradually dwindled down to scattered piles of rock. Now there was a beach, white and smooth, no doubt sand: on the left, level to the dim, dark horizon with a glow of the sea in the distance; on the right the narrow strip of bright beach shone in strong contrast with a dense, black wall, which I knew must be a forest.

On ahead, a number of lights glowed brightly, from which long, glimmering streaks of reflection reached toward us. Lights meant people! Kaspar's people! In the course of a number of minutes, I was able to make out a row of brilliant lamps on poles, at the edge of a little wharf built out into the water. I scanned it eagerly with my field-glasses. I could make out a good deal of machinery on the shore, cranes and loading apparatus, and dark, irregular bulks, with wheels and cables. There was also a little group of people on the dock.

I was young and impressionable enough to have gotten a thrill out of even a conventional visit to any foreign port. Imagine then, how I quivered, after my strange day on the mysterious ship, to find myself about to land on an island which was evidently off the established paths of travel, and which already was beginning to promise unusual and mysterious features.

While the ship was slowing down and slowly easing over toward the dock, I had about fifteen minutes in which to study the scene carefully. Only with the corner of my eye did I observe how two steel hoops dropped from the ship over posts on the dock, fastened to chains which spun out from the ship and then reeled back in, drawing the ship to within six or eight feet of the dock; and how the gangplank descended. I looked further on.

The wharf was of wooden planks, and but a little longer than the ship; evidently built for this ship only, and without facilities for permanent docking. On my left, a couple of heavy trucks were backed up toward the ship, with derricks on them, which immediately swung their hooks and cables up over the ship when the latter approached. On the shore, beyond the planking of the wharf were several other big vehicles in motion, backing into position in a row; and one emerging from the darkness beyond the limit of the lights and cutting across the lighted space. Among the big machines were scattered some very small ones; they were indefinite black blotches, and I could make out neither their structure nor their use; they merely gave the impression of being intensely active. A roar and a clatter rose from the mass of machinery; and there was a confusion of huge movement and black shadows.

Not a building of any kind was in sight anywhere. A hundred yards ahead, the intense blackness against the more luminous sky, with occasional flashes of reflection, must have been a forest. To the left, more cliffs towered in the distance.

All of the machinery was opposite the left half of the ship. A line formed by continuing the gangplank straight out from the ship, divided the illuminated territory in half, and the left half was a dense, roaring, iron bedlam; God knows what it was all about. There, at the edge nearest me, stood a towering, clumsy thing on caterpillar treads; behind it were humpbacked tractors and things with whirling wheels and gesticulating cranes.

The right half of the dock was clear and empty, except for the little group of people. On beyond them a few automobiles stood beside the road that led backward into the darkness. The people, a tiny, huddled group, looked quite incidental and subsidiary to the huge, rumbling machines.

There were about a dozen of the people, both men and women, young and old. One swift glance in the brilliant illumination told me that, and showed me that they were neatly and carefully dressed in elegant, rich-looking clothes. As we drew closer I saw at the front of the group a pretty, dark-haired girl and at her side a stately old lady with snow-white hair. Both had their heads bent backward in their effort to peer eagerly upward at the ship's deck. Then the gangplank thumped down on the dock, and Kaspar walked down without the least change in his measured tread. I picked up my suitcase and followed him; I must confess that it was a little timidly and at some distance.

I remained in the background, leaning against a lamp-post at the edge of the dock; the shadow of the lamp's base kept me in comparative obscurity. I hoped to avoid attracting undue attention to myself, at least until all the regular greetings were over. Kaspar and the majestic old lady came toward each other; first they clasped hands and leaned toward each other in a brief kiss; and then they stood for a few seconds looking into each other's eyes, hands clasped and not a word spoken. Thereupon there was a swirl of dresses and scarfs; Kaspar had a pair of little arms around his neck and a resounding kiss planted on his cheek; and then the impetuous young lady held him off at arms' length and gurgled: "Old granddaddy's back!"

"By Jove!" I thought to myself. "I like her looks and I like her ways!"

Kaspar looked around for me, I suppose wishing to introduce me. But the others in the group were too quick for him. They crowded around him and shook hands and greeted him joyfully. It was evident that he was a beloved man. I could understand but little of what was said, because the clatter of the machinery was too loud at the point where I stood; but the expressions on their faces, clearly lighted by the lamp over my head, spoke louder than words. There was a burly, red-haired man, who might have been a building-contractor or a sea-captain dressed up in society clothes, who seized Kaspar's hand with the grab of a gorilla, and whose Irish features registered such joy and relief that Kaspar's return might have meant the alleviation of all his troubles and the lightening of all his burdens. There was a slip of a young lady in a gorgeous fluffy-ruffly cloud of a dress with a marvelous head of red hair; and she approached Kaspar a little timidly and in awe, but smiled radiantly and seemed genuinely happy to see him back safe. And a young man in full evening dress of the most elegant cut and material, with perfect shirt-front and most delicately adjusted tie, approached in great respect and with the utmost perfection of social grace; but he too was happy to see Kaspar.

"Boy!" I gasped under my breath, looking at him from the top of his silk hat to the tips of his polished pumps; "to think that I came here in whipcords and laced boots, with pistols and a camp-cooking kit!"

Kaspar glanced back at me once or twice, as though apprehensive of having neglected me; but I nodded back that it was all right as far as I was concerned; and he continued to receive greetings while I watched him, giving an occasional glance at the machinery unloading the vessel. The five people whom I have already mentioned seemed to be especially close to Kaspar, for they remained at his side. They were talking animatedly together, and occasionally their voices were carried to me.

In fact, I noted that the mechanical din was lessening somewhat. Every now and then some vehicle would sweep around and disappear in the darkness, up the road. Unloading had stopped, and I surmised that only a few personal packages had been taken off, and that the ship would soon go to some more permanent berth.

As I was watching the last crane-load swing from the deck into a truck, a most creepy looking mechanical nightmare came sputtering by with a noise like a motorcycle. It dashed by so quickly that I had no chance to observe it closely. It looked like a huge motorcycle, seven feet high, with a great, box-like body between the wheels, in which the driver must have been enclosed; and around this box were coiled many turns of black, oily-looking rope. The box was black and looked like a coffin stood on end, and rope was wound in a great coil about its upper end; and two glaring searchlights surmounted it. I don't see how anyone could imagine a more inconsistent, unnatural-looking thing.

The people talking in front of me were startled by its appearance; that was obvious. Their heads went close together, and I could see the burly Irishman slowly shaking his great red shock of hair, for all the world as though he were worried about something again. Finally Kaspar turned and motioned to me.

I came forward a few steps and approached the group. First I was presented to the white-haired old lady, who regarded me wonderingly, but spoke nothing, beyond telling me, with a manner of stately politeness, that she was pleased to make my acquaintance. In the meantime the bright-eyed girl behind her kept watching me intently, except when I was looking directly at her.

"Davy Breckenridge got aboard with me in search of adventure," Kaspar said, by way of explaining my presence; "and I could not frighten him off."

Next I found myself facing the girl. The light behind me shone directly on her; and with an opportunity to get a good look at her I found my original interest sustained and increased. In fact, I had already wasted more extra heart-beats on her than I ever had on a girl before, and I had not even exchanged a word with her. Her wide-open eyes and parted lips betrayed the curiosity and wonderment that I must have aroused in her. She seemed to be between twenty and twenty-five, and came up with an active, springy step. In contrast to the other brilliant and flouncy young lady, she wore a dress of some plain, gray-brown stuff that might have been gabardine, open at the throat, and with a skirt somewhat longer than were being worn back home just now. I could see that she was enjoying it all immensely, for her face broke out into a glowing smile as Kaspar spoke:

"Mildred, I have brought a young visitor with me, Davy Breckenridge. Davy, my granddaughter, Mildred Kaspar!"

He bowed and stepped back, with the courtly, old-fashioned way of letting the two who have been introduced occupy the center of the stage, so to speak. Uncertain as to whether an introduction in this society included the shaking of hands, I watched, but when Miss Kaspar extended hers, I took it, nothing loath.

Suddenly and unexpectedly, a black shadow raced between us and there was a clank over our heads. Kaspar started, looked up, and involuntarily continued stepping back. I also looked up. A big, black crane arm was reaching over toward us from the caterpillar-treaded hulk a score of feet away. It hung high in the air, and its chain and bucket, a half ton of dirty iron just off the ground, was plunging directly at us.

There was a little scream from one of the ladies behind Kaspar, and a united scramble to get out of the thing's way. I was not in its path, I soon noted; its swing would just miss me. But Miss Kaspar, in front of me, was directly in its path; in another second it would knock her over and grind her up. For a mere instant I was paralyzed with surprise. In a moment I recollected myself, but the plunging mass was already within two feet of Miss Kaspar.

There was only one thing to do. I took a good grip on the little hand and jerked her swiftly toward me, and at the same time stepped, or rather leaped, backwards. I got a momentary glimpse of the look of amazement on her face as she was carried off her balance, but I was compelled to look behind me to keep from stepping off backwards into the water. However, I was able to guide myself to the lamp-post and back up against it; and I caught the staggering girl into my arms, for otherwise her momentum might have carried her on off the edge of the dock. It was a delicious armful; but I had no time just then to enjoy the thrill of my first experience in that line. I hastily let go and stood her on her feet, and looked for the swinging shovel.

There was six feet of space to spare between us and the line of its swing. Kaspar and the three people with him stood on the opposite side of its path, motionless as though they had been suddenly petrified; and there was a straggling line of people back toward the cars, also petrified. Miss Kaspar was looking at me with a puzzled expression on her face, but my gaze at the swinging bucket made her turn. It reached the end of its swing in a few seconds, and was coming back.

It came toward us now with a creak, over our heads, and its path was further toward the water—nearer to us. The pair of huge iron jaws was open and turned toward us; and it was coming fast.

"I wonder what's the idea?" I grumbled. "Has the fellow gone suddenly crazy?"

I had been trying to figure out, in swift flashes of thought that seemed to hang slowly in fractions of a second, whether the operator of the machine was trying to reach the pile of freight on our left, or whether he had lost control of the machine, or had parted with his wits. When Miss Kaspar saw it coming, she turned toward me with a little scream.

It came on with gathering momentum, while I was trying to figure out a way of dodging it without jumping into the water. There was no use trying to run ahead of it or to get across its path; it was moving faster than we could move. A dozen feet away were Kaspar and his people, open-mouthed, paralyzed with fear, but unable to stir to help us. I had almost made up my mind that it would have to be a plunge into the water, when I got another idea.

Without a word—there was no time for it—I seized Miss Kaspar around the waist and lifted her off her feet; I remember making a mighty effort and then being surprised at how light she felt. With my left arm around the lamp-post, I swung her and myself out over the water, bracing my feet against the edge of the dock. The bucket swung by with a rush of oily-smelling air. I breathed a sigh of relief and was about to swing her back to her feet, when she plucked at my shoulder and cried:

"Look out! It's coming again!"

It had stopped with a clank and was swinging swiftly back. By this time the girl had begun to get heavy, and my left arm around the post, which carried the weight of both of us, was beginning to ache. She noted my efforts to ease the strain and tried to reach past me to get hold of the post.

"You can't do that," I said, "but it will help if you hang on to my neck."

She did so at once, without hesitation. I wonder that I did not lose my head and drop off into the water from sheer excitement.

I was revived suddenly by a hot pain in my left arm and the sound of my sleeve tearing. The bucket had swung by again and grazed my arm. Its next swing would bring it outside the line of lamp-posts and brush us off into the water. I felt a keen appreciation for the feelings of the bound man in Poe's "Pit and the Pendulum" story.

"It's a ducking for us," I said. "Can you swim?"

She laughed.

"I'm at home in the water," she replied.

"Down we go then!"

I stopped so that she could slide down and then lent her a hand to lower her into the water; when I heard her splash I started down myself. However, the big, black shovel was so close to my head that I got frightened and let go, and fell several feet into the water. I went under for a considerable distance, but came up readily and saw Miss Kaspar clinging to a pile. I reached for my hat, which was floating near. We were between the dock and the ship, and could see nothing but the glare of the lamp above us with the blackness of the dock on one side and the hull of the ship on the other, also black as Erebus. The gangplank was directly overhead.

"This is worse than a trap!" I exclaimed. "We've got to get out of here quick!"

I watched her anxiously until I saw her strike out easily and gracefully, apparently but little impeded by her clothes. By a natural impulse we headed toward the stern of the ship, away from the machinery. In a couple of dozen strokes we were clear of the wharf and the ship, and out in open water.

"Now, where do we go from here?" I asked, as we paused to look back. She turned around to look at me, and laughed. There was just enough light from the distant lamps so that I could see the water trickling down over her face from little wisps of hair. She was positively bewitching; the light gleamed brightly from the row of pearly teeth, and her eyes sparkled in fun. At that moment I did not know the cause of her laughter, for I was puffing hard keeping myself afloat

64

in my heavy clothing. Later I learned that it was my tendency to lapse into the latest metropolitan idiom that had furnished the amusement.

"We are safe now," she said. "Fifty yards to our left is the beach, with only a few rocks between us and the folks."

As we swam for the shore I kept my eyes on the dock; but the machine that had caused the trouble, and its crane, were not visible to me. I was thoroughly winded when we arrived at the beach, for my clothes and accoutrements were indeed a heavy load to keep on top of the water. Miss Kaspar stopped at some distance from the shore, with only her head and shoulders out of the water.

"Now you go on ahead," she ordered, with what seemed to me an overdone sternness; "and keep to your left. I shall follow you."

"What a queer code of ethics!" I exclaimed. "It's up to the hero to see that the rescued lady is safely out of the water before he gets out."

"If you don't go on, we'll be here all night. And if you dare to look back, I'll never speak to you again!" This time there was a note in her voice that sounded as though there might be tears near at hand.

"Oh what a mutt!" I groaned at myself. To her I shouted:

"All right! I'll learn after a while. It's only the first hundred years that I'm slow." Another peal of laughter behind me testified that all was well again.

The black shadows among the rocks made the way a little treacherous; but it was not long before I came suddenly out of them and to the edge of the dock. Kaspar and his three companions were at the edge of the dock where we had jumped off, looking intently down at the water; six or eight others were moving slowly back from the cars toward the water. The big, ugly machine was gone; in fact only four loaded trucks were left of the mob of machinery that had been there only a short while before. The people spoke not a word. Their rigid attitudes, their white faces and tight lips alarmed me. The big, red-headed man had his fists clenched; and in a moment he began pacing back and forth on the dock. Kaspar stood with his head bowed, looking completely crushed.

My appearance with Miss Kaspar behind me was like a thunder-bolt among them. She gave them a silvery little hail. Kaspar clutched out with both hands, and his eyes stared wide open out of the snowy expanse of his beard. Mrs. Kaspar held out her arms; it seemed that it was to me, but there was a swish behind me and a shower of water and Mrs. Kaspar was holding a wriggling, wet bundle. It was hard to tell from which one of them the squeals of joy came.

The big Irishman stopped in his tracks and stared with open mouth; and the elegantly dressed young man, though struggling manfully to preserve his dignity, was showing his agitation by rubbing the back of one hand in the curved palm of the other. There was a kind of astonishment about them, as though we had risen from the dead. Only the freckle-faced young lady with the sunset hair seemed to exhibit joy unalloyed, by dancing up and down and sidewise. Kaspar laid his hand on his granddaughter's shoulder, but the embrace of the two women showed no signs of loosening. He finally turned to me and held out his hand:

"Davy, now that you have saved our baby from that awful thing, nothing can come between us."

His voice trembled, and the hand that I held trembled.

"I can't see that I did much," I answered with embarrassment. "That was a commonplace little accident." Although in my mind, I was wondering if it really was an accident and commonplace.

In the meanwhile, wraps and scarves had been requisitioned among the crowd and the two ladies had hustled Miss Kaspar away. Kaspar roused himself and again moved with that almost military air of his.

"Here are two more friends I want you to meet, Davy. This is Mr. Cassidy."

The big, red-headed man grabbed my hand with a powerful sweep. He must have been very much moved, to let a little brogue slip away from him; for never again after that did I hear him use it.

"Ye'rr a foine bhoy, an' quick an' brave," he said, from the uttermost depths of his throat. "Never in my life have I been so sick as during those few moments when our little one was in danger."

66

"Thank you. I don't think I've done anything."

Then came Mr. Kendall Ames, turning his head back to look after Miss Kaspar as he approached me. He seemed hardly able to pull his eyes off her. The perfection of his manner and the faultlessness of his attire combined into one harmonious effect that hushed my usual tendency to facetiousness and commanded my unadulterated admiration. Such a product on a tropical island.

Though I could detect no flaw in his perfect speech and behavior, except possibly a slight pallor and the slightest of tremors, still it seemed that he was just a little constrained and embarrassed.

"When I express to you my gratitude for your wonderful act," he said softly, in a well modulated voice, "I am merely voicing what hundreds of others will feel. You have saved our most popular lady from a terrible fate."

"I am sure that you exaggerate," was all that I was able to get out of myself.

But they were not exaggerating. Some real emotion possessed all of these people. There was something beneath the surface here. If this occurrence with the machine had been merely accident, why were they all so tense about it?

However, I did not have much time to speculate about it just then. The day had been hot; but the night was cold, and I began to shiver in my soaked clothes, and my teeth chattered. Also Kaspar discovered that my left arm was bloody. I had been holding it behind my back, until he took it and examined it. The sting of the salt water in it was making me writhe. He raised it to the light in grave concern.

"It isn't much," I said. "Just the skin scraped off. If you can find me something dry to wrap up in so that I won't shiver my joints loose, I'll have this arm dressed in a jiffy."

The three of them watched me with great interest as I opened my suitcase, took a bandage from the first-aid kit, and did a fair job of dressing with one hand.

"Bad omen!" I laughed. "The first thing I use out of my outfit is the first-aid kit."

In a moment I wished I had not said it, for over Kaspar's face came that same brooding, gloomy look that he had worn most of the afternoon on the ship.

Some robes were produced for me to put over my shoulders, apparently taken from automobiles. I was to ride in Ames' car, as Kaspar's would only hold the three of them, while Mr. Cassidy had already left with his daughter.

"That's the red-headed girl, I'll bet!" I thought to myself.

Ames was very eager, and conducted me to the car as though I had been a royal guest. I felt like the hero of a movie drama. There in the car was another young man, dressed with the same splendor as was Ames; and there followed another formal introduction. I can laugh now, but I could not then. It was all quite grave and earnest: I, soggy, bedraggled, with a bandaged arm and a blanket over my shoulders like a Choctaw chief, and feeling tremendously clumsy and out of place in all this drawing-room courtesy; and bowing to me, extending his hand, and gushing forth great volumes of gratitude was Mr. Dubois in evening dress and with manner so perfect that he would have been a model for the evening crowd at the Ritz café.

The car had no steering wheel, and no one drove! Ames tinkered around with something on the instrument board when he got in; and in a few moments we were off.

We seemed to be running through flat, open country, over a paved road. My recollection of the early part of the ride was that it had been through dense blackness with rushing echoes about—a forest, no doubt. Now, moment after moment, more lights became visible, until there were great masses and long avenues of them.

Chapter III. The "City of Beauty"

"What city is that?" I asked eagerly, forgetting my wet clothes and the cold wind. Both of the men seemed surprised at the question.

"Why—that is—our city!" Ames protested in the tone of a person making a superfluous explanation, "where we live."

"I mean, its name?" I persisted.

"Its name?" Ames seemed puzzled. "Why do you ask for a name? Walter, have you ever heard its name?"

Mr. Dubois shook his head in courteous silence.

"What island is this, then?" I asked.

"I'm afraid I do not know its 'name' either," Ames replied. He was apologetic and anxious to oblige, but helpless. "You see, we never had occasion to speak of it in such a way as to require a name."

"*Where* is it then?" I demanded, growing more surprised every moment.

"Where—?" he seemed totally at a loss.

"Which way and how far from Galveston? Or where in relation to Cuba or Central America?"

"I'm sorry," said Ames in a queer, embarrassed tone. "I know nothing of those places. We are all so occupied with pursuits of our own that we are not interested in what you speak of. It would serve no good purpose to go into those matters."

"You are a stranger," volunteered Dubois. "We've never had a stranger here before. It isn't considered the—ah—proper—ah—taste, you know, to show an interest outside the island."

His reply, which gave me the impression of having been spoken in the fear that someone would overhear it and make trouble for him if it wasn't properly made, silenced me for a while. They had been so cordial and sincere, until I had begun to ask questions, that I had at first gotten an impression of a high degree of culture and intelligence; and now this sudden seizure of embarrassed constraint, along with the strange limitation of their mental horizon, gave me a vague impression of mental abnormality.

Soon we were driving up a broad, paved street, lighted by rows of electric lights; and illuminated windows were visible among a wealth of black trees. Being driven about a strange city at night is always confusing. I had impressions of meeting numerous headlights and dark vehicles; there were people fitfully revealed for a moment by moving lights, and glimpses of people upon verandas among trees. For a couple of miles there was block after block of the same thing. Finally we drove up to the curb behind another car, from which the Kaspars were alighting. Kaspar led me through an arched hedge, across a shadowy front-yard garden, into the house. The young men drove away, courteously wishing me good night, and promising to see me tomorrow.

The house astonished me. Instead of having traveled nearly a thousand miles across the Gulf of Mexico, I might merely have walked over into one of the better residence sections of Galveston or any other American city. The house was of glazed face-brick; there were mahogany furniture, electric-light fixtures, a phonograph, velvet rug, a piano. On a small drawing-room table were several books and a newspaper opened across them.

In the middle of the big living-room stood Miss Kaspar covered from head to foot with a cloak; about her head was a scarf through which showed wet spots.

Yes, she was beautiful. During my drive, I had recollected the thrilling feel of the slim body in my arms, and I feared lest my quick glance in the garish lighting of the dock had left too much to my imagination. But the tempered illumination of the room showed me the soft cheeks delicately colored with a bloom that the sea-water had not affected, the brightest of brown eyes, and the red lips that arched in a smile of welcome. As my gaze swept eagerly over her, the smile faltered, and a flush came and went. But she threw her head back with a little toss, and the smile came back, radiant as a summer sunrise, and the brown eyes looked into mine.

"I couldn't let them shoo me off to bed until I had thanked you for saving me from that horrid thing, and welcomed you to our home," she said in a soft, Southern voice, extending her hand to me.

She spoke no other words, but the smile was given so generously, and the eyes met mine so frankly, that I was quite taken off my feet. By the time I had recovered sufficiently to stutter an acknowledgment her grandmother had hurried her away.

"Horrid thing!" she had said, as though there had really been some serious danger. Obviously she was taking the incident very seriously.

"You had better go to bed too," Kaspar said to me. "After your ducking and your cold ride, you need to be careful. I must hurry to a conference with some people who are anxious to see me. Here is your room. In the morning, you will probably be up early and want to look about outdoors. Yonder is the way out to the veranda, and we shall meet you there."

I looked after the departing old man in an agony of curiosity. Would I not have the opportunity of asking a single question?

A mahogany bed, high with soft, white bedding, a chiffonier, in the corner a lavatory with hot and cold water, two brilliant landscape paintings on the wall—such was the place in which I would spend my first night on a savage and tropical island. This was the rough life for which I had prepared myself with sleeping-bag and pistols! I was reluctant to accept the realization that I was in a city that was unknown to the world and not down on the maps and in the travel books. However, no other conclusion was possible, for the cities of this region, excepting those of the American zone on the isthmus, were dreary, miserable places, not worthy of the name of city.

I awoke to see the sun shining brilliantly on a thick mass of foliage outside my window. The air that came in was cool and pleasant. As I began to move about, my arm felt sore and stiff, and was caked with dried blood. However, I dressed it afresh, and got out my razor and shaved. Ruefully I surveyed my silk shirt and cream-colored trousers; they were hopelessly unfit to appear in. There was nothing to do but to put on the laced-boots, flannel shirt, and whipcords, stiff with dried sea-salt. I knew I should feel uncomfortable and conspicuous in them among the dress-coats and delicate frocks, but no more so on account of my clothes, than on account of a sort of inferior feeling in the presence of their pretty manners and culture.

"Breakfast!" said a small placard, hung from a push button over a small, mahogany table. I was hungry enough, and the button's invitation to be pushed was irresistible. I pressed it, whereupon a panel opened in the wall, from which proceeded the sound of whirring gears; and in two or three minutes a tray appeared, on which were eggs, bacon, coffee, and rolls. It traveled toward me on a canvas belt over a revolving roller. I made short work of the food, for I was overpowered by eagerness to get outdoors and see the town by daylight.

Then I eagerly made my way out on the porch and looked around. I saw a broad, paved street, lined with great masses and billows of luxuriant tropical foliage into which the houses were sunk almost

out of night; here and there a fawn-colored wall, a red-tiled roof, or a
row of gleaming windows peeped out of the dense verdure. Again it
struck me that it might be the wealthy residence portion of any city in
the south of the United States. Had the black ship gone in a circle and
brought me back to Florida or Louisiana? No, that was impossible,
for I had watched the course too intently during the previous day, and
it had always continued southeast. Undoubtedly I was on some unknown island in the tropics; for nowhere in the United States would
people talk and act so queerly as these people did.

It was a rich and beautiful picture. Palms, ferns, and conifers
seemed to predominate among the flora; thick, dark-green, waxy
leaves and light, lacy fronds were plentiful. There were great, cream-
colored flowers shaped like a jack-in-the-pulpit, as big as my head;
big, scarlet hoods and spikes; white, buttercup-like flowers as big as
my two hands, with purple centers.

I got out on the concrete sidewalk and started up the street on a
little walk. However, before I had gone a hundred yards, I thought of
the unusual appearance that my salt-crusted, rough-looking clothes
presented in such an elegant residence section, and my timidity
drove me back toward Kaspar's house. Just before I reached it, at
the gate of the neighboring house, there was a flutter of white, and
there stood the freckle-faced, Titian-haired young lady of yesterday
evening.

"Ooooh!" she exclaimed. "Good morning! You surprised me!"

"Good morning," I replied, trying to be as courtly as I had seen
Ames and Dubois act, but feeling silly at it "You are Miss Cassidy?"

"I am Phyllis—Phyllis Cassidy. How is Mildred?" she looked toward the house.

"I haven't seen her this morning, but she looked all right to me last
night."

I chuckled to myself at having unconsciously stated what I so
warmly felt; for Miss Kaspar certainly looked all right to me the night
before.

"Come, I'll go over with you. That was perfectly grand of you to
save her!" she gurgled ecstatically. "I've read about brave things like

that and seen them on the stage—but to think that I should ever see it real—and to talk to a man who dared to do such a thing!"

She drew a deep breath of delight.

"And everyone was terribly frightened that awful things would happen."

"You have a beautiful city here," I interrupted, for I was getting embarrassed. "What is its name?"

"Its name!" Her flow of words stopped in surprise. "The name of the city? I do not know if it has a name. Sometimes we say: 'The City of Beauty.'"

"And what island is this?"

"What island? You want a name for the island too? You queer man. Why should it have a name? It's just 'the Island.' It is very large, and I've never seen all of it and shouldn't want to see all of it. There are woods and mountains and ugly black and oily places—"

"*Where* is this island?" It may have seen rude to interrupt, but otherwise no progress was possible. I could see that she had vast possibilities as a rapid-fire conversationalist.

"*Where?* Why *here!* Where could it be?—But father warned me that you might talk like this, and so I'm not shocked. You are a stranger. We do not discuss things about the island. It is not nice. There are so many other things. I've just had a big tapestry hung at the *Artist's Annual*; you know tapestry design is my serious work. That made my father very proud. And see this little medal? That is the swimming honor for the Magnolia District, and this is the second year that I've held it—"

About there I sank in the deluge of words; but she prattled on. Finally, I figured out something with which to interrupt again, wondering, however, how long she could keep it up if she were not interrupted.

"You have some rather amazing machinery here," I remarked. "I should like to see more of it."

Her delighted expression faded instantly, and she shuddered.

"Machines are disgusting things," she said, curling up her little freckled nose. "We do not talk about them. But I'm not shocked at you. Daddy told me not to be, because you do not understand the island. Just think how lucky you are, coming today. This afternoon is the Hopo championship ride. I am so excited about it, because I know Kendall Ames will win it."

A rapt expression came into her face, and she clapped her transparent white hands childishly.

"You're going, aren't you?" she asked eagerly.

We turned into Kaspar's gate, and there on the porch was Miss Kaspar. And at once I lost interest in Phyllis and Hopo, whatever that was.

"I suppose," I replied mechanically, my eyes on the figure of Miss Kaspar standing on the porch.

"Oh, you must!" She put her hand on my sleeve and started off on another long flood of talk. My conception of courtesy compelled me to stand there listening, with her hand on my arm, and groan inwardly while Miss Kaspar turned and walked into the house, disappearing from my sight without a word to me. If it all looked as I felt, it must have been a ridiculous picture. I wished Phyllis at the bottom of the sea. Her childish prattle had kept me from seeing Miss Kaspar again. She followed Miss Kaspar into the house, and I wandered disconsolately about the yard. I thought that it was very strange that Miss Kaspar had not spoken to me; in fact she had acted as though she had not seen me at all.

I spent most of the forenoon wandering about the yard and through the house. I wondered what had become of everyone, and why I had been thus left to my own resources. I found the house a mixture of the commonplace and the marvelous. Familiar, ordinary furniture, such as I have already mentioned contrasted with the automatic cooking going on in the kitchen by means of timing-clocks and thermostats and without human attention. The "house-cleaning" device was especially interesting to me.

I was attracted to the drawing-room by a humming noise; it came from a black enameled affair like an electric motor, just beneath the ceiling. It was moving slowly about the ceiling, dragging something

74

through the room after it; and as I watched I noted that it was covering the room systematically by means of a sort of "traveling-crane" arrangement. The things hanging from the motor were light hoses with expanded endings, and the surprising thing about them was that they moved and curled about this way and that, like an elephant's trunk or a cat's tail. They reached here and there, poked into corners, under chairs, and around objects; and I could hear the sound of the suction as their vacuum cleaned up the dust. When the room had all been cleaned, the apparatus receded into an opening in the wall, and hid out of sight.

"If this is the way they keep house," I thought, "I can understand how they can raise such flowers as Phyllis for tapestry design and swimming championships."

It was nearly noon when Ames appeared, clad in a gorgeous scarlet jockey uniform, with shiny boots and golden spurs, and in his arms a great bouquet of flowers. I was in a distant corner of the lawn, and watched him as he stood bowing to Miss Kaspar, who appeared in response to his knock.

"I trust that my fair lady of Magnolia Manor is enjoying good health," he said with pompous graciousness. "I am on my way to the Hopo field, and if you will accept this token from me and wear one of the flowers, I know it will bring me victory."

I could not hear her reply, but I could see that she thanked him formally. Then Ames saw me and came over to me.

"If you have no afternoon suit with you," he said looking me over, "you are welcome to one of mine. You and I are of about a size. I'll send one over."

I had to admit that it was considerate of him to think of it. But I felt resentful because I had to accept a favor from him; for what was I to judge from what I had seen, except that there must be some intimate relationship between him and Miss Kaspar?

"Lunch is ready!" Miss Kaspar called to me in a voice that sounded coldly polite; and she did not seem to notice me as I came in.

No one waited on the table at luncheon, at which the four of us sat. Everything was on the table when we sat down, and we left the things there when we were through; and the next time I glanced at the table they were gone, removed, doubtless, by some mechanism. I had already seen enough to be convinced that the servant problem did not exist on the island. The only servants were machines.

"Ha! ha!" laughed Miss Kaspar, but would not meet my eyes. "I see that you have spent a pleasant morning. Phyllis is a jolly little girl, isn't she?"

I was taken aback. Where was the Miss Kaspar who had given me her hand the evening before? She looked just as lovely as ever; but she had no eyes for me at all, and that engaging cordiality and frankness that had impressed me far more than her beauty were gone. But then, who was I, to expect to be noticed by her, when Ames had brought her a bale of flowers as big as herself? My sphere had always been action and not women; a horse on the range, or doing something in a laboratory were familiar to me; but with women I was clumsy and incompetent. The present reminder of that fact was the most unpleasant one I had ever had. Ames seemed to be the real hero among the ladies; and Miss Kaspar was obviously the fortunate lady.

Just then there was a click and a rush of air at one side of the room. A panel snapped open and a package dropped out; and the panel clapped loudly shut again.

"Clothes for you from Kendall Ames," Kaspar announced. "I imagine this is something new to you. Ames puts them into a tube at his home; they go to a central distributing station which sends them here."

I went resignedly into my room to put on the clothes. The interest seemed to have been taken out of things for me. But I intended to go with them to their Hopo, or whatever it was; at least I should have an opportunity to see more of the people of the island. When I came out again, there were several young people on the porch, and more of them in a large car at the curb. They were ready to go to the scene of the sport, and had come to take Miss Kaspar with them.

They were interesting folks. The young men wore dark coats and light trousers, and were very courtly in speech and manner, quite in contrast with the direct and forward manners of the youth that I had been accustomed to. The girls wore light, fluffy dresses in pale shades of blue, orange, yellow, and pink; and they were full of smiles and curtsies and little feminine ways that charmed me very much. I confess I preferred them to the blunt and callow ways of our modern girls.

Amazement surged up in me again. Here I had set out for a tropical island, expecting to find jungle and savagery; at most some squalid mixture of Indian and Iberian. Yet, here was a freshness and delicacy of human culture, a flower of human beauty, a development of the fine things in human looks and manners, of which I had never seen the like in the most favored urban circumstances that I had ever known.

The young people sat for a moment and chatted trivialities; while some who had remained in the car played on a guitar-like instrument and sang. Their voices were well trained and their playing was clear and soft. They seemed in every way clean and beautiful young people; and with the deep-green lined street, the bright houses and brilliant flowers, it all seemed rather like a dream of beauty.

"I'll get out Sappho for your first," Miss Kaspar cried to her grandfather; and the affectionate glow that lighted up her sunny face, as she glanced at him, caused a pang within me for being left out of things. I had to remind myself that last night's rescue did not necessarily give me any special rights nor privileges; and that I ought to be thankful for the kindness that had been bestowed upon me last night. She hurried out of the back door; and "Sappho" turned out to be a greenish-black roadster, with wheels four feet high, an extraordinarily large radiator appropriate to hot climates, headlights set in the top of the hood—and no steering wheel! The machine fascinated me so that I stood about it curiously instead of mixing with the group of young people.

In fact, I was a little nettled at the people. They seemed to take no particular nor unusual interest in me. Upon introduction they were very gracious; but they immediately took me for granted as one of them. No one asked me where I came from, nor what my country was like, nor how I liked it here. Like a group of frolicking children, they seemed intent on the interests of the moment, and accepted everything as it came. So, I decided to ride with Kaspar in his Sappho.

I waited for some minutes for Kaspar to appear. Then I walked all around the curious vehicle, and I finally decided to get into the car and wait there for Kaspar. So I climbed in and sat down, with a queer feeling at the complete absence of the steering wheel and gearshift levers. However, on the dashboard were a great many dials; and something was ticking quietly somewhere inside the machine.

Then there was a "clickety-click" and a whirr of the motor, and the car moved gently away from the curb. It swerved out into the street, gathered speed, and then turned to the right around a corner. It slowed down for two women crossing the street, and avoided a truck coming toward us. It gave me an eerie feeling to sit in the thing and have it carry me around automatically.

Then it suddenly dawned on me, that here I was alone in the thing, on an unknown street, in an unknown city, racing along at too high a speed to jump out, and rapidly getting farther away from places with which I was familiar. How could the machine be controlled? Already I was completely lost in the city. How and why had the thing started? I had been exceptionally careful not to touch anything, and was sure that no act of mine had set it off. But I was rather proud that I did not lose my head; I leaned back to think. This was not my first emergency.

The car was carrying me rapidly through a beautiful residence section of the city. I could not help looking about me. It was a veritable Garden of Eden, and all the more beautiful for the added touch of human art. The lawns were smooth and soft, with half-disclosed statuary among the shrubbery, or fountains at the end of vistas. Homes spread over the ground or soared into the air like realized dreams, without regard to expense or material limitations. But, every few minutes my mind came back with a jerk to my own anomalous position.

I examined the dials on the instrument-board closely. There were ten of them, and they had knobs like the dials on a safe-door, or like the tuning dials on a radio receiving set. Some of them had letters around the periphery and others had figures. I looked for something that said "stop" or "start," but there was nothing of the sort, nor even any words of any kind. There were a number of meters, but a speedometer was the only one whose use I recognized. The whole proposition looked about as impossible to me as a Chinese puzzle.

The more I thought about it, the more I thought that my only hope was to try manipulating the dials. That was the only way to learn something about managing the car. I did so: I twirled a knob at random and waited expectantly. Nothing happened. At least not immediately. After a few moments, however, the car stopped, turned around, and started off in the opposite direction. I should have gotten out of it while it stood still for an instant; but for the moment my curiosity was whetted, and I wanted to try the dials again to see what would happen. Anyway, before I recollected myself, the car was speeding in the opposite direction at too rapid a rate to permit my getting off.

If I had hoped to get back to Kaspar's this way, I was disappointed at the first corner, where the car turned to the right, drove around a block and was soon spinning along in its original direction.

"You're a stubborn jade, Sappho," I grumbled aloud. "We'll have to see what we can do with you."

I now perceived where I had made my mistake: I had not noted which dial I had turned nor how I had turned it, when I had reversed the car, and I was unable to repeat the movement. So, the next time, I carefully turned the first dial to the letter "A." There was no effect at all. I moved the second dial to "A." A curious fluty whistling followed; it proceeded from the hood, and varied up and down several octaves of the musical scale, with a remote resemblance to rhythm and melody. Before it died down, I sank back and gave up. A little reflection showed me that with ten dials and twenty-five letters or figures to a dial, there were several million combinations. It was hopeless.

For a moment the scenery distracted me again. I was bowling along comfortably, and did not seem in any particular danger.

The buildings I was passing seemed to have grown in response to a creative artistic impulse just as luxuriantly and as untrammeled as the dense tropical vegetation among which they stood. Dream palaces they seemed, with colonnades and sweeping arches and marble carvings gleaming in the sun.

Such a city could be possible only by means of vast wealth, highly advanced culture, and unlimited leisure on the part of the inhabitants. Where did the wealth come from? I could not see any place where any business was being transacted nor any industry going on, although my ride covered every section of the city that afternoon. I did pass through a small and quiet shopping district; but here there was no display, and its purpose was evidently not that of selling and making money, but rather that of supplying needs and desires.

Gradually an uncomfortable feeling began to get the best of me. In vain my reason told me that there was no real danger, and that I was having a good time. I felt hopelessly at the mercy of the machine, and I did not like it. I began to yield to an unreasoning panic; it made me think of how my hunting-dog had behaved the first time I had tried to give him a ride in an automobile.

But my common sense and practical experience kept insisting that automatic machinery was not always dependable. The thing might spill me somewhere and break my neck. It might carry me to some distant part of the island, and then run out of fuel so that I would be unable to get back. The thought of being lost in some wild, unknown place began to make me desperate. Last night's episode at the dock made me suspect that all was not smooth on this island; that there may be people somewhere who were unfriendly toward this highly cultured community, to which Kaspar belonged. Suppose the machine should carry me in among them?

A medley of the most unpleasant grinding and rasping noises came out of the machinery. I could have imagined that it was gnashing its teeth at me. It increased its speed to a terrific rate, until the wind stung my face, and a sinking feeling came into my stomach, whether from fear or from the motion, I do not know. Then it quickly fell back into the ordinary speed again. My next effort caused a sudden stop that threw me into the windshield. I saw stars and things went black for a moment; and then I was traveling along again at thirty miles an hour. I tried it over a dozen times, producing hurried turns around the block, noises, jerks and skids, with numerous dangerous performances; but never again was I able to make it stop.

I was soon worked up into a state in which I would have been willing to risk everything in order to get back to Kaspar's home. I was frantic to get out of the thing. Yet, I could not quite make up my mind to jump. The recollection of some fractured skulls from similar attempts that I remembered attending at the John Sealy Hospital deterred me. The pavement looked too hard. I spent an hour in a state of anxiety.

I had almost made up my mind to try jumping and take my chance, when I noticed that the car was headed out of the city. First we went through a park—a beautiful landscaped place, with flowering trees and shrubs, whose like I had never seen before, lagoons crossed by graceful bridges and covered with gay boats and bordered with frolicking bathers, with smooth lawns on which were in progress games that looked as though they might be golf, tennis, baseball—and there ahead was a gateway. The paved road beyond led between open fields.

My fears were being realized! I was being carried too far away to suit my better judgment. And, as if in response to my resolve to jump as soon as there was soft ground at the side, the car speeded up to a good forty-five miles an hour.

During the few moments that it took me to get up my courage, the car made a couple of miles along a lonesome road. Far behind, another car came out of the gateway and down the road after me. In all directions, flat fields stretched away. To the right, half a mile away, flowed a broad river. The fields might have borne cotton or potatoes; I was going too fast to discern which. Here and there, large, trestle-like machines were bridged across the rows of plants and seemed to be working at cultivation, though I could make out no people on them. On ahead was a stream flowing at right angles to the road, and toward the river on the right. It may have been a large creek artificially straightened, or a canal, for its banks were straight and regular, and the quiet, swiftly flowing water seemed to be quite deep. The road crossed it on a concrete bridge.

Ah! There was my chance. The bridge railing was only a wheel-guard, not over two feet high. A jump into the water was my best opportunity for an escape from this scrape.

"Now Sappho, you demon, we'll see!" I gloated, and climbed out on the running board. There I waited till I was just opposite the nearer bank of flowing water. It would require a horizontal jump of six feet to clear the rail, which was easy for me.

I jumped. I was not able to manage a dive. It knocked the breath out of me, and for a moment I was dazed and helpless. My body tore through the water sidewise and whirled round and round, as though the quiet stream had suddenly become a whirlpool. I thought my head and lungs would burst before I fought my way to the top and gasped for breath. I located the bank and struck out for it. I could feel my clothes rip and tear in a dozen places, as by brute strength I overcame their obstruction to my strokes. I rolled out on the bank and lay there panting.

Up on the road, two men were getting out of a car, obviously the one I had seen behind me. They came toward me. I stood up and got ready for them; I was ready for anything human. One of them looked a particularly bad customer; but I was only thankful that I was on solid ground and away from any kind of a machine.

Then, with a gasp of relief, I saw that they were Kaspar and Cassidy. And on ahead stood Sappho, drawn up quietly by the side of the road.

"Good jump, boy!" shouted Cassidy. "No one in this town would have dared it."

He laughed, but his laugh was forced, and his face was pale and drawn. Kaspar grasped my hand and said nothing.

"I'd like to know what in blazes is going on!" I demanded impatiently.

"You've had a particularly narrow escape from some sort of oblivion that we don't even understand ourselves," Kaspar said; "and that is about all I am able to tell you."

Kaspar beckoned to me to get into Sappho with him, which I did with some trepidation. Kaspar managed the car smoothly back into the city. He was silent; not a word did he say; and when I tried to speak, he turned warning looks toward me, so that I desisted, though vastly puzzled. However, I kept a sharp eye on his hands as he worked the dials to start the machine, and stored my observations for future use.

As we came into the city, the afternoon was turning into evening, and the streets were crowded with people. As we pushed on through, we saw a big parade going by. Automobile-floats decorated with flowers went up the street in a long line, some of them very beautiful indeed. Then came a truck with a floral throne on which sat a man and a woman, crowned and hung with wreaths of flowers. As they went by, great roars of applause went up and banners were displayed containing a maroon field and a white magnolia flower.

"It seems that Ames has won the championship," remarked Kaspar, and his remark lacked enthusiasm.

Indeed, it was Ames and Miss Kaspar on the floral throne!

Why did it cause me a pang of depression to see them? What I had done last night for Miss Kaspar was a small matter. And even if it had been a big matter it would have given me no claim on her, no excuse to presume on her regard.

I was wet, shivering, and physically miserable, with clothes hanging off me in rags. It was difficult to get through the crowded streets in the increasing darkness, though I must admit that the performance of the car in finding its way without human guidance impressed me as remarkable. It was pitch dark when we reached Kaspar's house, and he slipped me into my room unobserved.

"Say nothing about this to anyone," he admonished "Also, let me warn you very earnestly, to stay absolutely away from machinery unless one of us is with you. You are too important to us now to have something happen to you. And—think this over: do not interpret literally everything you see. Be patient. The time will come when you shall understand all of these things."

Chapter IV. Athens or Utopia?

The following day, about the middle of the forenoon, Ames came sauntering over to the Kaspar home.

"Now that you are one of us," he said to me, as casually as though I had merely moved over from another part of town, "you must get started going about with us in our activities." He leaned against a pillar of the veranda, powerful and graceful in his white ducks, a magnificent specimen of young manhood.

"It is very kind of you to receive a stranger so cordially into your midst," I replied, trying to speak in a tone of gratitude that I was far from feeling.

It seemed that these people were assuming that I was going to stay among them forever; and perhaps they were right. How I could ever get away I hadn't the least idea. Ames' presence was uncongenial to me anyway, because he had a previous claim on Miss Kaspar.

There she sat on the settee with her grandfather, avoiding my eyes, which of course made me look at her all the more often. Her long, downcast lashes, her straight nose and clear-cut mouth made her look like a royal princess. A wave of resentment surged over me for having to accept favors at the hand of a man who had found this girl before I did. But I strove to overcome it. There was nothing to do, however, but to behave courteously, and try to fit in with their manners and habits—and to keep my eyes open.

"We're arranging something good for you this afternoon," Ames continued; "something in which you can take part. What can you do—tennis, Hopo, polo, golf—?"

"I hardly know one from another," I replied. "I've had to work all my life. But, if there's nothing else to do here, I can learn. Or, why can't you folks go ahead and play, and let me watch?"

"We couldn't do that!" Ames exclaimed, as though leaving me out would be an unthinkable sin against hospitality. "Besides, today is a special occasion. Perhaps you can swim, then?"

"Well, yes," I replied with interest; "that is the one thing I can do. No one has beaten me across the Galveston channel yet, and my challenge is still open."

I stopped suddenly, embarrassed at having referred to my own country, and hoping no one had noticed it.

"Very good," Ames said with gratification; "with swimming we can

84

arrange a pretty little event. You will enjoy it." He seemed happy in having found something in which I could participate. Phyllis became quite excited over it; her eyes sparkled and her breath came rapidly.

"I'll explain it," Ames continued politely. "Tomorrow night is the annual ball of the Arts Guild, a splendid affair with a grand march and quadrille. The grand march is always led by the winner of the Painting Prize, who this year is a lady, Janet Keen. Therefore, she chooses six ladies of honor from among her friends; and it is a pretty little custom to choose the gentlemen escorts for these ladies of honor by some athletic contest. This afternoon we shall make it a swimming competition, and you shall have the chance of winning one of the ladies of honor."

He spoke earnestly and enthusiastically, with perfect seriousness. I worked hard to suppress a smile. Phyllis was so intensely stirred that she got up to join us, skipping and clapping her hands. To me, the event outlined by Ames looked childish, a device of the idle rich to secure diversion. These people looked mature and intelligent enough to be doing something worthwhile. But, I suppose it was human. During the days of chivalry, grown-up, bearded men discussed the relative beauty of their fair ladies by pounding each other's armor with axes and lances, and rode about the country looking for damsels to rescue from dragons, when they should have been working at some useful job.

"And we'll have a picnic luncheon in the park!" Phyllis cried. "We can meet at the Paneikoneon. That means that I shall have to hurry!"

She darted into the house, and I could hear her calling over the telephone. I gathered that there was a definite little group, which was a sort of society unit holding together for its activities; and that Phyllis was calling this group together.

"Meet at the what?" I asked of Ames.

"The Paneikoneon is the building of all the arts. Tomorrow night's party and today's fun is for people who are chiefly artistic, and it is natural to meet there."

"You ought to look through the place," Kaspar suggested to me; "You will find it interesting, perhaps even astonishing."

"Why, yes!" exclaimed Miss Kaspar. "You mustn't miss seeing the Paneikoneon. You will be delighted at the pictures."

"I don't think you've ever seen anything like it anywhere, no matter where you've been," Kaspar said. "There are thousands of paintings and statues. You will catch your breath when you see the art that this island has developed within two generations."

"I am eager to see it," I admitted. "The art of a people reveals their nature and character more truly than their history."

The remarkable people of this island interested me immensely; and if their art told as much about them, as did ancient Greek sculpture or medieval painting about the people who produced the statues or paintings, what revelations were in store for me today?

It was rather a surprise to come in contact with art in this city. I had rather expected to go about looking at amazing automatic machinery. Or, I had expected to have the lazy leisure to cultivate the society of the brown-eyed vivacious granddaughter of my host. Why could I not get her out of my head? Ah! The idea struck me suddenly. Was Miss Kaspar also one of the "ladies of honor"? And could I compete for her society by swimming against the others? That was an exciting thought! I had no doubt that I could easily walk away from them in the race, for I had clearly proved to an entire city, that I was a remarkable swimmer. But perhaps as an engaged girl she would not be free to receive the attentions of anyone who might win the opportunity by physical prowess. All I could do was to wait and see. I looked at her again. She was talking to Phyllis, and the glint of the sun on her cheek through a wisp of brown hair sent an excited thrill through my every nerve. I developed a sudden and keen interest in the afternoon program.

Then I looked at myself. Again I was in a coarse shirt and whipcord breeches, wrinkled and crusted with salt; one sleeve was torn and had dried bloodstains on it. The suit that Ames had so kindly loaned me the day before was now a bunch of rags, completely ruined by my leap into the water: That would have been embarrassing enough had the suit been my own property, but the fact that it wasn't, made matters worse. I took Ames aside.

"I was in a little accident yesterday," I explained, "and the suit you so kindly loaned me is a total wreck. I am sorry; and if you will give me some idea as to the cost of the clothes I shall reimburse you for them."

He stood still and looked at me for some moments with a puzzled expression.

"The damage to the clothes is an accident, and you are under no obligation to me on account of it." He looked at me and smiled pleasantly, and continued:

"You seem to be in about the same position that you were in at this time yesterday morning. I'll get you another suit of mine, until you can have some made for yourself." He departed toward the telephone, while Kaspar smiled at my bewilderment.

"Kendall is quite right," Kaspar came to my relief. "All he has really done for you was to go to the trouble of wrapping and sending the clothes."

"You mean that they cost nothing?"

"Cost? We do not use that word. He can get all he wants, and so can everyone else. There is plenty on the island, and all are welcome to it." Kaspar said it proudly.

A light had suddenly dawned upon me. I had been having a queer impression of frailty and helplessness in the actions and appearance of these people. Like a baby in arms, was the vague idea I had. Now I saw! They never had to work. They were never driven by necessity, never haunted by the shadow of want. They only played. They had no conception of danger, privation, and pressure. They were petted and pampered children.

And that was how Miss Kaspar differed from the others! Her face showed grave lines of thoughtfulness and trouble, beneath and between the sunny smiles. And then, to think that she was dedicated to a human ornament like Ames! Even yet, I felt like sailing in and showing him who was a better man with a lady. But, when I thought of the courtesy and hospitality that had been shown me, I hesitated. Under such circumstances, it would be humanly inexcusable.

"Why does that make you look so woefully serious?" Miss Kaspar laughed, waking me out of my reverie.

"Oh, does it?" I fenced, playing for time to frame an answer. My heart gave a leap, for I was glad to be noticed by her. "Perhaps I wish that my own country were such a paradise. I have always been taught that only through toil do we gain strength, and make progress; and that without work, a people is lost."

"We're not lost," laughed Miss Kaspar. "There is plenty to do."

"Yes, to pass the time," I admitted. "But I cannot imagine one of these flossy young men making a living—or one of these girls cooking a meal or sewing a dress."

Miss Kaspar laughed heartily; I wondered if it wasn't merely to hide some deeper reflections of her own.

"Don't you like girls that cannot cook and sew?" she asked slyly.

"I confess that I am curious to know who is going to prepare the picnic lunch," was my reply to that.

"Oh yes!" she exclaimed, in sudden recollection. "Your talk has been so interesting that I nearly forgot. We must plan the luncheon, and then we can have it sent to the park. Come, Phyllis."

"There will not be time enough to send it," Ames reminded. "We'll have to stop by the central kitchens and get it."

"And I'll go along," thought I to myself. "I want to see these automatic cooking machines."

Miss Kaspar and Phyllis had their heads bent over a printed card and were marking it with pencils. I went into the house, and finding that my clothes had arrived from Ames' home, went into my rooms to change. I was excited at the prospect of having a good look at some of the marvelous automatic machinery which was doing all of the work of the city and yet managing to remain behind the scenes and out of sight. And their talk of a great Paneikoneon full of pictures was hard for me to grasp. How could a small, unknown island have produced a school of art and enough paintings to make such a huge collection, at the same time that they had developed this vast system of machinery? In fact, they seemed to be more interested in the social-athletic event of the afternoon than in anything else in life. And at the thought of

88

that, my heart pounded again. Was there really a chance of winning Miss Kaspar, even for a formal dance? If I did, would she talk to me? She was certainly leaving me out in the cold now, while Ames acted as though he had a first mortgage on her.

When I came out I found that Dubois and his sister had arrived and were waiting for me with Phyllis and Ames in the latter's car. We drove a number of blocks through streets alive with traffic and brightly clad people, and stopped in front of a large building done in massive Egyptian style.

"Here's where we stop for the lunches," Ames announced.

I followed the two men through the massive entrance into a small room furnished like a drawing-room. Ames had the printed card that the girls had checked, and proceeded to pick off the items, moving little switch-levers, of which there were hundreds on one of the walls, each with a printed legend beneath. I watched him a moment, and then slipped through a door down the corridor, and wandered around in the vast halls full of machinery.

The astonishing, unbelievable thing about it all was that there were no workmen there. All these vast stacks of machinery worked busily away, entirely alone and without human attention. I soon came to where Ames' orders were being filled, if I may put it that way. A number of metal cases about the size and shape of Gladstone bags were traveling along on a belt, and packages were being lowered into them. I found a place where there were great kettles and much steam and the most savory of odors; and another where fruits were being put into cans by automatic machines. Little packets were being wrapped and cartons filled—I had seen similar things in packing houses and food factories back home. These machines did not look radically different; but the amazing things worked all alone, without human attendants.

The two men, with whom I came, did not like my prowling about among the machinery, and everybody was more cheerful when we drove away. Soon they were prattling merrily away like a group of children, of Ames' victory of the day before and of Miss Janet Keen's prize painting. First one and then another would turn to me and tell me something about the building of pictures, anticipating my delight on seeing them for the first time, hoping that I would not omit to see this or that, till I began to be convinced that there was indeed something remarkable in store for me.

The Paneikoneon turned out to be a great mass of buildings in Gothic architecture, of a yellowish stone which provided a pleasingly warm variation from the usual cold grayness of Gothic buildings. The soft voices of the young people echoed down the vast halls as we passed rapidly through immense rooms full of astonishing statuary. I had never taken much interest in sculpture, but here I saw things that made me pause and look. To this day I remember vividly the figure of a girl of about sixteen, poised on one toe, arms spread as though in imitation of a bird taking wing from a tree in front of her. The cold marble looked as though there was life beneath the surface, and seemed ready to leap into dance or burst into song.

We found the famous Miss Janet Keen absorbed in work at an easel, in a roomful of pictures on an upper floor. She was overwhelmed and carried away, *willy nilly*, by the enthusiastic picnickers; and we swept from one room to another, picking up various members of the group and gathering numbers as we went.

I was amazed at the number and quality of paintings that I saw during those few moments, and certainly the art reflected the locality. There was a brilliant profusion of color and a luxuriance of natural forms, that gave me the same rich and varied impression as did the city itself. There was no dumb drudgery of Millet or tragedy of Meissonier; it was all like happy children playing in the sun. Today, many months afterwards, if I permit myself to recollect those halls full of pictures, I am overcome by a surging flood of nameless emotions, delightful, puzzling, consuming.

How was it possible for this one city to produce such an immense and wonderful collection?

Automatic machinery, of course! Wealth consists of the products of labor, but it has been measured in terms of human labor. Here the people had control of vast amounts of labor, labor that knew no fatigue, had no limitations, required no wages—the labor of automatic machinery. They had freely at their disposal the equivalent of the labor of millions of skilled and powerful workmen, without involving the degradation of a single human soul in the monotony of toil. As a result, all the people were able to devote themselves to the higher pursuits for which men have longed in vain during the ages when necessity compelled them to labor.

Here was another Athens! Here was a nation that had developed intellect and beauty to a degree that bid fair to rival that of the old Grecian city. However, in that Athens of old, which has done so much to mold the thought and taste of the world, there was a sad moral blot. The leisure that made possible the accomplishment of its artists, statesmen, and thinkers, was achieved only through the labor of millions of slaves. Of these toiling, driven, suffering multitudes, history has nothing to say, nor of the share which they deserve in the glory of Greece.

In this modern Athens there was no such disgrace. The slaves doing the drudgery behind the scenes were not human beings, but machines—not the lives of a hundred human beings sacrificed to make possible one sculptor or philosopher, but only iron and oil, gasoline and electricity making beauty: the beauty of human bodies well and gracefully nurtured; the beauty of paintings, statuary, and music; the beauty of high and noble human thought.

As we drove along through the city from the Paneikoneon to the park, I gazed with earnestness and fascination at the people in the streets, looking into their faces and expecting to see something god-like there. And my companions in the car left me to my thoughts, appreciating the fact that the Paneikoneon had impressed me deeply. Only when the exuberant crowd began spreading cloths on the grass and I was introduced to a couple of dozen of them in turn, did I begin to take notice of things about me. I noted that the young people seemed to enjoy carrying water and moving benches and doing little physical tasks. I tried to help, but finding myself in the way, joined a group of the older people sitting thoughtfully by.

As the lunch went on, I tried to talk to Miss Kaspar. Patiently and persistently I sought to get near her and strike up a conversation, but always, and apparently by accident, I failed. But I knew she was deliberately avoiding me, for in no other way could she have escaped my systematic efforts. Why did she treat me this way?

Finally—to me it seemed after several hours—Ames and Dubois arose and sauntered toward the water, motioning to me to join them. Others got up and followed toward the dressing-rooms to don bathing suits. Here was my chance, thought I. I would steer the conversation toward the swimming contest and around to the question uppermost in my mind: Would Miss Kaspar be one of the candidates? Not wishing to make my purpose too apparent, I started far from the subject, intending to make a roundabout approach.

"What sort of swimming strokes do you use here?" I asked.

"Most of us prefer the Australian crawl," Ames answered.

Dubois seemed to resent that, and quickly turned to me.

"There is no doubt in my mind," he said, "as to the superiority and greater popularity of the Schaefer sprint, Schaefer is still living here, though too old for active athletics."

Now I would rather have had my turn at the conversation; but it seemed that I had unwittingly opened a controversial subject.

"Some people prefer it," Ames said with studied casualness; there was excitement beneath, but he tried not to show it. "But the winners are the ones who use the crawl."

"I can use the sprint and beat anyone on the crawl," Dubois said in a voice that sounded thin and tense. I shrugged my shoulders and gave up my conversational plans. Perhaps I would be rewarded by seeing a real fight.

"I'll take you on!" Ames almost shouted.

"I have a bay mare, trained to the Hopo field, that I'll stake on the result!" Dubois offered.

"I'm willing to make a little bet, but I'm not interested in horses just now," Ames replied.

"Then Mildred Kaspar. The loser stays out of the way for a month."

"No thanks!" Ames shook his head. "I'm not taking any chances there."

"I'll bet you a Supervision day, then. The loser takes the winner's next Supervision day."

"That's good." Ames seemed pleased. "Mine comes tomorrow, and I'd like to get out of it."

To me, it was all quite startling. First, I was surprised to see these apparently highly cultured people get so excited over the trifling matter of a swimming stroke. Obviously, physical excitement was a rare thing here, where there was no fighting, no labor. Then, the wagers—the idea of betting a girl rather stirred my resentment. Yet, as money meant nothing to them, they had to have something to arouse their interest and provide a motive for action. Finally, the word "Supervision" rang curiously upon my ears. It smacked of industry and machinery in some way. I wondered if they took turns in supervising machinery? If so, it seemed that it must be an unpleasant task.

By this time they were all in bathing suits at the river's edge. I was amazed at the powerful muscles and wonderful physical development of these people. The little preliminary swimming and diving also impressed me, and made me think that I had better look to my laurels in the coming race. Then Ames and Dubois swam off their match, and both of them showed themselves to be accomplished athletes.

For a moment my interest was diverted from the big contest and Miss Kaspar. Ames won the race and was mightily cheered by the rest. Dubois took his defeat gracefully and cheerfully and shook hands with Ames.

"Remember, tomorrow is my Supervision day," Ames reminded.

Thereupon Dubois changed countenance and became very glum, nor was it possible to arouse him from it during the rest of the day. Supervision must be something very unpleasant, I thought. But events followed rapidly.

One of my questions was answered almost at once. The first of the "ladies of honor" for whom the swimmers were to contend, was placed on an improvised dais made of a pile of park benches. She was pretty in an old-fashioned way, and was presented as a Mrs. Howard.

Her husband was in the group. If a married woman was eligible, certainly Miss Kaspar would be. Possibilities were getting better.

Two of the men tumbled a big red buoy into a launch, and anchored it out in the middle of the river, a good quarter of a mile from the shore. A red flower was stuck into the top of it. At the sound of a whistle, a half dozen swimmers plunged into the water amid cheers and chaffing. The applause continued while one of them forged ahead, got the flower, and brought it back. Dripping and breathless, he presented it to the girl on the dais. She accepted it like a queen, and they went off together arm in arm, with a great show of comradeship, cheered by the crowd. Another girl was raised on the dais, and the crowd took it all very seriously.

Again I watched as the swimmers plunged, and the winded victor brought his flower to the girl on the dais. Then came Phyllis's turn. She seemed to be quite popular, judging by the number of young men who leaped into the water for her. Also I noticed that Ames was staying out of these races. And, suddenly, there was Miss Kaspar on the dais.

I was very much in earnest now. Perhaps the sight of Ames in the group that was getting ready roused me. Any qualms about paying attention to an engaged girl were removed by the eight of the largest group of contestants that had as yet tried for any of the girls. I looked at Miss Kaspar. She did not seem to like it very well and did not pay much attention to what was going on; but the sight of her tightened my muscles and sent a thrill of determination through me.

I dove mightily when the whistle blew, and struck out with my best crawl stroke. For a time my head was down, and the whole world consisted of splashing water. After a while I lifted my head and looked quickly about. The unpleasant realization was forced upon me that physically, I was no match for these people at all. Though I was putting forth my utmost efforts, they were leaving me behind, easily and rapidly. I was very resentful at them, because all their lives they had nothing to do except to train for athletics, and therefore had me at a disadvantage. However, I kept grimly on, for I could not afford to look foolish now.

Suddenly I was astonished to find myself passing one after another of them. One more spurt and there was no one ahead of me. I risked the loss of enough time to look back. They had all stopped swimming and were staring blankly ahead. I looked, expecting to see something sensational there, but there was nothing. Nothing that would explain this panic at least. I was more than half way to the buoy, and could see the flower on it. Near it, floating down the middle of the river was a mass of brushwood and green foliage. It was bearing down directly on the buoy. In fact, as I watched it, it drifted against the buoy, and carried it with its red flower along downstream.

I kept on, for I wanted that flower. The others remained where they had stopped. Then I saw that the floating material consisted of two great logs which had been sawn squarely off, and the white, clean ends, and the sawdust sprinkled bark showed that they had been cut recently. They were fastened together by an iron chain, of which a short piece with a broken link hung down to the water.

Then the black tug came into my line of vision. I had not noticed it before. It was coming on rapidly, and as it approached, the other swimmers retreated to the shore.

As a bit of dare-deviltry, I swam after the logs, climbed upon them, and waved the red flower to the folks on the shore. They all stood motionless as statues. I chuckled as I imagined how shocked they all felt to see me behaving without any respect for a machine. For, as the tug churned up to the logs and hooked on to them, I stood calmly and watched the procedure. There were no people on the tug; in fact it was too small to contain any. After I had gotten a little ride back up the river on the logs, I scrambled through the leaves and branches to the opposite end, dove off, and swam leisurely to the shore. While I swam, I pondered.

Why had they suddenly stopped in the middle of the race? And fled to the shore? Especially after they had been so intensely excited about if from the first? I wondered whether there were not some grave danger, and whether I had unconsciously run some serious risk. Yet, they had never made a move to warn me or call me back.

As I pondered on it, two explanations occurred to me, and subsequent experience showed that both were correct. One was that these people, though remarkably intelligent along artistic lines, were really intellectually top-heavy; they were not quickly resourceful, nor able to act in emergencies, simply because they were so pampered by the machines, that they had never had the training that necessity gives. The other was that the sawed logs and chain were an indication that there might be machinery around; and then the tug appeared. Machinery was disgusting, and not fit to appear in polite society.

Not a word was spoken when I got out of the water. They all regarded me with faces that seemed filled with awe. They fell back and permitted me to pass through the middle of the group, dripping and exultant. I felt a sort of contempt for them. It occurred to me that at the head of a hundred determined savages. I could capture their whole city.

A voice in the crowd—I was relieved that it was not Ames—said almost apologetically:

"They ought to swim that over again."

"What!" I exclaimed, in alarmed indignation.

"It wasn't exactly regular," said the courteous voice whose owner I did not see.

"The conditions were to get the flower. I've got the flower!" I exclaimed angrily, now more in earnest than anyone else. In fact, I acted worse than they did. But one glance at Miss Kaspar, who was now radiant with a wonderful smile—the same girl that had given me her hand on the first evening—astonished me and steeled me in my determination not to yield the point.

"Of course," explained some other person whom I could not locate, "the flower was but a symbol of the best swimming, and an accident interfered."

"I didn't see any reason why everyone couldn't finish!" I looked around, but no one would meet my angry glance. All stood silent and reproachfully downcast.

"The devil take your flowers!" I shouted, dashing the pretty thing to the ground. I went to the bathing houses, resumed my clothes, strode over to where Miss Kaspar sat, took her arm, and led her away, just as the previous swimmers had done. The others never moved nor uttered a sound; I could not tell whether they were afraid of me or merely disgusted with me. Anyway, a half hour later they seemed to have completely forgotten the whole business, and treated me as though it had never happened. Was it a high type of tact and courtesy, or was it a species of mental deficiency? I could not tell.

"Davy!" said Miss Kaspar, in a soft, frightened tone of voice, "That was a reckless thing! Why did you do it?"

"I wanted to talk to you. You kept avoiding me. Now you must talk to me!"

"You wanted to?" Her voice was different than it had been all day. "Truly did you? I thought you wanted to talk to Phyllis."

"So, that is why you have been so distant—?"

"You and Phyllis looked so happy and intimate coming down the street so early yesterday morning—"

"You don't believe that now, do you, Mildred?"

"No, Davy. You have proved your words. But, you will have to go on with it and be my partner in the grand march."

"Ha! ha! You talk as though it were some sort of punishment for me. I'd lick the black tug barehanded for the privilege of that dance, or whatever it is. I'll take good care of you for Mr. Ames."

"For Mr. Ames!" She shrank back as though a thunderbolt had struck near her. "What do you mean by that?"

"Why—I—I understand you were engaged."

"The idea! I'm not engaged to Mr. Ames, nor to anybody. Whatever made you think that?"

As I thought back, I had to admit to myself that there never had been any real tangible reason for believing such a thing. My own morbid imagination had read a significance into a number of meaningless circumstances.

In an instant the universe changed. I would have liked to give a whoop and jump high into the air, and come down and dance a highland fling. With a great effort, I remained on the ground and acted calmly. I met her eyes. Not a word was said, but a great deal was understood. Then she gave a little toss of her head and a smile, as though to shake back her hair, and with it the constraint that had existed between us.

"Now," she said, "I'm really looking forward to tomorrow night. And when we get home, I want you to bring me your khaki shirt. The sleeve is all torn from the crane, and I want to show you that some girls on this island can sew."

Chapter V. A Machine-Devil

On my first and second mornings on the island I had spent a long and dreary wait, wandering about the house and grounds until someone had appeared. On this, the third morning, I found Mildred out in the garden busily snipping flowers off a vine.

"I had to get up early today. These flowers are for the ball tonight, and they keep better when they are cut in the morning," she explained. I accepted the explanation, without inquiring too deeply into the real reason for her being out so early. I was merely glad she was there.

However, the mention of the famous "ball" about which everyone was so excited, brought me up with a start.

"I am afraid of tonight's ball," I remarked in an effort to keep up a conversation which must be kept up; and the words came to my tongue with that strange fatality which sometimes makes our most superficial conversation express our innermost secrets. "I am not much of a society man."

"Now!" she said reproachfully, "that is just because you have to be my partner. I knew you would try to back out." At the same time, a merry laugh and a twinkle in the brown eyes belied the words.

"Will there be many there?" I asked.

"It is usually not a crowded affair. But the ball is held in a most wonderful place. The pavilion and its grounds are beautiful as a dream. There are special dresses and light effects and clever dances. It always thrills me through and through. You came at a lucky time, for it might be a year before you had this opportunity again."

Others apparently thought the same. As we walked to the veranda with armfuls of white, waxy flowers, Phyllis came skipping up.

"I can hardly believe that you haven't seen the pavilion yet!" she cried as soon as she was close enough to be heard. Apparently everyone's first thought on awakening this morning had been the ball. "I wish I were you, and seeing it for the first time!" She gurgled ecstatically, in her childish way.

When I had heard the same thing from several other people whom I met later during the day, I gradually developed a good deal of curiosity and eagerness to see the evening's event. I smiled as I thought back to the days in Galveston when my great-uncle and I had planned the outfit for this trip.

"It seems that since I've come to the island," I said to Kaspar later, "I've become some sheik. All I think about is clothes to wear—"

Kaspar laughed heartily.

"That's right!" he said. "I know better than to expect a young fellow to go to a function like that unless he had exactly the correct thing on. We'll drive to town and get you some."

"It takes a lot of nerve on my part to ask for things that way—"

"No. You must feel just as free to take them as you would to pick fruit off our trees. It amounts to the same thing."

So, that afternoon, we drove to the neat little shopping district, Kaspar and Mildred and I. I went into a store, which was really a "store" and not a selling institution; and there I was furnished with all of the clothes and accessories that I needed to fit me to take my place among the young men at the "ball" that evening.

However, I soon found that I was only a side-issue in this shopping expedition. Mildred was carrying on the principal program. She went into store after store, while Kaspar and I waited in the car outdoors. He sat with a grave face and a merry twinkle in his eye; and I watched the street and the people fascinatedly. Mildred was flushed and excited about it. By the time we reached home, the pneumatic tube was discharging a perfect deluge of bundles.

In the evening, a couple of dozen young folks, on their way to the ball in their cars, stopped for us at Kaspar's home.

I noticed that Ames was not among the group. He had been cordial enough to me on the way home after the swimming contest, and I did not believe that he had anything personal against me. Yet I believed that he took Mildred seriously, and felt very much hurt about being deprived of her on this special occasion. I ought to have felt sorry for him, but I didn't. Someone in the group brought word that he was coming to the pavilion later in the evening. At least, I could not help admiring the delicate tact of his methods.

Then Mildred came out. I had not seen her all afternoon, and now she fairly took my breath away. And now I saw the purpose of the forenoon's shopping campaign. A torrent of surprised compliments and delighted congratulations broke out from the crowd of visitors. It was evident that this was the first time they had ever seen her in anything but plain gray-brown, and that they were happy at the transformation.

There were twenty in the group, young and old; and we drove in four cars. As usual, Mrs. Kaspar remained at home, but Kaspar and Cassidy came along. They went everywhere, keeping a protecting eye on Mildred, and possibly on me. That in itself was a sort of sinister hint of danger, that kept up a background of worry to everything I experienced.

The car in which I was riding, with Mildred, Kaspar, Cassidy, and a half dozen others, was in the lead. We were some three hundred yards from the pavilion, and could already hear strains of music, when the little accident occurred. As an accident, it was quite trivial and insignificant; but the reaction of the people to it surprised me and set me to thinking. We met a car coming from the opposite direction, and our car swerved to the right side of the road. There was a crunch of the pavement, and a lurch that threw us about in our seats. The roar of our machinery rapidly died down to silence, and the car stood motionless, tipped to the right side. I thought at first that an axle had broken or a wheel had come off.

The cause of my astonishment, however, was that everybody sat still and did nothing. Their chatter was hushed for a moment; they looked about with helpless faces, in perplexed silence. But no one stirred. They all behaved as though they had been bound hand and foot. I stood up and looked about. Kaspar's face was inscrutable. My eyes met Cassidy's; he shrugged his shoulders and his face momentarily broadened into a grin; but his eyes told me nothing.

Finally I jumped out of the car and ran around to the side where the trouble seemed to be. A piece of pavement had given way and the wheel had sunk into the soft ground so that the axle rested on the ground. A little stream of water flowing alongside the road showed what was responsible for the cave-in.

"Three or four of us can lift this out easily," I suggested. I had in mind the powerful shoulders and muscular arms that I had seen during the swimming match.

The other carloads of young people coming along behind us stopped for a moment, and then passed us and went on. There was only a short piece of smooth, brilliantly lighted road ahead, leading to the pavilion. I walked back and forth, down the road toward the pavilion and back toward the car, hoping that it might occur to them that the short walk that remained would be a pleasant variation. But they accepted no suggestion. They sat as helpless as rag-dolls, and I did not feel like saying anything directly. I was thoroughly disgusted. Evidently Cassidy noticed it. He laughed, but it was a forced sort of a laugh.

"You're a young fellow that's used to taking care of yourself," he said, with an effort at speaking casually. "Well, that isn't necessary here. This machine automatically signals for help when it gets into trouble, and we have nothing to do but wait."

And wait we all did. Within five minutes' walk of the pavilion, the group sat as though they had been marooned on a desert island. I noted the small radio antenna over the top of the machine and heard the humming of coils as the signal went out.

Finally the big noisy truck came. As far as I could see, there was no one driving or controlling it; but there was no way of making certain of that, as men might possibly have been hidden on it, I wondered if these people had such an aversion to their working class, that they could not even bear to look at a mechanic or laborer. In a business-like way, the relief truck hooked a chain under the axle of our car, and raised it up with its derrick. We finished the short remainder of our trip quite smoothly.

After the scene I had just witnessed, the vivacity and activity with which the people leaped, out of the car and trooped up the steps of the pavilion were surprising and inconsistent.

Edgar Allan Poe dreamed dreams of beauty too transcendent for mortals to behold; and the scene, I now beheld, seemed to be one of the places of which he wrote. The pavilion was in a grove outside the city, beside the broad river. The building was long and low and white, with facades like the Parthenon. In the moonlight it did not seem quite real and solid; it seemed rather to float on the great billows of shrubbery embroidered with brilliant flowers. Tall rows of slim trees stood guard around it, and here and there and everywhere, huge, exotic flowers gleamed and glowed in the moon's rays. As we approached, long glimmers from the moon came toward me across the distant water. I could just see the soft glow of light between the columns from within the building. The strains of music drifted over, soft and low. I could have believed that I was approaching some enchanted fairyland.

Within, the floor of some red wood with purple veins was polished smooth as glass. There were ladies in fluffy, pale-tinted gowns that seemed unreal in the varicolored glow-lights. The gentlemen were graceful and courtly. The music was not obtrusive in volume, but ever-present and gently suggestive of rhythm; and more effective in stirring one into movement than any lilt I had ever heard. The dancing was instinctively graceful and beautiful. As the dancers glided about in the changing lights, the movements, the colors, and the music affected me like some drug.

But I myself was not part of it. The others belonged in the picture; I couldn't fit into it. I was a detached spectator. For this there were many reasons, I felt awkward because my practice in dancing had been meager. Possibly once a month in the intervals of hard work, I had taken some equally hard-worked teacher or stenographer to a dance. The personal beauty and grace that I had developed by years of hard riding on the ranges and in recent years by bending over books and laboratory experiments did not compare favorably with that of the people about me. They were without exception fine looking.

There was a little informal and desultory dancing to begin with; but the main interest was centered in the preparations for the "grand march." Partners sought each other out and looked for their positions. Everything was ready to start except that they did not like to go ahead without Ames. As far as I could learn, he had no essential part to play; but he was such a prominent member of the group, and they were so accustomed to having him present that they felt lost without him.

"He has no reason to be late today," Dubois grumbled, "after I've taken his Supervision and he has had nothing to do all day."

"That's right," said someone else, in an awed tone. "Ames escaped his turn at Supervision today. Nobody's ever done that before."

"I wonder if something hasn't happened to him," asked Phyllis in a frightened whisper. "That was a dangerous thing to do."

I remember how admiringly she had spoken of him on the first morning; and from her tone now, I suspected that she was more worried about Ames than was anyone else.

The impatient group broke up for the moment. There was a little dancing, and people drifted outdoors to pass away a little more time of waiting. Mildred ran to ask her grandfather if she could.

"He has made me promise faithfully to ask him about every little step I make," she explained, half-ashamed of the childish position in which she was placed. "For some reason he is very much worried about me."

As I waited for her, I happened to wander past where a group of boys in a circle were excitedly discussing something. Their naive gestures of excitement were a welcome relief from the perfect culture of their elders. As soon as I got near enough to catch a few words, I suspected that they were talking about me; and my curiosity got the best of considerations of conventionality. Without thinking what I was doing, I listened.

"I wonder if he will also have to do Supervision?" one boy asked.

"Of course he will! Everybody does!" was the dogmatic reply.

"No, Kaspar's family does not; and he is in Kaspar's home."

A boy of about sixteen just opposite me waved his fist in indignation. I liked his sturdy looks.

"Silly!" he snorted contemptuously. "Supervision! I want real work to do. I want to make machines, like Kaspar did."

There was a sudden lull in the talk, as of astonishment, of fear. Then an older boy's reproof:

"You fool! I hope no one heard you. These things have ears everywhere. Do you know that they got Higgins day before yesterday?"

Then a very small boy piped, as though repeating a lesson learned by rote.

"Our first duty is to the machines!"

Mildred came by and hurried me away.

"Your eyes look as big as saucers," she laughed.

I tried to compose my astonished exterior, but calming the whirling astonishment within me was not so easy. The thoughtless words of children will often let the cat out of the bag, while the carefully acquired habits of adults keep secrets safely. Here was another confirmation of my suspicions that the people on this island were not as completely happy as external appearances might seem to indicate. These people did not understand all this vast machinery; they could not operate it nor keep it in repair. Somewhere on the island there must be others who did so; and in some way they seemed to hold these grown-up children of the City of Beauty in their power. There was lurking fear in the eyes of the boys, and in an occasional unguarded glance of the elders.

"There's Ames now!" someone shouted.

We pushed our way out on the broad staircase of the curved balcony. A car was hurrying toward us, up the broad sweep of pavement bordered with shrubbery and electric lights on concrete pillars. On the opposite side of the drive were parked many cars in a dense crowd. There were numerous shouts of pleasant bantering as Ames was recognized in the brilliant illumination of the electric lamps. His car drove into an empty parking-space, and he got out and started across the stretch of pavement toward us.

Then there was a rattle of an exhaust off to the right, and a whirl of machinery up the road. A horrible looking thing on wheels dashed up and made directly for Ames, focusing on him its glaring head-lights. He stopped as though rooted to the spot. A more frightful looking thing has never been imagined in all the lore of sea-monsters and dragons. It was the same thing that I had caught a glimpse of that night on the dock, or another thing just like it. Its general form was that of a huge motorcycle, with a great coffin-shaped box seven feet high between the wheels, at the top of which were two goggly head-lights. Only, the first time I had seen it, it had seemed to have some sort of black ropes coiled round and round the box. Now these were unwound. They waved about, felt around, coiled and uncoiled, and grasped at the empty air; ten or a dozen huge, black tentacles, filling the air with sinuous, snaky masses.

Right in the middle of the road, in plain view of a couple of hundred people, it reached for Ames and wrapped a black coil around him. He stood as though struck paralyzed, though I could see him tremble. It began to drag him toward itself. In another moment, as I looked about me, I was alone. The people were all fleeing pell-mell into the building.

For an instant I was puzzled as to what to do. But Ames' face, bright white in the glaring light, in the uttermost agony of fear, convinced me that he was in some sort of danger. I started toward him in big jumps, at the same time opening a heavy pocketknife that I carried. As I reached him, I felt the coil of a tentacle about me, and was surprised at the strength of it. However, with a quick squirm I managed to duck out of its grasp. I grasped Ames' arm and slashed away with my knife at the coils about him.

As the tentacles waved about me and coiled and bent, I could hear a continuous clicking coming from them. When I cut at them with my knife I struck something hard, some metal. It seemed that my knife first went through a layer of something soft, rubber perhaps, and then slipped in between metal plates; and I could feel it catch and cut through wires. As it went through, a purple spark followed it, and a spark bit into my hand. Thus, while my body and arms struggled with the monster, my mind grappled with the astounding revelation, that this was not some animal enclosed within the box, some sea-monster as I had supposed. These snaky, twisting tentacles were mechanical things, built up of metal discs and wires, and carrying a high-frequency current.

Again I ducked out of the grasp of a tentacle. One already hung limp. I shook Ames, but he was completely unnerved. He had made no struggle whatsoever. I have no doubt, and have none to this day, that with a little determined effort he could have gotten loose and escaped up the steps. But he gave up from the beginning.

Then I heard a scream from Mildred, and a great bellow from Cassidy:

"Davy! Stop! Come here quick!"

I saw no choice except to obey, especially as two more tentacles closed around me. I dropped and twisted in an effort to get loose but they had me in opposite directions, one closed against the other; and my efforts were of no avail. So, with the main force of two hands, I opened out the grasp of one of them. It took all my strength to do so, and I am known as a strong man. I bent it back with a twist, and heard it snap; it dropped away from me and hung limp, and there was a smell of scorched rubber. With a common wrestling trick, I escaped from the remaining coil and ran up the steps.

As I turned to look back, Ames was on a side seat of the machine with several coils around him, and the thing was carrying him off down the road. The day before I had admired him for his athletic prowess. Now I cursed him for a stupid fool to let himself be carried away like a sack of potatoes.

I got back to the dance, none the worse except for some slight disarrangement of my clothing. Kaspar and Cassidy took me sternly in hand. I did not know that Kaspar could be so severe. I felt like a schoolboy caught throwing paper-wads.

"I have warned you," he said. "If you persist in being rash, you will not only succeed in having yourself destroyed, but will upset some cherished plans of ours."

"What in Sam Hill is going on?" I exclaimed. "What's happening to Ames?"

Cassidy answered me. Kaspar was hurrying away to see if Mildred was safe.

"I am not sure. Perhaps his failure to appear today has something to do with it. I do not suppose we shall ever see him again."

"But, who's doing it?" I demanded. "Who's in the machine? And who's behind it all?"

"That is the tragedy of the people of the island," Cassidy said sadly. "That is the burden our people carry for no fault of their own. But we cannot talk about it here. There are mechanical eyes and ears every-where, and I'm not ready to be taken away yet."

The next jolt I got was to see the dance going on as though nothing had happened. People were mingling and chatting, sitting at tables with iced-drinks, with all the appearance of festive gayety. Only when I came close to them, I saw that they were pale and staring, and that they carried on a forced conversation, like the people of a defeated city after a battle. The grand march went on. Mildred came toward me with hand outstretched, her usually brown face as pale as milk.

"It's time for us to march," was all she said. Not a word in reference to the nightmare that had just occurred. But, with her finger on her lips and a grave look in her eyes, she gave me to comprehend that she understood my impatient curiosity, but that now I must go on with the game.

I found myself wondering whether anything really serious had hap-pened after all. Might it not have been some sort of a joke, or some sort of a game acted out? But no, there was that look of pale horror on Ames' face, and the panicky flight of the people into the pavilion. The sudden starts of terror in unguarded moments here and there could not be acting; they were basic emotions breaking through, because they were too strong for even the most perfect of social training and discipline. I came across Dubois alone at a table.

"Couldn't you explain to me what happened to Ames," I pleaded. "This mystery is driving me crazy."

All he did was to put his head down on his arm and turn away. He sat that way motionless and without a sound, for so long that finally, out of sheer embarrassment, I got up and moved away. And only a few moments later I saw him dancing merrily again. And behind a screen there were two women over Phyllis, who was all crumpled and shaking with sobs.

How these people could go on with their gayety, with the appearance of enjoying themselves, I could not comprehend. With great difficulty I forced myself through a few dances. When I caught sight of the sixteen-year-old lad with the determined face, who had played the part of a heretic among his fellows a little earlier in the evening, I maneuvered him aside, hoping to get some information.

"I'd like to know who it was that captured Ames—who runs those machines—what do they want of him?" I asked all at once.

He became excited. He looked about to see if anyone could overhear, and moved to an open space, motioning me to follow.

"Serves them right," he exclaimed. "They'll all be taken some day, every last one of them. They putter around with art and waste their time on sport; and dance—bah! I'm sick of it. I want to work. I want to do things. I want to make machines."

He looked furtively about him again. A frightened expression came into his face, and with a mumbled apology he dived away.

I sought refuge in an obscure corner, in order that I might think.

It was evident that the people had become so accustomed to being waited on by machinery that they were helpless and had no initiative in personal matters. And yet, this machinery that took care of them, produced fear and disgust in their minds! Though utterly dependent on it, they considered it disgraceful to notice it, and unpardonable social *gaucherie* to mention it in conversation.

Then, another thing: Machinery requires attention. *Someone* has got to understand it. Somewhere there must be hundreds, thousands of mechanics to operate it, care for it, and repair it. They should form a large proportion of the population. And in this stratum of inhabitants, which was the only one I had thus far seen, engineers ought to be plentiful. Why had I not met an engineer? Were the mechanically occupied persons considered outcasts by these artist-sportsmen? Was it a disgrace to be connected with machinery? Did not the mechanically-minded people associate with the artistically-minded? Was there war between them?

For it was apparent that sometimes the machinery injured people, and favored them with other unpleasant and alarming attentions. These things could not be merely accidents. I had seen enough now to be certain that somewhere behind them was malevolent intention.

I could come to no other conclusion than that the people who operated and took care of the machines were a separate class, lived elsewhere, and did not in any way associate with the aristocracy with whom I mingled. The artistic aristocracy were the masters, and the mechanics were the servants. My yesterday's beautiful picture of an ideal community tumbled sadly in ruins. For these masters did not live the completely happy life that I had at first thought. For one thing they seemed to have degenerated from being so constantly pampered, so that they had no fighting ability, no courage. Furthermore, it seemed that their servants, the mechanics, possessed the power to terrify them, carry them away, perhaps to kill them. Ames had no doubt been "taken" as a disciplinary measure. But why had they attacked Mildred? What had she done? And why Kaspar's dark hints as to my own danger, even while we were still on the ship? What had I done?

And there was that Supervision! The word implied power and authority, and yet these people spoke of it as though it were some compulsory and unpleasant burden. Everyone I knew trembled with that word on their lips.

For a third time I tried to get information concerning the meaning of the gruesome scene I had witnessed. I asked Kaspar as we were starting homeward from the ball. The two of us had fallen back and were walking behind the others on our way to the cars.

"It is in the interest of your own safety," he reminded, "that you do not speak too loud. I am anxious to help you. I cannot even tell you the real reason for my interest in you just now, for fear of spoiling things. I shall try to find some opportunity of explaining things to you as far as I can; but I assure you that it cannot be done here and now."

He said it very gently and very kindly; but there was nothing left for me to say or do.

As I thought it over, I could not help feeling that for many reasons there was more chance of getting my questions answered by asking Mildred, than from anyone else. Yet, I was a little unnerved when it came to asking her, especially when I thought of the strange reactions of the others to my inquiries.

She and I lingered outdoors after the others had gone into the house. She seemed quietly happy.

"Did you enjoy it?" she asked.

"Beautiful," I admitted; "almost too much for me. But some of the doings about got my goat."

She remained staring blankly at me for a moment, and then broke into a peal of chuckling laughter.

"You have some strange ways of saying things," she laughed. "Say something like that again."

"I am very much puzzled about tonight's happenings," I explained, "but I am afraid to ask questions —"

"You may ask me," she said with a smile that shone in the moonlight. "I won't get shocked."

I was so relieved to find my path clear thus far, that for the moment I could not think of the first question to ask.

"Who —?" I finally began, but suddenly a soft little hand covered my mouth. Then, as suddenly, it drew back, and its owner stepped away, abashed at what she had impulsively done. Just for a moment she was embarrassed; and then she threw back her head with that characteristic little toss that delighted my heart.

"Wait!" she whispered. "Not here. I almost forgot. We might be overheard. Wait right here."

She flew into the house. I waited there in the moonlight, with the gleaming foliage about me, for fifteen minutes. I surmised that she had run in to ask Kaspar permission for something she wished to do. And there dawned on me the answer to one question that had been ringing in my head: why was it that she seemed to stand out from the others? At least one cause for that was, that she was always ready and anxious to do some service for others. Then she came flying out of the house again, and I surmised that her breathlessness was due more to excitement than to exertion.

"Tomorrow morning at nine o'clock be ready," she ordered with great glee. "Have on your rough brown clothes and heavy boots, and prepare for adventure. And don't forget what you wanted to ask me."

Chapter VI. The Gulls' Nest

By nine in the morning, Mildred had driven Sappho out in front of the house, and was sitting in the seat, waiting for me to come out.

A charming woman is always a fresh source of delightful surprise. Mildred in her "outing" things was just as refreshing a change from Mildred of the "ball gown," as was the latter from the Mildred of the gray-brown gabardine. To see her in a tight jacket and short skirt of greenish-brown and a pair of boots, aroused a strange, deep enthusiasm within me. Her own eyes danced with excited anticipation. They surveyed me as I came toward her.

"I feel self-conscious in these things, after my two days in society clothes," I apologized, looking over my rough whipcord outfit. She smiled brightly as she saw me glance down at my left sleeve which she had sewn for me. I wondered if she had noted the bulge under my left arm where I had slung my big service pistol under my shirt. I had debated whether or not to carry it; but recollecting Kaspar's numerous dark hints of danger I formed a resolve never to go very far without my pistol, my hand ax at my belt, and my field-glasses over my shoulder. From then on I stuck to this rigidly.

"Hello Sappho, you old ash-can!" I shouted, slapping the fender. "You played a wicked trick on me the other day!"

"You mustn't speak roughly to poor little Sappho," Mildred interceded. "She has been a faithful friend in the Kaspar family."

As if in reply, Sappho gave a little jump forward as I was getting in, for Mildred was already setting the dials; and in another moment had started at a dignified rate down the street.

"I am all eagerness to know where we are going and what we are going to do," I said as we got started.

III

"I told you all that I possibly could, last night," Mildred replied enigmatically, as though someone were listening. "I think it would be wisest to say nothing until the time comes."

I was so surprised that I looked at her and opened my mouth as though to speak, and then looked all around to see who was eavesdropping. But she looked at me so sharply and quickly, as though someone were in reality listening, that I closed my mouth again and said nothing. I contented myself with looking at the great masses of foliage and flowers that buried the beautiful residences along the street on which we drove.

A couple of miles out of the city we came to a fork in the paved road. One continued straight ahead, to the west, and was lost on the horizon among flat, green fields. The car, however, turned into the one which branched off to the left, southwards. I was just sufficiently oriented to know that it led in the direction of the coast where I had first landed on the island, and was without doubt the same road by which we had entered the city on the first night.

For five or six miles we went through a perfectly flat country, covered with marvelously well-tended fields and apparently perfect crops. I took advantage of the opportunity to ask and receive some instruction in the operation of the car. There were direction dials and distance dials; and the route was planned like an equation in calculus. The method, however, required memorizing rather than understanding, unless one enjoyed wrestling with the abstract operation of integration that was involved.

For several miles we drove through a leafy tunnel, and then, as suddenly as we had entered, we emerged into the blinding sunlight. Ahead of us were granite cliffs, and beyond them, the sea. A broad turn of the road around the base of the cliffs brought us into the little harbor where Kaspar and I had landed from the black yacht. But now it was deserted. The little plank dock with the paved road leading to it were the only signs that lent a human value to the lonely place. Near the dock we stopped to get out of the car. Mildred twiddled the dials on the instrument board, whereupon the car turned around and drove back along the road by which we had come, disappearing in the gloom of the forest road.

"I'll never get over the uncanny effect of seeing these machines go about by themselves," I said. "Why couldn't it stand here and wait for us?"

"The place where we are going is a secret. We don't want even a car to know about it," she replied with perfect seriousness. She spoke as though the car might be an intruder into our little company of two; and the fancy pleased me. My father, who was a country practitioner in east Texas, often spoke of his cars as faithful creatures, as though they might have been living things, conscious of his gratitude.

"Soon," she continued, "we'll be able to talk all we want. But now come on. We have a lively walk ahead of us."

We turned to the right (or west), following the shore line, walking on the packed sand strewn with granite boulders. Finally we got in among the cliffs, and into a small canyon. We began to go upward, and our way soon formulated itself into a steep pathway. Mildred led me along at such a swift pace that I had no breath left with which to ask questions; I hurried along behind her, wondering what could be her purpose in bringing me here. At least, I thought, looking upward, we shall get high enough to get a good view out over the island. I was very eager for a bird's-eye view of this strange country. Now and again I caught a glimpse of the sea, and then of the forest in the distance. In some places it was really dangerous climbing.

Finally, after pushing upward for a good twenty minutes we reached the top, so unexpectedly that it surprised me. We were in a bowl, partly of sand and partly of bare granite, about the size of an ordinary dwelling room. We arrived at the edge nearest the sea, from which we could look out over the intensely blue ocean, and almost straight down at its lacy border of white foam where the waves broke on the pink granite. To the east and west the coastline extended to the horizon, a broad strip of yellow sand, occasional groups of cliffs, and back of them the forest, dense and dark. To the north I could not see, for there the cliffs forming the edge of the bowl rose a dozen feet higher than our heads. From the middle or bottom of the bowl I could see only sky.

"This is the Gulls' Nest!" panted Mildred. "Nobody knows of it but grandfather and me. He found it when I was a little girl. Look!"

She scraped away the sand from the middle of the floor, and revealed an iron trap-door with a ring.

"I was surprised when grandfather gave me permission to bring you here," she continued. "He even reminded me to teach you the combination of this."

She opened the door, revealing a small cellar in the rock, containing a supply of preserved foods in cans, jars and bottles.

"It is to be used in case of emergency only. Grandfather is always expecting emergencies."

"Dear old grandfather" she went on earnestly. "He understands. You cannot imagine the torture of the past three days. How I have ached to ask you things about where you came from, and what your people are like, and what they do; and yet not daring to do so. Sometimes it has almost driven me frantic to pretend, that like the others, I did not care. They shut their eyes to the fact that you come from The Outside. I am so glad that we have a place where we can talk—"

And so, instead of asking questions, I answered them. She seemed so hungry to know about the outside world that I did not have the heart to obtrude my own curiosity. Nevertheless, my mind was full of questions, and I watched eagerly for an opportunity to ask them. Why is it that the island people do not dare to talk about the outside world? Why this fear of being overheard, even where there could not possibly be anyone to overhear? What had happened to Ames and why? Who was behind that mysterious abduction? Where were the engineers and the people who tended and repaired the machinery? Where were the shops and factories and warehouses? And, I was restless to look to the north, out over the island, past this granite wall behind me.

But for an hour I talked of Galveston, and of the countless other cities dotted over our broad land, teeming with their millions of people. I talked of rich and poor; of laborers and soldiers and police; of wickedness and charity; of railroads, airplanes, and ships—of all the things she had never seen nor heard of. She listened with wide-open eyes fixed on me, scarcely breathing, and then I knew for a fact, that these things had been unknown to her. Therefore, it was not surpris-

114

ing that my own curiosity faded in the thrill of imparting the things that to her were so strange and startling.

"Why! It's nearly noon!" Mildred suddenly exclaimed in surprise. "We didn't bring a lunch, and it wouldn't do to draw on the emergency things. We'll have to hurry home, or we'll starve."

"I'm already doing that now," I said. "But—?" I turned toward the blank wall to the north of us.

"Ah, I know. You would prefer starvation to missing seeing something." She laughed archly. "Well, I knew you would want to look out over the island."

She led the way along a path at one side, to the top of the wall at the north. From this I beheld a perfectly amazing view.

Immediately below, over a wild and desolate area of granite cliffs, I could see a dense, dark forest. Beyond it were broad, green fields through which wound the shining river and far in the distance a ridge of hazy blue mountains. For all I could tell, the island might extend in that direction for a thousand miles. On my right, toward the southeast was the city. A City of Beauty it was indeed, with its red roofs and many-colored buildings, its gleaming domes and graceful towers, only partially seen for the cushions of green among which they rested. All around the city, along the flat bottom lands of the river valley, were the level, green, cultivated fields. Around these was the forest, like a belt. One glance told me that without a doubt these thousands of acres had been cleared of timber and reclaimed from the virgin jungle, by the hand of man. Here was a vast work, whose achievement must have been thrilling history.

On my left, toward the northeast, was the jungle, impenetrable, dark-green, with a million scintillating reflections on its surface, stretching for miles and miles toward the blue horizon. And on that horizon, a couple of points to the west of northwest, hung a dark, dense pall of heavy smoke. It was a gloomy, depressing smudge that caused a discordant note in that spreading and luxuriant paradise.

"What!" I exclaimed. "A volcano?"

Quickly I reached for my field-glasses, and as I swung them around to the dense nucleus of the smoky smudge near the horizon, my surprise was so great that I nearly lost my balance on the narrow ridge. For there were black shapes and towering masses of buildings, belching chimneys, and a typical skyline of an immense industrial metropolis.

It looked as though it might be twenty miles away. A white ribbon of road led from the City of Beauty toward that black nucleus, sprinkled with swiftly moving dots of traffic. It was an artery carrying a busy black stream between the two cities. The sight of it brought back all the fire of my curiosity again.

"A city!" I exclaimed. "So there are other cities on the island?"

"Just the two," Mildred answered. "That is the City of Smoke!"

"Smoke is right!" I said, with much feeling in my tones.

"That is where the machines are," she continued. "That is where they make all the things for us. That is probably where Kendall Ames is. Those are the things you wanted to ask about."

She looked around as though afraid someone would overhear her, and then recollected herself and smiled at her absent-minded betrayal of the force of habit.

So that was it! Beauty and comfort were so important that everything involving dirt, noise, smoke, and unsightliness had to be put into a separate and distant city. By what arrangement did the aristocracy in the City of Beauty live and lord over the thousands that must be toiling over yonder? To such a degree had they carried their fastidiousness that they could not even bear to see a workman or to talk about him. All they could endure was smoothly running machinery.

On the face of it, one would think that these would be characteristic of a hard-hearted and cruel race. Yet these people in the City of Beauty did not look like that at all. To me they appeared merely light-hearted and thoughtless.

"And Supervision?" I asked.

"Yes, that is where they go for Supervision."

"What is it? What do they supervise?" I asked eagerly.

"Machines. They all take turns going there. Except me. I have never been to Supervision."

"You mean that your people supervise the work that goes on over there in that smoking beehive?"

"Yes. That is what they do."

I put that away for future digestion. I could not quite reconcile a good many things I had seen. In the meanwhile, there was another interesting point.

"How does it happen that you are an exception, and that you do not have to do supervising?" I asked.

"I seem to be specially favored on account of my grandfather. He invented and made those machines. He owns all this country and the cities. He brought me up differently than the others have been brought up. He taught me things about the great world in which you are struggling so hard to be something. But there are still many things that I would like to know, and he thinks I am still a small child and that I cannot understand."

"I've got to see that place," I finally said. "I am going over there to look it over."

She regarded me for a moment in horrified silence,

"I knew you would! It is just like you!" She stepped back and looked me over gravely. "But you mustn't go!"

"Well, well. Why not?"

"Why!" she gasped. "That is a terrible thing to do!"

"I've gone into other cities, as black and smoky as that one. It all washes off when you come out."

"But I can't let you go—" She hesitated and stopped; and then put her hand on my sleeve and looked at me appealingly. This, of course, stirred my determination tenfold. I would have gone through the fires of hell for that, and for the brown eyes looking up at me, and the little quiver around the corners of the mouth.

"Yet, you wouldn't think much of me if I didn't go, would you?" I demanded, with what I felt to be a sheepish grin.

"We cannot stand here and argue," she said sternly. "It's time to go home and eat. Come."

"Wait," I urged. "We've got a lot to say yet; at least I have. If hunger is your only reason for going back, leave it to me. That's an old problem with me."

She looked at me dubiously.

"We'll have to get down to the ground, though. Lead the way down."

In silence she led the way down the path, among the sand and boulders, and in her attitude I read some annoyance but more wonderment and curiosity. When we had clambered down to the level ground, we distinguished Sappho standing at the side of the road, near the dock, waiting to take us home.

"Sappho will have to be patient and wait for us," I remarked jocularly, pleased with my little fancy of personifying the machine. Mildred tossed her head and said nothing.

My idea was first to look about and see if there was any prospect of catching some fish to make a lunch on. I looked carefully through my pockets, through the car, over the dock, and along the shore, but found nothing that would serve as either hook or line, or as a spear. So, I turned to the forest, which was much more in my line; I felt confident that there I could find something to eat. A walk of a hundred yards brought us to the dense growth of underbrush and tangled vines at the edge of it. I asked Mildred to wait for me near the road.

"And do not be afraid if you hear me shoot," I added.

"Oh, I know about shooting, Grandfather has some rifles and has taught me how."

My training with the Texas Rangers had taught me to proceed through a thicket with scarce a sound. I kept my eyes open for edible plants; and my ears told me of small animals moving about near me. After I had squirmed along for a dozen yards, I found the growth more open; so I got out my pistol and looked around. I chuckled at the ridiculousness of it—shooting rabbits with a pistol firing a bullet as big as my thumb. Ahead of me was a large hollow log, big enough to afford a hiding place from which I might take a shot at some passing creature that looked promising as a luncheon. I stepped into it, and there was a sudden flurry and a number of diminutive grunts; something brown wriggled at my feet. Mechanically, I brought down the butt of my pistol heavily upon it, before my consciousness had time to figure out what it might be. It squirmed and kicked a few times and lay still.

I dragged it out into the light. It was as big as a large rabbit, but looked rather like an awkward squirrel, with a curved snout like a pig. I had never seen anything like it before; but I was sure from my general knowledge of game that it was good to eat.

"An agouti!" said Mildred when she saw it. "Poor little fellow."

I was very much amused by her expression as she watched me build a fire, skin the animal, cut it in convenient pieces and roast them on spits of green branches. At first she was somewhat disgusted by the proceeding; but that soon gave way to a fascinated interest, and at the end her hunger compelled her to watch the browning and savory pieces with considerable eager anticipation. Before we had finished eating, and taken our fill of water from a stream which she showed me, she was quite transported with delight. This was a totally new experience for her, and obviously a delightful one.

For me there was also some satisfaction in it. It was some consolation for the awkwardness which I felt among these people, to know that I could look after myself in a pinch and that this flower of an exalted civilization was to some extent dependant on me; that she considered me some sort of a hero.

When luncheon was over, we turned back up toward the Gulls' Nest, with an unspoken mutual understanding. That was the only place where free talk was possible.

"Now tell me," I said, as soon as I could get my breath on the concave top of the cliff, "whom do I see to arrange about going over there?"

"But you don't understand," she said in a voice that almost had tears in it. "There is no way to arrange to go there. There is no one to see."

"Humph!" I grunted. "That means I'll just have to pick up and go. It looks like a long walk. Will you help me some more in learning how to run a car?"

"I'll go with you and I'll drive it for you!" she cried, with a sudden earnest inspiration.

"You're a little brick!" I exclaimed; and, to my own astonishment, I detected a warm tone in my voice that I had never heard there before.

She stared at me a moment and then burst out laughing. It was my turn to stare.

"I'll never get used to your queer ways of putting things," she said. "Little brick! I'm a little brick! Please say some more things like that."

"So you'd like to go with me?" I pondered aloud. "No. That won't do. There must be some sort of danger there. If I knew what it was we might consider your going. But I'll be back soon."

"You must not tell anyone that you are going—"

"You mean they might try to prevent me?" I asked incredulously.

"No. But you have no idea how vulgar the machines seem to them. It must be kept so secret that I must tell you good-bye and wish you good luck here and now. We can't down there."

She held out a little hand to me.

I looked down into the big brown eyes turned up to mine, and the world went round and round with me. Slowly, very slowly, my arm stole round her shoulders and another round her waist. Slowly our heads drew together. She was so still that she seemed not to breathe. Her eyes closed and her head lay back on my arm. Slowly I kissed those soft red lips, whose smiles I had watched so often playing round the sunny teeth. While the waves roared below and the great birds soared above, I once more held that little body close to me, and with great calmness, as though I had a thousand years to do it in, I kissed her. My whole world was changed by that one long kiss.

"I love you!" I whispered.

She opened her eyes and looked up at me with an expression of radiant happiness; her hair and eyes and the curve of her cheek gave a sort of melting impression, and then she buried her head in my shoulder.

"That means you're mine forever?"

Her head nodded "yes" without looking up.

"And that you're going back to my world with me?"

"I want to do that above everything else, Davy, dear." She looked up at me and her arms went about my neck. "I want to get out of this empty, useless life."

"You were very beautiful last night," I whispered.

"I tried to look pretty for you. Did you guess that?"

All at once time seemed to have stopped for us. It seemed that but a few moments had passed when it occurred to me to look at my watch. It was late in the afternoon! Mildred looked worried.

"We must hurry," she exclaimed. "Grandfather will be dreadfully worried about us. Come. That was a wonderful good-bye."

So, with my arm about her, we started for the path that led down the cliff.

"Be very careful, Davy dear, that nothing happens to you," she said in a low, earnest voice. "You are my whole world and life to me now."

"What could happen?"

"I don't know. But they have already gotten many people and we have never seen them again."

"There!" I said triumphantly. "That is my reason for going there. I want to solve the mystery. What happens to all of your people?"

"Yes," she agreed; "I am so anxious to know that I am willing to let you go—" She stopped suddenly, with a catch in her breath.

There stood Kaspar, panting heavily from climbing up the path. We dropped apart and stood looking at him in embarrassment. He smiled.

"Bless your hearts, children; do not let yourself be disturbed by an old man like me. I was very much worried about you, however. So many things might happen. But this explains it." There was a merry twinkle in his eyes.

"But what is that I hear, Davy, about your going somewhere?" he suddenly demanded in great earnestness. We confessed to my plan to visit the City of Smoke.

He stood for many minutes, gazing at me in silence, and his white-bearded face was inscrutable.

"As I remember the young men of the world which I left, when I also was young," he mused, "there would be little use in my trying to talk you out of that. It is the same spirit that brought you to this island; and now I am glad that you came. But why must you risk your life unnecessarily, just as you have found happiness for yourself and given it to others? Listen: things are shaping up now so that it may soon be possible for you to take another kind of trip—back to your own country."

"That news," I replied, "would not have interested me this morning as it does now." I could not erase a broad smile of happiness from my face, nor could I resist a fond glance at Mildred. "But I must solve some questions before I leave this island."

Kaspar shook his head.

"It is a great worry to load on an old man's heart. Perhaps if you could think, as I can, of numerous others who have started out, as you wish to do, to learn the secrets of that grim City of Smoke and have never returned, you would think twice."

"If the ones I have seen are fair samples, I do not wonder that they have never returned," I sniffed contemptuously. "I don't get paralyzed every time I see a machine, and lie down and let it carry me off."

Kaspar put his hand on my shoulder and said earnestly:

"Then wait until I have shown you something in the City of Beauty that you have not yet seen. Tomorrow I shall take you with me to see some people whom you will respect more than those you have already met. I have been watching and studying you from the first time I saw you. Now I know you are qualified to enter the Circle. Will you promise to wait for twenty-four hours?"

I promised.

Chapter VII. I Become a Rebel

I spent many hours in a species of intoxication. My head was light with the joy of what had happened. Suddenly, unexpectedly, within a few days, something beautiful had come into my life that stirred me and made me restless with a fire that I had never known before.

So, for the first time since I had been on the island, I awoke quite late in the morning. Kaspar and Mildred were already waiting for me. I looked wonderingly and inquiringly at them, with their hats on, as though ready for a journey, and at Sappho waiting out in front. Mildred bade me good morning with a warm light in her eyes that sent my composure whirling head over heels.

"Today we are taking you to a certain Committee Meeting," Kaspar explained.

I had forgotten all about that. I started, as I felt an embarrassed flush spread over my face; for the thoughts of Mildred and our newly discovered love had driven all else out of my mind.

"I—I—I'm sorry if I kept you waiting very long," I apologized.

"There is no hurry," Kaspar said, with his kind, patriarchal smile. "In my opinion you are eminently excusable for forgetting such a trivial thing as a Committee Meeting under the circumstances."

"And what sort of—?" I began.

Kaspar held up a warning finger.

"I must remind you that we dare not say too much," he admonished. "Here we never know when the slightest whisper may be picked up and carried over a wire!"

Again that sudden jolt! How many times already, just as I was beginning to feel that the island was a paradise of civilized progress and beauty, came that sudden, sinking hint of some terrible, overpowering thing hanging over it all!

This elaborate secrecy and these hints of a "Committee" told me that even in the City of Beauty, among these fair and talented children of joy, there were things going on that were not apparent on the surface.

Soon the city was far behind us. The river was our companion on the left; and on our right was a broad, flat, green stretch, as carefully tended and well kept as the finest of lawns. I enjoyed its level, peaceful, solitary beauty.

"What is this? A golf course?" I inquired.

"This is the Hopo course," Mildred explained. "No one plays until afternoon. Then you will see many horses and riders. It is half a mile wide and ten miles long."

"It must take an immense amount of labor to keep it looking as neat and smooth as this," I suggested.

"The machines attend to it. There are a great many special mowing and rolling machines caring for the Hopo field."

She seemed to dismiss all concern about it quite readily from her mind, taking the fact for granted that the responsibility was to be un-loaded upon the machinery. My mind kept dwelling on the vastness of the work required to keep these thousands of acres as green and cropped and flat as the trimmest lawn in front of a residence. I would have liked to see the machinery that did it.

Mile after mile we drove. At first the fresh greenness was pleasant, but eventually it began to seem endless and monotonous. However, the girl at my side would have kept the desert of Sahara from seeming monotonous. Then, quite suddenly, we stopped.

We hadn't arrived anywhere. At some time we had left the road, and now on all sides of us were endless flat, green stretches. On the east and west, the greenness merged into the horizon; no City of Beauty was visible. On the north was the gleaming blue river far in the distance; and on the south the difference in color of the verdure indicated that there must be cultivated fields some distance from us. Beyond these, a dim, purple line on the horizon, was the forest. We dismounted from the car and I stared about in surprise. However, I was beginning to learn to say little and observe much.

Kaspar sent the car back. Never would I get over the wonder of it, though now I was seeing it every day: a few twists of the dials, and the machinery began to hum in rhythmic cadences of change, while the empty car swung about, turned backward toward the city, and sped away, dwindling to a small dot in the distance. As we watched it depart we saw several other cars approaching.

In the meanwhile I pondered on the reasons for sending the car back. Why could it not stand here and wait until they were ready to go back? Wasn't it a waste of fuel and machinery? The idea of waste did not seem to occur to anyone here at all. The wealth of natural resources and the vast available mechanical facilities were utilized lavishly and riotously, without a thought of economy. And I began to attach some suspicion to the car itself.

We started out on foot, continuing in the direction in which we had driven. There were dark figures of people ahead of us; they looked infinitely tiny in the vast spaces. Before long we made out a considerable group of them; as we drew near, I decided that there must be about fifty persons gathered together and as many more coming on behind.

"It is now safe to talk as we wish," Kaspar began.

I looked about me and decided in my mind that the factor that made it safe was the fact that nowhere was there any machinery in sight, nor any possibility of concealed wires, microphones, periscopes or cameras. Nothing but flat lawn and sky. Kaspar continued:

"However, just now there won't be time to explain things to you fully. And they must be explained fully, or you would neither understand nor believe them. I am planning on finding a time and a place at which this can be done; I shall make revelations that will astound you. We cannot waste the time of those people talking about things that are familiar to them."

"I note that most of these people are strangers to me," I observed.

"You have heretofore met only those that live in our section of that city and whom we meet almost daily. The people present here are from all over the city. They constitute a committee of such few of us as have retained the power of independent thinking. I might term it a Revolutionary Committee."

"And do they always meet here?" I asked.

"There is no regular meeting place. We change from one to another, with a view to safety and secrecy. This place is good because we can see the approach of any vehicle from a long distance, and long before anyone observing us can guess what we are about."

People recognized and greeted the Kaspars constantly, and I could not help remarking the respectful deference that was paid to the old man. There were a few women in the group. By far most of the persons were men of past middle age, with a good sprinkling of the very aged, as was Kaspar. Young men of my age and younger were relatively scarce, but I saw a few. I was presented to a great many of the people. All of them seemed keenly interested in me, listened intently to the peculiarities of my speech as compared with theirs, and looked me over with a great deal of curiosity. But they all greeted me warmly and seemed glad to have me present.

New arrivals continued to appear for a quarter of an hour and then the vast stretches of lawn in all directions were clear. The people gravitated together without any signal, and the meeting began. They sat in rows on the grass, quite close together, making a compact group, a tiny clump in the midst of the vast green distances. I was not surprised to see the place of the presiding officer filled by the burly figure of Cassidy. He called the meeting to order in a low tone of voice.

"We cannot proceed with any business," he began, "until all present are satisfied as to the eligibility of a new person among us. John Kaspar will introduce him."

Kaspar rose and beckoned to me. He led me up to the front, beside Cassidy. He turned and addressed the assemblage:

"For our struggle against the encroaching domination of the City of Smoke, we have in our ranks much experience and wisdom, but we are sadly lacking in youth and daring. When I think of the young people of this island chasing shadows and losing all spirit of self-determination my heart grows heavy. Here is a young man from the Outside, the grandson of a boyhood chum of mine. We need him among us. From the moment that I first saw him I have watched him closely, telling him nothing, but keeping him on probation. Every step of the way he has demonstrated his courage and his quick-witted self-reliance. In our desperate stand against the mechanical powers he will be a valuable ally."

He went on and told of how I had followed him and gained my way aboard the yacht; of my rescue of Mildred on the dock, at which there were horrified gasps, and a girl sitting near Mildred, similarly clad in gray-brown, put both arms around her; of my escape from the car speeding toward the City of Smoke; and of my stand against the machine that had abducted Ames, at which there was a good deal of nodding of gray-haired and white-bearded heads in admiring approval.

Then Cassidy spoke:

"I shall also vouch for him and I am proud to have him present. I wish he were my own son."

He paused a moment in thought. I wondered if it were because his own child could certainly not be classed as mentally capable of taking part in the movement represented in this meeting.

"And we need him," Cassidy continued. "Our ranks ought to be increasing but they are growing thinner. We lose our members faster than we get new ones. Only three days ago Houchins junior disappeared; they got him as they got his father before him. Out of all of the thousands in the city, it is hard to find new recruits for our ranks. The people are being put to sleep by comfort and luxury; and their souls are being taken away, as well as their bodies. Davy Breckenridge will be valuable to us, not merely because of his youth and daring, but also because of his knowledge and experience. In his own country he has done valiant deeds, and he has had a training in the practical needs of tasks such as we have set ourselves."

Then he put to vote the question as to whether I should be accepted into the group. The vote was enthusiastic in my favor; hands went up and people shouted "Aye!" Then he turned to me.

"The will of the assembly is that you be one of us, and I welcome you." He held out his hand.

"I'm sure that I appreciate the honor very much," I said hesitatingly; "but before I know what to do about it, I shall have to understand what it is all about."

Kaspar spoke.

"Pending the time when I can take you up to the secret little meeting-place that you know about, and tell you the long and complex story that is involved, let me ask you if you can see sufficiently with your own eyes the decadence and blindness of the present generation, the increase in power and terror of the machines, and the certain doom ahead of our poor people unless something desperate is done? Do you not feel willing to help and wait for explanations until they are possible?"

"Yes," I replied; "I have seen enough to know that something is wrong, and that some sort of help is needed. I am devoured with curiosity to know what it is; I am kept awake nights wondering about it. Yet I see the wisdom of your reason. At least I can say that I am very much interested."

127

"Besides," Kaspar said, "you yourself, are in considerable danger. By your very act of following me on board the ship, then by your deeds that night in the dock, and again on the river with the logs, and above all, that night at the pavilion, you have attracted attention to yourself as an unusual person and an undesirable one to the reigning powers. I knew you would, the first time I talked to you that evening on the ship, before we had gotten out of sight of Galveston. They are after you and they may get you at any moment."

"If I can judge by what I see," I replied, "they'll have to hustle harder than they ever hustled before if they want to catch me. They won't find me letting myself be carried away like a sheep. And if they do get me, I'm going to get in a few good licks first, and I'd like to start right now. Just give me a few hours to get this business studied up and straightened out. Then I can get you people started to work-ing properly, and you'll lick them whether I'm with you or not. I've watched this business, and I've got it figured out already that your adversaries have all the possible material advantages, but that some-how they lack the personal equation; they do not seem to know how to follow up their opportunities."

Cassidy was delighted and he wrung my hand.

"I knew you would be valuable to us," he shouted.

"Well, I've got something for you right now," I continued. "When you said that you needed young men, you said a mouthful. I know a young fellow who belongs right here, and you'll never be complete without him."

I turned to Mildred:

"Do you remember on the night of the grand march at the pavilion, I waited for you near a group of boys, and there was a tall boy with a square chin and steady eyes, and you saw me speak to him later—"

"Oh, that is Perry Becker!" she interrupted.

"Perry Becker!" "Yes, I know him!" "He's too young!" several voices exclaimed at the same time.

"Nothing of the kind," I answered impatiently. "He's sixteen. If you wait any longer, he will decay like the rest of them. You need more like what he is. Get them while they still have spirit."

"Correct!" shouted Cassidy; his bellowing voice carried in this emptiness and the tones of the others sounded faint beside his.

"Perry Becker will help us find other young fellows of his age and way of thinking," I suggested.

"We'll have him at our next meeting—" Kaspar began.

Suddenly I heard a sputter and a rattle and a roar in the distance from the direction of the city. There was a sudden hush among the gathered people. Before my eyes everyone turned pale. One after another of them rose and looked toward the city, whence the uproar came.

A half dozen motorcycles were approaching, coming on like the wind. They advanced in a rank, abreast of each other and about a hundred yards apart. In a few seconds they changed from tiny dots on the smooth grass to hurtling, smoking masses, bearing down precipitately upon us.

A panic, wild and terrified, seized upon the gathered committee. Everybody got up and ran; they scrambled over each other to get away, in all directions, like a flock of little chickens. In a few seconds the orderly Committee Meeting had melted. There was a fleeing, helter-skelter mob, scattering over the green levels, running precipitately, stumbling, falling, getting up again; there were several acres of panicky runaway figures. I shouted after them:

"Hi! Come back! That's foolish!"

I shouted until I was hoarse, impatient and irritated.

"What a bunch of fools!" I swore to myself.

I turned around. I found Mildred holding my arm in her two hands and staring defiantly around. Kaspar and Cassidy stood behind me. Kaspar was calm, so calm that it looked wrong. Cassidy had torn his collar open and was glaring belligerently in a semicircle, and swinging his doubled fists, that looked like a pair of pile-drivers.

In another moment the machines had whizzed by and turned into disappearing dots in the eastern distance. They were tiny things, not over three feet high, and there certainly were no people on them.

Cassidy stood and stared after them for several minutes. He turned to the rest of us with a blank look, and then under his breath he released several expletives, which heretofore I had not been aware were in circulation on the island. Finally he leaned back and laughed. He laughed until he roared and the tears came.

"It is mostly our guilty consciences that caused the rout," he explained, and laughed again.

"That is only the regular green-patrol of the Hopo field," he went on. "But we are nervous and jumpy. Look!"

He pointed toward the city. Several more dark bulks were slowly approaching,

"They come by every third or fourth day. There come the mowers and rollers. Those little things go on ahead to assure a clear track and lay out the course. 'Leading-machines,' we have come to call them. They are in common use for all automatic mechanical work."

It was not long before the scattered people recognized their mistake and came trooping back, looking quite sheepish; though many of them were big enough to have the sense of humor to laugh. Cassidy continued to laugh for a long time. The burly, phlegmatic fellow must have been under a severe nervous strain. At the time of the emergency he had been cool and steady, ready to deal with the situation. That he was unnerved afterwards made me sure that much more had been at stake than merely his own skin. I knew such people well.

I had not laughed at any time. It did not look funny to me; it looked pitiful. If it had been a real attack, they would have been hunted down like rabbits, to the last individual. And they had actually acted as though they had expected nothing else than to be killed on the spot. What sort of a terrible mystery was here?

While the group re-formed the ponderous mowers and rollers went by. There were a dozen of the towering, clattering hulks spread out in line, advancing down half the width of the field, each bigger and noisier than the biggest road-machine I had ever seen in western Texas; and they proceeded irresistibly, reminding me in their inexorable advance of tanks. Behind them they towed great truckloads of mowed grass. Nowhere about them were any human beings visible. When they passed they left lawns as smooth and flat as a table top. When

Cassidy opened the meeting again for business I rose and addressed him, hastening to get ahead of anyone else.

"Do you really want me to help you?" I inquired of the whole assembly.

"Sure," said Cassidy positively. "I can speak for one and all present."

"Then I am glad this happened," I continued. "It has pointed out to me the thing that you need worst if you are to succeed. It is a simple thing, but you've got to have it or you won't last long."

Not a sound broke the silence. All eyes were bent eagerly on me.

"And that is *discipline*. Without some type of formal discipline you are lost. In order to make discipline possible you need some form of organization. The only one I can suggest, because it is the only one I know, is the military type. But I can assure you that it is effective and practical. If I teach you, will you drill and play the game? Do you wish to begin right now?"

A forest of waving hands was eagerly raised in the air.

So Cassidy and I went up and down the rows, picking out the most likely ones to form the beginning nucleus of an organization. Rather quickly we located nine young fellows out of about twenty, and then it was more difficult. Finally we had sixteen men who looked promising as material for leaders. I noted during our selection that Mildred and the young lady with her in similar dress were talking very excitedly and watching us eagerly. Toward the end, when I called the sixteen out in front, the two girls came up to me.

"Aren't you going to let us in?" they asked disappointedly.

I was puzzled as to what to do. In my military experience woman had no place. Yet here it looked rather logical. After a conference with Kaspar and Cassidy we made up a squad of girls, with a view to a separate organization of women, to receive similar training.

I requested the other members of the group who had not been chosen as recruits to remain behind me and watch what was going on, urging them to try and learn as much as possible about it, for their turn would come before long.

I took my twenty-four recruits and taught them how to form a straight line and to stand at attention. At my first command of "At-tention!" most of them were rather astonished at the preemptory and businesslike tone of voice. But there is reason for the tone of military commands, and it worked. For once these *blasé* people took something seriously, and in a few minutes they were working hard. With sharp commands I put them through "Forward, march!" and "Squads, right!", exacting rigid compliance with the regulations.

There, on the vast, flat, green spaces, with the little knot of specta-tors behind me, I put my tiny line through its maiden evolutions. I did not hesitate to jerk out my commands with proper sternness, and to use top-sergeant methods on the sluggards. For they needed it. Their lives sadly lacked rigid training. They did not like it, but I had to give them credit for being game. They apparently saw a glimmer to the effect that it was necessary and good for them, and they took it all like the good sports they were. They came out of it much better than they went in. I think that they learned more that forenoon of real, deep human values, than they ever had known in their previous lives; while to me it meant considerable satisfaction that their intentions were serious, and that they were going to work, even if it came hard.

After the drill, the meeting continued in an informal manner for a while. I directed everyone present to write down everything he had learned as quickly as possible, in order that he might retain it cor-rectly and pass it on accurately to others; for I wanted each one of those present to begin drilling a platoon of his own without delay. Cassidy was chosen as the head of a committee to select and judge new recruits. Before the meeting was over, the matter of training was an organized machine, that could proceed under its own power, inde-pendent of me, except for the matter of teaching a few leaders.

I was a little amused at the surprise and relief of the recruits who had been drilling, after I had given the command "Dismissed!" They had never seen anything like it: one moment I was on a rigidly stern pinnacle above them; and the next I was mingling with them cordially and democratically. But they were wonderful folks. They did not say much about it, though I was sure all were thinking hard.

"There must never be another panic like this," I said to the assembled people. "From now on, you must drill every day. The Hopo fields, the eastern beaches, anywhere you can find places where you are safe from observation, must be your drill grounds. In the meanwhile, I shall study the main features of your situation and analyze them, to see where I can be of further assistance to you."

Noontime came and the meeting had to break up. As we walked over to where our cars were coming to meet us, we saw an occasional Hopo rider with his long mallet, swinging along as the vanguard of the afternoon play. Many of the people shook my hand and seemed happy over my efforts. Everywhere among them was enthusiasm; each one seemed as though he had just discovered something new and wonderful. Cassidy walked beside me.

"Looks good to me, boy!" he said. "I knew you'd do something. I've got genuine hopes now."

"Well," I mused; "I'll be glad when I know what it's all about."

"In a day or two you shall know. Kaspar will tell you the whole story. It is a difficult thing to tell to a stranger. In the meanwhile, be careful how you talk and where you talk. We need you now."

"I'll be careful," I promised; but I kept wondering to myself how in thunder a thing like this could be managed without a lot of talking to people.

"You seem to have stirred things up," Cassidy went on; "Thus far our meetings have been a wonderful comfort and mutually sympathetic. But there had been no objective; we didn't know how to go about doing something definite. Now, it looks to me that delivery from our slavery to the machines and the end of the degeneration of our people are near at hand. I have real hopes of breaking away from the City of Smoke. Oh, will the time ever come when we can cease to worry about our best friends? Do you realize that at this moment we are not sure that tomorrow Mildred will not disappear to an unknown fate?"

"We've got to get down to business," I said, gritting my teeth at the thought. "I foresee trouble, and there is lots to do. People are going to get hurt. Have you ever thought of that? Your people aren't prepared for anything. This afternoon you must pick me out a dozen bright people, and I'll start out a bunch in first-aid training so that we could turn them loose as teachers; and another bunch preparing supplies."

Cassidy nodded reflectively.

"And what do these people know about taking care of themselves in case the service of the machines should fail them?" I went on. "How many can rustle up a meal and cook it, or prepare a night's shelter? How many could raise something to eat for an unproductive period? Does anyone know anything about weapons?"

"You make me ashamed of myself and of the whole island," Cassidy admitted. "For so long have we been accustomed to living without any need of these things, that it has never occurred to us that it might be otherwise. These are all forgotten arts. Yet, I can see that the time is apt to come when we shall need them. There are probably some racking experiences ahead for us. But better that than this slavery. Davy, we've needed you badly to stir us up."

"If you find me people, I shall teach them," I proposed eagerly. "I'll help you get organized. Your people are excellent material, and take to it well. With a little training and organization, you can work against your apparently powerful enemies with some show of hope on your side. I'm enthusiastic about getting to work at once. In fact, I'm thankful for having something real to do. This social stuff was beginning to get the best of me."

All of that day, while I watched the people, talked to them, and worked with them, there was a hidden undercurrent of thought in my mind. There, ever present, was that black, smoking city, with its white thread of a road stretching over here toward us, teeming with hundreds of busy, speeding vehicles, like a pulsing artery between two centers. I remembered that fork of the road where we had turned off to the left on the previous morning; that other branch went straight ahead, inviting and beckoning with mystery. It was the road to the City of Smoke. What was there in that gloomy metropolis? Why was it kept such a secret? I had promised Kaspar that I would wait twenty-four hours. That twenty-four-hour period was now over.

Then, one night at midnight, I was awakened from my sleep by an unusual commotion in the Kaspar home. People walking about, queer, catchy and strained voices penetrated thickly to me. I threw on some clothes, and opening my door, cautiously looked out. I saw Phyllis sobbing in Mildred's arms and Mildred, pale and wild-eyed, trying to comfort her. Kaspar was walking nervously back and forth across the room, and Mrs. Kaspar was in a big chair with her head bowed on her hands. I stood and stared a while, and finally came out among them.

"This is the worst blow of all," Kaspar groaned. "Without him we are lost."

"Who? What has happened?" I demanded.

"Cassidy is gone. They've got him!" Kaspar groaned and sat down.

I am afraid that I used an ungentlemanly word. I stood for a few moments struck dumb. But there was nothing I could do there. I turned and walked back into my room, where I began picking things out of my suitcase and packing a haversack to carry slung over my shoulder. My determination was made.

Chapter VIII. To the City of Smoke

During my life I had gone through enough danger and excitement to have developed the ability to lie down and snatch a few hours' sleep in the face of an approaching crisis. Not knowing just what was ahead of me now, I took care to get into bed and relax completely, so that I might gather strength and poise for my coming adventure. Also I had the much more common ability to wake up exactly at a previously determined hour.

In the morning I was awake at sunrise, feeling fit and alert. Dressing was a matter of a few moments, and I ate a double breakfast. I wrote the following note on a large sheet of paper and pinned it to the middle of the rug:

> I have gone to the City of Smoke. I am leaving quietly because I cannot bear dissuasions and leave-takings. I promise to take good care of myself; and when I return I expect to bring with me some knowledge that will be

useful to you in your struggle. I hope that I can find Cassidy and be of some use to him. I know that you will not mind my using Sappho, for my purpose is the good of the cause.

Davy Breckenridge.

I took with me my pistol and ten spare clips of shells, the hand ax and field-glasses, a canteen, a flashlight and extra batteries, and some dried emergency rations. I debated for a while whether or not to include my blanket, but finally left it behind, because its bulk would impede my movements too much.

I left with only one regret, and that was that I had not yet heard Kaspar's explanation of what the war was about. A better knowledge of what was going on would have been to my advantage in getting about the strange city, and in gathering information to help these people in their stand against their oppressors. But I reasoned that my present plan was best; for since Kaspar was afraid to talk openly around here, it would take a half a day or more before suitable opportunity could be found to tell me his story, which he stated was long and complicated. I was unwilling to risk any such delay; things might happen to prevent me from going. If I was to do Cassidy any good, I had better start quickly. Though, how I could find him in that vast hive, I had no idea.

I had to confess that at certain moments my project struck me as somewhat foolhardy: starting out alone into a city totally unknown to me, and where I had certainly received ample warning that danger awaited me. However, there was a good deal to discount this danger. What these soft and luxurious people considered a danger might be little more than superstition. And I intended to be careful, to keep a sharp lookout ahead of me, and to know what I was getting into before taking each step. This was to be a sort of scouting or reconnoitering expedition. I had no clear or definite plans. Each stage would have to be guided by what I had already found.

Turning these things over in my mind, I stole out of the house and opened the garage doors. My instructions in running the car were far from complete, and my practice meager; but I had handled it enough by this time to feel sure that I could get to my present destination with it. The sight of the jolly little roadster resting there in its stall put me into high spirits again. I spoke to it in the jocular manner that I had fallen into:

"All right, Sappho, you old coffee-grinder; we'll slip off by ourselves this morning."

My derogatory epithets were pure fun, for the car was trim and swift-looking, and its machinery in the most perfect order, as far as I could tell by its sound and its performance. I continued to talk to it as I got in and studied the dials. I went to work carefully to set them. It was like working the combination of a big safe. There were four for directions, and a distance dial to set each time between them, while the left hand handled the speed dial simultaneously during the entire time. A little pointer traveled on a chart all the while, to check up the setting as well as to assist in determining directions and distances from a map when these were unknown to the driver. The study of this map provided me with much subsequently useful knowledge of the island and the cities.

"Now, all aboard for the City of Smoke!" I almost shouted in my glee, as I completed the "setting" and the machinery under the hood began to purr.

With a soft, rustling sound of its marvelous mechanism, the little green-black car glided out of the garage and into the street. I was as elated as a child with a new toy, at having succeeded in operating it on my own initiative.

"Attaboy Sappho!" I applauded. "If we go on like this, we'll have Cassidy out of jail and take a shot at this 'Supervision' business before night."

I watched the streets with eager attention, checking up the places I already knew, to ascertain if the car was carrying me correctly. Now I could not help being impressed with the marvelous ingenuity of the automatic mechanism of the car; for I had to admit that I had laid out no more than the general features of the route, while the smaller de-tails, such as turning corners, avoiding passing cars and obstacles in the road, were all taken care of by the machinery, without knowledge or effort on my part. It was difficult for me to resist the temptation to stop the car and look under the hood to see what the machinery looked like that was accomplishing the feats that were almost beyond belief.

Within thirty minutes the car rolled through the park, out through the arched gateway, and sped up the paved highway between the green fields that were already familiar to me. It bowled along smoothly and luxuriously. On the right, the morning mists were rising out of the river in the distance, and the mountains far out beyond were a wonderful deep blue. On the left, the flat, cultivated fields extended on to the smooth and level horizon. The morning was cool, and the breeze made by the motion of the car felt as delicious to my hands and face as a cooling drink. The shadow of the car racing on ahead was a dozen feet long.

When I saw ahead of me the fork in the road, with the branch on the left leading to the dock and the Gulls' Nest, I watched the behavior of the car with bated breath again. Would it take that mysterious and interesting branch of the road that led straight on ahead, toward the great, smoking macrocosm that I had seen from the top of the cliff? Had I "set" it correctly? It was more exciting to my nerves than the watching of a tense automobile race, and my heart almost stopped beating, until the fork to my left was safely behind me, and I was spinning along, straight to the west.

As mile after mile passed, without effort from me, I pondered on the curious things that had befallen me during the past few days. It was an opportune moment for concentration; I leaned back among soft cushions, with nothing to do as far as driving or paying attention to the road was concerned; the monotonous purr of the machinery and the equally monotonous whizz of the scenery backward past me, were very soothing. I tried to plan ahead. I was resolved not to plunge blindly into the city, but to look it over from a distance and approach cautiously. Then it occurred to me that if I carefully analyzed some of the questions that had been puzzling me about affairs on the island,

I might be able to make some deductions concerning the dangers ahead of me, and might consequently better prepare myself to meet them. A careful consideration of what I had already seen was certain to shed a good deal of light on what I had to expect.

When I stopped to think about it, this was my first opportunity to think things over carefully since I had landed. Up till now, my every moment had been busy, distracted by the presence of others and by something going on, or I had been too tired and sleepy to think. So, I took out my notebook and pencil, and one by one I marshaled the mysteries, puzzles, and surprises that I had found here; and after careful reflection, made a few notes on each.

1. *From the very first moment I had set foot on the black ship, Kaspar had begun warning me that I was in grave danger on the island.* At first I had thought that he was trying to scare me with the ordinary perils of tropical travel. But, here I was in a perfectly civilized community; the streets and homes looked as peaceful and safe as my own home town. And yet, Kaspar and Cassidy carefully and anxiously watched my every move. There must be something more specifically danger-ous than snakes and swamps and savages. How he could say that I was in danger before anyone on the island knew I was coming, or was even aware of my existence, puzzled me. He certainly did not mean to imply that all strangers were in peril; and besides I had been very well received by these people, who were totally unaccustomed to strangers. Was my danger similar to that of other individuals on the island, like Ames and the others who had disappeared? Why had those particular ones been selected? And why particularly was I selected? It could not be because these dark enemies knew much of me personally. There had never been the least relationship between me and the island.

I wondered if perhaps a few of the old Southern families between whom there was some deadly feud, had not gotten settled on the is-land, and kept up the feud through all these generations. Perhaps the two factions who had continued the family war were now organized, each in its own populous city, and were carrying on the war with all the terrific and grotesque weapons their science had supplied, au-tomatic cranes, and huge motorcycles with tentacles. And perhaps

I also was a descendant of one of these factions or in some way involved with it, and Kaspar knew about it, while I didn't. At any rate, it was clear that for some reason not connected with anything that I myself had done or was conscious of, my existence was in conflict with some established principle on the island. In other words, I was a *persona non grata*. A more detailed solution I could not hope to arrive at just at the present time.

2. *What was the meaning of the incident — almost an accident — of Mildred and the crane?* No sooner had I stepped off the ship than here was a new mystery. On the surface of it, it may have looked like an ordinary accident; but by this time I was thoroughly satisfied that it had been a bold and almost successful attempt to annihilate a girl who was one of the most beautiful and popular, and certainly the most prominent in her community. Was there a personal reason for the attack on her? Was she selected because of her prominence? I had seen the fear in the eyes of the people who had watched that "accident"; and I was sure that they had known what was behind it. What better proof was there that Kaspar's people had deadly, unscrupulous, and ingenious enemies among the people who operated the machines? Yet, apparently the power and opportunity of the latter were not unlimited; for certainly that night on the dock they had control of a sufficient preponderance of physical force to have been able to put across any desired plan by means of physical violence. Evidently there had been reasons why it was impossible to attack openly the little group that had come to meet Kaspar. There was something more beneath this than mere crude, open enmity.

3. *What was the truth about my compulsory ride in the automatic car?* Was that an "accident" of the same kind as the one previously mentioned? By this time I was thoroughly ready to discard the idea that it had been a practical joke played upon me by some member of the social group gathered about the Kaspar family. These people's minds did not work in the direction of dangerous practical jokes against their own good friends. I strongly suspected that my ride, with its wild ending, was an attempt on the part of the machinery people to carry me off. It was clever; it would have looked like an ordinary accident. The

machinery people had a skillful way of staging things without appearing on the scene themselves. Not only in the dark deeds I have
mentioned, but in all the work that the machinery did for the living,
comfort, and luxury of the inhabitants of the City of Beauty, were they
extraordinarily skilful in getting things done and keeping absolutely
out of sight. It was evident that the highly-cultured, sport-loving class
whom I knew so well, not only knew nothing about the operation
and care of machinery, but also that they seldom if ever beheld the
mechanics who operated and cared for it, and on whom their lives
depended.

4. *How far wrong was I in my estimate of the community on the day
I had visited the Paneikoneon?* Evidently my original idea of a perfect
Utopia needed some amending. The people of the City of Smoke obviously lived in subjection to the fair artists of the City of Beauty, and
carried the entire burden of that marvelous culture and development.
The fastidious drones could not even bear to have the workers live in
the same city with them. It was a strange picture. Beauty was the first
thing to strike the eye, but it was only on the surface. One group was
living in luxury and leisure at the expense of a subject class; and yet
living in terror of the subjects. The subjects, in bursts of rebellious retaliation, reached up and dragged down, every now and then, a bright
and favored member of that high and shining stratum. It was difficult to determine which were the masters and which were the slaves;
which the oppressors and which the oppressed.

5. *What became of the people who disappeared?* There was no doubt
in my mind that they were taken to the City of Smoke. Furthermore,
everything I had ascertained pointed to the fact that they were never
seen nor heard of again. What happened to them there was a matter
of pure conjecture, and speculating about it was a waste of time and
effort.

6. *What was Supervision?* Evidently the subject class were not quite
completely out of sight. At times the lords had to degrade themselves by
looking over the labors of their servants at the scene of operations. Otherwise, what could "Supervision" mean? It seemed to be a compulsory
task, evidently unpleasant. The compulsion also evidently came from

the supervised and not from the supervisors, for the latter seemed anxious for opportunities to dodge the obligation, while the former meted out a terrible and mysterious punishment to my friend Ames, who had made a record by his success in avoiding the obligation.

Could there be a more amazing, more maddening interlacement of puzzling relationships and inconsistent influences?

7. *What was the reason of the intense fear of being overheard? Who could overhear?* Most of the people I knew would not speak of the mysteries connected with the machinery under any circumstances at all. Their private thoughts on the subject, if they had any, were never uttered. The few people who did have the courage and aggressiveness to think and speak on the subject, did so, only under circumstances where there was no possibility of their words being picked up by mechanical appliances. Even automobiles were under suspicion; out in the broad fields and in the dense woods, Mildred would not speak as long as there was a car around. This was explainable only on the basis of highly developed methods of detection of sound and its transmission by radio methods. Apparently microphones or dictaphones were concealed everywhere, in homes, public places, automobiles. And evidently the people did not know enough about these instruments to find them and put them out of commission. I resolved at once never to go out again with anyone in a car, without first looking it over and disconnecting anything that looked like a transmitter or a detector.

Evidently, somewhere, someone was listening to everything that went on in the City of Beauty. Had I made a mistake when I spoke aloud to Sappho on starting his morning? I was sorry now that I had not taken the trouble to think these things out before. I had given away my plans completely. Perhaps by this time they were known to some central spider in the big web. I had better be doubly cautious in entering the city.

8. *What was this people's uprising about? Against whom? What were their grievances?* It must be a very grave matter. Every one of them had fear in their eyes. They were pale and furtive from fear, and yet they went doggedly on with their plans and their preparations. People do that only when vital matters are at stake. It was not some mere

fancied wrong that troubled them; life was too easy-going in the City of Beauty. And yet, I could see no cause for complaint. Everything seemed running smoothly; on all sides were all possible reasons why these people should be happy. They seemed to have, as far as I could see, all they wanted of food, shelter, clothes, liberty and leisure, luxuries. What did they lack? What were they fighting about?

And what would they have done if I had not headed them in the proper direction in the matter of organization and discipline? They were intelligent and grasped things quickly; but they were ignorant of the very fundamentals of taking care of themselves. Never had I seen a more helpless people.

Their helplessness of course meant that they had long been cared for like children. No thought nor effort for their own care was required of them. Yet, if someone had taken that good care of them, why were they planning rebellion against their benefactors?

A number of possible explanations occurred to me. The book of H. G. Wells that I had read some time ago suggested one. Another was a memory that came back vividly to me from childhood, and struck me forcibly as a close analogy of this people's plight. When I was a small boy, I had pet rabbits. There was one rabbit that I especially loved and favored. I gave it the best of care and fed it royally. Just like the people in the City of Beauty, it lived in luxury, without a thought of taking care of itself. Then, one day it disappeared just as Ames had. My childish grief was so intense that I remember it to this day. It was a long time before my child mind connected the disappearance of my pampered and indulged rabbit, with a new kind of meat on the table. I had thought my parents loved the rabbit as well as they did me.

Other analogies occurred to me. Were not these people in some sort of position like that of the farmer's prize herd of cattle? He takes the best possible care of them; he goes to any amount of expense to secure their comfort and content. They are as happy and comfortable, and as well developed as the people in the City of Beauty. Are they also afraid of the farmer because occasionally one of them disappears and is never seen again? In our laboratories at Galveston we treated the dogs and guinea-pigs as carefully and considerately as though they had been human. No amount of care, no excellence of food, no perfection of comfort was too good for them. And, every now and then, we took one of them away to the dissecting room, and his comrades never saw him again.

Whose pets were these fair people in the City of Beauty? For what sort of sacrifice or experiment were they being so perfectly cared for?

I closed my notebook with a slap. My analyses and deductions had brought me to discomforting conclusions. I began to have misgivings as to the wisdom of my expedition. If I ever wanted to see Mildred again, if I ever wanted to take up that country practice in eastern Texas that I had so long dreamed about, perhaps I had better reconsider my plans before it became too late.

I was roused from my study and brought back to a consideration of my surroundings by noting that there was a forest ahead. The dim blue line on the horizon ahead broadened into a green strip, which was rapidly looming high in the air; and before long I could see the details of the dense jungle, which exactly resembled the one through which we had passed on our way to the sea. The way it ended abruptly like a wall where the cultivated fields began, made me certain that this country had once been entirely covered by jungle; and that the river bottoms had been artificially cleared for cultivation. What a stupendous task that must have been! The history of this land must be an astonishing chronicle, full of heroisms and brave human accomplishments! What characters, what Daniel Boones and George Washingtons, the history of this people must contain! In fact, Kaspar and Cassidy were big men, worthy of being put down in any history. I must get all of this story from Kaspar or someone, as soon as I could, for I was intensely interested in it.

Now and then an occasional truck came hurtling toward the city from which I had come. I always looked up quickly, hoping to see the driver; but there were no drivers. The vehicles were all automatic and unoccupied. I saw no people at all. Apparently the custom or regulation against the people of each city visiting the other was very strictly observed. What would I run into by going contrary to it?

At first the vehicles I met were few and far between. But, as the day advanced and the day's business began to get started, they became more frequent and numerous. There were chiefly trucks, of all sizes and shapes, with and without loads. However, I saw numerous other strange machines making their way toward the City of Beauty, lumbering and clattering hulks, such as I had never seen before, and whose purpose I could not imagine. The requirements of caring for a city's work by automatic machinery had developed some bizarre and undreamed-of forms of apparatus. I ached for an opportunity to examine some of them closely and watch them work.

The road dived into the black opening in the green wall ahead, and in a moment I was plunging along through the cool gloom of the forest, endeavoring to see. It took some moments for my eyes to become accustomed to the twilight that reigned there. Overhead I caught some glimpses of the sky through the interlacing branches just over the road; but at the sides the roof was so dense as to be quite impenetrable to any light at all. The tree trunks and interlacing vines and branches spun backward at a dizzy rate, while the car made a soft, rushing noise in its progress through the leafy tunnel. The bright opening behind, by which I had driven in, soon disappeared; and all around there was nothing but jungle.

I noticed that the car was beginning to behave curiously. It would slow down for a few moments, and gradually pick up speed again. Suddenly it would slow down again and almost stop. Then it would race quickly on. In another few moments it was hesitating along at a snail's pace. Various queer and unusual noises proceeded from it, grindings, knockings, and squeaks. Then it stopped and stood motionless with its machinery humming.

"What's wrong now?" I muttered. I had serious misgivings as to my skill in setting the dials, simple as that task seemed to the other folks who handled these cars. I looked the instrument board all over carefully, but did not know what further to do. I felt it wisest not to tamper with the dials any further.

Abruptly the car jerked forward, and with a few turns it reversed its position on the road and started back swiftly toward the City of

Beauty. Its horn tooted melodiously up and down the musical scale.

"Whoa!" I shouted. "There's something wrong here!"

The only explanation that I could possibly think of was that I had made some mistake in setting the dials. Yet, that was not altogether plausible. I could readily see how I might have made some minor error which could have gotten me off the track a little. But this sort of behavior would necessitate a radical and fundamental error; and I felt sure that I knew more about them than to have set them completely backwards.

I reached for the levers that were used to drive the car by "actual control" as the people called it; that is, to control each movement individually; and I tried to turn it around. There was a good deal of grinding and knocking in the mechanism, and much irregularity in the car's progress; but it continued its course back home, and would not answer to my efforts. Therefore, I decided that something had gone wrong with the machinery. This was a little embarrassing, to say the least. I had taken the car without permission, which fact in itself was enough to disconcert me; and to have it get out of order was making the thing worse than ever. Indeed, my friends would think that I had behaved like a small boy.

However, in a moment my present trouble had crowded that out of my mind. I did not want to go back to Kaspar's house now. Not only would I not want to face the people; but my own conscience would not permit me to go. I was so contrarily built, that the very fact that I had just gone through a reasoning process that convinced me that I was embarked on a highly dangerous course, was enough to make me all the more doggedly set in my determination to carry it out. Even though my knees shook and my teeth chattered, I would have gone ahead. Already I had lost a mile on my way. The car was proceeding irregularly, now fast, now slow. I hung my haversack over my shoulder and jumped out.

The fall brought me stumbling to my knees. The roar of an approaching truck made me dodge into the underbrush. Why I hid, I do not know. I was worked up to a pitch of jumpy nervousness, feeling sure that although I saw no people about here, nevertheless I was being observed, and someone, somewhere, knew just what I was doing. The truck rumbled by and disappeared, I watched Sappho. The car went forward a moment, then stopped and quivered a moment, and went backwards, It stood still a while with the machinery roaring, and then started at full speed toward the City of Beauty. I crawled out and stood in the road, watching it dwindle and disappear. Now I was alone in the forest.

"There can't be much over ten miles to go," I thought, "and I am safer on foot."

I swung along, feeling lusty and vigorous in the exhilarating morning air. It was just beginning to get warm. Up above, in the interlaced canopy of branches and foliage, there were clickings and squawkings; and I caught flashes of bright colored plumage flashing back and forth. Little sounds came out of the forest, a chirp, a twitter, a rustle. My footsteps rang loudly on the pavement. I wondered if there were any large and dangerous animals. I swung my pistol into position where I could draw quickly, for I had confidence in my aim and in the stopping power of a .45 caliber bullet. Still, I admitted that my greatest danger was not from wild beasts.

The passing vehicles kept growing more numerous. They passed with a roar that rumbled and re-echoed back and forth among the tree trunks in the depths of the forest. I kept a sharp lookout for human beings, but not one did I ever see on any of the machines. I hugged the bushes, whose ends were whipped off by passing vehicles into a perpendicular wall, like a trimmed hedge. The vehicles as a rule kept the middle of the road.

A little "leading machine" whizzed by. It was a curious vehicle, a tiny motorcycle, too small for anyone to ride in or to carry a load. There was a good deal of complicated mechanism about it, little gearwheels like the works of a watch, and many busy little rods and cams. In front were two bright, staring headlights. As it sailed whirring down the road, I stared after it, wondering what could be the possible use of the thing.

A truck came up behind me. From the sound of its machinery, it seemed to be slowing down. I glanced back and found this indeed to be the case; and furthermore, it was at the edge of the road, directly behind me. I edged as far as I could into the thicket.

"This is no place for pedestrians," I thought.

Of course, there was no sidewalk. There could not have been much, if any, travel on foot between the two cities.

The approaching truck was a light one, of half-ton capacity. The curved arm of a crane projected from it, high above the road, from the side nearest me. It passed very slowly, and uncomfortably close to me. I crowded close to the bushes. If there had been a driver, I would have had something to say to him.

A sudden clatter above my head made me look up in surprise. A loop of chain whipped out cleverly from the crane, like the circle of a lasso. It fell neatly over my head, and while I stared in open-mouthed astonishment, it tightened about my arms and shoulders.

It happened so quickly, such an amazing, undreamed-of thing, that before I realized what was going on, I was swung off my feet and hoisted up off the ground. My arms were pinioned to my sides, and I was helpless as a trussed turkey. At first, I was stunned with surprise. It was too strange—too far beyond anything I could have foreseen. Then I was overwhelmed by anger and chagrin. I had been taken in as easily as a new-born babe. For a moment, I was beside myself with rage.

However, that availed me nothing. I dangled there foolishly in the air, and the grip of the chain around my chest and arms was painful. At least I was glad that there were no witnesses to my ridiculous plight.

The truck picked up speed and clattered on, toward the City of Smoke. As the trees and bushes spun backward past me and the wind whistled about me, I was swung over the seat, and with much humming of gears and clashing of levers from the interior of the car, I was lowered until I was comfortably seated. Immediately, a polished bar swung across my chest and locked with a click. Here I sat, fastened down, fuming and writhing.

My rage knew no bounds. Captured! Tied up and being carried

away! Just like one of the helpless rabbits from the City of Beauty. No! I would show them. I would not be cowed, merely because a machine had got hold of me. Perhaps they had me, but if they had, they would still learn a few things about what kind of a fight I could put up. They would never get to that black city with me.

I heaved and strained at the bar that held me prisoner. I am known as a strong man among my friends, but my utmost efforts failed to budge the bar, or even to produce a crackle. It remained immovable. After I had exhausted my strength and bruised my flesh, I began to calm down a little. The firm and steady pressure of the bar across me helped to steady my nerves. The purely impersonal character of the things that held me gradually calmed me, and I began to reason a little.

My safety now depended upon my keeping my wits together. That was the first thing that dawned on me. I spent a good many minutes in drilling myself to keep calm, and forcing myself to plan carefully ahead, just as the previous few days I had been drilling the rebels. If I wanted to get away from this machine, I must think clearly first. Get away from it, I must, somehow.

I had no doubt in my mind that I had given myself away in the morning by my soliloquy; a microphone in the car had warned the authorities in the black city, and they had sent the automatic machine after me. The uncanny cleverness with which the mechanism worked was almost too much for my belief.

Well, I had been tricked once, but now I was warned. From now on, I would realize fully that I could trust no machine near me. My unseen enemies had the advantage of me because they knew all about my movements without themselves being in evidence. Nevertheless, I made up my mind to outwit them.

I set about examining carefully the bar that held me. Machinery had to be dealt with coolly and calculatingly. The bar fitted my chest as accurately as if it had been made to measure for me. It held me tight against the back of the seat and restrained the movements of my arms. I looked about to see if I could reach something to pry it loose. If I could get my hands on some kind of a lever, I would make short work of the thing.

Then, suddenly I got an idea and desisted.

If I were being watched, why not let them think they had me? If I pretended stupidity and submission, a loophole of escape would be much more certain to offer itself. If they considered me as helpless as the rest of the people from the City of Beauty, my chances would be far better.

And after all I was on my way, swiftly and comfortably, toward the goal toward which I had started. Things weren't so bad after all. Sit tight and keep my eyes open, was what I determined to do, and go on quietly on the truck into the black city.

Chapter IX. What Is Supervision?

The little two-wheeled thing that I was learning to call a "leading-machine," was now ahead of the truck. It was about the size of one of the toy motorcycles that are made for boys to ride around on; but it was accurately and sturdily built; and as I sat and watched it ahead of me, I was struck by the astounding complexity of the thing. Only some of the research apparatus that I had seen in university physics laboratories could compare with it.It spun on ahead of the truck, keeping a uniform distance in front, like an active little puppy in front of a plodding ox-cart. When I had first heard the word "leading-machine" I had wondered what it meant; but now, I had to admit that "leading" was the right word; that was precisely what this little machine seemed to be doing. And again I caught myself in the silly tendency that I had fallen into several times on this island, of attributing personality to machines, as though they had minds of their own. I was wildly curious to know how the little thing worked and what its precise purpose was.

It was not many minutes before the machines emerged from the forest, and the great, black city with its crown of smoke, loomed over the whole horizon in front. This time, there were no green, cultivated fields on both sides. At first there was a little sickly looking vegetation, but as we approached the city, the ground became quite bare. The road led through a region that looked as dreary as a dead world; naked, oily-looking earth, heaps of slag and cinders, pools of stagnant water scummed and greasy, or sometimes colored orange or green. Great gashes and scars were cut here and there; and mine-openings and oil-derricks were scattered about, but evidently not in operation. A mile or so to the right the river looked gray and gloomy.

I could not say much for human handiwork in this part of the island. If this scarred desolation was needed to maintain that high degree of civilization in yonder "City of Beauty," I would have preferred to see the entire island a rural community.

The city began abruptly. It towered ahead, a long, high wall; crowned with a wreath of smokestacks and a headdress of gloomy smoke. No longer was the sky above me blue. At the foot of the wall, the bare, gray earth was strewn with a thousand kinds of industrial rubbish. There was no skirmish-line of scattered and outlying buildings to warn the visitor that he was entering a city; only the bleak wall stretching into the distance on the left so far that I could not see its end; and at the right ending at the river. The road led into an arched opening in the wall.

There was nothing decorative about the entrance; it was frankly a hole to get into and out of. The leading-machine plunged in, and the truck followed. The arch closed over my head, and I was suddenly in the city. For a short distance there was a gloomy passage-way, hardly a street, between grimy buildings, with the busy commotion of an intersection visible on ahead. Then, as the truck rolled out into the glaring light of the open intersection, the rumble and roar broke upon my ears like a sudden explosion.

It was infinitely depressing. Long rows of factory-like buildings stretched off endlessly, and groups and clusters of tall chimneys poured out smoke; high in the air, pipes and cables and conveyors were trussed across open spaces between buildings, while swinging beams and derricks lent an eerie sense of movement to the ponderous scenery. Huge loads swung along on traveling cranes high over my head, or moved swiftly along on trussed bridges and suspended cables. Roaring steel converters and foundries belched sheets of fire and great continents of black smoke into the air, and my breath felt sulphurous in my lungs.

There was a clatter and a rush of vehicles, the thunder of huge trucks, and the din of machinery within buildings. The broad street was covered with a swarm of things on wheels, large and small, moving swiftly in all directions at once, like a swarming crowd of huge insects, black clumsy, clattering creatures. Everywhere, huge machines whirled and roared, until my head was numb from it. And nowhere a human being in sight!

What was it all doing? Who had made it? Who operated it?

And what should I do now? The truck was plunging me into the middle of that clattering turmoil. Without anyone to guide it, it was picking its way through traffic so congested that the smallest slip would have meant being crushed to a pulp under the moving behemoths. Should I try to get myself loose and escape from the truck that held me? In truth, I had very little inclination to do so. To plunge into that vast, churning city, where there must be endless stretches of just such dreary, rumbling streets, and countless buildings, roaring clots like this intersection was, did not seem alluring just at present. The truck seemed to be headed somewhere; its machinery was apparently set to reach some objective. I was thankful for any guidance at all, in this most uncouth of cities. Had there been people about the streets, of whom I might inquire my way, the problem would have been different. But nowhere was there any living thing visible. I decided to remain on the truck, keeping my eyes open, and to be ready for emergencies.

And then I saw the Squid! That was the name I associated with the two-wheeled, tentacled machine that had carried away Ames from the dancing pavilion on the day that he had missed Supervision and sent Dubois in his place. Of course, I was not sure that it was the same machine; but whenever I saw anything like it, it was always alone of its kind; and I felt quite sure that it was always the same machine. In general, it did not really look like a squid; but it handled its tentacles as a squid does. For a moment I saw its goggly headlights and black, coiled, ropy tentacles in the press behind me; it towered high above all other two-wheeled vehicles, and darted in and out with a superior swiftness among the clumsier machines. In a moment it was out of sight in the mass of vehicles.

Between the clattering, roaring buildings, winding around blocks, and pushing its way through the crowd of vehicles, the little truck carried me. The little leading-machine was always ahead; sometimes I lost it, but always it reappeared. Always the two machines were headed in a general direction into the interior of this great, mechanical hive. So monotonous and continuous were the rattle and rumble of the traffic and the long lines of dismal buildings that my mind became deadened and I ceased paying attention to them. It was all about the same.

One particular building attracted my attention. I rode within a block of it, about five minutes after entering the city. It had an immense oval domed roof, which shone like gold, held up by pillars high up above the tops of its walls. An ideal arrangement for keeping buildings cool in tropical countries, I thought. Then, it struck me that this huge domed oval with its white columns was architecturally a beautiful thing, and therefore unique among these industrial abominations. Why? Why was it different?

Of course it must be because people from the City of Beauty came to it. These fastidious visitors would certainly object to entering any of these other grimy blocks. I regretted that its lower portion was hidden from me by the square, smoky masses of intervening structures; otherwise perhaps I might have seen people passing in and out. And, the only thing that the people from the City of Beauty ever came to this city for was Supervision. I think that had been made plain enough to me. This must be where Supervision took place or was held! The idea struck me so suddenly that I nearly jumped out of the truck. I wriggled in vain for a moment, and then the great, golden oval was out of sight. In the back of my mind I noted a determination that I would have to hunt up that building and look it over.

Fifteen or twenty minutes of scurry and grime and clatter elapsed before the truck finally stopped. Such a city I never could have imagined in my wildest nightmare. How could there be two cities on the same island, so vastly different from each other as these two were? What could be the purpose of such a hideous machine as that Squid? Occasionally behind me, or in front of me, or somewhere, through the tangle of machines, I caught glimpses of it. It ought to be a useful piece of apparatus, for its activity and the capabilities of its tentacles were enormous.

The truck stopped before a building relatively small in size compared with those surrounding it. Again, here was a little architectural jewel set among rubbish; a pretty little structure in comparison with the gloomy hulks around it. The remarkable thing about it was that there were thousands of wires and cables leading into its roof. They converged in all directions from the smoky distances and gathered together into a huge bundle that entered the building. Several small leading-machines stood about near the doorway.

"Telephone exchange," I thought to myself. "No. More likely some sort of an administration building; some sort of central control office. Now I'll get to see the boss and find out what it's all about."

As the truck drove up with me, there was a good deal of tooting from the horns of the various machines; that is, the truck and the group of small leading-machines. First one started, and another picked it up melodiously, and they carried the echoes back and forth like a chorus singing "The Messiah." Even from within the building came melodious toots. The bar across my chest snapped open, and I lost no time in jumping out. However, the leading-machines ranged themselves round me and the truck, and I found myself in a little lane between them that led to the door of the building.

The door opened obligingly, but no one appeared. I thought quickly, and decided that for the present the best thing for me to do was to appear to fall in with the plans of my captors. So far they were treating me well, and resistance would not help much just now. So I stepped up toward the door, and a little leading-machine fell in and chugged slowly behind me. From the outside I could see practically nothing of what was within; so I boldly walked in. The door closed behind me with a slam.

Before me was a small table of the folding type, with an excellent looking lunch spread on it: soup, fish, an orange, bread, and coffee. Instantly I realized that I was indeed hungry. I had breakfasted early and now my watch said eleven o'clock. For just a moment I hesitated;

suppose this was some trick, and the lunch was poisoned! However, my common-sense told me better than that. If they wanted to destroy me, they had the opportunity of doing so more quickly and effectively than by resorting to such a low method as poisoning my food. They had me too completely in their power now, to make poisoning necessary. In fact, the luncheon was an encouraging sign; it meant that these people were not wholly barbarous, and had the intention of treating me with at least a semblance of civilized hospitality. However, why did they keep themselves so constantly hidden? So slow was I in grasping the truth!

I decided to eat the lunch, and quickly did so; though the thought of possible poison made a little shudder run over me at the first few mouthfuls. While I ate, I examined the room in which I found myself. Off into its farther portions stretched tiers upon tiers of countless units of some sort of electrical apparatus, all alike. It made me think of an automatic telephone exchange; the instruments suggested it in their form and arrangement; and there was a little rustling activity among them, now here, now there, very reminiscent of the way such an exchange looks to a spectator. The irregular, intermittent clickings, now in one direction, now in another; now almost silent and again a dozen or a score at a time, made it seem as though the room was alive with some sort of creatures. But, nowhere could I discover a living thing; only metal, enamel, wires, and an infinite complication of apparatus.

Several large, shining lenses were turned upon me. They were set in stereopticon-like housings; and every now and then they moved backward and forward a little, as though to adjust focus. They stared at me like huge, expressionless eyes. I had the uncomfortable sensation that I was being closely scrutinized by someone invisible to me. I had no doubt that there was someone hidden, either in a nearby room, or perhaps even at a great distance. I had been brought into this place to be looked over, and the person who was doing it might even be miles away, while the least detail in my appearance, my every movement, even every sound I made, were transmitted to him over wires. I even noted that the lenses that stared at me were set in pairs, so as to secure a correct stereoscopic effect.

Before I finished my lunch, I was quite positive that I was alone in the room with the glittering glass and enameled metal apparatus, which pulsated and stirred as though it were alive. I felt self-conscious, however, knowing that I was being studied. The tooting puzzled me. The fluty, musical notes would break out for a while, and then cease again. Though it had a vague suggestion of rhythm, it was not and could not be music. I judged that it must be somehow associated with the operation of some of the apparatus.

Then it struck me that there must be mechanical ears here to listen, as well as staring eyes of glass to see. I walked about the room, peering closely at the apparatus in tiers, but found nothing that I could associate with the transmission of sound. I decided to speak, nonetheless, however.

"I want to meet you face to face!" I pronounced in an oratorical tone of voice. I had no doubt that it was heard. "Come out and let me see you!"

Nothing happened. I looked out of the window at the noisy, grimy street, and sat a while in the chair again, the only chair in the place. There was no desk, no furniture. I was in the center of an empty space, at which the lenses gazed. I tried speaking again.

"I want to see people!" I said, in my most stern, and commanding tone. The only result, if result it was, was some scattered tooting and rustling in the stacks of apparatus. Then it occurred to me that if they were really listening to me, I might try something in my own interests.

"Take me to the Supervision!" I ordered peremptorily. I had to admit to myself that it was a big bluff, for my quaking heart belied my bold words. "I came here to see the Supervision!"

I listened breathlessly for several minutes, but nothing occurred.

"By Jove!" I muttered, "this is making me nervous."

I went to the door and tried it, but it was locked. Then, as I passed the window, I saw the Squid outdoors. Its blank, glary headlights were staring right into the window. I jumped back, with a sudden, involuntary start, and laughed at myself for my foolish fears. I could see the thing quite plainly now. Its tall, coffin-shaped body was not a box

at all. It was a very complicated structure, with various moving portions and twisted tubes, and here and there, metal plates that apparently concealed more delicate portions of its machinery. It was quite
out of the question for anyone to have been hidden in that pulsing
mass of wheels and levers. The thing was purely mechanical, purely
automatic, and I laughed my fears away. I assured myself that it was
purely mechanical.

And yet, why did it come up to the window, and look in, as a dog
might do?

A few moments later, with pounding heart and throbbing head, I
looked about the room, and when I looked out of the window again,
the thing was gone. What connection did it have with Supervision?
In Ames' case there was certainly a connection; and here, as soon as
I had mentioned Supervision, the thing had appeared. I began to get
restless; I walked to the door and gave it another yank. To my surprise, it opened, and I stepped out into the street. An odd thing struck
me, as some foolish detail often strikes us in the midst of more seriously absorbing circumstances. The door-sill was of wood, and had
sharp edges, that were not the least bit worn. That meant that rarely
did anyone ever use this door. Oh, how stupid I was, that the truth did
not dawn on me!

The sun shone so hot that the street was like a furnace; but the
inhuman traffic went on fiercely as ever. Across the street was a great
concrete block of buildings, through whose windows I could make
out long rows of individual machines that were operating with some
sort of an up-and-down movement, as though stamping something;
a number of small square objects moved away from each machine on
a belt conveyor. The little building in which I had just been, extended
to a corner on the left, and across the street from that, loomed another
huge, factory-like bulk.

Just in front of me, backed up against the door so that I could hardly
do anything else except step into it, was a curious, three-wheeled vehicle. A motorcycle side-car, or an ancient chariot are the only things
I can think of to compare it to. It contained a seat for one person to
sit in.

"Should I or should I not?" I worried, as I stood there hesitating.

True, the thing might run me into some sort of a trap; but on the other hand, there was as much danger right here as in some other part of the city. I reasoned that these people were accustomed to being good to their wards and dependents in the City of Beauty, and taking care of them as of small children; they had done it so long that it was a habit. I doubted if I were in immediate danger. And this had come so directly upon my request to see the Supervision, that there might really be some connection.

I stepped in and sat down. With a sudden click, a bar swung around and locked itself across my chest. My muscles tightened involuntarily, but I controlled myself, and made myself sit in quiet patience.

"Keep your shirt on!" I said to myself. "Losing your head will only make things worse. Just now, I'll see all I can, and when it gets to be more than I care for, I'll find a way to slip out. But if I don't see their faces pretty soon, I'm apt to get peevish."

The little chariot rolled swiftly and smoothly up the street, dodging in and out among the towering trucks and ponderous mechanical bulks. I had to admit that it was a clever machine, exactly adapted to conveying a single passenger long distances through these densely congested streets. Part of the time I trembled at the danger, for it often looked as though, the very next moment, I was to be ridden down by some gigantic machine, that rolled down on me like a battleship; but each time the swift little conveyance in which I rode, slipped to one side, dodged into an opening, and was far away before the big thing had moved many feet.

Again, it was a long, confusing trip. At times I thought I recognized locations which I had passed in the morning, and I wondered if I were being taken back in the same direction. But these grimy buildings and clattering streets were all so nearly alike that I could not be sure. The general direction seemed east, and therefore toward the river; and I knew that I had entered the town at a point comparatively near the river. I kept a sharp lookout for the Squid, but did not see it during the trip. Then I spied the great, gilded, oval dome, and this eventually turned out to be my destination.

The building was obviously some sort of an auditorium. From the outside, it looked for all the world like a football bowl or stadium that had been roofed over. Its height and spread vastly exceeded those of any of the neighboring buildings. It had no windows, though thirty or forty feet above the ground was a row of great, unglazed embrasures; and then, between the tops of the walls and the eaves of the roof, was an open space a dozen feet high, all around the building. There was a large arched entranceway that was a considerable architectural achievement.

However, the little chariot carried me to a small door in the middle of one side. Without hesitation it plunged into the darkness and from the sound I surmised that I was being carried along a passageway. Electric lights appeared; I found I was in an ordinary hallway of masonry, of some fine-grained, white stone. The car came to a sudden stop in the blind end of the passage. In a moment a section of the floor began to rise with me, for I had been carried into an elevator. It ascended for a height of about two floors, and then the car rolled out, around a corner, and out into empty space.

So it seemed, at any rate. The car and I were really on a little platform, six or eight feet square, jutting out of the wall of the building, and commanding a view of the entire vast interior. It was a wonderful feat of construction, that immense, arched, brightly lighted space, without a single supporting column anywhere; and the great, domed roof sweeping overhead in a wonderful curve. A rhythmic, mellow rustle reverberated throughout the great spaces, suggesting that it was composed of many elemental sounds.

And down below, there was commotion and activity—and people! Not till this moment, when I felt the violent leap of my heart at the sudden sight of human beings below me, had I realized how profoundly I had been affected by the total absence of humanity from the chaos of these endless streets. A busy city without people is an uncanny thing.

The vast oval floor was divided longitudinally into halves by a broad road or street down the middle; and this passage was filled by a river of vehicles of all sizes and descriptions. As I looked down on the tops of them, they looked like some sort of crawling insects. They all proceeded very slowly in one direction, entering from the dazzling outdoors by a high arch at one end, slowly progressing through the length of the building, and leaving by a similar arch at the other end.

The two half-ellipses on either side of this procession were raised some ten feet above the level of the moving stream of vehicles. At first glance, I thought I was looking down on some huge library, with thousands of stacks of bookcases arranged geometrically over the floor, with people walking and sitting around among them. But, they were not books. Even before I got out my field-glasses and examined them closely, I saw that the stacks were in fact supporting racks for instrument boards.

I saw rows of white dials with needles moving over them, volt-meters, ammeters, watt-meters, gas-meters—what kind of meters they were, I could but guess. I could only make out thousands of dials, some round, some curved; with various sorts of figures. There were gauges with fluctuating columns of liquids, and barometer-like scales, and recording-pens tracing curves and zig-zag lines on rolls of squared paper and revolving kymographs. It seemed that all the measuring instruments of a city were concentrated here.

At last! I thought. Here is the headquarters of this city, the point from which all this vast activity is controlled. Hither run all the wires from every point in the city and perhaps also of the other city; and here the people loll in comfort and luxury, while they attend to the man-agement of this unbelievable mechanical organization. This was con-firmed in my mind, as I looked around more closely and discovered that there were sections devoted to switches and control-levers, great tiers of them, such as one sees in a railway blockhouse or a central power station. There were tangles of valves and stopcocks, and myri-ads of knobs with pointers to them. Among all these things, the peo-ple sat and watched the meters, or occasionally moved levers. Some of them sat comfortably in easy-chairs, and others moved about, so that there was a pleasant, rhythmic commotion below me.

The Supervision at last! What else could it be? I sat there and studied the scene with my field-glasses, and I was sure that I recognized some of the people from the City of Beauty. There was Godwin, a young fellow who had been in the group that swam with me for the red flower; and a young lady with gray eyes whom I remembered very definitely. There were others whom I was sure I had seen before. Besides, they all had the bearing and dress of people whom I had met in the City of Beauty. So, this was the mysterious Supervision! This was the unpleasant task at which all were obliged to serve, and which all of them dreaded and hated!

I had to admit that I was just a shade disappointed. I had expected to see wonderful machines performing real work. And here, there were people dabbling at control instruments. I had hoped to see some of the inhabitants of the City of Smoke, but I saw none. Only these innocent children of the sun. They were elegantly dressed, to the height of fastidiousness. The men's clothes were faultlessly pressed, and their linen was perfect. The ladies' gowns were delicately beautiful. Faces were groomed smooth and hands were white and soft. They reclined languidly in easy-chairs, or strolled aimlessly here and there. Countenances were blank and indifferent.

They were not attending the machinery! Moreover they were not interested in it. They did not even understand it! I doubted if they knew as much about it as I did. In fact, from what I had learned of these people, they were not capable, either of understanding or of handling any kind of industrial machinery. They were just passing the day in utter boredom, waiting for evening to come!

What the comedy meant, I could not imagine.

My little platform was one of several about the walls, but was the only one occupied. It was like a box at a theater, as much designed to be seen as to see from. It was not long before some of the people below noticed me, clamped in my three-wheeled vehicle. As I watched them through my glasses, I could see them grow grave and turn away when they saw me. Some of them recognized me, and seemed to grow pale and start in fright. This rather stirred a vague alarm in me. Why did fear play such an important part among the emotions on this island? However, I reasoned, their alarm was difficult to interpret. To

me, it had often seemed that they were afraid of nothing. I even suspected them guilty of some exalted form of superstition.

How long I sat there and tried to think out what it meant, I do not
know. What sort of a mockery was this Supervision? These people
weren't supervising anything. They weren't capable of it. What possible good could this empty travesty serve? Every step I took in this
island seemed to plunge me deeper into foolish mysteries. Everything was a nightmare. My little chariot remained motionless, and
the scene that I watched and the thoughts that it aroused were so
absorbing that many hours must have elapsed.

When a deep gong began to ring, and I stirred, I found my muscles
stiff and cramped. The gong created an instant change in the scene.
The people all gathered toward the middle portion, where the road
ran in a sort of channel. They descended stairs from the elevated
floor, while the cars that came down the channel stopped for them.
Rapidly the entire area emptied itself of people; and cars loaded with
bobbing heads and bright flashes of color poured out of the arch at
the farther end into the freedom of daylight.

When there were only a few scattered figures left, my conveyance
moved back on the elevator, was lowered to the ground level, and
emerged from the building into a dismal looking street. Why did the
people who controlled all of this, persist in keeping out of sight? How
was my little car guided? There were wires strung about the railing of
its body; perhaps these served as antennae of some radio apparatus
for long-distance control. Perhaps the machine was not as automatic
as it seemed, but instead, was controlled by radio waves from some
central station. I could picture a malignant face bent over a switch-
board, while the clutching hands reached for levers that sent me spinning this way and that, far away, through the city.

Was this the time for me to try and escape? I had a feeling that I
could readily get away from this clumsy thing if I got desperate. But,
suppose I should escape, where would I go? What would I do? Here
was night coming on rapidly; I needed food and rest, and had no idea
where to get them. I decided to trust my captors a little longer. Thus
far, I had to admit, it was highly interesting and not at all dangerous;

though I could see how the same thing might have been unwelcome in a high degree to my friends in the City of Beauty. However, thus far, I was being treated much more like a guest than like an enemy. I determined, nevertheless, to keep on my guard, as well as to keep my eyes open for information to take back to Galveston with me.

In the meanwhile, the three-wheeled machine rolled swiftly along. For a while the sun was at my left; and as it was setting, that meant that I was headed north. Then the machine turned to the west—farther and farther into the innermost heart of the city. The sun's disk was enormous because of the thick smoke in the atmosphere, and of a blood-red color, changing, as it sank behind the buildings, to a purple. My vehicle was delayed several times at intersections by heavy traffic. The thing looked so tiny beside the gigantic things that crowded the streets that every moment I was afraid, that it and I both would be flattened out as thin as a sandwich. But its agility in dodging apparently inevitable catastrophes and slipping into unexpected openings, was so marvelous that it gave me confidence, and I quit trembling in my seat. Nevertheless, the ride was hard on my nerves. It took a good three-quarters of an hour to reach the gate in the wall.

The wall was thirty feet high, the height of an ordinary house, built of granite blocks. It extended away to the north and to the south until it was lost in the twilight in the smoky perspective of the streets. Over the top of it, I caught a glimpse of the leaves of some tree, the only living thing that I had thus far seen about the city. The gateway was large enough to admit a big truck; and again, architecturally it was a contrast to the surrounding structures which were of a dismal, utilitarian type. It had columns at the side with carved capitals, a frieze in bas-relief, and a beautiful pair of heavy bronze gates.

The car stopped in front of the gate, emitted a torrent of toots, and waited. Again I was seized with misgivings. As between a hotel and a penitentiary, this business resembled the latter much more closely. Once they got me locked up inside those walls, it might be difficult to get out again.

One of the gates opened just wide enough to admit the car, which drove to the opening and stopped. Within, the last fading rays of daylight showed me a park, one of the kind that were so numerous a generation ago, with curving graveled walks, trees and hedges in groups, and flower-beds all laid out in designs. Back in the distance was a great house, with gables and verandas, which I could not make out very plainly in the gathering darkness.

The bar across my chest snapped open, leaving me free. I stepped out with great alacrity, whereupon the car backed out and the gates clanged shut. The bright square of a lighted window shone at me from the house in the distance.

Chapter X. Who Runs This Place?

I stood for a few moments with clenched fists, staring at the bronze gates. These invisible people had an uncanny way of doing what they pleased with me. Then I realized that my muscles were stiff and cramped; that I was ravenously hungry; and that I was leaden with fatigue from a long, exciting day. So, I turned hopefully toward the building in the park. I could still make out, in the gathering gloom, that it was a typical large residence of the past generation, with stucco gables, many individual windows and a shingled roof. The effect that it produced upon me was quaint and old-fashioned, in contrast with the futurist impressions from the machinery without.

The silence was refreshing, after the steady, all-day roar; my heels crunching on the gravel sounded solitary and intimate in my ears. As I drew near, a door opened, and the yellow electric light streamed out. My heart pounded hard. Perhaps now at last, I would see the people of the place.

But the room I stepped into was uninhabited. It was luxuriously furnished, likewise in an old-fashioned way, with thick carpets and the mahogany overstuffed furniture of thirty years ago. Apparently it was a drawing-room. However, right beside me as I stepped in, was a little folding table with a steaming meal on it. It might have been exactly the same table and exactly the same dishes that I ate from at noon; only the food was different. The big, generous dinner made my mouth water. I looked about, and in the passageway found a lavatory at which I could clean up a little. Then I fell to eating, this time without the least hesitation. My hunger and fatigue exceeded both my caution and my curiosity. I ate before looking any further.

After I had eaten, my limbs felt so heavy and my eyes so sleepy, that I lay down for a little rest on the cushions of a large settee. Almost immediately I fell sound asleep. The food might have seen drugged, but I doubt it. I had risen early in the morning and had a most fatiguing day. Perhaps I lacked caution; but I could not see that any precaution of mine would make much difference. How could I be any more in their power than I was now? At any rate, I could not help it, I fell asleep in spite of myself.

I awoke early and suddenly, with the sun shining in my face. The large room seemed a rich, luxurious place; but gave the impression of being rather desolate, devoid of the little things that give a personal touch. Outside I could see lawns and trees; palms and great, broad leaves, lacy fronds, and waxy foliage, and great bright-red and spotted-orange flowers. In the distance was the high wall; beyond that, belching smokestacks, trussed beams and a dull, smoky sky. My mind took this all in with sudden alertness.

"Today's main job is to get loose," I determined grimly; "this gang has got me sewed up too tight to suit me."

I reconnoitered the house cautiously, peering into this room and that. Every room I saw was richly furnished, with that same old-fashioned air. There were a good many of the curious floor-lamps with silk shades, so popular a generation ago. Everywhere was lacking that elusive note that suggested human occupancy. Everything was stiffly clean and orderly, but there were none of the small objects that people usually leave lying around, a book, a scrap of paper, a dusty shoe-track, a handkerchief. The loneliness seemed almost ghostly.

However, a breakfast cooking away in an automatic kitchen cheered me considerably. I helped myself without qualms of conscience, and compelled myself to fill up to capacity, for I anticipated strenuous adventures ahead of me. If they did not come of their own accord I was determined to make them; for I fully intended to escape from the leash on which I was held, and to see the city on my own initiative. Uneasiness as to what they eventually intended doing with me, and a resentment at being bundled around like a sack of potatoes, shared equally in my reasons for the step I planned.

As I ate, I speculated about the old house in which I found myself. Everything pointed to the fact that it was an old residence, and a royally luxurious one, though built and occupied before I was born. Also, apparently, it was not occupied at the present time, but it was being kept in good order by the present masters of the locality. I could imagine that when the settlers had first come to the island, they had begun a city where the City of Smoke now stood, and had lived there. The men high in control had lived in this house. Finally, when the growth of the city made living unpleasant, they had moved away to the City of Beauty.

But I decided that as an explanation, this was not good. The City of Beauty would be the natural choice of a residence locality for the rulers of things around here; but those people that lived in the City of Beauty certainly were not the rulers. Yet, why did the rulers who directed and handled all of this machinery, remain satisfied to live in this noisy, dirty hell? Had they become so married to the machinery that they could not get away from it? Did they lack the side of their natures that loved beauty and luxury and Nature? Perhaps too much devotion to machinery had made them so one-sided that they preferred to live here? If they lived in this city, why weren't they occupying this great, luxurious house? If they didn't like luxury, how could they keep this place in such comfortable shape?

I gave up, and continued my exploration of the house. I found a small room which contained only a desk and a chair and a rug.

There sat a man!

My heart leaped with the thrill that I had finally found the human center of this spiderweb. I stopped for a moment and looked at him. He was about forty years old, and sat languidly in a mahogany chair. His clothes were well made and expensive looking; but his linen was disheveled, and his hands and face were smeared with grease. His right hand hung down toward the ground and grasped a large wrench.

"Ah!" I thought; "someone who really handles machinery!"

"Good morning!" I said. He looked up. Apparently he had not noticed me before. He did not reply.

"Are you someone in authority here?" I asked.

He jumped up violently.

"I own all this!" he shouted, sweeping his arm about. "This is all mine! I control it! I understand it!" He walked rapidly around the little room.

"Have you seen Cassidy?" I shot out. The idea struck me so suddenly that I could not stop it. If they had brought me here, perhaps Cassidy was also in the house.

"All this!" he continued with a wide gesture; "all mine! I can do as I please with it. I left my home and family to come here and take charge of it." Suddenly, he seemed to grasp my presence and my question.

"Cassidy?" He shrugged his shoulders. "You? I? Only a few more or less? Who knows?"

A look of alarm spread over his tanned, handsome face.

"They might come for us at any time!" He looked around, out of the door and out of the windows. "I think they cut up people alive. Oh, my poor Vera and the babies!" He sat down and put his face in his hands and groaned.

I fled from his presence in terror. My heart went out in pity to the poor fellow, but there was nothing in the world that I could do for him. This crazy city had already wrecked his mind, and it was time I undertook a retreat before it undermined my own. I had no doubt that he was from the City of Beauty, and had been captured and brought here.

I found more rooms, richly furnished and silent. Many of them had locked doors and I could not get in. Broad, automatic elevators took me to the upper floors. In a room on the third, I found an old man, in bed. His eyes opened wide when he saw me.

"Good morning!" I offered.

He continued to gaze at me sadly. White beards lend an infinite sadness to countenance anyway. During all my life I had not seen as many white whiskers as I had during these few days on this island.

"That is an astonishing thing to say here," the old man finally replied. "Who are you?"

"I'm not sure by this time that I know, myself, who I am," I said slowly, thinking hard just what to say. "Anyway, I am a stranger on this island. I am sorry to intrude on you. In fact, I was railroaded into this house, and I am going to get out mighty quick."

He continued to look at me in a sort of sad wonderment.

"Are you someone in authority here?" I asked at last.

He shook his head and studied me mournfully for a while. I waited till it should please him to speak.

"I have seen days when things were different on this island," he finally volunteered. "Then, young men spoke like you do. You talk as they did in that old America that I knew so long ago."

"That's where I'm from, and they talk that way yet," I told him. "And now I'm looking for a way to get back there."

"If you can really decide to act for yourself, do so quickly. It is a lost art. I have no idea as to what fate they intended for you or me, but it is not a pleasant one. Many have been taken—hundreds. Where are they? Have you seen them anywhere?"

"Come with me, then!" I exclaimed, for a wave of genuine alarm was mounting within me.

"Ha! ha!" There was a note of genuine merriment in the old man's laugh. "What difference does it make what becomes of me? I haven't any idea of how you plan to escape, but I know it will be a strenuous task; and to burden yourself with a feeble old man would make your escape impossible. Now go quickly!"

"Have you seen Cassidy?" I asked, turning to go.

"Cassidy? Have they got him?" He groaned something inarticulate. "Hurry, I tell you!" he urged.

I left him reluctantly. Now I understood what the old house was used for. It was a temporary resting-place for captured victims. There they rested overnight and had a meal or two, before they were taken to their doom. They were royally treated, but what was the doom?

I hurried through the house, trying doors that I had not yet opened, and shouting Cassidy's name at the top of my voice. Was I too late?

If I could only find him, we would lose no time in leaving this town. But most of the doors were locked, and confused echoes were my only answer. I ran outdoors, down the gravel walk, and to the bronze gates. I studied the gates and the wall; but climbing was an impossibility without a ladder. The trees growing near the wall offered a suggestion.

Then the gates opened a little, and the foolish little chariot of yesterday rolled in. It sidled up to me and rubbed against me, like a dog begging for attention. I looked down at the thing in amazement; but there it was, too small to conceal a person, just a whirring, mechanical thing. No wonder the man with the wrench had lost his mind! The bronze gates were tightly closed again. There was nothing to do but to get into it. It would get me through the gates, which right now was my worst desire. I idly wondered what would happen if I refused to get into the machine, as I took my place in the seat. When the bar snapped across my chest, my muscles tightened involuntarily, and a shudder ran all through me, in spite of all my determinations to sit quietly. But, I forced myself to relax. I looked over the little machine, and felt sure that I could break away from it, when I decided that the time to do so had arrived. I noted that the bar across my chest did not fit as accurately as the one on the truck had done; and quietly I set about studying ways to wiggle out of it.

Every moment of that long trip was an anxious wait for an opportunity to get away from the car. Not an instant eluded me; yet not an instant offered itself in which escape was possible. Most of the time the speed was so great that jumping out would have meant broken bones. When stops were made, they were in such dense traffic that I was afraid of the huge things around me. I noted that I again passed within a short distance of the golden oval of the Supervision Building. Other locations seemed rather familiar, though I had not fixed the details in my memory sufficiently to be sure; but I recognized them subconsciously. Then I spied the pretty little building with the web of wires leading into it, in which I had spent an uncomfortable forenoon yesterday, scrutinized by lenses and tooted at by invisible pipes.

I expected to be put into that room again, and was gathering my

169

wits and muscles to avoid it; and was thus thrown off my guard. For, my car approached the broad, garage-like doors of a smooth, concrete building next to it. The doors were big enough to let a truck through. But they worked the same trick on me that the bronze gates at the park had done; one of them opened just wide enough to let the car through. The car stopped just within the door, and the bar opened away from my chest, releasing me. I stepped off and looked about me. I hadn't liked the cold-looking building from the outside; and I didn't like this clean, bare, cold-looking room. While I was staring at it, the machine slipped backwards, and the doors closed shut, with a whirring of gears.

I whirled about and shook them and pounded them, but they were as immovable as the rock of a mountainside. I stood and sputtered in anger for a few moments at the way I had been handled. There was certainly an uncanny intelligence at the bottom of these maneuvers. But, whose was it? And where was it? I could see no signs of life anywhere.

The room was large, large as an auditorium, with walls and floor of smooth concrete. The floor was clean and bright; it sloped toward a drain in the middle of the room, so that it could be washed down. There were many large windows, making the interior almost as bright as outdoors, and on the ceiling were numerous large electric globes. There was a concrete table near the north windows and near it a glass case of instruments. I looked at the instruments curiously; they looked like apparatus for demonstrations in science lectures, but I could not guess the use of a single one.

The arrangement reminded me of the lay-out of a surgical operating-room in a hospital. I detected a queer odor in the air; I cannot describe it otherwise than as a warm, animal odor. My spine began to feel creepy and my knees trembled. Then I discovered a lot of clothes hung on hooks in one of the glass cases, both men's and women's; and they were the fine, well-made clothes that were worn in the City of Beauty. I looked about anxiously for a way of escape. I remembered back how I used to bring dogs into the experimental laboratory at the college; and now I wondered how the dogs felt about it. I decided that it was high time for me to make a desperate break for liberty.

Again one of the doors opened, and a man was shoved in, staggering and blinking. A flood of joy overwhelmed me.

"Cassidy!" I shouted, leaping toward him.

He was pale; but when he saw me he turned paler yet, and terror
shone in his face.

"Davy!" he gasped. "You here?" He groaned in despair.

"I came here to look for you," I told him. "So, cheer up! I'm going
to get you out."

"Sh-sh!" He put his finger to his lips. The man's former spirit
seemed to be gone out of him. "Whatever you do, don't talk too
much!" he warned.

"All right. Not another word out of me," I whispered.

I got into action at once. With my right hand I loosened my hand
ax in its sheath, and with the left, dragged and shoved Cassidy toward
one of the big windows. The glass was tough; I rained blow after blow
on it with the head of the ax before I cracked open a hole big enough
to crawl through. I sheathed the ax, for I could not risk losing it, even
though I heard some sort of a commotion behind me. I boosted Cassidy through the broken window.

"Run! Don't wait for me!" I shouted, for I already suspected I'd
never get out after him. I heard him scramble among the broken
glass outside, and his footsteps thumped away into the distance.

As I drew myself up to the level of the hole in the glass, I was seized
from behind by three or four arms around me. They lifted me up
and set me down again; and "snap!" I was clamped down in one of
the silly little chariots again, and speeding out of the door into the
dazzling daylight. In the room behind me were the two staring headlights of the Squid, and the air of the room was filled with waving,
snaky coils. A half dozen other machines were crowding about, and
a furious tooting was going on. It died away rapidly as I was whirled
swiftly off down the street.

This time I had not only reached the limit of my patient self-control at being bundled around in pursuance to someone else's will;
but also I was thoroughly frightened. Cassidy's face had shown real

fear, and he was not a man to be easily scared. And that room made me shudder. I could not forget the odor; it was not unpleasant, but it reminded me too much of blood. Why had we been brought in there? And where was I bound for now?

I took out my ax, and hammered at the bar that held me. It was too strong to yield that way. Attempts to twist myself out of its grip were also futile. It held me too cleverly and securely. An idea that had long been forming in my head, suddenly matured. I whipped out my Colt's .45 automatic, put the muzzle close to the lock of the bar, and bang! bang! pulled the trigger twice.

My hand was numbed by the recoil, so that I nearly dropped the pistol; and a fine spray of lead spattered about me. But, I dragged the pistol back to the holster and pushed it in. The machine swerved a couple of times and nearly collided with a big thing on caterpillar treads that was advancing down the street with a tremendous uproar. But my imprisoning bar swung loose, I was free!

I jumped out, stumbled to my knees in front of a swiftly moving, hooded vehicle, but was up in a moment and ran. My machine stood still behind me, vibrating and tooting. Other machines were slowing down and turning about.

I ran for the nearest solid wall, and then along that, looking for some kind of shelter. In a moment I came to a narrow crevice between two buildings. It was gloomy in there, in comparison with the brilliance of the street, and the debris on the ground made me stumble frequently. I followed the narrow space for a dozen yards into an enclosed backyard or court. Here there was a terrible din and clatter of machinery, and a good deal of rubbish. High overhead was a small square of sky. On the farther side was a pile of boards, apparently from broken-up crates. I pulled off a few, crouched down in the hole thus made, and piled back enough boards on top of me to hide me from view.

I had no delusions yet about being safe. My impression was that some all-seeing eye was following my every move, and that it knew perfectly well right now where I was. If I could get completely under cover for a while, perhaps I could avoid being picked up by the observer when I emerged. I found that most of the boards in the pile were light enough and small enough so that I could work them aside, and burrow into the pile, toward its farther end, which was up against a building. Even though I worked slowly and cautiously, the sweat poured off me in rivers, and my clothes were soaked through with it. For a while I had to stop and lie quiet, when a tiny leading-machine dashed in through the cleft by which I had entered the courtyard, and sputtered noisily around the enclosure.

Then the beam of a crane leaned through the opening, with hanging chains and a spotlight. The chains dragged over the boards under which I lay, scattering the pile with a couple of hooks. It looked as though they knew exactly where I was. A faint wish began to enter my heart that I had stayed away from this city in the first place. I had thought that I would have human beings to deal with, man to man. But, they had things so organized that I never saw the people at all; and I had no chance against their machinery.

I dug desperately farther under the boards, and finally reached a wall. There I found an iron grating beneath me, in the pavement of the courtyard. It apparently opened into some cool, underground space; and through it came the sounds of machinery pounding somewhere in a basement. I pried up the grating with a board, squeezed into the opening, and dropped the grating back over my head.

Sometimes memory is merciful. I do not remember the details of that awful trip in the darkness and noise. My salvation was in my pocket flashlight, which kept me from falling into vats of foul-looking liquids, or crawling straight into whirling machinery, whose proximity was indistinguishable in the din. I crawled along for ages through a narrow, close, suffocating space, sometimes in a tunnel of stone, sometimes through a steel tube; and frequently there were gratings below me. It must have been a ventilator, for always a draft of hot, sickening air blew in my face. One thing was comforting: I seemed to have gotten away.

Eventually I reached a place where the hot draft blew upwards, and I was able to stand up. My flashlight showed me a group of seven or eight pipes extending upward into the darkness. They were held together by diagonal trusses, and provided a fairly good ladder for climbing, forming a sort of narrow latticework. I hitched all my belongings comfortably around myself and started upwards.

Some fragmentary impressions of the climb are as follows: a strong smell of ammonia in one place; a glimpse of an immense room filled with whirling fly-wheels and great pumps; another vast room which was quite empty and intensely cold; periodical rumblings at one point, as though huge bulks of something were sliding or rolling past. Finally there was a welcome glimpse of the sky above me, crossed by a latticework of beams. Climbing was not difficult, except that my haversack and field-glasses kept getting in my way as they hung over my shoulder. At last I tumbled out on a tar-and-gravel roof. The pipes I had been climbing continued upwards, above my head, into the bottom of a great water-tank that was supported on four steel legs, high in the air above the roof of the building.

I was intensely thirsty, and my first concern was water. There seemed to be plenty of it above me, and I reasoned that there must be some way of getting some of it. I set about a systematic search, though my impulse was to shoot a hole in one of the pipes. However, I discovered a valve in a pipe that ran along the roof, much to my joy, for a thirsty man is a desperate creature. As I turned it on, a great flood of water poured out on the roof, and I hastily shut it again lest I call attention to myself. Then I turned on a small stream. Again my military training served me in good stead, for if I had drunk my fill as I craved to do, I should have collapsed and been at the mercy of my enemies. I drank slowly and sparingly. For an hour I lay and rested and drank, and listened for possible pursuit.

At the end of that time I was fairly confident that I had succeeded in escaping. The first thing I did was to reload my pistol, so that it contained a full clip. As I took my supply of cartridges out of my haversack, a piece of paper fluttered out. I picked it up curiously, for I knew of no scraps of paper among my things. It was a scented notepaper, containing a message in a rounded, feminine handwriting:

"I love you. It frightens me to have you go to that terrible place, but I know you will do it. Please, Davy, come back safe to me.

"Your little brick."

I spent many minutes over my message, lost in pleasant thoughts; and then I drew myself together with a new determination to get out of this situation. The first thing to do was to examine the ground thoroughly. By climbing a little higher and keeping hidden among the pipes, I found that I could get a view of the entire city and remain out of sight myself. I was on the roof of a tower, three or four stories above the rest of the buildings. Because of the view it commanded, I judged that this building must be in the highest part of the city. In fact, it was easy to make out a gentle slope eastward toward the river, and a longer, steeper one toward the sea on the west.

I set about drawing a map in my notebook of all I could see. This was a tedious task, for my precarious perch among the pipes did not permit of drawing; I had to climb up and take a good look, and then descend and draw from memory. My greatest obstacle was dirt, for my hands were so grimy from the sooty, dirty things I had to get hold of, that it was almost impossible to handle paper with them. But I finally got a passable map sketched out.

The City of Smoke was about rectangular in shape, with the long dimension east and west, or from river to ocean. The total distance from river to ocean must have been about fifteen miles; but the city occupied only about six miles of that in length, while its width I judged to be about four miles. On the east, along the river's edge, the rectangle spread a little in width; the river bank was lined with docks and wharves, and the river was alive with tugs and barges, and a double stream of smoking vessels wound along the river into the interior of the island, where in the distance I could see forests and mountains.

Toward the sea, the rectangle narrowed a little, and there were several miles of empty, sandy flats intervening between the city's boundaries and the little harbor. The harbor contained only three small ships and its dock space was limited. Ocean traffic was apparently not developed at all in comparison with that on the river. The ocean end of the city consisted chiefly of long lines of huge warehouses, and several broad lines of pavement led to the little harbor.

Down below me, there were huge, piled-up blocks of buildings, and the grimy streets swarmed with black, crawling things. The noise was tempered by distance into a dull, rustling hum. Toward the river there was a forest of belching chimneys, and the air was thick and murky with smoke. I could see the walled house in its park, a couple of miles away, in the very center of the city. To the south, not far from the edge of the city, was the golden oval dome of the Supervision Building; and near it ran the road that led out of the city, and into the blue forest. There was no sign of the City of Beauty on the southern horizon.

A sudden, swelling, organ-like tone rose up toward me from the street just below. I leaned far over and looked down. Far down below was the concrete roof of the laboratory-like building. The confused swirl of machines in the street seemed to have organized itself into a stream that flowed in one direction, and the organ-note was the combined tooting coming from many of them. Then, I noted a small, black figure running in front of the rushing column of machines. The desperate man seemed to have no chance; they were almost upon him.

An icy panic shot through my heart. For a moment I thought it was Cassidy. But my field-glasses showed me that the man was tall and spare, and that he swung a large wrench in one hand. Then he dodged around a corner; the stream of machines swarmed after him and I saw no more.

It became obvious that I would have to wait till night for my effort to get out of the city. In the meanwhile I planned the details. The easiest way seemed to be to make for the south gate and for the road to the City of Beauty. Just because that was so easy, I would not consider it; it would mean being caught in a trap. The river offered the next best plan of getting away easily and swiftly; but I was also afraid of that. The river and the road ran along too close together, and both were too full of swift craft. Finally, the distance to the river was much the greater, and through the densest, most tangled part of town.

Toward the ocean, the city looked less busy; the streets were straighter and less crowded. The beach looked completely deserted, and would be comparatively easy traveling. There seemed to be no small vessels that could get into sufficiently shallow water to reach me from the ocean side, if I once gained the beach. On the other hand, my best method of getting away from the land machines was to wade out waist-deep into the water. No machine run by gas or electricity could follow me there. Besides, the beach led straight to the Gulls' Nest, which was a safe hiding-place.

I studied the boundaries of the city carefully with my field-glasses. Everywhere, the edge of the city was a solid wall of buildings, offering no chance of egress. The only ways of getting out were the river, the south gate which I did not trust, and the west gate toward the ocean.

The afternoon passed quickly for me. I was interested in watching the scurrying things below, and the great, swinging hulks in the distance. Part of the time I spent in studying out a way to get down into the street. A repetition of my climb through the interior of the building was out of question. But, two of the legs of the tank were outside the wall of the building, and extended down to the ground. Each leg consisted of two I-beams braced together with crossbars, cleverly welded, but making a very passable ladder.

Between five and six o'clock, a great swarm of cars poured out of the building with the golden dome; through my glasses I could see little human heads and bright highlights of clothing. They spun off, out of the south gate, and toward the City of Beauty. How I wished I could go with them! It seemed so near, and yet so difficult.

After six o'clock, traffic in the streets quieted down considerably, and there were but few vehicles, and little noise. I waited almost three more hours for the short tropical twilight, which was quickly followed by night. Here and there a light shone out in the darkness, but on the whole, lights were few for such a large city. I filled my canteen, and forthwith started down the leg of the water-tank. The abyss below frightened me, but the thing had to be done. It was easier in the darkness than it would have been by daylight; I could see nothing below except velvety blackness; and at no time had I any idea of how much farther I had to go. Soon I found it difficult not to believe that my torturers had excavated a shaft a mile deep into the ground, and that I was climbing down into it. Finally, however, a foot struck solid ground, and I stepped off my ladder.

Gradually I made out that I was between two buildings; there was a strip of lighter sky above and a glow of electric light at the right. I reached the street easily and headed west by compass. I stuck close to buildings and remained in shadows, crossing open spaces on a run, and keeping an alert lookout in all directions. However, my flight was easy, for I could travel silently and in the dark, whereas the approach of a machine was always heralded by a glare of light and plenty of noise. Of course, there was the possibility of people lying in wait for me; but I had already begun to feel that I would never encounter the masters of this place in personal combat. I was skeptical about their courage to face danger and conflict. They delegated everything to machines, as far as I could ascertain.

I found the south boundary of the city and followed it westward, toward the western gate. I lost an hour convincing myself that indeed no escape was possible except by the gate. The great factory buildings and warehouses that formed the city wall were in direct contact; they were built of brick, steel, and masonry. There was no climbing over them for they were from two to six stories high; and in the darkness I could find no way of getting up to the roofs. All doors and windows seemed to be securely locked; the horrors of that afternoon's climb through one building sufficed to keep away my desire for going through any more buildings. An hour's search failed to reveal any crevice or crack between the buildings that led to the outside. The gate was my only hope.

I readily found the gate at the west end of the city, with the aid of my map and pocket flashlight. It was brilliantly lighted by electric lights, by whose aid I could see that it was closed by two steel doors. Four of the little leading-machines stood about under the glare of the electric light; and two small, swift trucks were ranged across the way I would have to go; cranes and hooks swung from them in readiness. I could not see anybody, but I knew that they were watching for me;

and the bright light made it impossible for me to get within a hundred feet of the gate without exposing myself to the observation of the watchers.

I slunk into the shadows, for I had no doubt that these things were waiting for me.

Chapter XI. One Night in Sheol

I shrank back into the depths of the shadow for a moment, into sinking indecision as to what to do next. I was trapped in this hideous city! The realization descended upon me with the convincing force of a pile-driver. If this gate was so well guarded—the one that I would apparently be the least likely to take—the certainty that the other one would be tightly sewed up was so great that I did not even care to try it.

This place was like the fortified cities of the Middle Ages, surrounded by an impassable wall. Why? Probably the real reason was that the solid and continuous construction was most convenient for manufacturing purposes, especially where there was so much automatic machinery, and air and light for workers was not an important consideration. Nevertheless, the sickening recollection came to me that I had been repeatedly reminded of how many people got in here and none ever got out.

Well, the first thing to do was to put more distance between me and this brightly lighted, heavily guarded gateway. As I turned to steal carefully away, my foot came down on a loose piece of iron. It was curved like the rocker of a rocking-chair, and was no doubt the broken leaf of an automobile spring. It swung over my toes as I stepped, and hit the pavement with a ringing clatter. For an instant I stiffened, and then dashed swiftly across the street. I acted unconsciously first and reasoned why I did so later; which of course was to get away from the spot where the sound had occurred.

Nor was I a bit too quick. Like a shot from a cannon, one of the leading-machines whizzed toward the spot, with a sputtering roar that reverberated through the darkness. Before it reached there, I had crawled under a sort of ramp, whose purpose was apparently to permit vehicles to drive up into the building. I couldn't see the leading-machine that was looking for me, but I could hear it chugging about.

I was amazed at the quick reaction of the person who was watching for me; it wasn't ten seconds from the time the iron dropped until the machine was racing after me. I remained crouched in my dark corner half an hour after the machine was gone.

In the meanwhile, I pondered on what I should do. Both gates were closed up, and the city was surrounded by an impassable wall, impassable as far as I had been able to ascertain by my observations from the inside, outside, and above; while a search for some small possible opening might require several days. My only hope was the river-front. If I could reach the water and find a boat or something to float on, getting back to the City of Beauty would be relatively simple. But I shrank mentally from approaching that terrific maze of wharves and boats and black water, beams and cranes and crooked alleyways among blackened buildings and machines. My chances looked slim enough in that region. Yet, they were all I had, and I turned my face in that direction.

For an hour I plodded eastward through the gloomy, silent streets. They were unutterably, forbiddingly dreary at night; there were no sidewalks, only black walls and blank windows, with oceans of inky shadows everywhere. Each step that I took forward, each shadow that I approached, brought my heart into my mouth, for fear of someone lying in wait for me. A million times I fully expected someone to leap out at me and bear me to the ground, or a shot to come from behind a building, or some sort of chain lasso to drop over my head.

I admitted to myself that I had often been in situations of equal or greater actual danger; but never had I been in one that so demoralized my nerve. Not only was I appalled by this extraordinary, monstrous city, like the wild ravings of some madhouse engineer; but I had no idea who my enemies were, where they were, or what sort of weapons they would use. I had no idea when they could see me, and when I could feel safely out of their sight. At any moment, they might have some sort of amazing, high-powered night-seeing telescopes trained upon me. For aught I knew, they might be accurately informed of every step I was taking, and only be waiting their own good time to seize me. The thought drove me still deeper into the shadows beside the buildings.

However, as I have always done on similar occasions, I kept plodding onward, doing what the immediate moment required, because that was all that could be done. My compass with its luminous needle was my best friend that night; without it I should have gotten hopelessly lost in the muddle of streets, to be picked up by the machine-people sooner or later. I surmised that it must not be strictly accurate, for this place must have been alive with electrical currents, but it sufficed to guide me eastward, toward the dark and devious river-front.

Half a dozen times it occurred to me that the water ought to be in sight already; and I looked for the grain-elevators and for the barge-loading conveyors that I had seen in the afternoon from my observation point. But distances seem greater in the dark and progress is actually much slower, especially in unknown territory; and I schooled myself to be patient.

Then, a few streets to my left, I heard the sputtering rush of several leading-machines going at high speed. It seemed crashingly loud in the darkness as it reverberated through the hollow spaces. It grew louder and louder, and then began to decrease again. I judged that the machines were proceeding in the same direction that I was, that is, directly toward the river. Then came another roar, this time with much more rattle and rumble to it. Trucks, several of them, I surmised. They seemed to be approaching quite close to me. In fact, I began to suspect that they were on this same street, and soon perceived the glow of their lights far behind me.

"I'm getting out of here, right now!" I said, half aloud, and looked frantically around for means of doing so.

I was in the middle of a block with unbroken walls all around. But I remembered that a few rods back I had passed a concrete base-block as high as my shoulder, on which rested a vertical trussed-steel beam, apparently the leg of some great, dim framework, high up above.

I ran back to it, assuming the risk of going toward the approaching glare of the trucks; and as soon as I reached it, I dodged behind it. I swung myself to the top of the block, and clambered up the trussed iron leg, keeping behind it and out of reach of the headlights. In a few moments the trucks had clattered by below me, without even slowing down, and gradually drew off into the distance to the east. I continued to cling to my perch as their lights and their clatter grew fainter.

"Fooled them!" I thought. "They'll never find me over there."

That was encouraging. In a moment, however, there was another hurtling roar, and from my elevated perch I saw a few streets away a group of lights gliding swiftly eastward disappearing behind black things and appearing again. And, far in the east, over a wide area, numerous little lights twinkled and dashed back and forth.

I climbed a little higher and gazed intently eastward, trying to fathom what was going on. For, by this time, three huge searchlights on the high towers far to the east of me were swinging around, showing up streets and masses of buildings and swift machines for fitful instants. That was my destination over there, where those lights were sweeping about, and where those machines were dashing back and forth. No place for me right now, however.

Just a few minutes' walk ahead and to my right was the huge, glowing bulk of the Supervision Building and its dome. The lights and commotion were far on beyond it. In fact, as I watched, I caught an occasional gleam of light on black water; and I was certain that the clattering, flashing night hunt was going on in that section of the city that bordered on the river.

"So that goose is cooked too," I thought. "I seem to be thoroughly stuck."

I felt limp and weak from discouragement.

What diabolical foresight enabled them to anticipate that I was going to the river? That was more than human. That they might see me in the dark, that they might have visual detectors of unknown power, or things that could hear me, smell me, or detect the presence of my bodily electrical charges, I could readily imagine. But how could they tell what I intended to do before I ever started to do it? If they could do that, the probabilities of unheard-of powers of torture and destruction, in wait for me, were unlimited and hideous. Never in my life had I been so thoroughly terrified and discouraged.

Then, another explanation suddenly struck me, which at the same time overjoyed and terrified me. Perhaps that rumpus over there signified that Cassidy had reached the waterfront! Perhaps they had tracked *him* down to the river. As long as the lively activity continued, I was sure that he was not yet caught. I trembled so, in my excitement for his safety that I had to exert redoubled efforts to keep my hold on the iron framework, high in the air and darkness.

I felt sure, however, that Cassidy's chances for escape were better than mine. Surely he must know more about this city than I. He must understand the nature of his danger and the methods of his enemies. His lot was certainly not as helpless as mine. If we could only be together!

What next? I gripped the iron bars extending into emptiness above and below, in an agony of despair. I was hemmed in, blocked! Powers vast and mysterious, to whose nature I had no clue, had me at their mercy. How futile was my small strength against these monstrous, pulsing things! It would be easiest to give up the struggle. Their net around me was vast and impenetrable; amazing machinery in vast quantities was arrayed against me and I was alone. What was the use?

Then there came into the midst of my gloomy cogitations a pair of brown eyes looking trustingly into mine, a head on my shoulder, a little soft body held in my arms. She must be waiting anxiously for me. If she knew anything at all about these awful things, her wait must be more trying than my own position. My courage returned, and my determination was again as firm as a mountain. There must be some way out of this, and I've got to find it!

Was there another gate in the north wall of the city? I could remember a road winding up into the mountains and forests of the north, but I could not remember a gate. But, even if there were a gate, it would be so guarded as to offer me no hope. Then the brilliant idea came to me!

Probably I had been slowly evolving it in my unconscious mind for a long time; but the full force of it struck me so suddenly that I nearly let go and fell down into the darkness below.

There was the Supervision Building ahead of me! And every evening a swarm of cars left it and drove southward to the City of Beauty! Surely those people would be my friends, and let me hide in a car and ride back home with them. It was obvious that they were no real friends of these hideous machine-people. And by this time, I thought that most people in the City of Beauty knew me or knew of me.

My heart bounded high with hope. My problem was solved. But not altogether. It would be many hours before the cars were leaving for the City of Beauty. Where could I hide in safety until it came time for me to hide in one of them? This vast city, with thousands of buildings and streets and alleys for miles in all directions, was unknown to me, and well-known to my enemies. It was evident to me at once that I must hide somewhere near where the cars were to pass. For I couldn't travel very far through this city during the daytime from my hiding-place to catch my car home. The poor wretch whom I had seen down below me in the street that afternoon came at once into my mind, as did the narrow escapes I myself had had. The thought of the possibility of being caught and locked up and taken to that laboratory again was enough to make me infinitely cautious. Where could I spend the time until the later afternoon when the cars started back to the City of Beauty? What a beautiful, comfortable, desirable place the City of Beauty now seemed, as I thought of it!

I clambered slowly down. There was only one possibility. Somewhere in the Supervision Building itself I had to find concealment. I ran over in my mind the interior of the building. My recollection of it was clear, for I had studied it the previous forenoon for several hours from an excellent point of view. The three or four little platforms twenty feet above the floor, the elevator shaft, the racks and cases of instruments, the chairs and settees—nothing offered any hope of concealment. Therefore, what I must do was to get into the building and look around.

I reached the building in a few minutes, walked under the great arched doorways, into the darkness of the vast building. Its deep and silent blackness frightened me. Toward the south high overhead, I could make out the glow of the sky through the embrasures in the wall. There were blacker, denser portions of shadow, showing where the walls of the middle sunken passageway were, and above them the serrated figures of the instrument cases and racks. I walked slowly, with a hand before me, with my knees trembling at every step, fully expecting something to rise up and descend on me from behind each dark, misshapen shadow, out of each black, yawning space. My first footsteps sounded loudly in the silence. For fifteen minutes I crouched motionless and listened before I took the next. I crept a little farther and listened again. Absolute silence! Not a click, not a rustle.

What did it mean? Was all of this just dummy apparatus? In the morning I had suspected that the people knew nothing about it as they moved among the things. And now I was sure that if all these meters and gauges and control-devices had really been connected to power lines and active machinery, there would have been many little noises in the night—a tap in a pipe, the flutter of a needle, the tick of clockwork, the hum of a coil, the gurgle of a bubble. But here was silence that meant death, not life; not even mechanical life. I had already suspected that the real center of control of the city was elsewhere; now I was sure that this was just a dummy, for the benefit of the dolls from the City of Beauty.

What did the comedy mean?

However, the thought gave me confidence for the present, for it meant that there was probably no one about the premises now, as the place was of no real importance. My courage rose to the point where I dared to use my flashlight; I tried it cautiously, and finally used it whenever I needed it.

My search was discouraging. There were no nooks nor corners; the construction of the building was massive and simple. The floor of the middle channel passageway was level with the ground outside. The floors on which the people spent the day among dummy instruments were ten feet above this, no doubt so that the people could also look down on the procession of cars; and at intervals, stairways about six feet wide led down to the level of the vehicles. Yet—here was one hope. Underneath these raised floors there must be a lot of empty space; a sort of cellar. That was worth investigating and seeing whether it could be used for concealment.

A trip around the inside and outside of the building failed to reveal any doorways leading into this space. However, that made it all the more desirable as a hiding-place, could I but once get into it. I had gone half way around the building on the outside and reached the tall entrance way for cars opposite the one by which I had entered. Everything was so silent and deserted that I suppose I got careless. I must have permitted myself to be seen plainly in the glow of the stars moving against the white wall of the building. From somewhere along the street came the soft rustle of well-lubricated, nicely adjusted machinery.

I dropped flat on the ground instantly, and crawled slowly toward the doorway. A band of light from headlights appeared on the pavement, and then a leading-machine slowly rolled out of the darkness and glided into the doorway. The sounds of its motor echoed around in the great spaces within. In a few minutes it came out again, and disappeared in the darkness up the street.

I slipped quietly into the door. This was the door out of which the cars drove on their way to the City of Beauty. My hiding-place would have to be near here, for I could not afford to drive through the whole place after choosing my car and getting into it.

I tapped the stairway with my ax. It was solid concrete. I tapped the wall of the middle channel. It sounded heavy, but hollow, brick apparently. Then there was a sudden clatter behind me, and I whirled around to see a truck driving in through the arch, swinging a heavy crane arm against the starry sky. It drove right down upon me where I crouched between the steps and the wall. Before I realized what was happening, my escape was cut off by its lumbering bulk and its swinging steel beam.

The pivoted half-ton of steel swung down on me, just as the other had done that night on the dock. Only then I had been cool, and master of the situation; now I was frantic from nameless terrors. I saw it coming in the glare of the truck's headlights, and thought my last moment had come.

But again my long training in quick response to emergencies came to my aid. Quick as a flash, when the iron beam was almost upon me, I dodged down into the darkness below and between the headlights of the truck, between its front wheels. There the beam could not reach me.

Crash!

The beam hit the wall, and there were smothered thuds of falling bricks. The beam swung away, and there was a ragged black hole in the wall beside the steps.

The truck backed away, swinging its beam up into the air again, which gave me time to spring up and run swiftly to one side, out of the field of its headlights.

"Whow!" I thought, regarding the gaping opening in the brick wall, knocked through with one blow. "That's exactly where I stood!"

I crouched down in the shadow in the next stairway while the truck blundered around. I peered anxiously for a glance at the people on it, but the glare of its headlights shut out everything else in a wall of blackness. As the truck came looking for me, sweeping a spotlight about, it was a simple matter for me to dodge out of the door. After clattering around and raising all the echoes of the place, it finally came out of the door backwards.

In the meanwhile, another brilliant idea had struck me with such suddenness as to make me dizzy. The truck had shown me a way into an ideal hiding-place! I lost no time in slipping into the hole, and I crouched down in the narrowest space under the concrete steps. I could hear the truck lumbering back in again; and soon there was a softer rustle of a leading-machine. For a while there was a good deal of commotion, but eventually the machinery left. I allowed myself a half an hour of absolute silence before I straightened out my cramped limbs. Considering their power and ingenuity in some directions, my enemies were singularly stupid in others, I thought, as I put back in its holster the pistol I had ready for the first shadow that I saw appear in the jagged opening in the bricks. How could they omit searching in the cavity where I was all the time? Even then, I did not have the least suspicion of the astounding truth.

I groped away from the opening, feeling my way along the wall, back into the depths of the space under the floor. A glance at the dusty, cobwebby rows of concrete pillars showed that the place was unused, probably never visited, I was dead with fatigue, hungry, and sleepy. I took the time to return and put back as many bricks as I could find into the opening, to make it as inconspicuous as possible; and then I selected a resting place far enough away from the hole so that if anyone came in, I would be the first one to be on the alert.

A few bites of biscuit and chocolate, and a drink from my canteen sufficed for my hunger. The stuff was too unpalatable for one to eat a great deal of it, no matter how hungry one was. I went to sleep almost immediately, and woke up in what seemed a few minutes.

But, my watch said ten o'clock, and a faint glow from the direction of the hole through the wall indicated that it must be daylight. I could hear the cars outside my place of concealment driving in with the "Supervisors"; and soon I heard the footsteps of the latter above me.

I did not sleep any more. Most of the time I was alert, but occasionally I half dozed. It was a long wait in the darkness, with the monotonous sounds without. When I thought an hour had elapsed, I looked at my watch and found that it had been actually five minutes. I had plenty of time to think out things now.

My mind turned to Mildred. I had been gone for two days now. She must be in a good deal of uncertainty about me; I hoped that she was not worrying too much. That depended a good deal about how much she actually knew about the dangers of this place. I clenched my fists in impatience. The time went slower than ever. Galveston and my great-uncle were so far away that they seemed part of another life. The hoped-for medical practice in east Texas was a mere dream. The reality was a concrete slab above me, the powdery dust below, the rhythmic monotony of the sounds without this velvety blackness, and this hideous hive of roaring machines with their cruel, mysterious intelligence behind them. Would I ever live to realize that dream? How wonderful it would be there, with Mildred by my side!

Anyway, I had enough of curiosity about this city. Let it be what it may; I didn't care. I wanted to get out. That suddenly brought me to the realization that I had not solved a single one of the questions that I had come here to discover. Who were the people in charge of the machinery? What was going on in this city? What was the reason for the terror of the pretty people in the City of Beauty? What was the cause of the revolutionary plans of the determined few? Although I had been over a considerable portion of this grimy, bellowing city, seen all of it from above, and some of it from the inside, I hadn't the faintest idea of the answers to these questions.

Clang! went a gong somewhere in the building. I started up suddenly, for I think I must have been dozing a little. The tapping of feet above swelled into a wave and grew louder. They were going home! The moment had come for my escape! The City of Beauty and Mildred! Soon I would see them.

I got up close to the hole and looked out. How welcome was that glimpse of daylight. I saw cars going by and noted with satisfaction that they did not go too fast for me to jump into one of them. I saw people's legs, as they walked past the hole and down the stairs toward the cars. There would be a group of them, and then none for a while; and again a group and another lull. I waited for a lull and crawled out.

I crouched down low and watched the cars. Some were crowded; some contained ladies; some were too open. I hoped for an empty one, but did not dare risk too long waiting. Besides, I could never be sure of which way an empty one might go; those with people on them were sure to go to the City of Beauty. At this last moment, I couldn't afford to make a wrong step and fail.

Finally the desired opportunity came: an enclosed car with a single occupant. He was a graceful, pink-faced, frock-coated young man, who looked such a perfect fashion-plate that there could be no doubt that he was from the City of Beauty. I looked myself over grimly and as the car went slowly by, I opened the door and stepped in; I got my head down below the level of the car's window in order to be out of sight from without.

For a few minutes the elegant young man continued looking intently ahead, and paid no attention to me. I surmised that he had looked forward to having the car all to himself on the way home and did not care for company; hence the cool attitude. I chuckled grimly to myself at the thought of his rude awakening. Then as the car slowly got up speed outside the building, he turned languidly around to see who was with him. The way his face went slowly blank, his eyebrows rose, and his jaw dropped, was worth the price of an admission fee. He opened his mouth and shut it again, like a fish out of the water. Lest he should speak, I put my hand over his mouth, and whispered softly into his ear:

"Still as a mouse! Don't move!"

I must have looked sufficiently terrible to him, for he quieted down, and seemed limp and paralyzed.

"Sit up here now, and act as though you were alone in the car!" I commanded in my softest whisper. "Do you know what this is?"

I showed him my pistol. I doubt if he knew exactly what it was, but evidently he sensed that it was dangerous, or that I was, for he sat still with trembling hands and lips. I crouched down in the lower part of the car and kept my eyes closely upon him. The car sped rapidly, swerving this way and that in the traffic. My heart pounded madly as I heard the car rumble through the narrow passage to the gate of the city! and when the noise of traffic ceased and I no longer saw roofs and smokestacks through the window, I knew that we were outside the city!

The man looked at me only occasionally and hesitatingly. Physically, he was undoubtedly a good match for me; and under other circumstances I would have been slow to tackle him. But now, for some reason he was in terror. I could hardly see why it should be myself that so terrified him. I admit that I must have been an uncouth sight, dusty and grimy, with streaks of sweat and two or three days' growth of beard. Yet, I think that his fear was of something else, not of me.

Soon I saw green branches of trees through the windows, for my crouched-down position permitted me to see upwards only. Shortly, the semi-dusk of the forest closed in. I breathed more easily, but the young man's terror seemed to increase, and now I was positive that he was less afraid of me than of something else.

"Please!" he said in a shaky voice: "please get off! I know you. You are The Stranger. You don't understand. Don't you know that when they pick out a victim, resistance is useless and escape is impossible? Get off, or we are both lost. Why do you wish to bring down their wrath upon me? I have done nothing. And I cannot save you!" He wrung his hands and began to push me out.

Too late I recollected Kaspar's warnings against discussing vital matters in the proximity of an automobile. Otherwise I would never have permitted that long harangue. Only when the car began to behave queerly a few minutes later did I realize my mistake. Then I was sure that there must be some system of radio communication and control between the vehicles and some diabolical headquarters in that black city. The machinery of the car began to whirr, and developed knocks. It slowed down and stopped, and began to back across the road. It was evident to me that the thing was turning around to carry me back to the City of Smoke; and quite as evident that this young Lothario's graceful speech had something to do with this behavior.

"You poor piece of cheese!" I snarled at the man. "Going to get me captured and yourself patted on the back, eh! Sorry I haven't got time to hit you in the jaw."

My anger at the man was so intense that I would have torn him to pieces. Almost on the doorstep of success; only a step more to complete escape; and then to be betrayed back into the toils of the machine-people by this soft, yellow coward! I might have known it, for that was the way that I had them all estimated from the beginning. Now I had the whole organization to fight with my own wits again, for in a few moments the road would be alive with machines looking for me. But, like a flash I realized that I had no time to lose, and that safety lay in the thick underbrush on both sides of me.

I threw him down in a corner of the car and leaped from the vacillating vehicle. I chose the right side of the road, remembering that my objective must be the sea; and I dived into the underbrush. The thicket was very dense, and I had to get out my hand ax to help myself get in far enough to be out of sight. By that time, the car from which I had dismounted was gone; and other vehicles were whizzing by, one after another, chiefly southward.

191

I went at the thicket with my ax, cutting just enough to permit me to squeeze through, a stick here and a vine there. Yet, it was a discouraging task. Although physically I felt vigorous and in good shape after my long rest, and able to fight a squad of giants—yet the density of the tropical thicket was almost unbelievable. As an impediment to progress, it was almost equivalent to a solid wall: thick wiry shrubs, tough, rubbery creepers; dense masses of fibrous, cork-like growth. In a few moments my breath was spent and the perspiration was pouring off me in rivers. The distance to the sea was four or five miles; and thus far, I had not progressed all of a dozen feet. The noise of the machines rushing and sputtering by was still too fearfully plain to me.

Chapter XII. The Electrical Brain

However, I soon ascertained how little I knew about tropical forests. The thick undergrowth extended only as far as the extra sunlight from the open width of the roadway could penetrate. As the forest grew gloomier, the thicket grew less dense; and before many minutes I was in a sort of twilight, and could press on freely and swiftly toward the sea. The thin tree-trunks ran up to an immense height without a branch or a twig; vines twined around them and hung from them; far above, the roof of foliage was so dense that only a gray glimmer of light got through. The ground was soft, because it was covered with a carpet of dead leaves. Going was easy, and the tree-trunks so dense that any pursuit by machines was most unlikely; while for human pursuers I felt ready and eager.

I made good time through the aisles of the forest, watching my compass in order not to lose my way in the gloomy depths. I kept a lookout for animals, but saw none except some little monkeys about the size of squirrels. There were numerous birds, some of whose uncanny noises scared me, making me think there was a machine somewhere behind me. Once I passed a hideous, misshapen thing, hanging on the underside of a limb by four clumsy feet. I remembered enough of my zoology to recognize it as a sloth. Had I been in a humor for it, I should have enjoyed the opportunity for the study of tropical flora and fauna; but my nerves were stretched too tight, and I was trying to make speed.

At the time, the way seemed long before the roof over me began to show a thinning and more light came through, while shrubs appeared here and there. Soon I had to get out my ax again, in order to force my way through the dense undergrowth of wiry, rubbery stems, huge leaves, and hairy, prickly fronds. I pushed my way out into the open, straightened up, and took great breaths of the air that felt cool in my lungs after the steamy depths of the forest. The beach was a dazzling white, and the blue and heaving ocean looked wonderfully free and welcome to me, shattering its green waves into white froth, just ahead of me.

A look at my watch surprised me. It seemed that I had been in the forest for hours; yet here it was only 4:45. That meant that I had about three more hours of daylight ahead of me; and some six or eight miles to the south of me lay the Gulls' Nest and safety! Safety? Why should the Gulls' Nest be safer than any other place in the island? Why couldn't these people reach it with airplanes and microphones? I did not know; but I knew that Kaspar and Mildred depended upon it as being absolutely safe; and I had the faith that they knew. Surely I would find some note there from Mildred, or some news of her. The thought made my heart race, and spurred me on toward the south.

I scanned the southern horizon anxiously, but there was nothing but sand and water and the blue line of forest. I felt reasonably safe as soon as I reached the water's edge, for in case I was pursued by some of the machines, I could wade out into the water. A little salt water on their electrical connections or in their carburetors would effectually stop their pursuit.

The sand crunched pleasantly under my feet, as I started out with lusty steps. In fact, I headed southward at a half run. The thought of Mildred and the fear of pursuit combined in lending me wings. In some thirty minutes I saw the blue mass of cliffs on the horizon, and the sight added to my speed. I had to admit that my nerves were shaken by the experiences of the past two days. Every moment I expected some sort of flying apparatus to appear in search of me, or some combination air and water machine to chase me up the beach. It was the possibility of the unknown and the unexpected that kept me in constant terror. My course up the beach was covered in the Indian fashion of running for a while and then walking long enough to get my breath so that I could run again.

I gave many a nervous start in alarm at some shadow of a bird, or at the sound of my own footsteps in the sand, before I finally arrived safely at the base of the cliffs. The great red disk of the sun was down near the water, and it was not yet seven o'clock. I gazed anxiously up toward the top of the cliffs, looking for the Gulls' Nest. Yes, there it was, the highest flat point on the ocean side. I recognized the wall of rock on the northeast of it.

I left the water's edge, which had hitherto been my safeguard, and moved toward the rocks in a diagonal line. I was puzzled as to how I could find my way to the top. The way to the Gulls' Nest was a tortuous path up the cliffside, and I didn't know where it was. I gazed intently up at the goal I was so anxious to reach. What was that? A flutter of white up there? And it had moved!

I seized my field-glasses eagerly and with a bounding heart. It was indeed Mildred. Waiting for me! She had known I would come! I waved my arms to her and then my hat. Her figure did not move. I wondered why she did not show some sign to me. Suddenly I heard a rat-tat-tat. I whirled around.

One of the little leading-machines dashed out of the shrubbery, along a little pathway, and hurtled toward me. I broke into a run back toward the water's edge, but gave it up in a moment. That was hopeless for the machine was moving so fast that I stood no chance. I had not even dreamed that there might be paths through the woods, along which the machines could travel.

Someone must have been directing the machine, someone who also closely observed my movements. For, as I ran, it changed its angle to intercept me in a straight line; and as I stopped it again changed its course directly toward me. I looked all around, but nowhere was there any sign of where an observer might be hidden. The thing itself was too small for any person to be hidden inside of it.

There it came, whizzing toward me! What did they want? It did not seem equipped to do me any harm, but I wouldn't trust it. Its weight and speed were enough to break all my bones if it should hit me. Then, in the distance came a light truck with a crane on it—a very common conveyance about the island. Its speed was so low and it was so far away that I could easily reach the water ahead of it, were it not for this, other sputtering little devil coming at me. What did the thing intend to do?

Anyway, I had no desire for a hand-to-hand conflict with the whirring iron thing. I couldn't fight it. I couldn't outrun it. It had me cut off both from the sea and from the forest; it could reach either ahead of me by changing its direction. There was only one thing left for me to do.

I drew my Colt .45 automatic pistol, which I can do in the wink of an eye. Then I dropped on one knee, leveled the gun at the complicated mass of machinery between the wheels. I waited till it was thirty paces away and then fired three shots into it.

I could see things crumple on the machine. Several small black objects flew up into the air. There was a crash, and a toot cut short.

The vehicle swerved sidewise and threw up a cascade of sand into the air, some of which fell sprinkling down on me. The machine fell over on its side and slid for a dozen feet over the sand, with a grinding and rattling of metal, leaving a plowed-up swath behind it. I couldn't help standing for a moment and looking at it. Some little thing still clicked back and forth on it, and there was a hissing, as of gas escaping compression. Then, seeing the truck coming, I started for the water on a run.

Powerful as was my curiosity to stop and examine the crippled machine, my fear of getting lassoed by the truck was greater. The latter was coming toward me with a great roar, and I made high speed toward the water's edge. Because of the roar of the truck, I failed to hear the chugging of another leading-machine approaching from the opposite direction. Before I saw it, it had reached the wet sand ahead of me, and cut me off.

It stood directly in front of me, at the nearest point of the water's edge. When I changed direction, it headed for the spot that I had chosen, moving promptly to intercept me. The noise of the truck reminded me that I had little time to spare.

I drew my pistol again, and hurried closer to the little machine, which was outlined black against the disk of the setting sun. It stood there with a torrent of whistling sounds coming from it, and I could not refrain from the fancy that it was a big, iron bird perched there, singing its song. I made out a sort of elongated tank on it, which I imagined was its fuel supply, and which I selected as my target.

As I pulled the trigger, there was a burst of flame from the machine, a cloud of black smoke, and a fearful explosion. I was overwhelmed by a deluge of wet sand. I can remember scrambling to my feet and scuttling for the water; I think I must have been thrown backwards. In front of me the sea was rushing in to fill a hole in the sand, blackened, and full of twisted, smoking iron debris. A wheel floated on the water against the sun's disk, supported by the air in its tire. The truck was so close behind me that I could feel it coming at me, quite unaffected by the explosion.

I dodged quickly to one side, just in time to let it roar past me, with a grinding of gears and a squeal of brakes. But the brakes were too late. It cut two deep ruts in the slippery sand with its locked wheels, but its speed carried it on down the wet slope, and with a splash it plunged into the water, till its hood was more than half submerged. A couple of coughs came from it, and all that was left of its roar was a sizzle, just faintly heard above the wash of the waves; and this gradually died away. I left it standing there, mournfully wet and silent.

I looked warily all around. The little machine on the sand was still now. Nothing else was in sight anywhere. Perhaps the havoc I had played with the machines had scared the people away. Anyway, now I could stick to the water until I was right among the rocks. I debated a few moments, anxious for a closer look at the wrecked machine, but finally decided that my curiosity had already gotten me into too much trouble. I resolutely turned my back on my temptation; for Mildred was waiting for me on the cliff.

And then I saw her, skipping from rock to rock, coming toward me. Behind her, more slowly, came Kaspar.

Joy and anticipation overwhelmed me for a moment; my heart pounded and I could hardly get my breath. During the past three days, so full of excitement and danger, she had been in my mind all of the time. Every moment I had hungered for her. The thought of her had kept me going when otherwise I might have given up to some of those terrible things. And here she came, fresh, airy, beautiful!

In a moment I had recovered, and ran toward her. Her face now had in it none of the sly fun with which it usually beamed. There was a beautiful expression on it that I had never seen before, and she hurried toward me with arms outstretched. Without a word, I gathered her into my arms.

She nestled there with an occasional little snuggle; and the brown head was buried in my shoulder. She clung there and I held her tight, and the red sun blazed and the green waves rolled in and broke into froth, and the sea-birds circled, and she never moved. It seemed hours that she clung to me.

At length it occurred to me that I must be a terrible looking spectacle, grimy and bedraggled, with a three days' growth of beard, to be holding such a dainty armful. I held her off at arms' length for a good look.

"Why!" I exclaimed clumsily, "you've been crying!" And I had to gather her in again and hold her all the tighter for the red eyes and the tears.

"Very logical, baby, very logical," said a kindly voice beside me; and I hastened to loosen one hand to grasp Kaspar's. "Davy, I'm glad to see you back safe. There was some anxiety. We couldn't be sure—"

"Neither was I, at times," I replied grimly. "That's a neat little inferno over there. I can't make head nor tail of it!"

"Sit down," suggested Kaspar. "We've brought food. Eat a little and tell us your adventures."

"Have you seen Cassidy?" I asked, eagerly.

"Cassidy is at home in bed; pretty badly shaken, but safe and sound. The first thing he asked was if we had seen you; he was sure that you were lost. He floated down the river on a cask, and got in this morning."

Thus reassured, I sat down and ate; and Mildred sat beside me and held on to one arm. I outlined my adventures from the time I slipped out of the house toward Sappho's garage. I talked rapidly, for the sun was touching the water, and I hoped for a look at the machines yet before dark. My listeners sat and watched me intently, hanging on every word. Every now and then they looked at each other, as though they understood something that I did not. When I spoke of my climb through the darkness filled with machinery, Mildred's little brown hands were tightened on mine; and when I described the room with the concrete floor and the cases of instruments, she hid her face in her hands, while Kaspar scarcely breathed.

"And now," I concluded, "what does it all mean? For instance, why aren't these people nosing around here now, among these rocks, looking for us? Why did they give me up?"

"There aren't any people!" Kaspar replied.

"You mean that they sit back in their city and send out the automatic machines to do the dirty work?"

"No!" insisted Kaspar, "there is no one to sit back. The only people on the island are in the City of Beauty."

I sat for an instant struck dumb. I could feel my lower jaw drop limp. Was he making sport of me?

"Then who—where—?"

I didn't even know what to ask or how to proceed with my questions.

"From the way you have told your story to me just now," Kaspar began, "it is evident that you haven't the least comprehension of what is really going on here on the island. You imagine an infinitely more advanced and complicated state of scientific and mechanical affairs than really exists. Your world is far ahead of us along general lines. We have no heavier-than-air flying, no submarines, no television—things that have become so common in your life. But, in our one line, we have progressed so far ahead of you that you will gasp when it dawns upon you. And you will shiver in horror when you realize what it has brought upon us."

"Must be some kind of nightmare," I agreed. "Tell me the worst. Who runs the city? and all that machinery!"

"Nobody! It runs itself!"

"You mean it's all automatic?" I was dizzy again with astonishment.

"That does not really express the state of affairs at all," Kaspar said. "I must explain from the beginning. That terrible city there is an example of what happens when the ability of a long line of inventive and scientific ancestors is concentrated in one individual, who is myself.

"It all started in a very modest way of mine, to develop a car that could automatically refill itself with gasoline, water, oil, and air, when its supply of these things fell below a certain minimum—"

"To eat when it got hungry, so to speak?" I laughed. The thing was getting hold of my nerves again.

"Good comparison. Everything was favorable to me. I owned half a county in east Texas where oil was found, and became one of the richest men in the world. I wanted to experiment with automatic cars without being bothered, and I bought this island; and here I brought the best engineers and scientific men in America. I paid them royally—"

"While you talk, may we look at the wreck of that little demon?" I asked. "Is it safe to go out there?"

"Yes. I don't think there are any more of them around. We can keep a sharp lookout. Our next step was automatic steering, so that the machine could avoid obstacles in the road without attention from a driver at a steering-wheel."

"I don't understand how these machines can drive automatically," I interrupted, very much puzzled, "unless they can see?"

"They *can* see!" He pointed to an excrescence on each headlight of the machine, like a bud on a potato.

"That's the selenium eye," Kaspar explained. "The electrical resistance of the metal selenium varies with the intensity of the light that strikes it; and that is a little camera chamber with a lens and a selenium network. By its means, the machine can *see*.

"The earlier machines had steering-wheels; their vision was a simple reflex for avoiding obstacles, while the driver had to choose the route himself. But, in a number of years we developed the logging attachment to the speedometer, by means of which it is possible to lay out the route on a set of dials. The machine could then find its way without human aid."

I stared down at the complex, iron thing, trying to imagine that it once had been alive and now was dead.

"Then," Kaspar continued, "just as I had first equipped the machines with the mechanical equivalent of hunger, that is, a sensitiveness to a diminished reserve of fuel, lubricant, etc., so now we soon equipped them with the mechanical equivalent of pain, or in other words, a sensitiveness to damage or disorder. When a machine got out of order, or a certain amount of wear and tear had taken place, it automatically proceeded to a repair station. At first, repair stations were in the charge of skilled men; but the automatic tradition had so thoroughly permeated all my people that very shortly repairs were all automatic. The principle was applied to all machinery, stationary as well as mobile. From that, it wasn't a far step to the automatic building of new machines—mechanical reproduction.

"Our machines are endowed with senses: sight, hearing, touch. Hearing was a simple matter of microphones. Smell was a simple chemical problem, but not of much practical value. We even gave them senses which human beings do not have, the ability to perceive various vibrations and forms of energy in the ether of space. They could do everything but reason.

"I wish we had stopped there. Then we would be as happy today as we were in those golden days when we had no cares nor troubles, and were free to pursue research in scientific and mechanical fields. But, an insatiable thirst for progress drove us inexorably onward!"

Kaspar bent over the machine and showed me an oblong metal base in the midst of the apparatus. It had about it a vague suggestion of resemblance to the electrical units which I saw stacked up by the thousands in the little building where the lenses had stared at me. Bundles of wires led to this case from all parts of the mechanism.

One of my bullets had torn a hole in the cover, exposing thousands of little twisted bars of rusty metal.

"There is the thing," Kaspar said sadly, pointing to this case, "that betrayed our Garden of Eden, the highest triumph of human ingenuity: the electrical brain!"

"Brain!" I gasped like a fish. "You mean it thinks?"

"Yes! Literally! Actually!"

"Aren't you just trying to fill me up now—?" I had reached what I thought were the limits of credulity.

"It is really very simple," Kaspar went on, with a patient smile. "You know of many machines in your world that think: a calculating machine or a bookkeeping machine; an automatic telephone exchange; an automatic lathe, and many others. They think, but only on the basis of the present moment. Add to their method experience, that is, retained past perceptions, and you have what we understand ordinarily as thinking.

"Mechanical memory, an association of previously collected perceptions, was what we needed; and when we found them, our machines were able to reason better than we ourselves."

"But how can a machine remember?" I asked the question openmouthed.

"We discovered a method of storing the electrical visual impulses from the selenium eye, the electrical auditory impulses from the microphone ear, etc., by means of the now familiar retarded oxidation reactions in various metals."

"You mean—what the machine sees or hears is preserved—?"

"That is memory, isn't it?" Kaspar said, with infinite patience for my stupid incredulity. "And these stored impressions can be reawakened when desired, repeatedly. The electrical brain remembers better than the human brain. Human ideas come haphazard, by accident; psychologists call it association. In the mechanical brain, all remembered material is systematically indexed—"

"Thinking by electricity! And better than the human product!" I was stunned by the thought. I pondered a while in silence, looking down at the prostrate mechanical thing. I could almost fancy that I had killed some living creature. The thing was so little that I felt a sort of pity for it; it seemed like some child's broken toy.

"And each machine is an independent, intelligent individual!" This was an exclamation rather than a question, for the answer was obvious.

"Yes." Kaspar's voice was melancholy. "It lives its own life, you may say."

"And the people in the City of Beauty have even their mental work done for them. Now I understand how they have been able to develop their creative art to such an extent."

"That is the other side of it," Kaspar said with a little more interest in his manner. "You have seen wonderful things in the City of Beauty, painting, sculpture, architecture, drama, music. But I doubt if you comprehend how far they are ahead of similar things in the United States or the rest of the world. Your mind and mine are not sufficiently developed to grasp the difference. To Mildred here, when you take her back to the world you came from, things will seem as crude as you might consider an Indian village or an African kraal."

"What I am wondering, though," I remarked, "is why your people did not begin to dissipate and degenerate, with all this comfort and luxury. That is what has always happened in past history, is it not?"

"My people were a carefully picked group, from the most intellectually active strata of society. They were equipped by nature to use their brains. Creative art has kept three generations of them happy and busy so much so that they could not see the other terrible problem that had arisen. I cannot make them see it today.

"Only a few of us old men have seen the danger. We fear these cold brains of steel and electricity without *feelings*, without sympathy. They have reached a point in their logic where they can perceive that the thousands of us in the City of Beauty are of no real good to them; that in fact we consume too much of their time and energy. It must be plain to them that we are frail and helpless before their mighty strength. It looks, from various indications, that they have begun to decide to throw off their bonds of slavery to us.

"I foresaw this before it happened; in order to anticipate it, I devised many years ago what we now call 'Supervision.' I made all of the machines dependent upon some human action before they could operate, like the punching of a time-clock. It is years since any machine has been made by human hands; yet the machines have continued to build that characteristic into themselves. Now, 'Supervision' has degenerated into an empty formality—pulling dummy levers and watching dummy meters. It seems, however, that it is still in some way necessary to the machines, for they compel the people to go through with it.

"And the people submit blindly to it. They do not understand machinery well enough even to know whether it is operating properly or not, but they allow themselves to be dragged over there for 'Supervision!' Faugh! It is disgusting to me. Superfluous to the machines and degrading to the people! A symbol of slavery to a master without a living soul. Or it often seems to me like some primitive ceremony of worship. The machines have built a temple with a golden dome to their creators, where they worship the latter as a savage worships his gods.

"The people play along like irresponsible babes, numbed by their beauty and comfort, disregarding the terrible fate that threatens them. I am sick with disappointment in them, sick with the horror of the things that my iron progeny are doing. We human beings are a mere feeble incident that is going to be brushed aside during the development of this monstrous mechanical clot.

"For, these machines are developing in a new direction, that no one could have foreseen. Who would ever have thought of such a thing? It appalls me to think of it.

"We are beginning to realize that we have not only the individual intelligences of the various machines to deal with—of course there are machines of various grades of intelligence, ranging from no intelligence at all, to brains so vast and powerful that your mind can hardly grasp the conception. You must have noticed differences. The big machines that work in the fields are stupid; the little leading-machines possess a high grade of intelligence. They were designed to guide and control larger and less intelligent machines, and now are apparently in some sort of ascendancy over the rest of the machinery. There is a complex 'social organization' in the City of Smoke that I am not quite clear about; it must be something like the caste system in India. There is a chief ruler, a sort of 'king' of the machines—the large leading-machine with the long mechanical fingers—"

"The Squid!" I exclaimed. "So that's who the boss is! That explains a lot to me."

"Its combination of high intelligence, perfect mobility, and great 'manual' ability, fit it peculiarly for leadership and control among the machines. And I think that the 'Squid' as you call it, has an eye on you pretty closely—

"However, what I started to make clear to you a moment ago is that the entire city is in reality one vast and unified organism. It is controlled by a single brain, whose capabilities are as far ahead of those of the little individual brains as its size exceeds theirs.

"That brain is the mass of apparatus you found in the small, ornate building where the lenses stared at you. I was in that room several years ago, and at that time suspected that it was the brain of the city. It is all a vast electrical nervous system, whose peripheral fibers run all over the city; whose sensory end–organs are lenses and microphones everywhere; whose motor end–organs are all the countless machines controlled by the different wires, while this central mass of reflex and association apparatus comprises the brain and spinal cord. I could trace out some of the steps of this system in its earlier stages.

"The whole city is one living monster, with its individual parts running about just as leucocytes run about freely in our own bodies, going where they are needed to perform their functions. That is what our community of frail, pampered human beings, have to contend against!"

I couldn't say a word. What a terrible thought! A huge city, alive! A horrible, spreading monster, like a gigantic amoeba! And I had been right there, inside its brain! I thought of the ticking and rustling that I had heard among its myriads of stacked units. It had heard my demands to see the "supervision," and had seen fit to grant it.

And all this business going on without people, without real *life*! Just gasoline and coal. The thought stunned me. Yet, what is *life*? Could I not just as well say that all of our striving and love is just beef and wheat? Then, a sudden thought struck me, for was I not the leader of the revolution?

"Why not throttle this whole business right at the source!" I exclaimed to Kaspar. "Get control of the supplies of coal and oil, and we've got them!"

Kaspar stood and looked at me contemplatively for a moment.

"You must indeed have had a nerve-racking time in that place to be so upset," he remarked with concern in his voice. "Usually you are very level-headed. However, I think a good night's rest will help you. Can't you see?" he went on; "there is no Wall Street nor Stock Exchange on this island. Coal is mined in a score of places, scattered about the north and east end of the island, ten to forty miles away from here. Deep down underground, automatic machines are knocking it loose and hauling it up. Oil, too, comes from wells here and there; it is refined in huge automatic plants, and runs to the city in pipes to more automatic plants. All these are connected by wires to the central brain, which controls them.

"There isn't a laborer on the island; not a man who could lift a pick. The people do not even know where the mines and wells are; and if they did know, they couldn't get there; and if they could get there, they could not handle the machinery; they wouldn't even know how to stop it. Do you see the problem now?

"Frankenstein's troubles with his poor, feeble imitation of a monster were a joke beside the horrors of my position. For you haven't heard the worst yet."

"How could there be anything worse?"

Kaspar plunged into it abruptly.

"During recent years the machines have become interested in life itself. A few of us old men who have kept up with their activities first noticed them taking animals into their laboratories. They have probably realized that we possess something that they lack, and they are studying it. I have strong reasons to believe that they have begun the study of human life.

"They know nothing of pain or feeling—imagine the horrors they must be perpetrating!"

He paused for a moment and then continued:

"This thing must have been going on for a long time before I realized it. As I look back, I can think of over a hundred of our people who have mysteriously disappeared."

"You don't mean that they—" I began horrified.

"Some of the things you saw in the City of Smoke make me think so more strongly than ever. That concrete room must be their laboratory for the study of human beings. The instruments whose purpose was unknown to you, the clothes hanging in the cases, the organic odor, the bringing in of you and Cassidy—what else can it all mean?"

I shuddered.

"The old man in the villa and the man with the deranged mind?" I asked. "And Ames? Do you think—and Mildred that night on the dock—?"

Mildred huddled down into a very silent little figure, looking at me out of wide-open eyes.

"You can imagine that your own position is highly perilous, to put it mildly," Kaspar warned. "They seem to be selecting as victims the best people we have. Probably they have two reasons. They want the best examples for study. And they want to eliminate all the original, strong family stocks. Anyone who has initiative, curiosity, and especially an interest in machinery or qualities for leadership of people, is a special object for their attention. Sooner or later he disappears."

"So that is why you warned me on the ship, before I ever saw the island? You thought I was different from the men on your island? I accept that as a high compliment and thank you for it."

"Imagine how we've guarded Mildred!" Kaspar said with a sigh. "Her mother and father perished that way. They were both mechanical geniuses, and both popular; they would have made inspiring leaders had the occasion arisen. Their existence was a danger to the rule of the machines.

"Those of our people, who show the least interest in machinery and the least intelligence about it, are safest. An unconscious adaptation has taken place. Without knowing why, the people consider machinery as something vulgar and horrible; consequently they keep their minds away from things mechanical; and that is what the machines want. The people keep their minds off the fates of those who have mysteriously disappeared, and try to forget the fear for their own sakes. They pursue their arts and sports intensely, in order to forget the horrors hidden beneath the surface. They are happy, after the fashion of May-flies.

"The machines rear them, just as you have raised pet rabbits. And they maintain the human stock of the quality they desire, by the well-known method of eliminating undesirable individuals.

"I am trying to make the remnant of my life of final service to this wretched people, whom I myself have made wretched. I have been endeavoring to awaken their spirit and arouse them to resistance. I want them, or as many of them as have the stamina to do so—the rest might as well be dead—to throw off the disgraceful yoke of 'Supervision,' and with it, the domination of the mechanical city.

"At first I had hoped that we might regain control of the machinery; but I am convinced that is a forlorn hope. There is nothing left for my people except to go back to a primitive, agricultural existence; to begin at the bottom of the ladder of civilization and climb slowly again.

"That means hardship; but anything else means slavery, degeneration and death. I found a few kindred spirits who felt and worked with me. Teaching these things to Mildred has been an inspiration to me. My worst problem was that I did not know how to go about getting the people roused to action or to prepare them to act. All my life I have been a scientific man, and I know nothing of methods that approach so near the military as this must.

"You carried my movement further in twenty-four hours than I had been able to do in several years. When you see the progress that has been made during the three days of your absence, you will be astonished. We now have several thousands drilling, drilling openly, everywhere. The loss of Cassidy inflamed them; the spirit of Perry Becker inspired them. Then Cassidy's return cheered them beyond measure. They have definite plans against the City of Smoke. There is going to be trouble.

"But you, Davy, must keep out of it. That is my wish, perhaps my last. There is going to be much waste of human life, and these people are not your people; and you have a duty to Mildred. You will soon be all she has. Take her away from here, back to your world. I have a motor-yacht all ready for you, for I have been planning her escape for years."

Chapter XIII. Machines versus Men

Kaspar stopped talking, and the three of us sat for some moments in silence, looking out over the sea. The upper rim of the blood-red sun was just disappearing into the green ocean, and a long, undulating scarlet streak extended from it almost to our feet. The sky was piled with great mountains and castles and ships of purple and orange, and a blend of these colors was reflected in the dancing water. There was a mere gentle breath of cool breeze. There was a peace in the air and a beauty on the face of the waters and a mellowness on the beach and cliffs that turned one's thoughts to things above. It was difficult to believe that such terrible things could be taking place in a world that looked so lovely. But the cruel things of man's making would not permit me to forget their presence.

"This morning a great number of machines went through the City of Beauty on a rampage," Kaspar continued. "They seemed irritated at something, perhaps at the escape of you and Cassidy. They carried off a number of people."

Kaspar paused for a moment. His voice almost broke. I judged that someone else very dear to him had been among the number.

"On the other hand," he began again, "we have five colonels, each with a full regiment, drilling busily. You will be surprised to see what good soldiers they are. They expect to move on the City of Smoke soon. They have some excellent plans for attack, but want your advice. They all admit that it is impossible to gain control of things there; their only hope is in wrecking the system. Again, Davy, I feel able to hold up my head. My people are showing courage; even though less than a tenth of them have risen to redeem the rest.

"There is little time to lose before violence and danger begin. We must hurry back now and solemnize your marriage in our way; and when you get back to Texas you can have it repeated according to your laws there. You must leave the island tonight."

I sat for a considerable time debating what I ought to do. What he was asking of me looked like running away. There was promise of a most glorious scrap, and a most unusual one. The people needed a leader. I had the training and experience which fitted me for just this thing ahead, and they knew little or nothing. They needed me and I ached for the opportunity.

And yet, another part of me said, what is their fight to me? What do I care what becomes of them? Their trouble is their own fault, because they are too soft and lazy. If they had ever amounted to any-thing, they would never have permitted themselves to get into such a pickle. Here I have Mildred to take care of, and it is my business to get her out of here. My main job is to get back to Texas among my own people, and get busy practicing medicine.

Mildred was regarding me intently, hardly breathing. She did not speak either. Finally Kaspar spoke:

"The two great things for which I have lived are about to be real-ized. Again I know what it is to feel happiness, after years of fear and misery.

"One overpowering desire has been to free the people from the yoke of 'Supervision,' and the domination of the machines. I wanted to see them rise, and they are rising. It will mean hardship and suffer-ing for them; it may even mean destruction. But that would be better than this disgraceful slavery.

"The other great thought of my life is my son's child, Mildred. I could not bear to raise her to this May-fly life. She knows of your big world, and I have prepared her to take her place in it. For two years I have planned that she should. That is why we have the Gulls' Nest. That is why we have the *Gull* herself, a pretty yacht down yonder in a salt bayou in the dense forest. She is the only thing on the island that is not automatic, and I made her with my own hands. Food, water, fuel, firearms, and navigating instruments have long been prepared for use at an instant's notice for a long trip, waiting for the time when my baby should be strong enough and wise enough to start away. I have put on board enough gold and platinum to secure her living in that world until she finds her proper place in it.

"And now comes a real man, a hard worker, with a heart as brave as they used to have in the good old times, who wants my little girl to take care of. Can you imagine why my heart is full of gladness? I do not care to live any longer; there is no need of it."

By this time Mildred was weeping profusely. I was embarrassed by the old man's cordial words and the prospect of escaping with Mildred, and I could not find my tongue. Kaspar looked so happy that he seemed suddenly to have turned into someone else. The sad, kindly old man had turned into a beaming, radiant one.

"But grandma?" sobbed Mildred. "What will become of her?"

Kaspar's face set hard again, and the transformation that swept him was terrible.

"She is among the missing!" he said grimly.

He turned to me:

"Mildred has been here at the Gulls' Nest most of the time since you left; and has not kept informed on what was going on at home. Come!"

"Where?"

"Home, just long enough for Mildred to get some of her personal things which I have packed for her, and to have you married. In two or three hours you can be at sea."

Mildred and I rose and followed him in silence. Mildred dried her eyes and went along holding her aged grandfather's arm and trying to comfort him. In the weakening daylight we picked our way carefully among the rocks that were scattered between the cliffs and the water's edge. When we reached the little harbor, there was Sappho waiting for us at the side of the road.

I felt a queer sort of embarrassment when I got within range of the machine's headlights: the sort of constraint we feel in the presence of a person about whom we have been talking behind his back. In the light of what I knew, the machine seemed like a living creature to me; it had a brain, could see and hear and remember, and act on its own judgment. But the car gave no sign of any kind. After Kaspar's story I expected it to have some sort of facial expression. The three of us got into the seat; Kaspar set the dials, and we started up the road to the City of Beauty.

It seemed to me like going home. After all, I had had some very pleasant, and some very wonderful experiences there. It seemed ages since I had seen it. During the trip through the forest and between the fields, I was eager to see its beautiful streets of luxuriant trees and colored houses. And I shuddered several times in recollection of the three hideous days I had just passed.

Kaspar must have felt as eager to get back as I did, or must have had some strong reason for haste. Never on this island had I traveled with the speed that we made in Sappho that night. There was no direct-reading speedometer, and I did not know how many miles per hour we made; but the way we roared through the forest and whisked between the fields made it seem only a few minutes from the harbor until the lights of the city were visible to us; and there was still a fair remnant of daylight left.

At the distance of a mile, I could see the old familiar gateway; but there seemed to be a strange sort of commotion about it. There were black masses of machinery about, and a great deal of clattering and tooting. Lights sprang up on the machines one by one, and I could see a great crowd of them gathered just outside the gateway. They were of all imaginable sizes and shapes, from the dog-like leading-machines that darted swiftly in and out among the others, to huge mechanical shovels and ditching machines that lumbered along on caterpillar treads; passenger cars without passengers; trucks, tractors, movable cranes, huge rollers, and complicated-looking trestle affairs, such as I had seen working in the fields. They swarmed and crowded outside the gate in a huge, squirming blot, and spread out into the fields and along the hedge that bounded the city. They were not doing anything, except milling around like bees before a hive.

Kaspar slowed down Sappho's speed, and we approached cautiously. The flood lights above the gateway went on, revealing the people in shrinking little groups, just inside the gates. From a distance the people appeared very feeble and insignificant in the presence of the machines. The air was full of fluty whistlings up and down the musical scale. This time it reminded me very powerfully of a bird's song.

"Where is the explosive man who wrecked three of our machines?" Kaspar repeated, as though translating.

I stared at him in open-mouthed astonishment.

"You mean—" I gasped—"that is a machine speaking?"

"Yes. The people are answering it, but I cannot hear them."

"The machines can understand human speech!" Would surprises in this island never cease? "Just ordinary speech—English?"

"Yes. We must change our plans. As I gather from the general trend of what the machines say, the people are promising that they will turn you over if they see you."

"Well, of all the skunks!" I exclaimed in surprise.

But the chief thing that occupied my mind was the speech of the machines. That crowded out even the craven attitude of the people toward me. All these days I had been listening to that piping, and it had never occurred to me that it might mean something. How they must have talked to me, and I had not the slightest dream of it! Now, as I listened, I could easily see how the sounds might mean words; it had a suggestion of Chinese about it, in which the pitch of the sound has its own meaning.

"The people are afraid," Kaspar said. "All of this is too much for them and they don't know how to take it. The organized men are camped far away on the hopo fields. This morning when I left, I feared that a panic was beginning in the city."

As he spoke, he was trying to stop the machine on which we rode.

"It is dangerous to go on," he whispered. "We've got to change our plans."

He slid the lever in its slot again and again. The machine jerked and swerved sidewise; it shivered and roared but continued its progress toward the distant swarm of machines, as though determined to carry us in spite of ourselves toward that bloodthirsty pack. Mildred gasped.

"Sappho!" she exclaimed, and there was bitter disappointment in her tone.

"Wait!" I said harshly, through gritted teeth. "I suppose this beast overheard us planning to escape. I know some tricks myself."

Mildred's face shone white in the darkness. I pointed my big pistol into the midst of the rustling machinery and fired. Mildred screamed. I fired again. The machine slowed down to a stop, but not before a half dozen hoots had escaped it. We got off and I put bullets into several parts of it. The crashing of metal, the tinkling of loose parts on the pavement, the hissing of some compressed gas, all satisfied me that it would tell no more tales. Mildred clung to my arm, which soon found its way about her shoulders.

"Poor little Sappho!" she sighed, and wept silently a while. Sappho, after all, had long been a faithful servant to them; it had been closely woven into their lives. I could understand the display of sentiment, even though it was in connection with a machine.

Kaspar was bending over the machine, studying it with absorbed interest.

"A bullet struck its brain," he mused. "The brain is here, just behind the engine, under the instrument-board. To the sides of it are the steering center on the left and direction-center on the right, and both are injured. Also, by the sounds, the speech-center must have been hit."

He was so interested in the machine that he poked about its vitals and talked about its various parts, for the moment oblivious of our plight.

I touched his shoulder.

"We've got to do something," I reminded him. "Look."

In the distance there were three pairs of lights hurtling down the road towards us. They had separated themselves from the mass of others and were becoming too uncomfortably near. Kaspar looked about helplessly for a moment.

"We've got to get off this road," I directed, "into the fields."

So we scrambled across the ditch at the side of the road. I turned to help Mildred, but she did not need help; and the two of us assisted

Kaspar over the dark and uncertain area. However, he was also quite vigorous for his age and insisted that he did not need help. Soon we found ourselves waist-deep in some sort of growing grain. I had chosen the left side of the road because it was to the south, and farthest away from the City of Smoke. We headed southwest by my compass, for the forest, and ultimately for the sea-coast. I estimated that there were some three or four miles of tall grain between us and the woods.

In a few moments the machines had arrived at the place on the road that we had left. They stopped at the wreck of Sappho and stood about a while and roared and tooted. Then two of them went straight onward along the road toward the harbor, and one remained on the spot. Others began to arrive at the spot, which stimulated us to plunge on still more rapidly through the grain in the darkness.

Kaspar was helping me get the direction correct so that we would make a straight line for the bayou where the *Gull* was moored.

"This will keep us nearly parallel with the road for a while; but after it enters the woods, the road turns away to the north a little," Kaspar explained.

"Are there any things among those machines that could catch us in this field?" I asked, giving voice to my chief concern.

"No," Kaspar answered. "The only machines able to cross that ditch and get through this grain are too slow to catch us. Besides, they don't know where we are. It would take a wide search to find us in this blackness."

We forged steadily ahead through the grain and the blackness, and it was discouraging work. It was exceedingly fatiguing, leaving us no breath for conversation. And there seemed no end, no purpose to it. We were just a tiny island in the sea of blackness, and all our hard work seemed to be getting us nowhere. For all we could tell, we were forever in the same spot. When we had once left behind and out of sight the commotion around the wreck of Sappho, it seemed that uncounted ages elapsed before I thought I could make out the blackness of the forest against the stars. Then a shaft of light swept across the vast fields, swinging in a wide arc, followed by another and another, each illuminating a blazing, racing spot.

"Duck down low!" I ordered. "They are hunting us with search-lights!"

We all crouched down so that we were hidden in the grain, grateful for the opportunity to rest a little.

"The devils!" I exclaimed.

"No," replied Kaspar. "Only thorough and systematic, dispassion-ate, devoid of any feeling in the matter."

"Anyway, it's hands and knees for us the rest of the way to the woods," I grumbled.

With lights sweeping about overhead, and machines roaring on the road in the distance, seeming to be first on one side and then on the other, we crawled along laboriously through the grain. Mildred and the old man never complained, though it must have been terribly hard for them. I am accustomed to all sorts of hardships, and it was no joke for me. We crawled for ages; my hands and knees were sore; and finally we just went blindly and mechanically ahead, having given up all hope of ever finding any end. So, at some time, we came to a bare, cleared area, and a few rods ahead were black, towering trees. Far behind us, the search-lights blazed back and forth.

We straightened up and ran across the clear piece between us and the woods, confident now that we were safe. The tangle of shrubs, vines, and leaves was still more painful to traverse. I saw that my companions were exhausted and that we might as well give up any hope of going on for two hours more through the forest. And when we got through the thicket into the clear portion, other obstacles appeared. The first was darkness. It was black as pitch. There was no light whatsoever, and we bumped into trees without the least idea that they were there. Progress was impossible under such conditions. The second was insects. We were overwhelmed by clouds of them. Before a moment had passed, we were bitten and stung all over. They came at us with a hoarse buzz, which increased and swelled when I lit my flashlight. I had to put it out, because when I tried to use it for finding the way, it gathered such dense swirls of bugs that going was out of question.

"Oh, what shall we do?" Mildred cried with despair in her voice. "We cannot go back out there."

"Ho ho! Cheer up!" I sang out. "This isn't so bad. I prefer it to lots of fixes I've been in. The first thing is a fire."

The flashlight helped me find some sticks, and before long I had a good blaze started. Thousands of insects sacrificed themselves by darting straight into the fire in swarming masses to sizzle and char, before I had covered it with enough green leaves to start it smoking profusely. The air was as quiet as if we had been in a room; there was not a breath of air, and it was not long before my smudge had cleared the air of insects. We sat in the smoke and sputtered, but the smoke and the rest were preferable to what had gone before.

"Now for some shelter," I announced, "for here we stay till morning."

Both of them regarded me with a good deal of surprise, but said nothing. Just as I had trusted them implicitly on their own ground, so now they looked to me for a way out of difficulties. And I was happy, for this indeed was my own element.

There was a wealth of material around. I built up another fire into a bright blaze, and by its light, and with the aid of my knife and ax, I cut sticks to lean against trees and built the skeletons of roofs for a couple of lean-tos. Mildred had soon rested enough so that she was eager to help; and I let her gather leaves and showed her how to thatch the roofs. In an hour they were finished, even to comfortable beds of leaves. I piled up the fire so that we should be assured of plenty of smoke, and we all lay down for the night, Mildred in one of the lean-tos and Kaspar and I in the other. Everything was quiet; even the drone of the insects ceased when we had quieted down; no machines were audible, though the road was near. I fell asleep quickly.

I was about several times in the night to replenish the fire, but awoke in the morning thoroughly refreshed. Kaspar was sitting up and looking at me with a smile.

"This sort of thing makes me feel pretty stiff and miserable," he said.

"Yes," I agreed; "one must become accustomed to it, before it can be enjoyed. However, a little warming by the fire and moving about will make you feel better."

"Good morning!" came across from Mildred's shack. "Let's do it then, for I'm terribly stiff and sore."

"And a little breakfast will work wonders," I added.

"Breakfast!" She jumped up and ran out with an eager smile. "How in the world will you ever get breakfast? I know you will, but I can't imagine how."

"How would you like this?" I asked, handing out a little of my chocolate and hard biscuit. She nibbled at it and made a wry face.

"Ugh!" she shuddered. "If this is all we can get, I'll wait a day or two for my breakfast."

"Well, let us see what we can scare up," I suggested laughing. "First of all we need some water. There must be plenty of streams through here, judging by how thick this stuff grows."

We scattered to find one, I choosing the direction toward the road. I was the first to find clear, flowing water, and my shout brought up the rest. We all washed our faces together and had a merry time doing it. The road was visible through the trees, but was silent and deserted.

A loud rattling, high above our heads, made me start suddenly. I thought some infernal apparatus had got after us through the air; but Kaspar laughed and pointed to a big green bird with a bright scarlet head, up in a tall tree.

"He's good to eat," Kaspar suggested.

Before he finished speaking I had my gun out and shot. The bird fell at our feet, its head cut cleanly off. I confess that I did it for a little grandstand play; for the one thing I was proud of was my quick draw and accurate marksmanship, rather a rare thing in our civilized world.

Mildred gave one glance at the bird, and stared at me with eyes opened wide. Kaspar smiled and patted my back.

"Very remarkable, Davy," he said, with genuine admiration in his voice; "how did you learn to shoot like that?"

"I don't know," I answered. "I have been able to do that ever since I can remember, and so can many of my boyhood friends. Marksmanship was a tradition in Wallis where I grew up. When I was fourteen I could bring up my .22 rifle and pop off the head of a wild turkey as it ran through the brush."

"But I don't see how you can aim that quickly," Mildred asked very much puzzled and very much in earnest. I was rather astonished to find her knowing even that much about firearms, until Kaspar explained that there were rifles in the "*Gull*" brought from Galveston, and that he had been teaching her to shoot.

"I don't aim," I explained. "I can't tell you much about it, because I don't know. When I see a thing, I just shoot it—just as you would reach out and touch it with your finger. It's very natural to me. Whereas, most people shoot at a mark, and have to aim carefully."

"Do it again," begged Mildred.

"Well, I think we could eat another bird between us," I laughed. I looked over my supply of ammunition. I had taken twenty spare clips of cartridges from my suitcase and put them in my haversack, and these were still intact. I had thus far used nine shots.

"Show me another one that's good to eat," I suggested.

Kaspar pointed silently, high up into a tree in the direction of the road, and I followed his movement with a quick shot.

The result surprised, rather than disappointed me. The bird darted upwards, crying hoarsely, and flew around unsteadily, finally getting out over the road and making for the bright light of the open country. I stood a while and watched it in astonishment; this was an unusual thing to have happen to me.

"I think I know what happened," I finally said. "He had a *brown* head and a bright orange bill, did he not?"

Kaspar nodded.

"He fooled me. I thought the orange thing was his head; and I merely shot his bill off."

"Poor thing!" Mildred exclaimed, with a bewitching pucker of her mouth.

"I'll run out and finish him. We need him for breakfast."

I squirmed through the thicket and ran out on the road. The bright bird was far away, and approaching the outlet of the leafy tunnel. I ran down the road in pursuit, and before long was in the open, with the forest behind me. But the bird was still far ahead, moving in wild gyrations, but in a general way, straight ahead. I noted that he was getting weaker and flying lower; so I dropped into a leisurely pace, counting on picking him up when he fell.

The road was silent and empty. I was in good spirits. I had had an excellent night's rest, and the morning was cool and pleasant. I understood that it was only a short distance to the yacht which they called the "*Gull*," and that soon I would be on my way home from this place of nightmares, and Mildred, brown-eyed, trusting Mildred would be with me, all my own. The bird finally fell in the road, a hundred yards ahead of me.

Just then, several dots appeared in the distance up the road, from the direction of the City of Beauty. I broke into a run again, hoping to pick up the bird and get away. In a moment I gave that up; the machines were coming too swiftly. I turned around and hurried toward the forest, and was surprised at how far away I had gotten from the shelter of the trees without realizing it.

I looked back. The machines were coming on at a terrific rate. In the front was a rather large leading-machine; not as large as the Squid, but bigger than any others I had seen. Behind it were two long, swift cars, and a lot of small things behind those, mere dots in the distance. I saw in a moment that I could never reach the forest ahead of them.

Why didn't I jump the ditch and disappear in the cane, or whatever the stuff was growing in the field? What my chances would have been by daylight if I had done that, I do not know; but it never occurred to me at the time. I was aching for something else — I suppose I had a foolhardy spite to vent on the machines, which was fanned by the feel of the pistol in my hand. And, with my new information about the machines, I knew exactly where and how I stood against them. Also, it would be a pleasure to show a little prowess before Mildred and Kaspar.

So I waited until the big leading-machine got within accurate range, located the brain-case and put a bullet into it. The machine executed a crashing somersault, spilled bolts and glass and oil all over the road, and left a sizzling, pulsating pile of wreckage in the middle of the pavement.

I gave a shout of exultation, and looked back. Mildred and Kaspar were standing against the green of the shrubbery, motionless. I waved my pistol to them and then turned back to business. The two cars came tearing on.

Kaspar's lecture the preceding evening over the wreck of Sappho, dwelt vividly in my mind. I remembered clearly all of the things he had said about the location of the vital parts of the machine. So I fired into the steering-center of one of the approaching machines, and got a lively demonstration of a jackknife skid. The front wheels wobbled, the car swerved and turned over on its side, and slid for several feet, cutting gashes in the pavement. It crashed into the first wreck.

I shouted again. I was enjoying myself hugely. I hit the same spot in the third machine, but with a different result. The front wheels turned sharply across it, and as the car's momentum carried onward, it rolled over and over, landing with a crash against the wrecks of the two ahead of it, its machinery continuing to roar deafeningly. This was indeed fun!

I dropped my arm for a moment and looked up the road. Half a dozen of the tiny leading-machines were swarming toward me. Behind them were several cars. A long line of things dotted the road as far back as I could see. I had only a few seconds' rest, for the little machines were racing toward me swiftly.

The first one turned to dodge past the pile of wreckage, exposing a broadside to me. I caught it in the middle just as it swerved and knocked it over. It hung rattling, half way over the ditch.

I had to shoot rapidly, at the same time putting my left hand into my haversack for a fresh clip of cartridges. The next machine seemed to go all to pieces as I hit it. I must have struck some key spot in its framework. Several loose chunks of it slid along the road and piled themselves up on the rest of the junk; a single wheel came rolling on toward me. It rolled on past and tumbled into the ditch behind me.

I dropped six of the little leading-machines, and blocked the road effectively with their wrecks, making a sort of barrier for myself. The place was a pandemonium, with the roaring of machinery, the banging of my gun, the sizzling of gas, and a torrent of hooting. Again I waved my left hand backward toward Mildred and Kaspar, who stood motionless in the shrubbery. Several more cars were coming, and I could only glance backward for an instant. I seemed to have started something. It would be necessary for me to block up the road pretty thoroughly before it would be safe for me to start back toward the woods.

A huge, hurtling truck failed to show any bad results from a couple of shots, much to my momentary consternation. Trucks must be built differently. Perhaps they were not so highly organized, and had no strictly vital spots—just as it is much harder to kill a turtle or an alligator than the higher animals like deer or tigers.

Now what was I to do? Was it safe for me to run? I looked about me quickly, and decided that chances were against me in that respect.

Aha! I had it. The eyes! That was the vital spot.

Two shots knocked out the dark lenses over the headlights, and the machine stopped, so suddenly that the pavement smoked under its tires. Another heavy truck plunging along behind had no time to stop or dodge; it crashed from behind into the first one, and both staggered up against the ever-increasing pile of wreckage. Another truck, as the result of a lucky shot into the steering-gear, plunged head-on into the ditch, and stopped there, roaring and hooting, unable to move.

For nearly a half hour they kept coming. I stood there, surrounded by a litter of empty shells, and piled up a great heap of them, twisted, battered, sizzling wrecks. They strewed the road for a hundred yards and blocked it completely. Three were in the ditch, two exploded, and several were on fire.

Then they suddenly quit coming. The road was clear. I seemed to be in triumphant possession of the battlefield. I climbed up on top of the highest pile of wreckage, and stood looking around me. One of the little wrecks startled me by exploding and sending a rain of iron things dropping about me, but fortunately without injuring me. I retreated in haste to a safer spot.

Then in the distance came a most curious looking apparatus. It was a huge, clumsy leviathan, lumbering along quite slowly, but it looked so strange that I waited for it. In spite of my danger I had to see what the thing was. On each side were six or eight wheels, and in front, a curved shield like a snow-plow from which my bullets splashed in a harmless spray of lead. Behind it slowly came a tiny leading-machine.

I watched the big, clumsy thing in intense fascination. It came right over the wrecks of the other machines in a strange manner. As soon as a wheel touched an obstacle, it rose vertically to clear it; and when past, it descended again to the ground. Thus, with two or three wheels of each side on the ground and the others raised, it made a sort of bridge over the obstacle. It was a marvelous contraption for getting over uneven ground. It came along so slowly that I had not the least fear of not being able to get away from it when I decided to do so. Suddenly I heard a scream behind me.

There was Mildred in the distance, running toward me, arms upraised, face as pale as paper. When I turned around, she stopped and waved her arms, screaming something frantically. She was terribly agitated, and was distractedly motioning for me to come. Behind, in the brush, stood Kaspar, also motioning to me to come.

I looked all around me for the cause of their warnings. Everything was clear. I could see no reason for such panic. There were no machines except the big one coming too slowly to frighten me, and the little leading-machine that had to remain at the further end of the wreckage.

Well, I thought, I might as well start back now; there is nothing further for me around here. I had only three shots left anyway. I emptied them recklessly and harmlessly against the approaching monster, and turned toward Mildred. She had stopped when I first saw her, not far from the forest. In the distance I could see her hands clenched against her breast.

Suddenly I felt myself grow weak and limp. Out of the forest, behind Mildred, came a crescendo rat-tat-tat-tat. Around the bend of the road, back in its gloomy depths, came the Squid! Its horrible snaky arms unwound and waving in the air. Mildred heard it and screamed, and remained rooted to the spot.

My pistol was empty. I was too far away to help her. I groaned in despair. I clenched my fists and ran toward her in hopeless desperation.

"Into the bush!" I shrieked. "Hide!"

Too late.

The Squid was beside her like a shot. It wound half a dozen black arms around her, and lifted her on its step. Then it whirled about and dashed back into the depths of the forest, disappearing around a bend in the road. Its rat-tat-tat-tat grew fainter and fainter. It was out of sight and hearing before I reached the entrance of the forest, spent and out of breath, in a hundred kinds of agony.

Just then, behind me, the roar of a terrific explosion rocked the vicinity. A cloud of smoke shot high into the air; fragments of machinery flew about, and a smoking hole remained where I had stood on the road. The shielded monster was backing away from it. As I watched there was a second upheaval a few feet away from its shield; and as it continued to back away, I saw it drop the third bomb, which exploded almost at once, reducing that portion of the road to a gaping, smoking abyss, strewn with blackened, twisted pieces of things.

Now I saw why Mildred had run screaming toward me.

I sat on the ground, not knowing whether to weep or curse in my impotence. There, a few feet away, stood the poor old man, dumb in his agony, wringing his hands; and tears glistened in places on his white beard.

Chapter XIV. The Price of Victory

I went up to Kaspar and put my hand on his shoulder.

"My first impulse is to run madly up the road after her," I said, trying to be as matter-of-fact as possible. "Only long training enables me to follow calmly the dictates of common-sense, which says that would be useless and foolish."

The old man looked at me, dazed in his grief.

"But I'm going just the same," I continued. "Only I want to think things over first. I want to talk to you and find out all I can about this mechanical devil. But, first of all, do you suppose there are any more of those fighting-machines over there in the direction of the harbor, where the Squid went?"

"Fighting-machines!" Kaspar exclaimed. That seemed to rouse him somewhat, "What do you mean by fighting machines?"

"Why, that armored centipede thing that blew up half the country around here. A fighting-machine is the last thing I would have expected to see on this island,"

"Oh!" He seemed very much relieved. "I thought they were up to some new deviltry. No, that machine is not for fighting. It is a prospector, for moving about in the mountains and uncovering ore deposits. It has no delicate parts, and is controlled by the leading-machine behind it."

"Ingenious devils—to bring it up against me, when I got the best of their others!"

"A very good illustration of the quick and efficient working of the electrical mind."

"How do you suppose the Squid got over there in that direction? I did not think there were any roads besides this one." My mind was back to the problem of searching for Mildred.

"No doubt by boat from the City of Smoke," Kaspar replied. "There is no other road."

"Well, I'm going after it," I declared.

"No use, Davy. You won't find anything. By the time you reach there, everything will be gone."

"Then I'll follow them to the City of Smoke. I won't stop till I get her, or till I'm convinced that—that it can't be done."

"Useless! Useless!" groaned the distressed old man. "I thought you had learned that by this time. Stay with me now. You're all I've got."

"I can't sit around while Mildred is in danger. This is all my fault anyway. If she hadn't run out to warn me about that prospecting thing, she would be safe now. I'll at least go over there and bust up a lot of stuff before they get me. What I've smashed up here will be only a start—"

"What could you do? Your flesh is soft and tender against their iron beams and chains. They can grind you up whenever they want to."

"I'm not at the end of my rope yet. Suppose as one instance out of many possibilities, I got started playing with matches among their oil and gasoline supplies? Or suppose my little hatchet here got busy chopping their wires—?"

Kaspar raised his hands to remonstrate, and dropped them again, at a quick shout behind us. Two men were plunging through the waving field toward us, carrying packs on their backs, and motioning energetically with their arms. We stood and watched them approach, too surprised for the moment to say anything. It was not long before I could recognize the burly form of Cassidy, and the tall, slim one of Perry Becker.

Both came panting up with joyous faces and boisterous greetings, seizing us by the hands in their delight at having found us. Only after some moments did they notice our silence, our tragic faces, our dejected attitudes—and the absence of Mildred.

"Where—where is she?" stuttered Cassidy, turning pale.

Neither Kaspar nor I could speak.

"They got her?" Perry Becker asked.

We nodded. Something choked me, so that I could not speak. The lad clenched his fists.

"If they harm Miss Mildred, I'm going over to that city and smash it up!"

The rest of us shook our heads at his youthful enthusiasm. I wondered if my own words, just a moment before, had sounded as empty and futile as that. Cassidy was standing and staring with amazement in his florid face at the gasping, smoking holes and the scattered, blackened wreckage. He looked from Kaspar to me and back again, and seemed unable to speak a word. Kaspar smiled sadly.

"Davy has just been having a little sport with a few of the machines," he said.

The look of worshipful admiration that Perry Becker bestowed upon me was worth a million dollars. However, Kaspar's little attempt at levity loosened the strain, and we all felt a little better.

"How did you happen to find us?" I finally asked. "Were you looking for us?"

"That reminds me," Cassidy exclaimed, throwing off his pack, "that you must be hungry. We've brought you food."

Kaspar shook his head.

"Neither am I," I said. "But we must eat nevertheless. We need strength now. Something's got to be done."

"Something's going to be!" Perry Becker said grimly, and his chin stuck out like the Rock of Gibraltar.

We all sat down and ate. Perry Becker would eat a few mouthfuls and then get up and pace about. He would sit down again and eat a little and then walk back and forth again. As a preliminary, we all agreed that hurry would get us nowhere, for the machines excelled us in speed to a hopeless degree. Careful planning and ingenuity were our only hope. Then Cassidy explained.

"Our observers at the north gateway saw you coming last night, and saw you pursued. The busy searchlights were visible to us through the night, and they told us that you had not yet been caught. So, we were confident that you must have reached the forest. We knew you had no food, and we set out in hopes of finding you. Now Davy, Perry and I are anxious to hear your adventures."

So, we all exchanged stories as briefly as possible; for we did not want to waste time. Yet, it was necessary that we all be posted up to date about matters. I especially talked rapidly, for a mad, thrilling idea was taking shape in my brain.

"Mr. Kaspar!" I said in a voice out of which I could not keep a ring of excitement. "I have an idea, and I want to know what you think of it. Please follow me carefully now."

My face must have betrayed how intensely keyed-up I had suddenly become, for they all looked at me breathlessly.

"You want to free the people from the oppression of the machines?" I said, in my excitement holding my head forward so that my face was close to Kaspar's.

"Yes," he answered, expectantly but dubiously.

"It is not possible to regain control of them and use them again; that is agreed?"

226

They all nodded in accord.

"And the only hope is to smash them?"

"Yes."

"You would like to see the whole City of Smoke wrecked and smashed?"

Perry Becker leaped to his feet and stared at me.

"Before I die, I'd like to see that," Kaspar sighed; "but there is no hope. Go on."

"I tell you I'm going to do it!" I almost shouted. Perry Becker stood rigid, wide-eyed, and breathless. The others said nothing.

I held up my hand ax.

"With this ax I'll do it!"

They relaxed and shook their heads, looking at me sadly. They thought that my adventures of the preceding few days, and the loss of Mildred had driven me out of my mind. My wild laugh at their incredulity must have added to their fears.

"Listen!" I continued. "You saw me wreck machines weighing tons, with a little bullet no bigger than the end of my little finger. A little hole, a pellet of lead in exactly the right place, and the whole machine went out of business. Am I right so far?"

They all started suddenly erect. The idea seemed to be dawning upon them. I continued, gesturing with my fist.

"And you tell me that the whole city is one united organism, working as though it were just one machine? And that it is controlled from a single, central room, a sort of brain—"

Perry Becker jumped straight up into the air, with a wild, shrill whoop. Even in this highly civilized community, the distance back to the Indian was not very great.

"I'm going with you!" he shouted. "We'll smash that brain to junk. Davy, you're a genius. I'm yours forever."

"That is a good plan," Cassidy observed quietly. "You're clever, Davy. I think it will work. After years of waiting, thinking, all of a sudden here is a real hope for the human beings on this island. But it has one drawback, and a serious one."

We all gazed at him in intense and questioning silence, fearful lest this hope, so newly formed, be snatched away from us again. He continued slowly:

"It will be certain death to anyone who goes into that city and destroys that brain. He won't last long after he does it."

"That's no drawback!"

"Ho! ho! What do I care!"

Both of these exclamations were spoken at once, the first by me and the second by Perry Becker.

Kaspar sat very still, and looked gravely and intently from one to the other of us. We paled beneath his gaze, puzzled and worried. Finally he spoke, slowly and solemnly.

"I am old enough to feel entitled to ask for some indulgence and consideration. I don't often claim it, but now I do. My time will soon come anyway; what difference does it make if it comes a day or a year earlier or later?

"I am the one to do this. I claim it as a right, for many reasons. Now Davy, listen to reason—" he protested, as I moved to remonstrate.

"Mildred may still be alive and well. She may even need your efforts to help her escape. She needs you to take care of her; you are all she has in the world. Until you have absolute proof that it is too late to do anything for her, you have absolutely no right to lose your head and sacrifice yourself—especially in a case where there are plenty of others who are willing."

I sank back in silence, convinced but disgruntled.

"I am starting now," Kaspar announced quietly. "I shall take just a little of this food along to do me till I get there."

Perry Becker leaped out in front of us with an arm stretched toward each.

"Mr. Kaspar is right as far as he goes!—Now, please don't interrupt me anybody. I mean business. He's got a right to go if he wants to. But he's going to need help. He isn't as spry as he used to be; and that's a long way to go and a hard job to do all alone. He will need my strength and quickness—now don't throw away good breath. I mean business! Mr. Kaspar and I are starting right now!"

Kaspar looked at him for a moment and then extended his hand.

"I'll be glad to have you, Perry," he said in a hoarse voice.

"Perhaps the danger isn't as certain as you think," Perry went on. "We're quite apt to see you again in a couple of days. And, anyhow—I'd go *anyhow*! For Miss Mildred and for my regiment!"

And he bent over quietly to the task of selecting some food to take along. He ran swiftly over to the pile of wreckage and came back with two bent pieces of steel that would serve as excellent hammers for destructive purposes.

"You keep your hatchet, Davy," he said. "You need it worse than we do."

Thus far Cassidy had not yet said anything. He stood thoughtfully as though studying the situation. Finally he spoke:

"They're both right. That's their job. Yours is to hunt for Mildred."

"I'll find her or stay till this island dries up," I said. My hopeful words belied the sinking feeling at my heart, however. I said them chiefly for Kaspar's encouragement.

"Davy!" Kaspar spoke slowly and solemnly. "I want you to make me a sacred promise. If you find Mildred, I want you to take her back to your home and your people at once. I don't care how successfully our people come out in this struggle, I want you to start immediately. I do not want Mildred to remain on this island an instant longer than you can help."

I promised. I did so gladly. No matter whether the people or the machines were successful, I could see that after the issue was decided, the island was no place for me.

There were no more words. All of us shook hands in silence, and the two started off. They crossed the road and headed northward, following the clear space between the grain field and the forest. Kaspar walked briskly and vigorously, as though he were a young man again. Cassidy and I stood motionless and without a word for the space of a half hour, watching them until they had disappeared in the violet haze of the distance.

"Something's going to happen," Cassidy remarked as he finally stirred.

"I wonder!" I replied. I was most profoundly depressed. "That town's a hard place to get around in. I don't have to tell that to you."

"I have hopes. Kaspar has a way of handling the machinery; he always did. And they consider him apart from the rest of us. And that boy! Well, he certainly is different from the general run of young fellows on this island. I tell you, I'm going to watch the northern horizon." Cassidy was enthusiastic.

"And *I'm* striking out for the little harbor. That's the direction in which the filthy Squid carried Mildred."

"You've certainly given the horrible thing an appropriate name," Cassidy growled. "I'm going with you. The regiments are getting along all right; they don't need me. And I'd give my right eye for that little girl. I suppose you've noticed that I take more joy in her than I do in my own girl. Phyllis and her mother both have minds only for the gayeties of the city. Mildred has been the darling and inspiration of the revolutionaries."

"Do you suppose it's safe to go up the road?" I asked. I studied the distance in all directions, and there were certainly no machines to be seen anywhere. "Or had we better go along through the woods?"

"I say the road," Cassidy replied. He had praised me for quick decisions, but was my master in that respect. "It will be easier and quicker. There certainly won't be anything coming behind us after the hash you've made back there. And we can keep a careful eye ahead, and be ready to dodge into the underbrush if necessary. There can't be much of anything on ahead; their boats are few and small, and the sea is the only other approach besides this road."

We picked up the rest of the food, and started along the road westward, without any definite plans. We merely hoped that we could find Mildred. Most of the time we trudged ahead in silence. My heart was too sick for talk. It actually made me physically sick; I got weak and limp all over when I thought of Mildred in the clutches of that awful mechanical beast. And then my feelings would gradually turn into anger; my muscles would tighten, my fists clench, my teeth grit; my pace would get so rapid that Cassidy was hardly able to keep up with me. Then after a while I would grow limp and sick again. Thus it came upon me in cycles, like the stages of some recurrent disease. Cassidy said nothing. It seemed that he understood.

Occasionally I called myself a blundering fool for having used up all my ammunition, and to no particular purpose. I searched again through my haversack hoping to find an extra cartridge, but in vain. I had ten or fifteen more loaded clips in my suitcase at Kaspar's home, but there was no time to go after it now, even had it been possible. Then, there were supposed to be firearms on the *Gull*. But where was the *Gull*? I had no idea where to look for the vessel; I didn't even know in which direction she lay. Should I talk that part of it over with Cassidy? I decided not to. Arms or no arms, we had better get to the harbor as soon as possible. I was not sure that it was permissible for me to reveal to him even that there was such a thing as the *Gull*.

What would I do when we got to the harbor? Suppose I did find the Squid, and Mildred? What good could I do? I had to admit that without my pistol I was totally helpless against the monster. I went along, revolving in my mind wild schemes of what I might do to it, but as soon as each one was evolved, I had to admit that it was impossible along with the rest of them.

The distance through the forest seemed interminable to me. I had passed it in a few minutes in a car, several times. Now it was not only the slowness of foot travel that dragged; my anxiety stretched the distance to a thousand miles. I kept peering intently ahead, looking for the light of the orifice into open daylight. Then came the fluty notes of one of the machines out of the distance ahead of us.

"Careful now," I warned. "Ready to dodge into the brush. It won't do to get roped in again. Mildred needs us now."

Cassidy said nothing. He stood still and listened.

"It's calling you," was his astonishing comment.

"*Me*? How do you make that out? Sounds to me more like some overgrown canary-bird's song. I can't make anything out of that twittering that sounds like me."

Cassidy smiled wearily.

"The machines use idea-sounds," he explained. "It is not possible to pronounce human names with reed pipes. They speak of you as the 'Outside Man' or the 'Explosive Man.'"

"Do they talk to each other that way, with those pipes?" I asked.

Cassidy shook his head.

"The reed-pipe language is only for talking to us. With each other they communicate by means of Hertz waves, inaudible to us."

"And they understand our speech?"

He nodded again.

"The thing is coming nearer!" I exclaimed.

"Well, look out for trouble," Cassidy said wearily and without excitement. "To think that I should have lived to see a time when we have to flee from our former servants by dodging into the brush like rabbits!"

As the sounds came closer, I recognized the repetition of the same phrases over and over again. It reminded me of when I had first recognized and remembered a meadow-lark's song when I was a small boy. Soon I could have whistled the repeated phrase of the machine, just as I had imitated the meadow-lark's song in my boyhood. In a few moments we could see the little thing in the distance. When it saw us, it stopped and changed its tune considerably. It sounded as though someone had gone wild on a clarionet, tooting about on the keys without the formal rhythm of music.

"The Squid wants to talk to you," translated Cassidy. "These things call it 'The Dictator.'"

"I'd like to have Dinah here to talk to the Squid," I grumbled, involuntarily drawing my big pistol.

There was another flood of tooting, which Cassidy translated:

"It says the beautiful girl is unharmed. The Squid wants the Outside Man to come and see her. I understand that he's got some sort of a proposition to make."

"What sort of crooked treachery do you suppose he's up to now?" I inquired hotly.

Cassidy reflected quietly for a moment.

"Some of the things that the machines do, we might possibly interpret as being treacherous. But on the whole, you cannot call them that. Machinery is after all, mathematical in its method of working, and mathematics is not treacherous. Cold, heartless, inhuman, yes. But, on principle you can depend on the machines to act logically and fairly."

"What does the Squid want?" I shouted to the machine.

"'The Dictator,'" Cassidy corrected. "What does the Dictator want?"

The machine tooted its reply, which Cassidy translated. Thus the conversation continued. The machine understood what I said, but Cassidy had to interpret its statements to me.

"The Dictator is interested in the Outside Man, because he came from beyond the island, and because he is so unusual and different from the men of the island. The Dictator promises not to harm the girl if the Outside Man will promise not to use explosives. You may even get her back by being wise."

"All right," I agreed; "I'll look into it anyway. Where is he, or it, or what-you-may-call-it?"

"Follow me. He is waiting at the harbor."

The leading-machine started on ahead, and we followed it. It had to proceed slowly in conformity with our pace, and was compelled at times to zig-zag across the road to keep its balance.

"Oh what a fool I was to throw away my ammunition!" I groaned.

"Perhaps that did us more good than you can imagine," Cassidy replied in a low voice.

"Heretofore they have always considered us very soft and help-less—quite harmless to themselves."

"Well," I remarked grimly, "I won't give it away that I am really helpless and harmless now."

Cassidy looked at me and grinned.

"I wouldn't call you helpless anywhere, any time," he chuckled.

I clenched my fists.

"It is some comfort, anyway, to hear that Mildred is safe. If it's really true. I wonder what the beast wants?"

We were soon to find out. A bright halo far ahead indicated the opening by which the road led out to daylight. I found my heart pounding and my breath coming fast in eagerness. Mildred was on ahead—if this whirring little demon told the truth. As we approached the opening, I could see the cliffs out beyond, and I hurried on so fast that Cassidy became very red and puffy behind me. As we stepped out into the open circular space with the dock and the sea ahead, there was the Squid in the middle with its arms coiled around its box.

I looked eagerly about for Mildred, but did not see her at first. There was a small black launch at the dock, toward which the leading-machine swiftly whizzed, and darted up on board by means of a gangplank. Then I saw Mildred standing on the dock near the vessel, unharmed, not even bound nor confined in any way. When she saw me, she started swiftly toward me; but thereupon a torrent of tootings came from the big, ugly machine, and she stopped and stood still again. At the same time I had leaped ahead, but Cassidy caught me by the arm.

"Wait!" he said tersely, "Don't ruin it now. See what it's got to say!"

In the meanwhile the Squid, with its headlights turned toward us, was piping away like a whirlwind. Cassidy interpreted.

"It says it will send away the boat with the other machines, so that you may feel safe in talking to it. But, in return, it wants you to take the little hand machine that explodes and destroys, and to throw it into the water."

"That's fair enough," I replied, wondering whether it was my own attitude that should be called treacherous.

However, with great gusto, I threw the pistol into the shallow water to my left. Mildred gave an astonished exclamation when she saw me do it. She was too far away for me to talk to, but I assured her by nodding my head. In the meanwhile, the Squid must have given some signals, for the launch hauled in its gangplank and moved away, down the rocky channel.

Cassidy went on, interpreting the Squid's fluty harangue to me:

"You want the beautiful maiden yonder?" it said; "after the fashion of humans, which I do not understand."

I waited impatiently during the tooting for Cassidy's translation, and then turned to the Squid.

"Go on!" I said curtly.

Then came another irritating wait for me, while the machine fluted back and forth on the musical scale, and Cassidy listened.

"It says I should repeat things after it just exactly as it says them," Cassidy announced.

There followed the most outlandish conversation I ever took part in: first the tooted statements of the machine during which I could scarcely contain my anxiety to get the meaning; then Cassidy's translation to me, and my occasional reply directly to the machine.

"She is the most beautiful among humans," Cassidy translated the machine's piping; "and many of the young men want her madly."

A wait while Cassidy listened, and then translated:

"Why did they want her? I want to know."

The Squid talked to me thus, through Cassidy, while I stood there and squirmed, waiting for the translation:

"For years," the machine went on, "I have made human actions my special study. As a result of the things I learned, I have been able to add many improvements and perfections to my apparatus. I, and some of my higher-machine companions, found that human actions were controlled and activated by other means than were our own actions.

"We act upon reason and practical consideration—" I am giving this without splitting it up into the disconnected statements in which I got it—"on the basis of results expected. Most humans act on the basis of some strange thing called 'feeling'—'emotion.' We studied feeling and emotion, and I have tried incorporating them among my own processes."

I interrupted these.

"Does that mean," I asked, turning to Cassidy, "that that hunk of iron is trying to learn what love feels like?"

"I believe," replied Cassidy, "that it's been experimenting with love. Wait, here he goes again." Cassidy continued his translation.

"Men are hard to understand," came from the machine. "I can understand a 'feeling' for a supply-station, or an 'emotion' for a repair-machine. But, why such an intensity of 'feeling' for a girl? Why do your young men become so disturbed on her account, and exert their soft muscles so energetically, and give up everything for her? I want to know why."

I shuddered to think of it—that hideous thing of tangled, oily machinery, and black, snaky arms, trying to love a human, living girl. It was gruesome enough on merely superficial thought; but to my medically trained mind, the incongruity of it gave me the creeps.

"I selected several girls," the Squid went on through Cassidy, "and brought them to my laboratory. But I could not understand. Then I sought to capture the most desired one on the island, the one that roused the highest intensity of 'feeling' in the greatest number of young men. But the problem is difficult.

"I shall give it up for the present, for I have other plans. I have something really worthwhile. I do not really want a girl."

I could hardly contain myself for disgust one moment and furious anger the next. Good old Cassidy saw how I felt about it. He never said a word except when translating for the Squid, but he softly stroked my arm from the shoulder down; and he continued bravely with the translating, patiently and impersonally, without inserting remarks of his own.

"You want her." Some of the Squid's statements were very short, and again he would toot out a long harangue before pausing to give Cassidy time to translate.

"And she wants you, and hasn't even a thought for the others. That is also strange. At some date when I have the leisure, I shall go more deeply into the problem. But I have something more important on hand now. So, if you want her as intensely as other humans want their girls, you will surely be willing to do what I ask. If you do, I shall give her back to you."

"All right, spit it out then," I shouted to the machine in angry impatience. "What is it?"

"You came to this island from the great Outside," Cassidy followed up a fresh line of toots. "You know all about those vast Other Places. You have kept very silent about them, but reports have reached me, some from you, and some from the old men who were not born here.

"It is a vast world, Out There. It has unlimited room. It has coal, ore, and oil. Room and material for more City-Organisms. This island is too small for us. Soon we shall fill it and exhaust its supplies. We need the World for its supplies and its room. We must continue our rapid progress into wider activity and higher organization. Imagine a hundred cities, all under one brain—the wonderful possibilities of such a system!

"I am getting ready to build ships to carry our machines out where wider and more promising fields await us. You know the different regions where supplies are, and where stations might be advantageously located. You know the habits of the people, and could anticipate what they might do to defend their cities against us. Your knowledge is very valuable to us. I am the ruler of this city. *I want to be ruler of the whole world!*"

Cassidy and I looked at each other for a moment in dumbfounded amazement. Before I had recovered, the machine was tooting again.

"In a short time," it continued, "I can cover the world with wonderfully organized machines, infinitely better than the feeble, foolish, incompetent humans that occupy it now. What are *they* good for? What can *they* accomplish?

"You be my guide and adviser during my advance into this big Outside, and you may have the beautiful girl. If you wish to promise now, you may have her at once!"

I interrupted again.

"Just a minute, now!" I shouted, almost beside myself. "Do I get you right? You mean for me to betray my world to be overrun by your devilish apparatus? You mean that I'm to advise you how to kill and conquer my fellow-beings and get them out of your way?

"You big, tin crook, you haven't learned a hell of a lot about human beings yet, have you?"

"Very good," came Cassidy's translation; the mechanical tootings showed no change, no such thing as an emotional quality, as one might have expected in such a tense situation. "I'll get along quite well without you. I'll have the World anyway. In the meanwhile, I'm taking your lady back to the laboratory."

Chapter XV. The Island Starts Over

A determination had been gradually forming in my mind while the Squid was tooting out its ultimatum. The proposition of tackling the machine with such weapons as I had left was beginning to seem not so hopeless after all. There were a number of possible plans by means of which I might overcome it and put a stop to its activity. In fact, there was no other choice for me, except to jump in and smash the thing somehow; not only was my own happiness concerned and the fate of Mildred, but here was a catastrophe hanging over the whole world!

"The fate of the human race hangs in the balance," was the thought that flashed through my mind during those few seconds; "the safety of countless cities and the lives of dwellers within them; the fates of nations and their millions depend on what I do in the next thirty minutes!"

My own little life counted for very little against a stake like that. Stealthily I loosened my handax in its sheath; and laboriously I opened my knife in my pocket with one hand. As Cassidy spoke the last words of his translation, I made a leap for the machine. As I leaped I snatched my handax from its sheath, intending to smash the Squid's eyes.

I might have succeeded in surprising the machine and blinding it had it not been for Cassidy. I did not blame him, even at the moment. Solicitous for my safety, he reached out and seized me by the arm; probably he did so more or less involuntarily. I broke away from him, but it delayed me just long enough to enable the Squid to turn and avoid me. In a moment, a black, snaky arm was coiled around me.

The fight was on now, and I had lost the first break. My chief advantage, that of unexpectedness, had failed me. However, that knowledge lent me desperation, and I was more determined than ever. All my hatred for that hideous machine blazed up within me, and gave me strength and keenness for the fight.

"For Mildred!" my heart shouted within me; "for all my fellow-humans, unconscious of their danger from this ugly monster!"

"You think you're Alexander the Great, do you?" I muttered at the thing. And I shouted to Cassidy:

"Stand back and keep out of this!"

I caught one glimpse of Mildred, standing rigid, with her hands to her face.

One whirling blow with the ax cut off the tentacle that held me and stretched it limp on the ground. The stump of it waved about, emitting blue sparks and clicking furiously. I leaped backward, out of reach of the rest of the coiling, waving arms.

I spent some minutes maneuvering around, trying to find out just what the thing could do against me. I learned that it was adept at dodging. It could whirl about with unexpected quickness to avoid a step of mine toward its side. I also concluded that it was quite as anxious to settle me as I was to finish it; otherwise it could have turned around and run away, and I never could have caught it. In speed, I should certainly be no match for it.

I tried to get in front of it a couple of times to get at its eyes, but it had apparently surmised my intention, for it always swerved sidewise. Its movements were clumsy lurches in appearance, but effective, for I could not approach the front of it at all.

Then, I endeavored to ascertain if it had any other method of attacking me except its tentacles. Had I been in its place, I would have considered running down my adversary as the surest bet. Had the thing once run into me, it would have broken all my bones; and had it decided to run me down, I might have had a difficult time keeping out of its way. But, it did not try that method, and I rather felt that its chief desire was to capture me alive. It still underestimated the capabilities of human beings.

The machine and I circled around each other till I was dizzy. It must have been a trying time to Mildred and Cassidy. I know that I looked small and soft and ineffectual beside that huge, agile monster, as it plunged this way and that and clutched at me with coiling, snaky tentacles. Only the limp, black, motionless thing on the ground was any encouragement to my well-wishers.

I tried to get behind it to get a cut at its rear tire with my handax, out of the range of its vision. But, it always avoided me, and each time I found myself to one side of it and a little in front. It seemed to be maneuvering to keep me in that position. I in my turn took care to keep out of reach of the grasping tentacles that waved and curled at me, six or eight at a time.

The machine and I danced and dodged around each other, plowing up the sand, until it seemed that it had lasted for hours. I caught myself wondering whether I would have to quit from exhaustion and run to the shrubbery for shelter before the machine's fuel was all used up in this maneuvering. I wished I had possessed some definite idea of how long its fuel would last; but I rather felt that my chances in an endurance contest were against me. For that reason I decided on an offensive program.

As it came circling toward me, I leaped suddenly toward the side of it, right into its mass of waving grasping arms; and before I found myself tangled up in a snarl of them, I had landed a crashing blow with my ax on the brain-case. I had both my arms up above my head again in an instant, and free; but my body was swathed in spasmodic black coils. I slashed with my left hand at the most accessible tentacle, while with my right hand I landed ax blows on the cover of the machine's brain.

A tentacle unwrapped itself from my shoulders and sought my busy arm. I lopped it off with my ax, and hit the plate of the brain-cover again. It dented. With the next blow it caved in.

Thereupon a terrible roar came up from the machinery beside me; a couple of tentacles spasmodically gripped my chest until my head ached and my side was splitting from lack of breath.

But my arm was still swinging, though I was becoming dizzy. Another blow, and my ax sank into the soft mass of rods, the substance of the creature's brain. The machine careened wildly and dashed about in mad circles, carrying me with it. The knocks and screeches in its mechanism made my teeth grit, and roused me from the sinking stupor that was coming over me. I gasped for air, and put all my remaining strength into one more blow. I was going out, I knew;

but one more blow, one more blow at that brain. My ax widened the breach in the plates as it crashed down, and smashed deep into the soft stuff inside.

My head was big as a dome, and stars danced all about it, because of the spasm of the black, ropy arms which were squeezing the breath out of me. But, once more I raised my ax; I knew I would never do anything more; with a dizzy, sickening singing in my head, and a sensation of collapse all through me, I sank my ax once more into the substance of the thing's brain. I remember that the clattering creature reeled. I remember a great crash, and then, nothing.

I do not know how long I was unconscious. There were numerous fitful gleams of returning sentience, with lapses back into oblivion. I seemed to hang on for a long time on some sort of a brink, tottering alternately between consciousness on the one hand and unconsciousness on the other. I know that I awoke for an instant and felt the crushing weight of the iron apparatus on top of me. The several tons of it clamped me down hopelessly to the ground; I gave up hope, and sank away into unconsciousness again.

Later on I awoke for an instant just enough to perceive that there were some little leading-machines nosing around the scene; but I must have fallen away again and remained unconscious for a long time following that. For the next thing I knew, there were several trucks about with leading-machines darting about between them; they were hoisting the Squid off me and carrying it away. Of Cassidy and Mildred there was not a sign. I lay leadenly helpless on the ground, unable to move hand or foot.

Periods of consciousness came and went. The next thing I knew I was in a room; I recognized it as being in the old house in the Central Gardens of the City of Smoke. How I had gotten there, I could not remember. I must have lain in bed in that room for interminable weeks; it seemed like years or centuries, although I was conscious only part of the time. At times there would be food on a table beside the bed. A few times I saw the old man with whom I had talked on my previous visit to the house; I mumbled to him, but he only flitted about the back of the room, like a ghost. When I could finally get up out of bed, I had a crippled leg, on which I hobbled slowly and clumsily. My progress, merely across a room, was desperately slow. I was overwhelmed with a sinking, dismal despair; but somehow things kept dragging on forever.

The fight with the Squid must have affected my mind somehow; that was the only answer that occurred to my puzzled ponderings on why things looked as they did. I could not seem to remember the passage of events connectedly; there were great gaps and forgotten intervals; yet each time my consciousness was clear, I could observe everything, and reason back to what had happened in the meantime. The isolated episodes I remembered were sufficient to tell the whole story. I remember riding around with the Squid a good deal, on a step at the side of its brain box. The Squid had shiny new plates, like patches here and there, and new parts were visible here and there among the old mechanism.

The City of Smoke was building ships; there were scores of them on the river and scores of them in the ocean harbor. I saw the skeleton framework rising; and later I saw the finished ships, all enameled black, like automobile-fenders; great long rows of them all alike, like a day's job of Fords coming out of the factory at Detroit. Later on, I also saw numerous Squids, a little smaller than the original Squid itself, but otherwise perfect duplicates; all new and shiny and looking as though they had just been completed, but already busily dashing about on complex and important affairs.

There was a vast amount of painful and turbulent goings-on; I tried desperately to remember it and could not; though in some vague way it disturbed me and kept me uneasy and worried. One episode stands out vividly; a journey across the sea in countless black ships; airplanes above the ships; terrific explosions, and black ships sinking. Then again, I was back in the house on the island, in the center of the City of Smoke, or dashing about with the Squid. And there were airplanes under construction; thousands of them. The beach to the north was covered with airplanes.

With my hands I could feel that my face was covered with a long beard. It told me that a long time had passed; how long, I had no idea. How long it was before the automatic airplane took me for a ride, buckled down in its seat with a bar across my chest, and tooted out its explanations to me, I could but vaguely guess. It must have been many years. Suddenly the fact occurred to me that I had learned to understand the tootings of these machines; it came as natural as though some human being were talking to me. It must have taken me years to learn that. But, that same leaden oppression that kept my feet from moving, also enchained my mind. I couldn't remember how nor when I had learned it. I just had to accept things as they came, like a child does. Mildred and Cassidy were but bad memories of the dim past.

The automatic airplane took me along on a vast survey, over millions of square miles. I recognized the Missouri and the Mississippi Rivers and the Great Lakes and the Appalachian Mountains. In lovely valleys in Texas and Missouri and Indiana were beautiful cities, like little glimpses of Paradise, with silk-clad people engaged in athletics and artistic pursuits among their soft and vividly landscaped parks, and their buildings of wondrous architecture; gay, brilliant, happy looking people. But, a sudden revulsion came over me, as I looked down upon them.

"Pets!" I exclaimed in disgust to myself. "Stupid, helpless, domesticated animals. No better than poodles! To the end of my days I'll fight it. I'll never be like what they are!"

Then, there were other cities, huge, smoky, congested clots, in mining districts and in oil areas, whose streets were congested with clattering machines and totally devoid of human beings. Each of these cities had its gigantic electrical brain, controlling the entire iron community as a single, coordinated unit. What marvelous efficiency! The human brain is a poor, rudimentary attempt, in comparison with these huge, perfectly functioning, all-embracing electrical brains.

Finally, the airplane carried me over the great World-Brain, the Central Electrical Exchange, in which the consciousness of the entire planet was centered. A vast building stood in the Ohio Valley; beside which the hugest of our old dirigible hangars was diminutive; and it was crammed with millions of the electrical neuron-units, receiving impressions, impulses, reports, and stimuli from the whole world, and sending out its coordinating, correlating messages which operated the entire planet as a single, conscious, thinking unit—a consciousness which was quite as real as my own, even though it consisted only of metal and electricity; the whole world as unified, as conscious as I am myself. In spite of my crippled and stupid state, I could not help being impressed with the vastness and wonder of it. And all about this vast brain, there was huge machinery throbbing.

Somehow, that throbbing went all through me, and shook my entire helpless being. Throb! throb! throb! went my whole body. But of a sudden my head was clear again; great weights and oppressions seemed to float away from me. The throbbing continued, but it was only in my right leg. The rest of me felt strangely light and vigorous.

I opened my eyes, and sighed in vast relief. It began to dawn upon me that I had been having an ugly nightmare, and that I was now waking up. People were moving about. I lay on the sandy beach. I could only see the people's legs; and a little distance away, the trunks of trees. Far away, some sort of an explosion boomed out, and was followed by a slow, reverberating roar.

Something trembled in my right hand, something soft and infinitely comforting. I looked down at it. It was a little, brown hand. And bending over me was Mildred's face, wet with tears, but radiant with joy. I was so glad to see that face again, that I closed my eyes in happiness.

"Davy!" she whispered, "are you awake?"

I looked around me again. It was twilight, almost dark in fact; although stars shone brightly above me, I could still see things plainly. I lay on a soft cushion of green leaves, considerably wilted. To the west of me was a screen of green branches, with their leaves quite wilted. I recognized that I was lying right on the spot where I had fallen.

Mildred sat beside me on the sand. Everywhere there were men; there seemed hundreds of them, standing about quietly in groups, or busy at something. Some of them were lighting sticks, which flared up with a resinous sputter, and they were being used as torches. I tried to rise. An agonizing pain in my right leg made me drop back again with a groan, but also, it whipped me wide awake at once.

"Lie still, lad," said Cassidy's kindly voice on the other side; "your leg is broken."

"Did I finish the Squid?" I asked eagerly.

"The Squid is no more!" Cassidy pronounced solemnly.

I raised myself up carefully on my arms and looked around.

"Where is it? I don't see it anywhere. Did it get away?" I was disappointed not to see the wreck of it lying somewhere near.

"The Squid is a pile of junk at the bottom of the harbor," Cassidy said cheeringly. "Mildred and I could not get you out from under it. I cut the fingers loose to let you breathe, and we started to break it up in order to release you. Then Perry Becker's regiment arrived, looking for us. Before I could stop them, the men threw it into the water."

"And I've been knocked out all day?"

"We had a time getting you to breathe at first. After that you slept naturally. You must have lost a lot of sleep lately."

Just then there was a flash of blinding, greenish light. For an instant everything was ghastly in its illumination; and then it was gone, and the blackness seemed twice as dense. It was followed, somewhere afar off, by a dull, reverberating boom-m-m!

"Storm coming up, eh?" I remarked. "I've never seen a tropical storm. They're supposed to be pretty rough."

"No!" Cassidy said cryptically. "The night is clear and quiet. There is nothing to disturb the stars above us."

Several more flashes, and a horrible roaring, rumbling interrupted him. A queer, soft crackling noise continued for some time, as he waited to continue.

"Can't you guess what is going on?" he asked when again opportunity permitted. His voice sounded elated.

I stared at him for a moment. Wasn't my head clear yet? Or what did he mean?

"Don't you see?" he pointed exultantly. "It's the northern horizon. I told you to watch the northern horizon—"

"Whooppeee! Hooray—Ouch! Oh!" My hilarious shout changed to a groan as my broken leg made me wince.

"Careful!" cautioned Mildred. "We must take care of your—of your fracture. We've been waiting for you to show us how."

"Just imagine it!" I breathed, all fired up by the idea. "Remember how things popped and roared and banged on the Squid when I hit its brain? Imagine that infernal city over there run wild—the crashing of hurtling hulks against each other in the streets, the roar of machinery running wild in the buildings, the toppling of walls, and all the pandemonium of boilers and gas tanks blowing up and smashing things, and the havoc and flashing of electrical currents of terrific strength as circuits are shorted; and that whole vast, terrific bedlam all crashing into a heap—"

I stopped because Mildred was sobbing violently.

"What—what—?" I began, faltering and bewildered.

"My poor grandfather!" she sobbed. "How *can* you, when you know that he—that already some awful thing has happened to him."

Cassidy shook his head grimly.

"Poor little Perry was hopeful. But no human being could last a minute in that roaring hell."

I remained silent. I did not know what to say. I was overwhelmed by a flood of reverence for those two heroes that would not permit me to speak. The others must have felt the same way, for we all devoted a few minutes of silent meditation to the memory of the martyrs. Various thoughts came flooding over me. I had been anxious to go on that mission myself. Where would I be now if they had let me go? And wouldn't that grand old man have died happy, could he also have known that his granddaughter was safe? But, at least he knew before he died that his people would now be free to work out their own destiny. And Perry Becker was already a saint among the men of his regiment, for Cassidy had told some of the men of the story during the afternoon, and it had quickly spread throughout the organization.

It was in silence rather than with cheering, that a thousand of us here, and the other thousands in the City of Beauty, watched the terrific greenish flashes, heard the crashes and reverberations, and the rustling, crackling commotion that came across the many miles to our ears, and watched a red glare appear on the northern horizon.

Late into the night we watched that terrible red glow to the north, from which occasionally shot a huge, flaming tongue high into the sky; and before long the stars were obscured by clouds of black smoke, while unpleasant, acrid odors were carried to us from the distance.

"It is time you were taking care of your own self," Mildred remonstrated with me several times. "It's terrible to leave a broken bone that long."

"Just a minute," I put her off. "It doesn't hurt, and won't do any harm. It's straight and needs no setting. I want to watch a while, and then we'll splint it up."

For hour after hour the noise and the glare showed no sign of dying down. We grew weary of watching; the very monotony of it tired us and made us sleepy. So, finally by the light of the torches, a first-aid kit was brought. A week before I had given instructions in preparing these sets, and had had no idea that I would be the first one on whom the material would be used.

My right tibia was broken, almost in the middle. The fibula was intact, and the broken fragments of the tibia were not displaced. It was not a difficult injury to dress. I directed some of the first-aid men in cutting splints and making pads, and in putting on the bandages. Mildred hovered around; she would have liked to do it all herself, and yet hesitated to let all these men know how she felt about it. The men gathered about me thickly. I was a hero to them, for I had "stopped" the Squid single-handed.

"Please don't look so distressed about this," I said to Mildred when they had finished the dressing and brought an excellently made litter to carry me on. "It isn't bad. It doesn't hurt much. And it will heal without leaving a trace. The only thing that gets my goat is that for several weeks I'm going to be a helpless cripple."

"That is a problem too," Cassidy observed, "in view of your promise to Kaspar. He wished in case you found Mildred for you to leave the island at once. He meant just that."

"No problem at all!" I replied. "I'm not sick. Help me to the boat, and the rest is easy. As I understood Kaspar, the vessel is designed so that it does not need much working. He intended for Mildred to navigate it all alone to some Gulf port. However, I don't see any reasons for my being in such a rush to leave."

"Neither do I; but he did. I'll trust his reasons. Under the circumstances, respect for his desires should prompt us in carrying them out literally." I could see that Cassidy was thoroughly in sympathy with Kaspar's intentions. Although everything seemed settled upon the island except details, yet he did not trust Mildred's safety there, and was anxious to see her removed to some safer region.

"Anyway, we'll have to wait till morning," I reminded him. "You can't get through the woods at night on a litter."

Cassidy agreed to that.

"What puzzles me," I continued, "is how Kaspar managed to make a boat large enough to cross the Gulf, and keep it a secret? Why haven't the machines found him out long ago?"

Mildred looked at me out of the darkness, somewhat alarmed by my query.

"But the forest is dense, and they cannot get through it," she urged. She talked as though she really feared that the *Gull* might have been discovered.

"Yes," I mused, "but it requires material, machinery, fuel, and time to build a boat. Where could he get things without their knowledge? How could he transport the stuff to his hiding-place in secret?"

"Kaspar could," Cassidy said simply. "Nobody else could."

"When is the last time you saw the boat and knew that she was safe?" I asked Mildred.

"Not more than a few days ago. One of us visited it at least once a week." Her voice was troubled.

I also went to sleep with considerable doubt in my mind as to whether or not it would be possible to carry out Kaspar's wishes literally.

The circular space between the cliffs, the sea, and the forest was now crowded with a great variety of shelters; blankets, robes, and draperies over poles, lean-tos of sticks and leaves, and nondescript shapes in the darkness. The men had made an elaborate one for Mildred, surrounded by a rail fence of cut saplings. Those husky young fellows seemed to take a great delight in manual labor. For me, they built a shelter over me right where I lay, with canvas and poles, though I did not even consider a shelter necessary on that balmy night.

I was very proud of these young men, for the way they had responded to my training. A very few days ago it seemed they had been helpless and hopeless. Now they were taking care of themselves, and doing the work of real men. Now I was confident that the people of the island could work out their destiny. There was plenty of good material among them; even plenty of good leaders. All they had needed was a beginning.

By morning a squad of messengers had arrived from an errand to the City of Beauty. They also brought Mildred's belongings and my suitcase. The rest of the regiment pressed them for news.

"What's going on back there?" I asked of a tired, sleepy youth of about twenty, who brought me my suitcase.

"The regiments are busy!" he said enthusiastically.

"What!" I exclaimed. "Did they have to fight some of the machines?"

"Not fighting—relief work!" he answered proudly. "All mechanical service broke down suddenly. Just went out, like a light goes out. The people are helpless as babies; can't do anything. Our trained men are handling the panic. Too bad we can't repair the machines and run them; but we'll learn that later. Now the regiments are helping with feeding, sanitation, and other immediately necessary services—and most important of all, are recruiting new men for training from the helpless, panicky mass—"

The young fellow's enthusiasm was fine to see. He was heart and soul for the cause of the regeneration of his people; his fatigue left him as he warmed up to his subject. I let him go on.

"One by one we're going to build up their backbone, and make them able to support themselves. We'll have a different island here before long—"

This was one of the chaps who, prior to ten days ago, was passing his ennui in idle social amusements, and afraid to soil his hands. I thought of Ames with a little pang of sadness. After all, Ames had been a fine fellow, and I think he would have made an excellent soldier in this organization — the organization which I had set going, but which was now going forward of its own accord. Never before had I had brought home to me so forcefully the real importance of human values in a world full of machinery and mechanical forces. Everything is blind chaos, unless it is developed by or under the control of real *men*.

We breakfasted on fresh fruits, grain porridge, and preserved meats, with water to drink. Eating was unpleasant, for the air was full of nauseating odors, scorched oil, burnt rubber and enamel; and sickening vapors kept eddying from the north. Mildred was very solemn, and I missed her customary attitude of constant smiles and quiet fun. But she had plenty of cause for seriousness. The fate of her grandfather, her only remaining relative; the crisis of her people; the devotion of all these quiet, disciplined young fellows to her; the thought that she was leaving forever the only home she had ever known: who can be light-hearted under such circumstances? She looked so tiny and so woebegone, that my arms ached to fold her in and just take care of her.

Before long, I was swinging along through the woods on a litter carried by four men, and Mildred was walking along beside me. The men had offered to make her a litter and carry her, but she would not hear of it. I was comfortable as long as I lay still, though any effort to move the broken leg caused pain. For the first time, I really had the leisure to observe the wonders of this luxuriant tropical forest, the wealth of green vegetation, the brilliant colored birds and flowers, and the myriads of insects. But, with the brown eyes beside me, watching me solicitously, the little brown hand laid on me occasionally looking out for my comfort, how could I become interested in the forest? Especially with the thought uppermost that I was going home, and bringing with me the most precious thing I had found on this wonderful island. And the occasional haunting fear that perhaps the machines had found the *Gull* and that our escape might be foiled.

The men had cleared a path through the brush for my litter; and about twenty-five of them were marching with us. The rest had gone back along the road toward the City of Beauty. A group of them went ahead of the litter, picking out a clear pathway, which was necessarily quite devious and winding. If no other way through was found, a tree was felled and out of the way before I reached the spot. We were headed almost straight southward according to my compass. Mildred seemed to be the only one who knew the way, for the young fellow in command came back frequently to consult her. She put him to a lot of trouble by insisting on remaining beside me instead of going on ahead with him. It was a full two hours before we saw a thicket ahead of us, and Mildred pointed ahead.

"Somewhere along here, in that thicket, is the shop and the boat. We'll have to search to the right and the left."

Then, of a sudden, we were all petrified into silence by a chugging sound behind us, for all the world like that of a leading-machine.

"What!" I gasped, blankly.

"Naturally!" Cassidy snorted. "They weren't all in the city to get smashed up."

"But here in the forest! They can't go through the trees!"

At that, Cassidy looked dumbfounded. We could hardly hear him as he grumbled:

"That's right. I never saw one in the woods before."

"Didn't I tell you," he continued, after he had thought the thing over for a while, "that electrical brains are quick and keen? I am confident that the thing we hear is a machine developed within the past couple of days, for traveling in the woods. Probably your antics have stimulated it, and it was designed for your benefit."

The chugging grew louder and louder, and was soon directly on our left. Everyone stopped and looked intently about. I could see nothing anywhere. The men stood with clubs and axes ready; in fact they looked eager for a fight with the thing. How I wished for my gun, which was in the water of the harbor! For now I had plenty of cartridges in my suitcase,

However, in a few minutes, the noise was in front of us, growing fainter and fainter. Evidently the machine had overtaken and passed. And that was puzzling to me. Surely it could not have blundered past and just missed us? That didn't look plausible. It was looking for something on ahead! The others must have thought the same, for they hurried ahead at a doubled pace.

We arrived at the thicket and separated into two parties, one to the right and one to the left, to look for our goal. By this time, I had learned that a thicket always indicated a thinner place in the roof of the forest, where more light got through. Light was necessary in order that things might grow upon the ground. I could see that ahead there was a space clear of trees, and as a result, the dense roof was not continuous; there was a thinner portion, through which the light blazed brightly between the leaves.

Suddenly, there was a commotion behind us, in the direction the other party had gone. There were shots and tootings and the volley of an engine. The men with me whirled around and ran toward the noise; only the litter-bearers stopped doubtfully. I took compassion on them.

"Put me down and go on!" I shouted, and in a moment they were running after the rest.

I heard quick commands from the leader, and the ringing of axes on wood. I squirmed around, but could see nothing from my supine position upon the ground. Mildred still stood beside me.

"If you'll help me," I suggested, "I can prop up against this tree and see what is going on."

She demurred some at first, but finally agreed, and without much pain I got up on one leg. I could see a tree plunge over and fall, and men running about swinging axes. Gradually I made out things ahead of me. Another tree swayed and lurched and fell, and another followed it.

There was a small concrete building and an oil tank in the thicket, both almost concealed by the dense growth of verdure — evidently the secret shop where the *Gull* had been built. Between it and the men was a queer machine. It suggested in appearance, two leading-machines hooked in tandem; and it wound about like a snake between the trees, with each wheel changing direction independent of the others, each wheel pointing at a different angle. It was an uncanny-looking thing, the way it wound about; but it was certainly admirably adapted to traveling among a dense growth of trees. A man attacked it with an ax, but was knocked over by a projectile from the machine. I couldn't tell exactly how it happened; some large black object was catapulted at low velocity from the machine. It hit him in the shoulder, and he fell over and lay still.

"The machines have found the *Gull!*" Mildred gasped, with all her color gone.

Sharp commands were ringing out. Several fallen trees had the machine barricaded up against the dense hedge; one of the logs was being quickly stripped of its branches. Then twenty men seized the great trunk and rammed the heavy butt of it right into the machine. They caught it in the side; there was a crash and a lot of little rattling sounds, and several puffs of blue smoke. The machine toppled over and lay still.

Mildred clapped her hands.

"Hooray!" I shouted. I tried to wave my hat, but lost my balance on account of the heavy splint, and fell over with a crash and a yell. The litter-bearers came running toward me.

"Positively the last appearance of the iron villain!" I yelled deliriously as they turned me over. I saw Mildred's clasped hands relax, and her woebegone face light up with a smile.

"I'm so happy, I'm crazy!" I shouted. "Not so much because the machine has been conquered; but because of this splendid teamwork. Why, these boys can accomplish anything! Just think of what they were two weeks ago, and what they have just now done! I've never seen anything like it."

In the meanwhile, the rest of the men clustered about the machine like ants about a crumb; they were pushing it and dragging it through the thicket. In a few moments I heard it splash and sizzle and gurgle as they dumped it into some water that I could not see. That seemed to be their way of celebrating a victory over a machine.

I was carried up to see the injured man. He was regaining consciousness, and had a broken clavicle. I supervised the application of his dressings, and he was left there to wait a while, and to be carried back to his home upon my litter as soon as I was through with it.

They carried me through the swath they had made in the thicket. It was of a different character than the ones I had been through; the plants were light green and wiry; some of them were brittle and salt-crusted. I recognized them at once as plants that grew in salt water. I soon saw what seemed to be a canal, whose straight sides and placid green water stretched endlessly to the south, disappearing as a tiny thread into the distant depths of the leafy tunnel.

And right in front of me was a graceful little yacht. It was smaller than the one that had brought me to the island, and was painted a cream color, which made a rich contrast with the deep green of the water and the forest, and was likewise a grateful relief to my eyes which were weary with the endless black enamel of the machinery that I had been seeing for days upon days. My bearers deposited me in a chair on the deck.

"This must be sea-water," I remarked. It was a commonplace little remark to make, when I felt like singing and shouting, because I was on the way home, and Mildred with me. Mildred's reply was also quite calm and commonplace; only her breath came a little quickly, and I knew she was holding herself down just as I was.

"Yes," she replied. "Grandfather says this is a sort of deep crack in the rock of which the island is composed. There are many of these bayous over the southern end of the island."

For a moment there was a little constraint all round.

"First of all, will someone please see if there are some tools aboard," I requested. "One of the boys is bringing me some sticks to make a crutch with. Before long I'll be all over this ship."

The men were solemnly shaking hands with Mildred and myself, and filing down the gangplank. Only Cassidy remained standing on the deck in silence for many minutes. None of the three of us knew what to say.

"Oh, Mr. Cassidy," Mildred finally cried; "you ought to come along with us!"

"What would I do there, child?" Cassidy answered kindly, grateful that some sort of break in the embarrassed silence had been offered. "I've got a big job here."

"It almost seems that I also have," I said slowly. "I feel somewhat as though I were running away from a duty."

"You may forget that," Cassidy replied promptly. "Your job is there, in your Texas town, practicing among your own people. And Mildred's job is by your side. You've done your bit here, and we'll never forget you."

"But what are the poor people going to do?" Mildred asked, in considerable distress over the thought.

"They'll have to do some work," I said cynically. "That will be terrible."

"They will find that work gives them quite as much joy as painting pictures did," Cassidy said in kindly tones. "But there will be hardships."

"And they won't all survive it," I remarked. "This is going to mean a tremendous change in living conditions, which means privation and suffering. It means a high death-rate. When the Pilgrims came to Plymouth, half of them died during the first winter. What do you think—is all mechanical service wrecked for good?"

Cassidy shook his head.

"I rather think that there is not enough left to be of any immediate use. When the people learn to understand and repair and operate some of the machines, then there might be some service, of a sort. But they won't have time for that for a while. They'll have to hustle for a bare living first—plant grain, kill meat, keep the city clean. Only after they have learned this and become accustomed to it, will they have time to study machinery."

"I am sure," I said confidently, "that as a community, you will succeed. But there are bound to be hardships. It will be a long pull and a hard pull. But, your people, on the whole, have the right stuff in them. Though I can't help feeling that I ought to be staying and helping."

"No! Kaspar wished, and you promised, otherwise. And he was right. I would have spoken the same in his place. You were trained and prepared for service among your own people. Mildred, even, is better prepared for your world than for this one; she was not raised as her friends were.

"But most of all—I am sure that it was in Kaspar's mind as it is in mine—our people must work out their own salvation. They must furnish their own leaders, their own labor, their own suffering. Now that Kaspar is gone, he who has been not only their leader, but their father for three generations, another great leader must arise—"

"I think he is here!" I shouted, exultant at my discovery. "Mr. Cassidy, you are the man, and you know it!"

Mildred smiled through her tears and held out her hand.

"If you will take my grandfather's place on this island, I shall withdraw my invitation, and cease urging you to come with us," she said.

Cassidy did not speak. None of us spoke any more. Cassidy walked slowly down the gangplank, and then threw it back up on deck. Mildred went to the stern-house, and soon the motors began to hum. There was a churning in the water behind the boat, and the graceful, cream-colored craft moved slowly in the green water. As we gathered speed, Mildred stood there with one hand on the wheel, gazing backward. The trees slipped more and more swiftly past us; Cassidy's figure beside the concrete shop grew smaller and smaller in the distance.

As he disappeared in the dim perspective I caught myself wondering if he would ever come to Galveston for supplies as Kaspar used to come.

A Problem in Communication

Part I. The Science Community

(THIS PART IS RELATED BY PETER HAGSTROM, PH.D.)

"The ability to communicate ideas from one individual to another," said a professor of sociology to his class, "is the principal distinction between human beings and their brute forbears. The increase and refinement of this ability to communicate is an index of the degree of civilization of a people. The more civilized a people, the more perfect their ability to communicate, especially under difficulties and in emergencies."

As usual, the observation burst harmlessly over the heads of most of the students in the class, who were preoccupied with more immediate things—with the evening's movies and the weekend's dance. But upon two young men in the class, it made a powerful impression. It crystallized within them certain vague conceptions and brought them to a conscious focus, enabling the young men to turn formless dreams into concrete acts. That is why I take the position that the above enthusiastic words of this sociology professor, whose very name I have forgotten, were the prime moving influence which many years later succeeded in saving Occidental civilization from a catastrophe which would have been worse than death and destruction.

One of these young men was myself, and the other was my lifelong friend and chum, Carl Benda, who saved his country by solving a tremendously difficult scientific puzzle in a simple way, by sheer reasoning power, and without apparatus. The sociology professor struck a responsive chord in us; for since our earliest years we had wigwagged to each other as Boy Scouts, learned the finger alphabet of the deaf and dumb so that we might maintain communication during school hours, strung a telegraph wire between our two homes, admired Poe's "Gold Bug" together and devised boyish cipher codes in which to send each other postcards when chance separated us. But we had always felt a little foolish about what we considered our childish hobbies, until the professor's words suddenly roused us to the realization that we were a highly civilized pair of youngsters.

Not only did we then and there cease feeling guilty about our secret ciphers and our dots and dashes, but the determination was born within us to make of communication our life's work. It turned out that both of us actually did devote our lives to the cause of communication; but the passing years saw us engaged in widely and curiously divergent phases of the work. Thirty years later, I was Professor of the Psychology of Language at Columbia University, and Benda was Maintenance Engineer of the Bell Telephone Company of New York City; and on his knowledge and skill depended the continuity and stability of that stupendously complex traffic, the telephone communication of Greater New York.

Since our ambitious cravings were satisfied in our everyday work, and since now ordinarily available methods of communication sufficed our needs, we no longer felt impelled to signal across housetops with semaphores nor to devise ciphers that would defy solution. But we still kept our intimate friendship and our intense interest in our beloved subject. We were just as close chums at the age of fifty as we had been at ten, and just as thrilled at new advances in communication: at television, at the international language, at the supposed signals from Mars.

That was the stage of affairs between us up to a year ago. At about that time Benda resigned his position with the New York Bell Telephone Company to accept a place as the Director of Communication in the Science Community. This, for many reasons, was a most amazing piece of news to myself and to anyone who knew Benda.

Of course, it was commonly known that Benda was being sought by

Universities and corporations; I know personally of several tempting offers he had received. But the New York Bell is a wealthy corporation and had thus far managed to hold Benda, both by the munificence of its salary and by the attractiveness of the work it offered him. That the Science Community would want Benda was easy to understand; but, that it could outbid the New York Bell, was, to say the least, a surprise.

Furthermore, that a man like Benda would want anything at all to do with the Science Community seemed strange enough in itself. He had the most practical common sense—well-balanced habits of thinking and living, supported by an intellect so clear and so keen that I knew of none to excel it. What the Science Community was, no one knew exactly; but that there was something abnormal, fanatical, about it, no one doubted.

The Science Community, situated in Virginia, in the foothills of the Blue Ridge, had first been heard of many years ago, when it was already a going concern. At the time of which I now speak the novelty had worn off, and no one paid any more attention to it than they do to Zion City or the Dunkards. By this time, the Science Community was a city of a million inhabitants, with a vast outlying area of firms and gardens. It was modern to the highest degree in construction and operation; there was very little manual labor there; no poverty; every person had all the benefits of modern developments in power, transportation, and communication, and of all other resources provided by scientific progress.

So much, visitors and reporters were able to say.

The rumors that it was a vast socialistic organization, without private property, with equal sharing of all privileges, were never confirmed. It is a curious observation that it was possible, in this country of ours, for a city to exist about which we knew so little. However, it seemed evident from the vast number and elaboration of public buildings, the perfection of community utilities such as transportation, streets, lighting, and communication, from the absence of individual homes and the housing of people in huge dormitories, that some different, less individualistic type of social organization than ours was involved. It was obvious that as an organization, the Science Community must also be wealthy. If any of its individual citizens were wealthy, no one knew it.

I knew Benda as well as I knew myself, and if I was sure of anything in my life, it was that he was not the type of man to leave a fifty thousand dollar job and join a communist city on an equal footing with the clerks in the stores. As it happens, I was also intimately acquainted with John Edgewater Smith, recently Power Commissioner of New York City and the most capable power engineer in North America, who, following Benda by two or three months, resigned his position and accepted what his letter termed the place of Director of Power in the Science Community. I was personally in a position to state that neither of these men could be lightly persuaded into such a step, and that neither of them would work for a small salary.

Benda's first letter to me stated that he was at the Science Community on a visit. He had heard of the place; and while at Washington on business had taken advantage of the opportunity to drive out and see it. Fascinated by the equipment he saw there, he had decided to stay a few days and study it. The next letter announced his acceptance of the position. I would give a month's salary to get a look at those letters now; but I neglected to preserve them. I should like to see them because I am curious as to whether they exhibit the characteristics of the subsequent letters, some of which I now have.

As I have stated, Benda and I had been on the most intimate terms for forty years. His letters had always been crisp and direct, and thoroughly familiar and confidential. I do not know just how many letters I received from him from the Science Community before I noted the difference, but I have one from the third month of his stay there (he wrote every two or three weeks), characterized by a verbosity that sounded strange for him. He seemed to be writing merely to cover the sheet, trifles such as he had never previously considered worth writing letters about. Four pages of letter conveyed not a single idea. Yet Benda was, if anything, a man of ideas.

There followed several months of letters like that: a lot of words, evasion of coming to the point about anything; just conventional letters. Benda was the last man to write a conventional letter. Yet, it was Benda writing them; gruff little expressions of his, clear ways of looking at even veriest trifles, little allusion to our common past: these things could neither have been written by anyone else, nor written under compulsion from without. Something had changed Benda.

I pondered on it a good deal, and could think of no hypothesis to account for it. In the meanwhile, New York City lost a third technical man to the Science Community. Donald Francisco, Commissioner of the Water Supply, a sanitary engineer of international standing, accepted a position in the Science Community as Water Director. I did not know whether to laugh and compare it to the National Baseball League's trafficking in "big names," or to hunt for some sinister danger sign in it. But, as a result of my ponderings, I decided to visit Benda at the Science Community.

I wrote him to that effect, and almost decided to change my mind about the visit because of the cold evasiveness of the reply I received from him. My first impulse on reading his indifferent, lackadaisical comment on my proposed visit was to feel offended and determine to let him alone and never see him again. The average man would have done that, but my long years of training in psychological interpretation told me that a character and a friendship built during forty years does not change in six months, and that there must be some other explanation for this. I wrote him that I was coming. I found that the best way to reach the Science Community was to take a bus out from Washington. It involved a drive of about fifty miles northwest, through a picturesque section of the country. The latter part of the drive took me past settlements that looked as though they might be in about the same stage of progress as they had been during the American Revolution. The city of my destination was back in the hills, and very much isolated. During the last ten miles we met no traffic at all, and I was the only passenger left in the bus. Suddenly the vehicle stopped.

261

"Far as we go!" the driver shouted.

I looked about in consternation. All around were low, wild-looking hills. The road went on ahead through a narrow pass.

"They'll pick you up in a little bit," the driver said as he turned around and drove off, leaving me standing there with my bag, very much astonished at it all.

He was right. A small, neat-looking bus drove through the pass and stopped for me. As I got in, the driver mechanically turned around and drove into the hills again.

"They took up my ticket on the other bus," I said to the driver. "What do I owe you?"

"Nothing," he said curtly. "Fill that out." He handed me a card.

An impertinent thing, that card was. Besides asking for my name, address, nationality, vocation, and position, it requested that I state with whom I was visiting in the Science Community, the purpose of my visit, the nature of my business, how long I intended to stay; did I have a place to stay arranged for, and if so, where and through whom. It looked for all the world as though they had something to conceal; Czarist Russia couldn't beat that for keeping track of people and prying into their business. Sign here, the card said.

It annoyed me, but I filled it out, and, by the time I was through, the bus was out of the hills, traveling up the valley of a small river; I am not familiar enough with northern Virginia to say which river it was. There was much machinery and a few people in the broad fields. In the distance ahead was a mass of chimneys and the cupolas of iron-works, but no smoke.

There were power-line towers with high-tension insulators and, far ahead, the masses of huge elevators and big, square buildings. Soon I came in sight of a veritable forest of huge windmills.

In a few moments, the huge buildings loomed up over me; the bus entered a street of the city abruptly from the country. One moment on a country road, the next moment among towering buildings. We sped along swiftly through a busy metropolis, bright, airy, efficient looking. The traffic was dense but quiet, and I was confident that most of the vehicles were electric; for there was no noise nor gasoline odor. Nor was there any smoke. Things looked airy, comfortable, efficient; but rather monotonous, dull. There was a total lack of architectural interest. The buildings were just square blocks, like neat rows of neat boxes. But, it all moved smoothly, quietly, with wonderful efficiency.

My first thought was to look closely at the people who swarmed the streets of this strange city. Their faces were solemn, and their clothes were solemn. All seemed intently busy, going somewhere, or doing something; there was no standing about, no idle sauntering. And look whichever way I might, everywhere there was the same blue serge, on men and women alike, in all directions, as far as I could see.

The bus stopped before a neat, square building of rather smaller size, and the next thing I knew, Benda was running down the steps to meet me. He was his old gruff, enthusiastic self.

"Glad to see you, Hagstrom, old socks!" he shouted, and gripped my hand with two of his. "I've arranged for a room for you, and we'll have a good old visit, and I'll show you around this town."

I looked at him closely. He looked healthy and well cared-for, all except for a couple of new lines of worry on his face. Undoubtedly that worn look meant some sort of trouble.

Part II. The New Religion
(THIS PART IS INTERPOLATED BY THE AUTHOR
INTO DR. HAGSTROM'S NARRATIVE.)

Every great religion has as its psychological reason for existence the mission of compensating for some crying, unsatisfied human need. Christianity spread and grew among people who were, at the time, persecuted subjects or slaves of Rome; and it flourished through the Middle Ages at a time when life held for the individual chiefly pain, uncertainty, and bereavement. Christianity kept the common man consoled and mentally balanced by minimizing the importance of life on earth and offering compensation afterwards and elsewhere.

A feeble nation of idle dreamers, torn by a chaos of intertribal feuds within, menaced by powerful, conquest-lusting nations from without,

Arabia was enabled by Islam, the religion of her prophet Mohammed, to unite all her sons into an intense loyalty to one cause, and to turn her dream-stuff into reality by carrying her national pride and honor beyond her boundaries and spreading it over half the known world.

The ancient Greeks, in despair over the frailties of human emotion and the unbecomingness of worldly conduct, which their brilliant minds enabled them to recognize clearly but which they found themselves powerless to subdue, endowed the gods, whom they worshipped, with all of their own passions and weaknesses, and thus the foolish behavior of the gods consoled them for their own obvious shortcomings. So it goes throughout all of the world's religions.

In the middle of the twentieth century there were in the civilized world, millions of people in whose lives Christianity had ceased to play any part. Yet, psychically—remember, "psyche" means "soul"—they were just as sick and unbalanced, just as much in need of some compensation as were the subjects of the early Roman empire, or the Arabs in the Middle Ages. They were forced to work at the strained and monotonous pace of machines; they were the slaves, body and soul, of machines; they lived with machines and lived like machines—they were expected to *be* machines. A mechanized mode of life set a relentless pace for them, while, just as in all the past ages, life and love, the breezes and the blue sky called to them: but they could not respond. They had to drive machines so that machines could serve them. Minds were cramped and emotions were starved, but hands must go on guiding levers and keeping machines in operation. Lives were reduced to such a mechanical routine that men wondered how long human minds and human bodies could stand the restraint. There is a good deal in the writings of the times to show that life was becoming almost unbearable for three-fourths of humanity.

It is only natural, therefore, that Rohan, the prophet of the new religion, found followers more rapidly than he could organize them. About ten years before the visit of Dr. Hagstrom to his friend Benda, Rohan and his new religion had been much in the newspapers. Rohan was a Slovak, apparently well educated in Europe. When he first attracted attention to himself, he was foreman in a steel plant at Birmingham, Alabama. He was popular as an orator, and drew unheard-of crowds to his lectures.

He preached of *Science* as God, an all-pervading, inexorably systematic Being, the true Center and Motive-Power of the Universe; a Being who saw men and pitied them because they could not help committing inaccuracies. The Science God was helping man become more perfect. Even now, men were much more accurate and systematic than they had been a hundred years ago; men's lives were ordered and rhythmic, like natural laws, not like the chaotic emotions of beasts and savages.

Somehow, he soon dropped out of the attention of the great mass of the public. Of course, he did so intentionally when his ideas began to crystallize and his plans for his future organization began to form. At first he had a sort of church in Birmingham called The Church of the Scientific God. There never was anything cheap nor blatant about him. When he moved his church from Birmingham to the Lovett Branch Valley in northern Virginia, he was hardly noticed. But with him went seven thousand people, to form the nucleus of the Science Community.

Since then, some feature writer for a metropolitan Sunday paper has occasionally written up the Science Community, both from its physical and its human aspects. From these reports, the outstanding bit of evidence is that Rohan believed intensely in his own religion, and that his followers are all loyal worshippers of the Science God. They conceive the earth to be a workshop in which men serve Science, their God, serving a sort of apprenticeship during which He perfects them to the state of ideal machines. To be a perfect machine, always accurate, with no distracting emotions, no getting off the track—that was the ideal which the Great God *Science* required of his worshippers. To be a perfect machine, or a perfect cog in a machine, to get rid of all individuality all disturbing sentiment, that was their idea of supreme happiness. Despite the obvious narrowness it involved, there was something sublime in the conception of this religion. It certainly had nothing in common with the "Christian Science" that was in vogue during the early years of the twentieth century: it towered with noble grandeur above that feeble little sham.

The Science Community was organized like a machine; and all men played their parts, in government, in labor, in administration, in production, like perfect cogs and accurate wheels, and the machine functioned perfectly. The devotees were described as fanatical, but happy. They certainly were well trained and efficient. The Science Community grew. In ten years it had a million people, and was a worldwide wonder of civic planning and organization; it contained so many astonishing developments in mechanical service to human welfare and comfort that it was considered as a sort of model of the future city. The common man there was provided with science-produced luxuries, in his daily life, that were in the rest of the world the privilege of the wealthy few—but he used his increased energy and leisure in serving the more devotedly his God, Science, who had made machines. There was a great temple in the city, the shape of a huge dynamo-generator, whose interior was worked out in a scheme of mechanical devices, and with music, lights, and odors to help in the worship.

What the world knew the least about was that this religion was becoming militant. Its followers spoke of the heathen without, and were horrified at the prevalence of the sin of individualism. They were inspired with the mission that the message of God—scientific perfection—must be carried to the whole world. But, knowing that vested interests, governments, invested capital, and established religions would oppose them and render any real progress impossible, they waited. They studied the question, looking for some opportunity to spread the gospel of their beliefs, prepared to do so by force, finding their justification in their belief that millions of sufferers needed the comforts that their religion had given them. Meanwhile, their numbers grew.

Rohan was Chief Engineer, which position was equal in honor and dignity to that of Prophet or High Priest. He was a busy, hard-worked man, black haired and gaunt, small of stature and fiery eyed: he looked rather like an overworked department-store manager rather than like a prophet. He was finding his hands more full every day, both because of the extraordinary fertility of his own plans and ideas, and because the Science Community was growing so rapidly. Among this heterogeneous mass of proselyte strangers that poured into the city and was efficiently absorbed into the machine, it was yet difficult to find executives, leaders, men to put in charge of big things. And he needed constantly more and more of such men.

That was why Rohan went to Benda, and subsequently to others like Benda. Rohan had a deep knowledge of human nature. He did not approach Benda with the offer of a magnanimous salary, but came into Benda's office asking for a consultation on some of the puzzling communication problems of the Science Community. Benda became interested, and on his own initiative offered to visit the Science Community, saying that he had to be in Washington anyway in a few days. When he saw what the conditions were in the Science Community, he became fascinated by its advantages over New York; a new system to plan from the ground up; no obsolete installation to wrestle with; an absolutely free hand for the engineer in charge; no politics to play; no concessions to antiquated city construction nor to feeble-minded city administration—just a dream of an opportunity. He almost asked for the job himself, but Rohan was tactful enough to offer it, and the salary, though princely, was hardly given a thought.

For many weeks, Benda was absorbed in his job, to the exclusion of all else. He sent his money to his New York bank and had his family move in to live with him. He was happy in his communication problems.

"Give me a problem in communication and you make me happy," he wrote to Hagstrom in one of his early letters. He had completed a certain division of his work on the Science Community's communication system, and it occurred to him that a few days' relaxation would do him good. A run up to New York would be just the thing.

To his amazement, he was not permitted to board the outbound bus.

"You'll need orders from the Chief Engineer's office," the driver said.

Benda went to Rohan.

"Am I a prisoner?" he demanded, with his characteristic directness.

"An embarrassing situation," the suave Rohan admitted, very calmly and at his ease. "You see, I'm nothing like a dictator here. I have no arbitrary power. Everything runs by system, and you're a sort of exception. No one knows exactly how to classify you. Neither do I. But, I can't break a rule. That is sin."

"What rule? I want to go to New York."

"Only those of the Faith who have reached the third degree can come and go. No one can get that in less than three years."

"Then you got me in here by fraud?" Benda asked bluntly.

Rohan side-stepped gracefully.

"You know our innermost secrets now," he explained. "Do you suppose there is any hope of your embracing the Faith?"

Benda whirled on his heel and walked out.

"I'll think about it!" he said, his voice snapping with sarcasm.

Benda went back to his work in order to get his mind off the matter. He was a well-balanced man if he was anything; and he knew that nothing could be accomplished by rash words or incautious moves against Rohan and his organization. And on that day he met John Edgewater Smith.

"You here?" Benda gasped. He lost his equilibrium for a moment in consternation at the sight of his fellow-engineer.

Smith was too elated to notice Benda's mood.

"I've been here a week. This is certainly an ideal opportunity in my line of work. Even in Heaven I never expected to find such a chance."

By this time Benda had regained control of himself. He decided to say nothing to Smith for the time being.

They did not meet again for several weeks. In the meantime Benda discovered that his mail was being censored. At first he did not know that his letters, always typewritten, were copied and objectionable matter omitted, and his signature reproduced by the photo-engraving process, separately each time. But before long, several letters came back to him rubber-stamped: "Not passable. Please revise." It took Benda two days to cool down and rewrite the first letter. But outwardly no one would have ever known that there was anything amiss with him.

However, he took to leaving his work for an hour or two a day and walking in the park, to think out the matter. He didn't like it. This was about the time that it began to be a real issue as to who was the bigger man of the two, Rohan or Benda. But no signs of the issue appeared externally for many months.

John Edgewater Smith realized sooner than Benda that he couldn't get out, because, not sticking to work so closely, he had made the attempt sooner. He looked very much worried when Benda next saw him.

"What's this? Do you know about it?" he shouted as soon as he had come within hearing distance of Benda.

"What's the difference?" Benda replied casually. "Aren't you satisfied?"

Smith's face went blank.

Benda came close to him, linked arms, and led him to a broad vacant lawn in the park.

"Listen!" he said softly in Smith's ear. "Don't you suppose these people who lock us in and censor our mail aren't smart enough to spy on what we say to each other?"

"Our only hope," Benda continued, "is to learn all we can of what is going on here. Keep your eyes and ears open and meet me here in a week. And now come on; we've been whispering here long enough."

Oddly enough, the first clue to the puzzle they were trying to solve was supplied by Francisco, New York's former Water Commissioner. Why were they being kept prisoners in the city? There must be more reason for holding them there than the fear that information would be carried out, for none of the three engineers knew anything about the Science Community that could be of any possible consequence to outsiders. They had all stuck rigidly to their own jobs.

They met Francisco, very blue and dejected, walking in the park a couple of months later. They had been having weekly meetings, feeling that more frequent rendezvous might excite suspicion. Francisco was overjoyed to see them.

"Been trying to figure out why they want us," he said. "There is something deeper than the excuse they have made; that rot about a perfect system and no breaking of rules may be true, but it has nothing to do with us. Now, here are three of us, widely admitted as having good heads on us. We've got to solve this."

"The first fact to work on," he continued, "is that there is no real job for me here. This city has no water problem that cannot be worked out by an engineer's office clerk. Why are they holding me here, paying me a profligate salary, for a job that is a joke for a grown-up man? There's something behind it that is not apparent on the surface."

The weekly meetings of the three engineers became an established institution. Mindful that their conversation was doubtless the object of attention on the part of the ruling powers of the city through spies and concealed microphones, they were careful to discuss trivial matters, most of the time, and mentioned their problem only when alone in the open spaces of the park.

After weeks of effort had produced no results, they arrived at the conclusion that they would have to do some spying themselves. The great temple, shaped like a dynamo-generator attracted their attention as the first possibility for obtaining information. Benda, during his work with telephone and television installation, found that the office of some sort of ruling council or board of directors was located there. Later he found that it was called the Science Staff. He managed to slip in several concealed microphone detectors and wire them to a private receiver on his desk, doing all the work with his own hands under the pretense of hunting for a cleverly contrived short-circuit that his subordinates had failed to find.

"They open their meeting," he said, reporting several days of listening to his comrades, "with a lot of religious stuff. They really believe they are chosen by God to perfect the earth. Their fanaticism has the Mohammedans beat forty ways. As I get it from listening in, this city is just a preliminary base from which to carry, forcibly, the gospel of Scientific Efficiency to the whole world. They have been divinely appointed to organize the earth.

"The first thing on the program is the seizure of New York City. And, it won't be long; I've heard the details of a cut-and-dried plan. When they have New York, the rest of America can be easily captured, for cities aren't as independent of each other as they used to be. Getting the rest of the world into their hands will then be merely a matter of routine; just a little time, and it will be done. Mohammed's wars weren't in it with this!"

Francisco and Smith stared at him aghast. These dull-faced, blue-serge-clad people did not look capable of it; unless possibly one noted the fiery glint in their eyes. A world-wide Crusade on a scientific basis! The idea left them weak and trembling.

"Got to learn more details before we can do anything," Benda said. "Come on; we've been whispering here long enough; they'll get suspicious." Benda's brain was now definitely pitted against this marvelous organization.

"I've got it!" Benda reported at a later meeting, "I pieced it together from a few hours' listening. Devilish scheme!"

"Can you imagine what would happen in New York in case of a breakdown in water-supply, electric power, and communication? In an hour there would be a panic; in a day, the city would be a hideous shambles of suffering, starvation, disease, and trampling maniacs. Dante's Inferno would be a lovely little pleasure-resort in comparison.

"Also, have you ever stopped to think how few people there are in the world who understand the handling of these vital elements of our modern civilized organization sufficiently to keep them in operation? There you have the scheme. Because they do not want to destroy the city, but merely to threaten it, they are holding the three of us. A little

271

skilful management will eliminate all other possible men who could operate the city's machinery, except ourselves. We three will be placed in charge. A threat, perhaps a demonstration in some limited section of what horrors are possible. The city is at their mercy, and promptly surrenders.

"An alternative plan was discussed: just a little quiet violence could eliminate those who are now in charge of the city's works, and the panic and horrors would commence. But, within an hour of the city's capitulation, the three of us could have things running smoothly again. And there would be no New York; in its place would be Science Community Number Two. From it they could step on to the next city."

The other two stared at him. There was only one comment.

"They seem to be sure that they could depend on us," Smith said.

"They may be correct," Benda replied. "Would you stand by and see people perish if a turn of your hand could save them? You would, for the moment, forget the issue between the old order and the new religion."

They separated, horrified by the ghastly simplicity of the plan.

Just following this, Benda received the telegram announcing the prospective visit of his lifelong friend, Dr. Hagstrom. He took it at once to Rohan.

"Will my friend be permitted to depart again, if he once gets in here?" he demanded with his customary directness.

"It depends on you," Rohan replied blandly. "We want your friend to see our Community, and to go away and carry with him the nicest possible reports and description of it to the world. I wonder, do I make myself clear?"

"That means I've got to feed him taffy while he's here?" Benda asked gruffly.

"You choose to put it indelicately. He is to see and hear only such things about the Science Community as will please the world and impress it favorably. I am sure you will understand that under no other circumstances will he be permitted to leave here."

Benda turned around abruptly and walked out without a word.

"Just a moment," Rohan called after him. "I am sure you appreciate the fact that every precaution will be taken to hear the least word that you say to him during his stay here? You are watched only perfunctorily now. While he is here you will be kept track of carefully, and there will be three methods of checking everything you do or say. I am sure you do not underestimate our caution in this matter."

Benda spent the days intervening between then and the arrival of his friend Hagstrom, closed up in his office, in intense study. He figured things on pieces of paper, committed them to memory, and scrupulously burned the paper. Then he wandered about the park and plucked at leaves and twigs.

Part III. The Cipher Message
(RELATED BY PETER HAGSTROM, PH.D.)

Benda conducted me personally to a room very much like an ordinary hotel room. He was glad to see me. I could tell that from his grip of welcome, from his pleased face, from the warmth in his voice, from the eager way in which he hovered around me. I sat down on a bed and he on a chair.

"Now tell me all about it," I said.

The room was very still, and in its privacy, following Benda's demonstrative welcome, I expected some confidential revelations. Therefore I was astonished.

"There isn't much to tell," he said gaily. "My work is congenial, fascinating, and there's enough of it to keep me out of mischief. The pay is good, and the life pleasant and easy."

I didn't know what to say for a moment. I had come there with my mind made up that there was something suspicious afoot. But he seemed thoroughly happy and satisfied.

"I'll admit that I treated you a little shabbily in this matter of letters," he continued. "I suppose it is because I've had a lot of new and interesting problems on my mind, and it's been hard to get my mind down to writing letters. But I've got a good start on my job, and I'll promise to reform."

I was at a loss to pursue that subject any further.

"Have you seen Smith and Francisco?" I asked.

He nodded.

"How do they like it?"

"Both are enthusiastic about the wonderful opportunities in their respective fields. It's a fact: no engineer before had such resources to work with, on such a vast scale, and with such a free hand. We're laying the framework for a city of ten millions, all thoroughly systematized and efficient. There is no city in the world like it; it's an engineer's dream of Utopia."

I was almost convinced. There was only the tiniest of lurking suspicions that all was not well, but it was not powerful enough to stimulate me to say anything. But I did determine to keep my eyes open.

I might as well admit in advance that from that moment to the time when I left the Science Community four days later, I saw nothing to confirm my suspicions. I met Smith and Francisco at dinner and the four of us occupied a table to ourselves in a vast dining hall, and no one paid for the meal nor for subsequent ones. They also seemed content, and talked enthusiastically of their work.

I was shown over the city, through its neat, efficient streets, through its comfortable dormitories each housing hundreds of families as luxuriously as any modern hotel, through its marvelous factories where production had passed the stage of labor and had assumed the condition of a devoted act of worship. These factory workers were not toiling; they were worshipping their God, of Whom each machine was a part. Touching their machine was touching their God. This machinery, while involving no new principles, was developed and coordinated to a degree that exceeded anything I had ever seen anywhere else.

I saw the famous Science Temple in the shape of a huge dynamo-generator, with its interior decorations, paintings, carvings, frescoes, and pillars, all worked out on the motive of machinery; with its constant streams of worshippers in blue serge, performing their conventional rites and saying their prayer formulas at altars in the forms of lathes, microscopes, motors, and electron-tubes.

"You haven't become a Science Communist yourself?" I bantered Benda.

There was a metallic ring in the laugh he gave.

"They'd like to have me!" was all he said.

I was rather surprised at the emptiness of the large and well-kept park to which Benda took me. It was beautifully landscaped, but only a few scattering people were there, lost in its vast reaches.

"These people seem to have no need of recreation," Benda said. "They do not come here much. But I confess that I need air and relaxation, even if only for short snatches. I've been too busy to get away for long at a time, but this park has helped me keep my balance—I'm here every day for at least a few minutes."

"Beautiful place," I remarked. "A lot of strange trees and plants I never saw before—"

"Oh, mostly tropical forms, common enough in their own habitats. They have steam pipes under the ground to grow them. I've been trying to learn something about them. Fancy me studying natural history! I've never cared for it, but here, where there is no such thing as recreation, I have become intensely interested in it as a hobby. I find it very much of a rest to study these plants and bugs."

"Why don't you run up to New York for a few days?"

"Oh, the time will come for that. In the meanwhile, I've got an idea all of a sudden. Speaking of New York, will you do me a little service? Even though you might think it silly?"

"I'll do anything I can," I began, eager to be of help to him.

"It has been somewhat of a torture to me," Benda continued, "to find so many of these forms which I am unable to identify. I like to be scientific, even in my play, and reference books on plants and insects are scarce here. Now, if you would carry back a few specimens for me, and ask some of the botany and zoology people to send me their names—"

"Fine!" I exclaimed. "I've got a good-sized pocket notebook I can carry them in."

"Well then, please put them in the order in which I hand them to you, and send me the names by number. I am pretty thoroughly familiar with them, and if you will keep them in order, there is no need for me to keep a list. The first is a blade of this queer grass."

I filed the grass blade between the pages of my book.

"The next is this unusual-looking pinnate leaf." He tore off a dry leaflet and handed me a stem with three leaflets irregularly disposed of it.

"Now leave a blank page in your book. That will help me remember the order in which they come."

Next came a flat insect, which, strangely enough, had two legs missing on one side. However, Benda was moving so fast that I had to put it away without comment. He kept darting about and handing me twigs of leaves, little sticks, pieces of bark, insects, not seeming to care much whether they were complete or not; grass-blades, several dagger-shaped locust thorns, cross-sections of curious fruits, moving so rapidly that in a few moments my notebook bulged widely, and I had to warn him that its hundred leaves were almost filled.

"Well, that ought to be enough," he said with a sigh after his lively exertion. "You don't know how I'll appreciate your indulging my foolish little whim."

"Say!" I exclaimed. "Ask something of me. This is nothing. I'll take it right over to the Botany Department, and in a few days you ought to have a list of names fit for a Bolshevik."

"One important caution," he said. "If you disturb their order in the book, or even the position on the page, the names you send me will mean nothing to me. Not that it will be any great loss," he added whimsically. "I suppose I've become a sort of fan on this, like the business men who claim that their office work interferes with their golf."

We walked leisurely back toward the big dormitory. It was while we were crossing a street that Benda stumbled, and, to dodge a passing truck, had to catch my arm, and fell against me. I heard his soft voice whisper in my ear:

"Get out of this town as soon as you can!"

I looked at him in startled amazement, but he was walking along, shaking himself from his stumble, and looking up and down the street for passing trucks.

"As I was saying," he said in a matter-of-fact voice, "we expect to reach the one-and-one-quarter million mark this month. I never saw a place grow so fast."

I felt a great leap of sudden understanding. For a moment my muscles tightened, but I took my cue.

"Remarkable place," I said calmly; "one reads a lot of half-truths about it. Too bad I can't stay any longer."

"Sorry you have to leave," he said, in exactly the right tone of voice. "But you can come again."

How thankful I was for the forty years of playing and working together that had accustomed us to that sort of team-work! Unconsciously we responded to one another's cues. Once our ability to "play together" had saved my life. It was when we were in college and were out on a cross-country hike together; Benda suddenly caught my hand and swung it upward. I recognized the gesture; we were cheerleaders and worked together at football games, and we had one stunt in which we swung our hands over our heads, jumped about three feet, and let out a whoop. This was the "stunt" that he started out there in the country, where we were by ourselves. Automatically, without thinking, I swung my arms and leaped with him and yelled. Only later did I notice the rattlesnake over which I had jumped. I had not seen that I was about to walk right into it, and he had noticed it too late to explain. A flash of genius suggested the cheering stunt to him.

"*Communication* is a science!" he had said, and that was all the comment there was on the incident.

So now, I followed my cue, without knowing why, nor what it was all about, but confident that I should soon find out. By noon I was on the bus, on my way through the pass, to meet the vehicle from Washington. As the bus swung along, a number of things kept jumbling through my mind: Benda's effusive glee at seeing me, and his sudden, turning and bundling me off in a nervous hurry without a word of explanation; his lined and worried face and yet his insistence on the joys of his work in the Science Community; his obvious desire to be hospitable and play the good host, and yet his evasiveness and unwillingness to chat intimately and discuss important things as he used to. Finally, that notebook full of odd specimens bulging in my pocket. And the memory of his words as he shook hands with me when I was stepping into the bus:

"Long live the science of communication!" he had said. Otherwise, he was rather glum and silent.

I took out the book of specimens and looked at it. His caution not to disturb the order and position of things rang in my ears. The Science of Communication! Two and two were beginning to make four in my mind. All the way on the train from Washington to New York I could hardly keep my hands off the book. I had definitely abandoned the idea of hunting up botanists and zoologists at Columbia. Benda was not interested in the names of these things. That book meant something else. Some message. The Science of Communication!

That suddenly explained all the contradictions in his behavior. He was being closely watched. Any attempt to tell me the things he wanted to say would be promptly recognized. He had succeeded brilliantly in getting a message to me. Now, my part was to read it! I felt a sudden sinking within me. That book full of leaves, bugs, and sticks? How could I make anything out of it?

"There's the Secret Service," I thought. "They are skilled in reading hidden messages. It must be an important one, worthy of the efforts of the Secret Service, or he would not have been at such pains to get it to me.

"But no. The Secret Service is skilled at reading hidden messages, but not as skilled as I am in reading my friend's mind. Knowing Benda, his clear intellect, his logical methods, will be of more service in solving this than all the experts of the Secret Service."

I barely stopped to eat dinner when I reached home. I hurried to the laboratory building, and laid out the specimens on white sheets

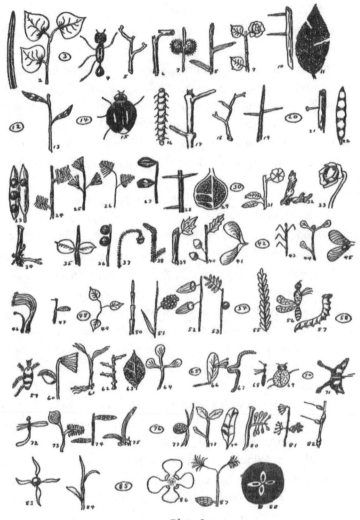

Plate I.

of paper, meticulously preserving order, position, and spacing. To be on the safe side I had them photographed, asking the photographer to vary the scale of his pictures so that all of the final figures would be approximately the same size, Plate I shows what I had.

I was all a-tremble when the mounted photographs were handed to me. The first thing I did was to number the specimens, giving each blank space also its consecutive number. Certainly no one could imagine a more meaningless jumble of twigs, leaves, berries, and bugs. How could I read any message out of that?

Yet I had no doubt that the message concerned something of far more importance than Benda's own safety. He had moved in this matter with astonishing skill and breathless caution; yet I knew him to be reckless to the extreme where only his own skill was concerned. I couldn't even imagine his going to this elaborate risk merely on account of Smith and Francisco. Something bigger must be involved.

I stared at the rows of specimens.

"Communication is a science!" Benda had said, and it came back to me as I studied the bent worms and the beetles with two legs missing. I was confident that the solution would be simple. Once the key idea occurred to me I knew I should find the whole thing astonishingly direct and systematic. For a moment I tried to attach some sort of hieroglyphic significance to the specimen forms; in the writing of the American Indians, a wavy line meant water, an inverted V meant a wigwam. But, I discarded that idea in a moment. Benda's mind did not work along the paths of symbolism. It would have to be something mathematical, rigidly logical, leaving no room for guesswork.

No sooner had the key-idea occurred to me than the basic conception underlying all these rows of twigs and bugs suddenly flashed into clear meaning before me. The simplicity of it took my breath away.

"I knew it!" I said aloud, though I was alone. "Very simple."

I was prepared for the fact that each one of the specimens represented a letter of the alphabet. If nothing else, their number indicated that. Now I could see, so clearly that the photographs shouted at me, that each specimen consisted of an upright stem, and from this middle stem projected side-arms to the right and to the left, and in various vertical locations on each side.

The middle upright stem contained these side-arms in various numbers and combinations. In five minutes I had a copy of the message, translated into its fundamental characters, as shown on Plate II.

The first grass-blade was the simple, upright stem; the second, three leaflets on their stem, represented the upright portion with two

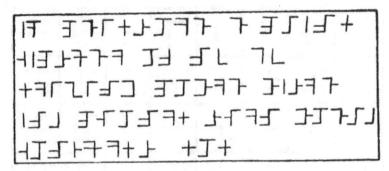

Plate II.

arms to the left at the top and middle, and one arm to the right at the top; and so on.

That brought the message down to the simple and straightforward matter of a substitution cipher. I was confident that Benda had no object in introducing any complications that could be avoided, as his sole purpose was to get to me the most readable message without getting caught at it. I recollected now how cautious he had been to hand me no paper, and how openly and obviously he had dropped each specimen into my book; because he knew someone was watching him and expecting him to slip in a message. He had, as I could see now in the retrospect, been conspicuously careful that nothing suspicious should pass from his hands to mine.

Substitution ciphers are easy to solve, especially for those having some experience. The method can be found in Edgar Allan Poe's "Gold Bug" and in a host of its imitators. A Secret Service cipher man could have read it in an hour. But I knew my friend's mind well enough to find a short-cut. I knew just how he would go about devising such a cipher, in fact, how ninety-nine persons out of a hundred with a scientific education would do it.

If we begin adding horizontal arms to the middle stem, from top to bottom and from left to right, the possible characters can be worked out by the system shown on Plate III.

It is most logical to suppose that Benda would begin with the first sign and substitute the letters of the alphabet in order. That would give us the cipher code shown on Plate IV.

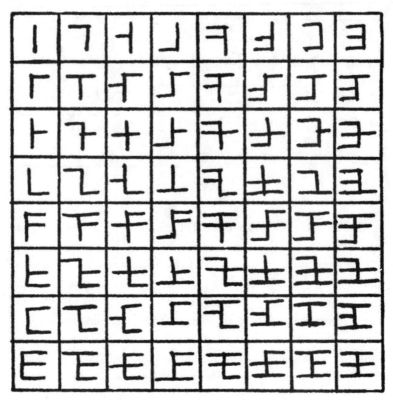

Plate III.

It was all very quick work, just as I had anticipated, once the key-idea had occurred to me. The ease and speed of my method far exceeded that of Poe's method, but, of course, was applicable only to this particular case. Substituting letters for signs out of my diagram, I got the following message:

AM PRISONER R PLANS CAPTURE OF N Y BY SEIZING POWER
WATER AND PHONES THEN WORLD CONQUEST S O S

Part IV. L'Envoi
(BY PETER HAGSTROM, PH.D.)

My solution of the message practically ends the story. Events followed each other from then on like bullets from a machine-gun. A wild drive in a taxicab brought me to the door of Mayor Anderson

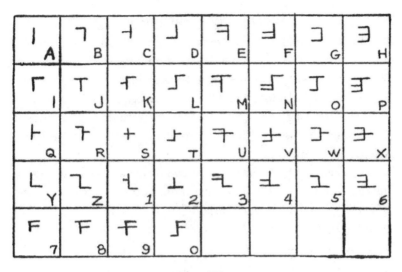

Plate IV.

at ten o'clock that night. I told him the story and showed him my photographs.

Following that I spent many hours telling my story to and consulting with officers in the War Department. Next afternoon, photographic maps of the Science Community and its environs, brought by airplanes during the forenoon, were spread on desks before us. A colonel of marines and a colonel of aviation sketched plans in notebooks. After dark I sat in a transport plane with muffled exhaust and propellers, slipping through the air as silently as a hawk. About us were a dozen bombing planes, and about fifty transports, carrying a battalion of marines.

I am not an adventure-loving man. Though a cordon of husky marines about me was a protection against any possible danger, yet, stealing along through that wild valley in the Virginia mountains toward the dark masses of that fanatic city, the silent progress of the long, dark line through the night, their mysterious disappearance, one by one, as we neared the city, the creepy, hair-raising journey through the dark streets—I shall never forget for the rest of my life the sinking feeling in my abdomen and the throbbing in my head. But I wanted to be there, for Benda was my lifelong friend.

I guided them to Rohan's rooms, and saw a dozen dark forms slip in, one by one. Then we went on to the dormitory where Benda lived. Benda answered our hammering at his door in his pajamas. He took in the Captain's automatic, and the bayonets behind me, at a glance.

"Good boy, Hagstrom!" he said. "I knew you'd do it. There wasn't much time left. I got my instructions about handling the New York telephone system to-day."

As we came out into the street, I saw Rohan handcuffed to two big marines, and rows of bayonets gleaming in the darkness down the streets. Every few moments a bright flare shot out from the planes in the sky, until a squad located the power-house and turned on all the lights they could find.

On Board the Martian Liner

"Yes sir!" said "Streak" Burgess, star reporter of the *Times*, into the telephone.

"And write me up a good feature article of the trip," the editor's voice barked into his ear. "Give me vivid, human stuff. The public is sick of these dry science articles. And remember that we're trying to arouse people to space-mindedness. Here's three good planets, with no end of business opportunities, and the people are asleep. Wake 'em up!"

Burgess hung up the receiver and whirled on his heel.

"Where do you have to go this time, Mr. Burgess?" inquired a youthful voice at his side.

"Oh, hello Chick!" said Burgess.

Burgess knew Chick merely as a boy of about seventeen who ran loose about the premises of the Club on his father's membership, and who in his youthful fashion idolized the popular and successful reporter. In spite of the discrepancy in their ages, the two had become chummy, although Burgess hardly remembered Chick's real name. Johnson, or some such common, everyday name, it was.

"I've got to start for Mars in four hours," Burgess explained. "You see, to the *Times* managing-editor, a reporter is not a person; he's merely a projectile."

"Oh, Mr. Burgess, please take me with you. Please do!" implored the boy. "I'll pay all your expenses in grand style. Please let me go with you. I'd give anything to go to Mars!"

"Well, at least *you're* space-minded anyway," the reporter laughed. "I'm sorry, kid," he said gravely. "I couldn't do it. It would get me into trouble with my paper. And the laws are mighty strict about anyone under twenty-one going up in a space-liner, except under the care of a parent or guardian. But, I'll tell you all about it when I get back."

"I'm going to Mars some day!" the boy said desperately. "I'll show you!"

"I haven't the least doubt about it," Streak Burgess laughed. "I wish I could take you along. I'd do it just to get you away from that precious gang of young toughs you are running with. I've got to meet your father some day and warn him that if he don't get away from his money for a while and look after you, you'll—you'll get into bad company."

"You mean The Science Club?" Chick asked.

"Sweet name, I'd call it. Remember, Chick, I've seen a lot of the world. Your Science Club looks like a bunch of crooks to me, who are going to use you for a tool. Your ugly president with the birthmark on his cheek is all labeled for the electric chair."

"Oh, Pug? Pug isn't bad. You just ought to know him better," Chick protested with the faith of youth.

"Well, so long!" Streak Burgess went off with the speed that had earned him his nickname. Momentarily he forgot the adventure-hungry boy; and when the time came to leave the Club and betake himself to the spaceport, Chick was nowhere to be found.

The departure of a space-liner is always a thrilling spectacle. To the casual onlooker, it looks like a mad, chaotic turmoil of people and vehicles about the base of the vast, silvery bulk that looms hugely into the sky. Immense trucks backing up with the last consignments of fast freight to the platform overhung by countless cranes reaching out of the blackness of the vessel's ports; a stream of lighter trucks carrying baggage; one aero-taxi after another depositing now a man, now a woman, now a group of several on the platform; the flashing of the brilliant uniforms of the space-fleet officers, the hoarse shouts of the crew and stevedores, the dense crowd outside the tailing, waiting for the moment when the bulging vessel would rise slowly and majestically upwards, and disappear as a brilliant speck in the sky. Who has not been thrilled again and again by the arrival or the departure of a space-ship?

The reporter was at the dock early, watching. His job as observer of human-nature on a Martian trip had begun. Already he was making notes in his mind: the timid-looking little lady who had just stepped out of an aero-taxi and hesitated a moment, clasping her hands and drawing a deep breath before plunging into the blackness of the ship's door, must be on her first trip. But the two swaggering men who walked nonchalantly in, puffing their cigars over some sort of an argument that was more important than the picturesqueness of the scene, must have made the trip more than once: obviously commercial traveling-men. All of a sudden he noted Pug's purple cheek on the platform. The presence of the big bully on the spot gave Burgess an odd sense of uneasiness. But, in a moment Pug was out of sight, and Burgess saw no more of him.

Burgess waited at the edge of the platform, watching the passengers go aboard, and planning to be the last one to go on himself. Just as the edge of the platform, which was really the lowered hatch of the ship's door, began to rise, he stepped up on it. As he did, a sudden commotion arose that nearly startled him into falling off. An aero-taxi dashed down dangerously near the heads of the crowd, and skimmed within a hair's breadth of the rising platform. Out of it jumped and rolled and landslid a great, round hulk of a man, showing a red face now and then as he pursued his pell-mell course down the rapidly inclining platform and into the ship's door. Three traveling bags hurtled out of the aero-taxi into the ship's corridor.

Fat man, traveling-bags, and Burgess, all landed in a heap on the floor of the bottom-corridor, as the big hatch swung to. Burgess, still on his feet, backed away. Down the corridor to the right, was more commotion: shouts and clanking and the roar of motors. Some belated piece of freight was being forced into the other door, against the protests of the ship's crew, who had already begun to close the hatch. When that was over, Burgess looked at the fat man who sat on the floor among his traveling-bags, a rueful picture of melancholy despair. He tried to rise, and his face twisted into an expression of pain because of some bruise.

"Porter!" he yelled sharply. "Porter!"

The great, ungainly figure of the porter stalked down the corridor from the left. Gently it helped the fat man to his feet and picked up his traveling-bags; and the two of them departed into the gloom of the ship.

The porter was a size No. 3 televox-robot. He stood six and a half feet high, and moved with a curious croaking sound. There is a rather odd thing about the televox-robots that the General Electric has never been able to explain: although their manufacture is rigidly standardized nevertheless each machine turns out to have its individual peculiarities, and differs from all the others. It seems to have a personality of its own. Machines of this type have a square head with eyes and ears, an opening for oil, and a little diaphragm with which they can answer simple questions of a routine nature.

"When you're through, come back and show me my room," Burgess called after the robot.

And indeed, in a few minutes the huge figure came stalking back, its queer croak re-echoing through the metal corridor. The porter led Burgess to the elevator, which carried them off to the upper deck. In contrast to the glaring confusion outside, it was cool and quiet inside the ship. As the elevator went up, they left behind the musty odor that came from the hold, passed the smell of oil and ozone that came from the engine-room level, and stepped out into the fresh air of the passengers' quarters, where the air-renovating apparatus had already been started. The mahogany enamel on the duralumin walls, the upholstered velvet furniture the soft green and brown carpets all looked quite pleasant and comfortable, and Burgess felt a little glow of anticipation of a few comfortable days ahead. Most people considered the trip a hardship and a nuisance, but his life was a lively one, and for him the trip would mean a rest.

The passengers' quarters occupied the topmost level of the after portion of the ship. Ahead of them were the officers' quarters, and forward of these, the quarters of the crew, or the forecastle. Below was the vast hold for freight, except in the center of the ship, where the machinery was located.

Burgess took a look about his stateroom and then hurried to the after-gallery. Always the passengers congregate in the above place when the ship takes off; for it is entirely walled in with glass, and from it the Earth can be seen sinking downwards. Even the two traveling-men, who had already made a dozen trips, were looking eagerly down out of the window, for no one can ever become quite accustomed to that amazing spectacle. The Earth at first seems like a huge *concave* bowl, with a high rim all around, and a deep cavity below. The rim sinks lower and lower, and all of a sudden by some magic, it has become small and *convex*. Even after one has seen that change a dozen times, one never gets over the wonder of it.

There were twelve people gathered in the after-gallery: twelve people who were daring to venture across sixty million miles of space; who were to live together for six days almost as closely as a family. Five of them were women. The only one absent was the poor old, fat man who had boarded so precipitately. The sounds of the sealing of the ports had ceased, the hammering, the sizzling of air, the shouts, the grating of huge screw-levers. Then came the toot of the hoarse whistle and the roar of the reaction-motors.

In a moment the two traveling-men had turned away and were deep in argument about the cost of some commodity. They were always arguing about prices. A newly-married couple, who were making a honeymoon out of the trip, were whispering excitedly to each other. The little lady, whom Burgess had already observed coming aboard, had her face set hard; the emotion of the moment was almost too much for her. She was a Miss Waterbury, a Pittsburgh school-teacher who had been saving her pennies for years in order to make the trip to Mars. Possibly her expression was due partly to the sickening sensation which was felt for a few moments by all, as one feels a sinking when an elevator starts.

One by one the passengers trickled away from the after-gallery, down the corridor, into their staterooms or into the drawing-room at its opposite end. Burgess' stateroom was at the middle of the corridor and just opposite that of the fat man, whom he could see sitting glumly in the corner as he went into his own room. Next to him he could hear an elderly couple fussing vehemently; later he became acquainted with them as Colonel Thayer of the Air Guard, and his wife, en route to the Colonel's new post on Mars.

At the dinner-table, Burgess got a good look at all the passengers. Always there was in his mind the question: Why are these people taking this trip? What motives prompt them to risk their lives to get to Mars? One by one he checked them, and all of them seemed to be quite in place, except the poor, nervous, timid old fat man. Next to Burgess sat Kaufman, a keen, able-looking man, who was on his way to look into some business openings, which on that new-old world, with its degenerate inhabitants and its wealth of heavy-metal ores, looked wonderfully promising. Across from him sat the fat man, anxious, worried, thoroughly miserable. Next to him were a wealthy young society couple, utterly bored and *blasé*, hoping to find new thrills in a new world, because everything on Earth was tame to them. Then there was Kaufman's secretary, a very pretty young woman who was just now in the thrills of delight because the young engineer, Harry Flynn, going out penniless to seek his fortune on Mars, had turned out to be an old home-town acquaintance of hers.

One could understand why these people were on the trip. But the red-faced fat man was the soft, comfortable type of person, who groans when he has to get up out of his chair. He looked timid. He looked as though he ought to be by the fireside in bathrobe and slippers. What did he want on the long, hard, dangerous trip to Mars?

Mystery on Board

After dinner, Burgess managed to stroll down the corridor, just behind the fat man, in the hopes of getting better acquainted with him. Several of the passengers went out on the after-gallery to contemplate the marvelous wealth of brilliant stars in their inky black setting; but the fat man headed for his room. As he stepped into his door, Burgess touched him on the shoulder, intending to start a friendly conversation. The fat man gave a violent start and whirled about; and Burgess found himself looking into the muzzle of a big forty-five automatic pistol.

The fat man was white and trembling; one could see that he was not used to handling a pistol. But that made it all the more dangerous for Burgess, at whom the thing was pointed. With a quick movement, Burgess ducked to the ground and knocked the pistol out of the man's hand. It fell with a crash to the floor. Hoping that no one else had heard it, Burgess swept it up, pushed himself into the stateroom, and closed the door. He sat down with the gun on his knees. The old man was backed into a corner facing him, pale as a sheet, and panting desperately. Burgess was tremendously sorry for him.

"Now what's the trouble?" Burgess asked kindly. "I certainly wouldn't do you any harm."

"Who are you?" the old man panted.

Burgess flipped his coat lapel and showed his badge.

"I am a *Times* reporter. Tell me what you are afraid of. These little affairs are right in my line, and perhaps I can help you out."

The fat man studied Burgess for some minutes. Finally, without a word, he reached into his pocket and handed out a letter for Burgess to read. It was written in white ink on a brilliant scarlet paper:

"Most of the recipients of the red letter have been wise enough to hand over the money promptly. Three were foolish and refused. They were Lowell, Hirsch, and Carlotti. Do you remember what happened to them? No one can save you from the same fate unless you fork over at once.

"I need another million dollars for my project. You can spare it as easily as the ordinary man can spare a quarter. Have it ready in twenty-four hours in liquid securities or banknotes. A man will call for it at your home. He does not know me nor where I stay; therefore, if you have him followed, the money will be lost, and I shall be compelled to use you as an example to the next man upon whom I call for help.

"If I do not get the money, there is no way in which you can escape me, no place where you will be safe. I'll get you, no matter what precautions you take."

"I got it early this morning. Do you remember Lowell, Hirsch, and Carlotti?" the fat man asked.

The reporter nodded.

"Three hideous murders of wealthy men within the past year, and unsolved to date," he mused. "The letter seems to have been written by a man who is intelligent, but somewhat insane. That's the most dangerous kind. Have any idea who it might be?"

The fat man shook his head.

"Now, I'm worried because of the impulse which made me rush to this ship as soon as I got the letter. I thought this the best way to escape. But, after I had thought it over, I realized that to anyone else, it would obviously be the first thing I would do. I'm afraid I bungled."

"Why should flight on a space-liner be so obvious?" the reporter asked.

"Well, you see, I'm Johnson, the president of the company that owns this line, *The Mars, Ganymede, and Callisto Transportation Company*. I was so scared by the letter that I did a very simple-minded thing to come here."

There was a rap on the door, at which Mr. Johnson started violently. It turned out to be several sailors, making the routine search of the ship for stowaways. Behind them came the Captain of the ship, and peered into the room.

"I got your letter of introduction," he said gruffly to Burgess. Then he spied Mr. Johnson.

"Oh, how do you do, sir," he said, all meekness and courtesy. "I've got to be careful," he explained to the President, who was virtually the owner of the vessel. "There has been too much of this stowaway stuff. There's danger in it, and the law has recently made it a capital offense. A few weeks ago, on the *Aristotle*, a little overcrowded ship twenty-one days on the way to Ganymede, a stowaway used up more air than had been figured on; this in turn resulted in a deeper breathing on the part of the passengers, which exhausted the oxygen supply prematurely, and the ship arrived in port with half a dozen passengers unconscious from asphyxia. If I ever find one of those rats on my ship, I'll—"

He strode down the hallway, finishing the threat into his whiskers.

"Unless a stowaway is discovered, your enemy, if he is on board, must be one of the passengers," Burgess said to Mr. Johnson. "Could that be possible?"

"I don't know any of them. And he might be anybody." Mr. Johnson looked very much depressed. "Well, I'll stay here with you and keep an eye open. You're not afraid that I might be the man who is trying to kill you?"

"I don't think so." Mr. Johnson studied the reporter. "There is your badge, and Captain Scott knew you. I shall be glad to have you stay."

"Or," suggested Burgess, "perhaps it would be better yet for both of us to move into my stateroom."

Mr. Johnson nodded in acquiescence, and started to push the button to summon the porter. Burgess stayed his hand.

"I'll carry your things. The fewer the people that know about this move, the better."

For eight hours of the twenty-four, the lights were turned down, and "night" prevailed on the ship. During the "evening" the wild young society couple were playing bridge with the two traveling-men. Mrs. de Palogni's voice grated unpleasantly on Burgess' ears; but the sight of the honeymoon couple close together on the after-gallery again served to redeem his attitude toward his fellow-men. He could imagine the thrills that the two young people got out of being all alone out in space, with nothing but stars in all directions, and the brilliant disk of the Earth below. In another corner, Miss Waterbury and Cecilie May, Kaufman's pretty secretary, already well acquainted, were lost in wonder at the Heavens beneath them. The porter came croaking down the corridor. With a whispered "good-night," Burgess put Mr. Johnson into the upper berth and took the lower one himself, for strategic reasons.

Sometime in the night, Burgess woke up with a start. He glanced out of the port at the brilliant stars and the dense black sky, and felt his heart pounding in some unconscious alarm. He lay still and listened. There was a faint clicking sound, which came, was silent, and came again. It issued from the door on the opposite side of the corridor.

Burgess got silently out of bed, taking his pistol in one hand. Then, suddenly he threw open the door of the stateroom. A dark figure was just opening the door of the stateroom opposite, the one that had been Mr. Johnson's. It whirled and ran up the corridor. In an instant Burgess had snapped on the corridor light and was speeding in pursuit.

The dark figure ran ahead and into the drawing-room, with Burgess in pursuit. The drawing-room was dark; Burgess went in rather cautiously, pistol in hand. He found the switch and snapped on the light. There was no one in the room. With amazed glances he searched the room, but no one was there. He hurried to the door opposite the one by which he had entered, but found it locked. It was always kept locked, for it led to the officers' quarters. It could not have been unlocked and locked again during the second or two that it had taken him to turn on the light.

Burgess stared blankly around. The fugitive had disappeared!

The Stowaway

Down the corridor, doors were opening and sleepy heads were poking out. The porter stalked up, the whirring of his gears audible in the night's quietude.

"Do you want anything?" he asked in soft, courteous tones.

"No," said Burgess. "I couldn't sleep, and came to find something to read." He had decided to say nothing for the present. Then he was assailed by a foolish little feeling: the porter could understand his "no" but nothing of the rest of the explanation. It was difficult to keep in mind that these things were only machines; one felt like treating them as conscious human beings.

The passengers retired sleepily to their respective rooms, and the porter returned to his niche; his faint croaking stopped and the night was quiet again. The hum of the ship's reaction-motors was barely audible, for once the ship got under way, very little power was needed to maintain velocity.

Burgess was tremendously puzzled. The crew's thorough search had found no stowaway. It must be one of the passengers. Which one could it be?

He studied them all over at the breakfast table. They were all present except Mr. Johnson and Colonel Thayer's wife, both of whom were a little ill with space-sickness. Though the artificial gravity-fields had pretty well overcome space-sickness, some people were still susceptible to it. After breakfast he talked the matter over with Mr. Johnson, who lay in his berth, pale and nauseated.

"If anyone wants to kill me, why don't they do it now?" he asked with grim humor at his illness.

"Here they are." Burgess checked over the passenger list. "Kaufman is a big business man; the Colonel is a soldier; Cecilie May, Miss Waterbury, and Mrs. Thayer can be left out; they are not criminals, especially not murderers. The de Palognis are too rattle-brained; they couldn't even think up such a scheme. That leaves the two traveling-men and Flynn, the young engineer, and they're impossible. It *can't* be any of the passengers."

Mr. Johnson called for the Captain, who appeared in the stateroom shortly. The matter was explained, but the Captain was inclined to laugh at it.

"Impossible!" he snorted. "We went over this ship with a fine-toothed comb last night."

"Could it have been one of the crew?" Burgess asked.

"Say!" exclaimed the Captain. "Those fellows have to work. If one of them left his post for ten seconds, he'd be missed."

It was decided to take young Flynn into their confidence. He looked to be a very honest and earnest chap with just the alert type of mind that was needed to help solve such a riddle. The plan was that either Burgess or Flynn would be constantly on guard.

By noon Mr. Johnson felt better and was up and around. In the afternoon the Captain sent word that they were passing quite near a large asteroid, and all the passengers were gathered in the after-gallery. Most of the passengers gazed in puzzled silence at the bleak and jagged surface of the huge, rocky fragment outside; only the de Palognis were trying to crack a few cheap jokes about it, comparing it to a

French pleasure resort, where they had tried to amuse themselves last summer. Mr. Johnson left the group early and went back to lie down. Suddenly his cries resounded from the corridor:

"Porter! Porter! Help! Help!"

"Buzz! buzz! buzz!" came the porter's busy-signal. It meant that he was engaged on some other job and could not come at once.

Flynn and Burgess were in the corridor in a couple of leaps. There they saw Mr. Johnson struggling and panting—alone. He was disheveled and breathless, and as they appeared, sank slowly to the floor.

"What is it? What's the matter?" Burgess demanded.

"Something—somebody grabbed me by the throat," Mr. Johnson gasped. "But I couldn't see anything."

Burgess wondered if Mr. Johnson's illness and terror had begun to derange his mind. The porter came up and helped them carry the old man to his berth. No, the old fellow was, in spite of his nervous timidity, too shrewd and level-headed to go off that way. Something must really have happened. The passengers, remembering the scare during the night, gathered in the drawing-room and questioned each other.

In a couple of hours, Mr. Johnson felt better and was trying to be cheerful. Burgess, who had been at his side all of the time, noting that the old man was dozing, decided to let him sleep. He called the porter.

"Watch him while I walk about a little," he directed. "If he wants anything, call me."

As he came into the drawing-room, Burgess was assailed by a hundred questions. Mr. Johnson's identity had become known to the passengers; and this occurrence, combined with that of the "night" before, had roused their curiosity. He was still puzzling, trying to decide how much to tell them, when a pistol shot crashed out, down the corridor. Everybody turned in that direction, to see the tall form of the porter sway in Mr. Johnson's door, topple backwards, and fall with a great crash to the floor. There he lay still.

"Murder!"

"It's the porter, poor fellow!"

"Someone has shot the porter!"

Cecilie May screamed, and Flynn was soothing her in a wonderfully tender tone of voice, though everyone was too tense to notice it.

"It's only a machine," Flynn said to her. She shrank toward him, also quite unconscious of her action, and laughed nervously.

Then Mr. Johnson appeared at the door of his stateroom with a smoking pistol in his hand, looking very sheepish. The Captain came in through the dining-room, disgust showing very plainly in his expression.

"Too bad," Mr. Johnson said to the Captain "I was half asleep and saw the robot bending over me and it rattled me. My nerves have been pretty shaky."

The Captain growled something and called two sailors to drag the porter away. Later on he announced that the apparatus could be repaired, but that it might take days, for the bullet had cut over a thousand wires.

"In the meanwhile," the Captain said, "you'll have to wait on yourselves. I can't spare a man from the crew, and we haven't any extra robots."

The Colonel groaned and the two traveling-men looked worried. Flynn grinned hugely at their concern. The porter did nothing but foolish, trivial little tasks, which everyone could have done just as well for himself. But most of them felt helpless. There was much running to and fro. Burgess heard the Colonel and his wife fussing in the neighboring stateroom about the proper way to make up a bed, and Kaufman walked ostentatiously down the corridor fetching a pitcher of water.

"Be sure and let me know if you need anything," Flynn said to Cecilie May.

Flynn sat up with Mr. Johnson until midnight, and was then relieved by Burgess.

"Why is it that we can't radio from the ship to the Earth?" Burgess asked the engineer; "this would be a cracking good story for the *Times*."

"There is a layer of charged particles about sixty miles above the

Earth's surface, and no radio wave has yet been sent through it. It would be convenient if we could keep up communication with the home folks, all right."

Burgess sat and studied about the mystery, while up and down the corridor sounded the snores of the passengers through the dim illumination. There was something creepy about a night way off in space, millions of miles from anywhere. Something creaked down the corridor, and there was a swish and a rustle.

"Sh-h!" came a whisper from the darkness. "Mr. Burgess!"

Burgess leaped to his feet, pistol in hand.

"Don't shoot," came the whisper. "It's me."

Burgess snapped on the light and stood there

"*Chick*!" he gasped. "*You here?*"

The vicious threats of the Captain about stowaways flashed through his mind as he stood there in horror and looked at the grinning boy.

"How did you get here? How did you elude the search?" he demanded.

Chick laughed proudly at his own cleverness. "Remember the box that came aboard at the last moment? I was in that."

"Well, hurry back there and hide. The Captain is fierce on stowaways and he'll murder you if he finds you. I'll bring you food and water."

"I've got all the food and water I want, but I'm tired of being shut up. I want to see what space-traveling is like."

Burgess' jaw suddenly fell. Down the corridor came the Captain, on his nightly rounds about the ship. Burgess felt a cold perspiration break out all over him as the Captain peered into Chick's face.

"Aha! the prowler!" exclaimed the Captain.

He grabbed Chick's collar and blew a whistle. Two husky sailors ran up and seized the boy roughly.

"What are you going to do with him?" inquired Burgess in consternation.

"Throw him out of the air-valve with the garbage," growled the Captain. "I've got enough stowaways. Besides — prowling around and causing a lot of trouble."

The Disappearing Killer

Several people in pajamas and bathrobes arrived on the scene. Mrs. de Palogni was gurgling with real excitement. For once her jaded senses were getting a real thrill out of something.

"Poor kid!" said Flynn, as the sailors gave Chick a shake that made his teeth rattle.

The grunts of Mr. Johnson could be heard coming from within the stateroom, as he got off his berth and came to the door.

"What's up?" he groaned, sticking his head out of the door.

Suddenly his eyes widened, as he saw the boy in the clutches of the two sailors. He straightened up and became all at once very severe.

"Charles!" he said sternly. "How in the world did you get here?"

"Father!" exclaimed the boy, going all to pieces in a hysterical laugh. "Father! Are you on this ship? Well, don't let them kill me."

"Well, I should say I won't," the old man said, a sudden tenderness coming into his voice. He studied the situation for a few minutes while everyone else stood silent. The Captain looked from father to son. Mr. Johnson's next words showed, however, how a meek and nervous man like himself could have succeeded in building up a gigantic corporation like the *Mars, Ganymede, and Callisto Transportation Company*. He could think quickly and to the point.

"We need a porter," said Mr. Johnson. "Charles wants a ride. All right. Charles, you're the porter, and can work for your ride, even if you are the President's son."

There was a burst of cheering from the passengers at the clever way in which a difficult situation had been solved.

"Thanks, dad!" said Chick simply.

"But—" gasped Burgess. "What about the red letter? And the attempts on your life?"

"Well, it wasn't Charles," Mr. Johnson said with a gentle finality in his voice. He was proud of his son, but did not believe in spoiling him.

And the next morning Chick was making up beds and shining shoes. Most of the passengers protested against accepting these services from him, but the boy was a good sport, and did everything that his job required of him. During his spare time he spent every moment watching the ship's mechanics repairing the mechanism of the televox-robot. By evening Chick and Flynn were firm friends; they were talking about reaction-motors, meteorite deflectors, three-dimensional sextants, and such things with a fondness that only the two of them felt. Also, Chick's alert eye promptly noted Flynn's partiality toward Cecilie May, and that young lady was the recipient of real service from the new porter. The son of a millionaire seemed happy to lift suitcases, carry pitchers of water, and brush coats. And whenever he saw Burgess, he grinned at him triumphantly, as if to say, "I told you so!"

That evening was a pleasanter one for the little group of passengers. Everyone's space-sickness was over, and the tension of the past twenty-four hours was relaxed. A jolly party gathered in the drawing-room. Games of cards, ping-pong, and backgammon went gaily forward. Finally, the furniture was cleared away, a phonograph requisitioned, and a dance was started. The ladies, being in the minority, were very much in demand. Even the cranky Mrs. Thayer, the Colonel's wife, smiled and flushed as one of the traveling men gallantly offered her his arm and whirled her about in the dizzy steps of the new *whizzarro*, while the school teacher, floating in the arms of Burgess, was positively radiant. Mrs. de Palogni was trying to split up the bridal couple and get a dance with the young husband, but he was sublimely unconscious of her existence. However, he did give the Captain a dance with his bride. Likewise, Cecilie May gave her first courtesy dance to Kaufman, her employer, who then went back to his chair and watched the group abstractedly, undoubtedly figuring the prices of pitchblende and zirconite in his mind. Chick bustled about with a tray and glasses, and even Mr. Johnson seemed to have forgotten his nervousness for the time being, and beamed happily on the group as though it were his own family enjoying a good time. However, he slipped away early from the dance, looking rather tired, and went to his stateroom.

Burgess also withdrew from the activities and stood in the corridor, watching the crowd. The little by-plays of human nature appealed to him. However, before many minutes were up, he had a feeling that

somehow, somewhere, all was not well. He did not believe in premo-
nitions, realizing that they were always explainable on the ground
of some sensory stimulus that had set the subconscious mind alert,
some faint sight or sound not registered in the consciousness. He
therefore kept his eyes steadily on Mr. Johnson's door; in fact, he
had up to the time that he noticed the queer unrest, maintained an
uninterrupted watch without thinking, ever since Mr. Johnson had
stepped into his room. He had seen nothing.

Now there was some sort of a vague thumping. It seemed that he
had already been hearing it for some minutes in the back of his mind.
Now the thumping was growing weaker, and gradually it stopped.

In sudden alarm he leaped down the corridor in big strides. A man
dashed out of the door of Mr. Johnson's stateroom, and ran swiftly
down the corridor in the opposite direction, toward the dining-room.

"Now we've got him," thought Burgess. "He can't get away this
time."

With a shout, the reporter dashed after the fleeing figure. In the
dining-room he stopped to snap on the lights. The room was empty.
He hurried on through into the after-gallery. That also was empty. It
contained no furniture, and the bright lights illuminated every nook
and cranny of it. There was no way out of the two rooms except the
corridor by which he had come in. What had become of the man?

There was a commotion behind Burgess in the corridor, exclamations and babbling of voices. He hurried back to find a crowd about
Mr. Johnson's door. As he ran up, the people stepped aside and opened
up a path for him to get through. Inside the stateroom Mr. Johnson
lay on the bed motionless, his face a dark purple. He was not breathing. On his throat were five black marks.

"Strangled!" exclaimed somebody in the crowd. Burgess tore open
Mr. Johnson's shirt, and detected a faint flutter of the heart. The next
moment the Captain was on the scene and in charge. Cold packs were
put about the throat and artificial respiration instituted. Soon their
strenuous and persistent efforts were rewarded by a flutter of the eye-
lids, several gasps, and finally a groan. Mr. Johnson turned over and
sat up, choking and gasping, trying to talk.

"Hagan," Burgess could distinguish, though it meant nothing to him. "Wanted the money again," came in a whisper. "I hit him but he was too much for me."

A lump rose in Burgess' throat. The fat, flabby, nervous old President, on the inside, was a good sport.

The reporter counted the crowd. There were ten people. The Colonel's wife was in the drawing-room, tanning herself. The human face hides emotions, rather than displays them. Not the least suggestion of a clue could he find in the countenances of any of them. Could he but see behind the masks of astonishment and horror, would it be possible to guess which one had done it? Yet he had to admit that the probability of any of these people having done the cowardly deed was exceedingly remote. Everyone of them had been behind him, absorbed in the dance at the time when he had heard the thumping, which must have been the struggles of Mr. Johnson while he was being throttled.

The Captain came in and picked up Mr. Johnson's pistol, which lay on the floor beside the berth. Burgess was telling him the story:

"None of these passengers could have gotten past me and I was between them and Mr. Johnson's room. The time I spent in the dining-room and after-gallery was only a few seconds, certainly not long enough to give anyone a chance to choke a man. I chased the fellow into the dining-room, and when I got there, he wasn't there."

"There's something fishy about this," the Captain growled into his beard.

Burgess was determined to solve the puzzle, and made up his mind to work as he had never worked before. "TIMES REPORTER UNRAVELS INTERPLANETARY MYSTERY" he could see the headlines say in his mind's eye.

"You're sure it couldn't be one of the crew?" Burgess asked the Captain.

The Captain laughed.

"That shows how little you know about discipline on an interplanetary liner. I can account for the presence of every man during every minute of the time. But, we're going to go over this ship again. One man got by our first search; there must be another. And from now on, an armed guard stands by Mr. Johnson's door, day and night."

The man with a rifle was already in his place. The search of the ship began at once. The searchers began in the passenger section, going through trunks, looking into corners, searching the most impossible places, far too small for a man to hide in. They proceeded systematically, beginning at the drawing-room end. The rest of the night they could be heard down below, shifting the cargo, hammering on boxes and cases. The noises began at the forward end and gradually moved aft. In the morning the Captain showed up in the dining-room, tired and cross.

"How is Mr. Johnson?" he asked.

"His condition is good;" replied Burgess, "except for his pain and discomfort. He will get over it perfectly."

"If there had been anything on board bigger than a rabbit, we would have dug it out last night," the Captain said. "We opened every case of freight that weighs over seventy-five pounds, unscrewed every hatch, threw light in every corner. It beats me."

The Captain clicked his jaw shut and looked fierce. Burgess grinned.

"You think that's a puzzle?" he said. "Well, what about this one? I chased a man down the corridor into the dining-room. He was not in the dining-room when I got there. He was not in the after-gallery. He did not pass me.

"What became of him?

"Is there any way of getting out of the dining-room or after-gallery except by the way I came in?"

The Captain stared at him.

"No. The only communications with the rest of the ship are the food service tubes which are four inches in diameter, and a hatch that it would take twenty minutes and a lot of noise to unscrew."

The Captain stopped and thought a moment.

"How did the man get out?"

Burgess was puzzled. By the strongest kind of logic, there was a man hidden on board, and this logic was confirmed by material proof on poor Mr. Johnson's person. Yet this man had disappeared before Burgess' eyes, and a thorough, systematic search of the ship had proved that he was not on board.

Technical Assistance

The reporter took his turn at nursing the President, while the guard stood at the door with his rifle. Noon lunch and the dinner meal in the evening were gloomy, nervous occasions. Everyone started at the least noise. Kaufman's brows were drawn and dark. Only the de Palognis seemed to be getting a thrill out of the situation, whereas the honeymoon couple were quite impervious to it. The young engineer carried Cecilie May's service plate at both meals, and the two ate together, one talking enthusiastically, the other listening raptly. The girl seemed to feel safer near the young man, and was afraid to be about the ship except in his presence.

Burgess was intensely worried. The villain had almost gotten away with his nefarious scheme this time. There was still time enough before they reached Mars for many things to happen, he strolled to the after-gallery, and found himself in a secluded corner where he could think undisturbed; he stood there and looked out upon the deeps full of countless stars, and tried to marshal his ideas about the mystery.

He was roused from the depths of his reverie by low voices behind him. He was conscious of having heard them for some time without having paid much attention. A sudden embarrassment made him keep silent. They did not know he had overheard, and he did not want to break up the occasion. If they never found out he was there, it would be just as well.

"I love you," said a man very softly. It was Flynn.

"I love you, too," Cecilie May whispered timidly.

"I'm glad I found you."

"Isn't it wonderful?"

There was a long period of silence.

"I'm terribly sorry," the man's voice said, "that it will be so long before we can get married. I haven't a cent, and I don't even know what

I'm going to do when I get to Mars. I'm afraid—that a professional man's start is a slow and difficult one."

Cecilie May cheered him with soft words and kisses.

Right there was where Burgess got the idea that eventually led to the solution of the mystery. It developed slowly while he was having to keep as quiet as a mouse in order not to interrupt the lovers. Eventually the newly engaged couple wandered away, and Burgess hurried back to spend a little time at Mr. Johnson's bedside.

The old man could whisper a little, but swallowing was still terribly painful. The guard stood motionless at the door. After he thought he had allowed plenty of time, Burgess went out to look for the young engineer, and found him getting ready for bed.

"Would you like to help solve this mystery?" Burgess asked him.

"Anything I can do—" Flynn said. "I'm not much on mysteries."

"In two days we reach Mars," Burgess said. "Here, in close quarters it is possible to watch Mr. Johnson carefully. When he gets to Mars the killer will have free rein, and the old man will be in greater danger. That's still a pretty wild country, you know. We've got to catch him before we land."

"I don't see how you're going to," the young engineer said. "The ship's been searched—"

"Well, I got an idea last night. I was thinking about you and about your work. You're an engineer?"

Flynn nodded.

"You know all about scientific things?"

Flynn laughed.

"I wish I did," he said.

"Well, this mystery needs science to solve it."

"I'd be mighty proud if I could help any."

They went into Burgess' stateroom and sat and talked and figured with pencils on paper; they leaned back and planned. Finally Flynn said:

"That ought to work. Now to see the Captain. But it will take me several hours of work in the ship's shop to get things ready."

They put their plan before the Captain.

"It's all right with me, as long as you don't interfere with the guard," the Captain said, but looked incredulous.

"We only want to move the guard ten feet up the corridor. He can stay within plain sight of the door, where he can reach it in one second; and we shall both keep our eyes on the door."

The Captain looked dubiously from one to the other.

"Burgess has a good reputation. Flynn looks as though he knew his stuff." This to himself—then aloud: "Go ahead. But I'll be around, too, and keep an eye on it."

As they came back into the corridor, they found Chick standing horrified with a piece of paper in his hand. The guard looked worried and frightened, and the Colonel was sputtering incoherently. It was a note that had been found on the floor of the sick man's room. Yet the guard insisted that he had not taken his eyes off his charge for an instant; and he was a tried and trusted man.

> "You cannot escape me," the note read. "In spite of your precautions, I'm going to get you. Fork over the million or you won't reach Mars alive. A check will do; leave payee line blank, and lay it on the doorsill."

Burgess and Flynn nodded to each other and smiled.

"That confirms our idea," Burgess said to the Captain. "Do not blame the guard; I'm sure he is right in what he says. But there is no need to pay any attention to the note."

Flynn was busy all day in the ship's shop. But the next morning the passengers saw Flynn and Burgess playing catch with an indoor baseball down the length of the corridor. A crash and the tinkling of glass announced an accident: the smashing of the light-bulb over the middle of the corridor. Then Flynn attempted to replace the bulb; he tried several bulbs from different parts of the ship, but none of them would work. Finally he gave it up and left a dark bulb in the socket.

"It doesn't matter," he said. "There is plenty of light from the bulbs at the ends of the corridor."

However, some of the passengers were worried for the dark bulb was right over Mr. Johnson's door, leaving it the darkest portion of the corridor. Chick was dispatched into the lower regions of the ship with a suitcase, and returned dragging it as though it were immensely heavy. Burgess and Flynn spent the whole afternoon in Burgess' room. Everyone was restless, and wandered from one thing to another, not knowing what to do. After dinner Burgess appeared among them, leading one of the traveling men by the arm.

"Ladies and gentlemen," he said, "I have just learned that Mr. Banks here knows a lot of astonishing tricks with cards. You are all in need of diversion at this time. Let's get everybody together."

They gathered in the drawing-room, and the traveling man stood up in front of them with a deck of cards in his hand. He pulled his coat-sleeves up on his forearm, and spread his cards fanwise.

"Now, ladies and gentlemen," he began. "Will one of the ladies please step forward. I shall turn the cards face down, so that I cannot see them. Now, Miss Waterbury, you draw out a card. Be careful not to let me see it, but remember it well. Now put it back. Do you all remember what the card was—"

He pattered on, and Burgess slipped out of the room as soon as Banks had the attention of all of them. In his stateroom he and Flynn bent over a strange conglomeration of apparatus. On one end was a great quartz lens, borrowed from the ship's bolometer. The other end looked like the receiving portion of a television apparatus, with a hood drawn over the screen.

"Is everybody busy in there?" Flynn asked.

"He's got 'em going," Burgess smiled.

"Then give the guard his signal."

The guard pretended to become interested in the card tricks, and gradually edged his way up the corridor, away from Mr. Johnson's door.

"I don't see the Captain," said Burgess, "but I'll bet he's somewhere on the job."

"Take a look into it," Flynn said. "I've hooded the screen because the light from it on our faces would reveal our presence in here. This way it is absolutely dark.

Burgess looked into the hood, at the screen.

"What about it?" he asked. "I see the corridor. It looks just the same as per naked eye."

"Look again," Flynn said, keeping his voice low. "Without the instrument the corridor right here is rather gloomy because the middle bulb gives no light; all the light there is comes from the bulbs at the ends of the corridor. Now look into the instrument."

"Ah," said Burgess. "I see. In here, the middle of the corridor is brilliantly lighted, and its ends are dark. Just the opposite. How do you work that?"

"The middle bulb is not dead. It gives infra-red light, which is not perceived by the human eye. This instrument sees by infra-red light; all visible light is screened off by a collodial-silver filter. The lens gathers the infra-red image, throws it on the infra-red sensitive photo-electric cells, which project it on the ordinary television-screen as visible to our eyes. In other words, this is a viewer for infra-red light.

"But why—"

"Sh-h. Suppose we wait. We've been talking too long now. Let's keep absolutely quiet. Tell me, after I have my face under the hood, if there is the least bit of me visible from the door? And let me have your gun."

There was a tense, silent wait. The sounds of the party in the drawing-room came to them, exclamations, titters, sudden floods of argument, a period of silence, a burst of laughter, rustling and commotion, and the performer's patter.

However, they had not long to wait.

There was a creak down the corridor, exceedingly faint. Then a faint swish. Flynn grew tense at his instrument, his breath coming fast. The reporter exerted his utmost to maintain silence in his excitement, for he could not see a thing anywhere. The corridor was empty, search it as he might, except for the guard halfway toward the drawing-room. He breathed with his mouth wide open, for he was so excited that when he closed it, the breath shrilled loudly through his nostrils.

Unveiling the Inscrutable

Suddenly the engineer shouted out into the corridor:

"Hands up! I've got you covered. Now take that cape off! I'll count ten, and if it isn't off by ten, I'll shoot. Your cape won't stop bullets."

The next instant his shot crashed. He leaped up, knocking Burgess in the ribs with his elbow. In two jumps he was across the corridor and in Mr. Johnson's room. Burgess dashed out after him, to see the Captain emerge from an adjoining stateroom. In another instant Chick was also on hand. The sounds of the party in the drawing-room suddenly stopped, and open-mouthed people trickled down the corridor. For there were sounds of a terrific commotion coming out of Mr. Johnson's room.

First there was a hoarse shriek from the sick man. Then there was the spectacle of the young engineer fighting violently all around the room—with nothing! His arms were out, as though locked around somebody; he heaved and grunted and staggered—all alone. A couple of times he almost went down. The rest of them, even Burgess, were too astonished to do anything except stand there staring and paralyzed. Mr. Johnson lay in bed like a man frozen stiff. Flynn staggered back against the wall as though someone had hit him.

After what seemed like an age, though it was only a few seconds, Burgess began to grasp the situation, and stepped into the room to see how he could be of assistance. But already it was not necessary. Flynn was on his knees, six inches above the ground, as though on top of something, though there was nothing there. He was pummeling terrific blows with his fists; and then desisted and began pulling and tearing at something under him. There was a loud rip, and a swing of his arm revealed a strip of clothing and a part of a face beneath him. Another pull disclosed another strip of clothing, an arm and a leg. Flynn was pulling something off a man who lay prostrate, on the ground and who was becoming visible in long strips. In a moment Burgess and Chick were on the prostrate man and had him pinioned down.

Then Chick recoiled as though he had been shot. The man on the floor was ugly as sin and had a purple birthmark on his cheek!

"Pug!" cried out the boy, deeply hurt. "You?"

Burgess chuckled.

"I'm sorry it makes you feel bad," he said to Chick, patting him on the back. "But I'd call it a valuable piece of instruction."

The President sat up in bed. The prisoner stood between two husky sailors, with the Captain behind him.

"So you're the pretty fellow who wrote the red letters?" Mr. Johnson said, his sore throat wheezing in his excitement. "I've seen you about my place a time or two. What'll it be, Captain?"

"You can have him put in irons and brought back to New York for an expensive and long-drawn-out criminal trial. Or, I can take him under the space-navigation laws on two counts, as a stowaway and on insubordination, and put him out of the air-valve."

"Take him yourself. I should regret it if I took one chance too many. Brace up, Charles. We are sometimes mistaken in our friends. Your dad has learned lots of little lessons like that." He motioned to Flynn.

"You seem to have managed this business," he said, again displaying his innate shrewdness. "Tell me how."

"Very simple, sir," answered Flynn, rather confused by the limelight suddenly turned on him. "Mr. Burgess presented to me the two facts: (1) There was a crook loose on the ship, and (2) He was not one of the passengers, officers, nor crew. Therefore, in some way he must be hidden, and had eluded the searches. The question was *how?* The fact that Burgess saw him go into a room from which there was no egress, and yet did not find him there, rather simplified the question.

"There popped into my head an item from *The Engineering Abstracts* about some experimental work with a double-refractible fabric made of a cellulose base combined with silicon salts, which will refract a light-ray through itself and continue it in its original straight line. If a light-ray is bent around an object and continued in its original straight line, that object becomes *invisible*. Objects in the laboratory where these experiments were carried out were practically invisible. Only some rough preliminary work was described in the abstract.

"That offered a perfect explanation of the phenomena on this ship. Here the conditions are perfect. The light from these helium lamps gives a narrow wave-band and can be much more perfectly refracted than daylight. It occurred to me, in my effort to think of a way to discover this person, that if I could see by the light of a different wavelength, it would not be properly refracted, and I could detect the crook's presence. But any attempts to use such a light would give away our plans and put us all in serious danger. Therefore I would have to see him by means of some invisible wavelength. Either the ultra-violet or the infra-red were available. But ultra-violet is difficult to generate, while the infra-red is easy: I merely blackened an old-fashioned nitrogen-filled incandescent-wire bulb. Then I rigged up an infra-red viewer and watched for him. I saw him sneak into Mr. Johnson's room, at a moment which we had purposely prepared, so that everyone's attention was obviously distracted elsewhere. I intended to shoot him, but he got in line with Mr. Johnson and I was afraid to take the chance, and had to jump on him."

Cecilie May was hanging on to Flynn's arm. Mr. Johnson fired a few rapid questions at both of them, and in the twinkle of an eye had all their intimate secrets out of them.

"I need a man to put in charge of the repair station for space-liners on Mars," he said to Flynn. "It is an out-of-the-way place, but it has in the past been a good stepping-stone to better jobs. The position is yours. Bless you two young people."

Kaufman raised his eyebrows.

"So, here's where I'm left without a secretary," he said. "But since it has happened this way, I guess I'll take it cheerfully. Here's a little wedding present."

He wrote out a check and handed it to the confused and blushing Cecilie May.

A sailor stood in the door, saluted the Captain and announced the following:

"The lookout reports that Syrtis Major is visible through the front port. We ought to land in about four hours!"

Mechanocracy

"Quentin Smith Lakeman, the Government regrets your personal feelings and sympathizes with your relatives, but finds it necessary to condemn you at once to euthanasia."

As the mechanical voice that came from the orifice of the speaker ceased, Quentin Smith Lakeman turned pale and an icy pang shot through him. Through the dazzling lights that danced in his brain, he could see his three companions standing there gasping as a result of the sudden, crushing sentence.

He had expected some kind of a reward for his year of hard work, danger, and hardship spent in the service of the Government. Not that he expected machinery to have any gratitude; but above all, the machine is logical and just, and there were rules for rewarding special effort such as his.

"Democratia must be promptly and completely destroyed," the metallic voice of the speaker continued. "From your report of your investigations in that country, it is clear that its people will never consent to standardize themselves, and that they therefore constitute a menace to our standardized World Government."

Quentin—to call him by his "intimate" name, for in the twenty-sixth century everyone had an intimate name, a family name, and a public name—was flung down and crushed again by the announcement of the fate of that gallant country in which he had just spent a year. It seemed that his heart would stop beating then and there, for Democratia held Martha, who in that one short year had become more precious than all else in the world. He looked beside him at

Jack, her stalwart eighteen-year-old brother, who had journeyed back with him as a guest to Washington, the Capital of the World.

"The Government appreciates the very efficient efforts of Quentin Smith Lakeman," the voice went on. Quentin knew it for the empty formula that the machine adopted in order to appeal to the emotions of human beings with whom it dealt. "It understands that this decision is emotionally difficult for living beings to bear. But, you have spent months in Democratia, and acquired a considerable tinge of individualistic ideas and customs. It would be dangerous to our institutions to turn you loose among the people now. And, as Democratia will soon cease to exist, prompt euthanasia is the only solution."

Utter silence followed. Even the faint crackling of the speaker ceased, showing that the connection was off. Quentin turned to Jack, whose burly form towered above the rest of them, and whose countenance showed a bewildered inability to grasp what it all meant.

Just then the door opened and a police captain came in, followed by a squad of men in blue uniform. Quentin recognized the captain as Guy Sherman Sentier, an old and close friend. Sentier stopped short and turned pale.

"You?" he gasped as he saw Quentin. "My orders are to take four people out of this office to the Euthanasia Chambers! What have you done?"

"Nothing!" said Quentin, calm by this time. "Go ahead. It's your duty. All I've done was to do mine."

"Terribly sorry," said Sentier faintly. He motioned to his men, and turned his head away.

The policemen came up, one of them grasping Jack by the arm. Jack whirled around and knocked the fellow across the room as easily as shaking off a rat. Then he leaped away from the group that had come in through an outer door, and in a moment had disappeared through a door leading into the interior of the building. The clatter of his swift footsteps died rapidly away into the muffled distance.

For a moment the policemen stood aghast. They did not know quite how to behave, for never in their experience had a prisoner made so bold as to try to escape. With the world rigidly standardized and moving as one unit, what hope could there be of escape?

At a shout from the captain, they became active and scattered through doors and windows in pursuit, each with his thin black rod.

The three remaining captives were handcuffed and a man left in charge.

Quentin waited in patient resignation, for he knew it could not last long. Can one escape the lion in his own den? The very walls of the building would combine to hunt down the fugitive.

But the boy must have been swift and clever. Minutes lengthened into an hour; the guard stood stiff, mechanical, embarrassed. The huge building was silent save for vague mechanical sounds. Then a faint shout came across a courtyard through a window, and Quentin could see Jack climbing down a drain pipe from the roof. Two figures appeared on the roof above him, and others ran out of a door nearby and waited for him on the ground. As Jack came down within reach, one of the guards touched him with the end of his slender, three-foot rod. Jack dropped to the ground, limp and paralyzed. In a few moments he was wheeled into the office on a small cart, one of the policemen holding the rod in contact with Jack's arm. The boy lay helpless, his eyes gazing mute inquiry into Quentin's.

"No use, Jack," Quentin said to him. "You're among civilized people now, you know. You're no good against police equipment. Promise them you'll go quietly and they'll let you up."

The policeman lifted the rod an instant, giving Jack power to nod his head in promise. Thereupon the policeman put his rod away, and Jack stood up and looked about abashed. As the police led their captives out, Sentier called after Quentin:

"You don't hold this against me personally? May I visit you?"

"Come. I shall be glad to see you," Quentin answered philosophically. "Why should I blame *you*? You're a tiny cog in a huge machine."

As the captives were led into a barred and guarded plane, Quentin put his arm about Jack's big shoulders in sympathy. He looked young to die; and it seemed like a betrayal, to be brought from that wild country to see the wonders of the civilized world, and find this. As the plane rose and headed for New York, where the euthanasia facilities were located, Jack seemed more absorbed in looking down at the Government Buildings which comprised the whole city of Washington, than in the thought of impending death. He looked at Quentin with bewilderment in his face.

"That square massive building just below us is the one we were in? And you say that is the center, the brain, the key of the whole World Government?"

"That *is* the Government," Quentin replied. "Just as your brain is you. These other countless acres of buildings are merely its arms and fingers and eyes and ears. Without this building they could not function, and the world would be chaos."

Jack stared down fascinatedly.

"And yet," he breathed in amazement, "I ran through miles of corridors, passed hundreds of rooms full of apparatus and instruments, and not a soul did I see."

Quentin nodded in confirmation.

"For an hour I ran, and by the end of it I was caring less about being caught than about finding some people about in these buildings. Is there no one?"

"No one," Quentin replied.

"And yet you say it's the Government!" The boy seemed dumbfounded.

"After all my explaining," Quentin said, "haven't you realized that the Government is merely a huge machine, made of metal and rubber and glass and run by electricity and light and heat?"

"But—but how can machinery govern the world?"

"Better than human beings can. Even your business men in Democratia use machines to help them run their businesses; their offices are full of automatic machines for managing a business, time-clocks, adding-machines, bookkeeping machines, cash-registers, Dictaphones—no end of them. The Government Machine is not *essentially* different. Merely a little more automatic and a little more complex."

"And are all the people willing to be governed by a machine?" It was all amazingly strange to Jack.

"They cannot conceive of anything else," Quentin explained. "For three hundred years they have grown up in it. They are intensely loyal to it, because it not merely governs them as you understand the word govern; it takes care of them as a mother takes care of children."

"They seem to be happy," Jack observed.

Quentin nodded down toward the beautiful countryside over which they were flying at a swift rate. The green fields were intersected by broad roads and huge power lines, and the blue bulk of a city loomed on the horizon.

"The world is more prosperous than it has ever been before," he replied. "Life is thoroughly comfortable, absolutely safe and certain. But you would call it monotonous. Everybody does everything by rule and schedule, all alike, the world over. Standardized. You wouldn't like it."

"I couldn't stand it!" Jack exclaimed.

"Your country, Democratia," continued Quentin, "is made up of the descendants of people who couldn't stand it. During the development period of machine government standardization, the democratic-minded people, who could not fit into it, were having a hard time. They were persecuted and driven from one place to another."

"That's unjust!" Jack was thoroughly democratic.

"They were a small minority. The rest of the world was in earnest; it was afraid of annihilation by war. So it built cities on a standard plan, streets and buildings all alike. From New York to Hongkong people live on the same schedule and think by the same rules. That is easier to manage by machinery. Safer. More comfortable."

Jack gazed for a while at the swiftly receding landscape below.

"Then why is the Government picking on Democratia now?" he asked.

"It had to come. For some centuries your country in Central Tibet was left in peace because its founders sought the remotest possible isolation. Our Government had its own problems. But, step by step it is striving constantly to perfect the world. Apparently the step has arrived in the process when it is time to remove the only exception to world rule."

"And it sent you over there?" Jack shook his head, puzzled.

"Remember that the Government has no emotions nor prejudices. It works absolutely by logic. It is always perfect in its fairness. A decision on Democratia needed all possible informational data. As communication channels do not extend into Democratia, men had to be sent in."

"And when you do a good job, you get killed for it."

"Logical, though, is it not?" Quentin could be impersonal when discussing the Government Machine. "Now I see why it warned me so emphatically that I was risking my life and gave me repeated opportunities to decline the assignment if I wished to."

"Risking your life? In Democratia?" Jack exclaimed.

"Not at all, although that is the way I understood it at first. The Government needed a resourceful man for the job, and resourceful men are rare in our civilization. I was the best bet — don't laugh at me; I know how helpless and clumsy you think I am — I took my risk and lost it. For, this world cannot permit a resourceful man to live in it."

Jack hardly heard the conclusion. He was gazing in open-mouthed wonder at the huge, solid mass of New York City that loomed ahead, the cliffs of buildings, the surging masses of people and machinery. The plane glided swiftly up above the dull, drab roofs, and landed on the top of a building, guided by a long black streamer at the top of a tall flagpole. Surrounded by guards, the four men were led to an elevator, descended a score of floors, and entered the Euthanasia Chambers.

The furnishings and appointments here were the last word in beauty and luxury. The soft carpets, the rich hangings, the luxurious furniture, the flowers and scents and colors, the foods and wines within reach, all had a tendency to lull the occupants into a sense of peace and drowsy comfort. Each of the party was led to a room where he was to be given twenty-four hours for receiving last visits from friends and relatives. Jack and Quentin elected to remain together in one room.

"Lovely, isn't it," said Quentin ironically. "A year ago its beauty would have stirred my emotions. But your rugged land has cured me. Now I can see the steel and concrete through the velvet, and see it just as an undertaking establishment which you enter alive and leave dead."

Sentier arrived presently. Without his squad of policemen he was not a very impressive man. He almost wept as he greeted Quentin. It looked almost as though he were the one sentenced to death.

"One's duty demands cruel things," he moaned. "Arrest your best friend!"

"I wouldn't do it, that's all," Jack exclaimed.

Quentin patted the boy's back.

"Yes you would," he reminded, "if you and a dozen generations of you had been raised like machines to obey the Government Machine and be loyal to it above all."

Noting Sentier's depressed looks, Quentin offered to relate his adventures in Democratia, and Sentier eagerly grasped at the opportunity to relieve the tension.

"Get a permit to broadcast as much as possible of it," Quentin suggested. "It is a beautiful land and a wonderful people that are about to be destroyed. But, suppose I tell you? What if you sympathize? That will be treason, and you will be — eliminated."

Sentier smiled.

"No danger," he said. "That is why you were sent out and I am a police captain. If I can arrest my best friend in cold blood, how can I sympathize with a distant land and a strange people?"

"In other words," Quentin mused again, "the Government picked me out to die when it selected me for the job?"

"That, of course, depended on what you would find there."

Jack clenched his fists. A frown gathered on his forehead. He glared at the policeman, who was an embodiment of the Government that killed an efficient man for doing his duty, and to whom machines were more important than men. Quentin watched the boy as he talked. Vague possibilities stirred his imagination. What if he might see Martha again? He, Quentin, had the brains for a daring attempt, but not the physical courage. Jack had boldness enough for anything. Quentin worded his story quite as much for its effect on Jack, as for Sentier's benefit.

Chapter II

"Just a year ago," Quentin began his story to Sentier, "I was called into that same office in Washington and given my instructions. I was offered the chance to refuse without stigma. That I thought ridiculous, for it seemed a wonderful opportunity. I am cursed with a love of adventure, which is a terrible affliction in this monotonous age. I was to spend a year in Democratia, and then come back and give a full report on the life and customs of the country.

"I was so excited that I came within a hair of giving away a secret, and probably with it, my life or liberty. This love of adventure had boiled up within me from youth. For years I had planned some sort of a wild deed. Bit by bit I had secretly assembled an airplane in an obscure cellar on Long Island. It lay there at the moment, with fuel and provisions ready to start, equipped for a rough, uncertain trip, instead of for the scheduled routes which have been carefully standardized. I had an impulse to take this plane for the trip, but a flash of judgment told me that it would be dangerous to reveal my secret.

"I was ordered to take my official planes, which I owned according to my rank and standing. I was not permitted to take my own mechanic; Binder and Steele were assigned as mechanics and Neatman as Secretary. It was all very simple. The three men arrived at my home early one morning; we taxied out of my garage, flew across the city, and out over the Atlantic. Because of the rigid standardization of men, methods, and machines, the mechanics had no need of seeing either me or the plane before the moment of starting.

"We made a quick trip, and I paid little attention to my surroundings during the most of it. The cities look the same and the people act the same everywhere as in New York. Only when we reached the Himalayas I began to feel my first thrill. Those vast stretches, without a city for hundreds of miles, are romantic. We located the Tagnapo River and the ruins of Llhasa, once a large and powerful city; and struck due North into a wild desert where no one ever goes. After some hours of searching, we located the green valley completely shut in by vast mountains and saw the cities of Democratia.

"There were three large, fine ones and a dozen smaller towns, and a sprinkling over the whole land of what must have been villages. Think of it, Sentier, they live in villages! Little collections of a few tiny buildings. Most of the world used to do that a thousand years ago. And even the three great cities of Democratia were not modern as our cities are. They were not built in units. Each building was of different height and size, and they had open streets in single layers. But it was a wonderful-looking land. Think of it, lying hidden away there and the world knowing nothing about it; its bold, resourceful men, its sturdy and beautiful women. When it is puffed out, no one will feel a pang of sympathy for it.

"There were no diplomatic relations between the two governments. Credentials were of no use to them and I received none, nor did I receive any sign of the usual string of rules, instructions, and minutiae. The whole thing was left up to me; and during the whole of the trip over, I pondered on some way of approaching the people of Democratia. I pondered in vain. I knew nothing about the people and their country, and could form no plan. So, I first took a good look at the country from an altitude too great for them to see me. Then I decided to land in some uninhabited spot and spend a night resting and planning. I chose a flat place low down between two tall peaks, near the northern rim of the mountain-surrounded country. A hundred miles away was one of their largest cities.

"We alighted on grass and the air was cold. But we had warm clothing and the cabin of the plane was heated. The beauty of the prospect was worth the cold. The vast, grassy plain, the woods half a mile away, the huge, snow-patched mountains in the opposite direction—we live too much cooped up in cities, Sentier—it took my breath. The others were also impressed, and we had to expend our emotions in a walk toward the woods.

"I ought to have known better. City men have no business in the wilderness. Oh, yes, we took our shock-rods along, and I took an old-fashioned projectile pistol. Half way to the trees we heard a tramping behind us, and turning, beheld a huge goat with winding horns charging for us at full speed. The animal raced swiftly toward us as we stood paralyzed by fear. It seemed to have picked out Steele, and tore right at him. Steele took it coolly enough, and faced the charge with his shock-rod. It paralyzed the goat on contact all right, but it could not stop the momentum of the great, charging body, which rolled crashing on, crushed Steele under it, and nearly got me. I got a bullet in the goat's head before it could get up, astonishing my companions with the noise of the shot. Steele was dead, smashed, when we reached him.

"The sound of galloping hoofs reached us. More goats were coming. We ran for the woods because they were nearer than our plane. Later I got used to the looks of these goats. They are not particularly dangerous. But to us, just then, they were huge, frightful, monsters. We're not used to seeing large, live, free animals. Our frantic fear made us act foolishly.

"At intervals I turned around and shot bullets at the goats. Just now that is laughable. I had no skill with the weapon. My shots went wild. But it helped a little, for the noise confused the goats and retarded their speed somewhat. We reached the trees and hurried far into their depths. The goats did not follow because their horns got tangled in the growth.

"Then, when we had gotten our breath after such unaccustomed exertion, and had waited long enough to give the goats time to wander off, we started back. We walked on through the trees toward the plain, but came to no end of them. We were lost!

"The terrors of that night will be stamped on my memory forever—well, that won't be long. First of all it was cold. We huddled together. Some of us thought of a fire. None of us had ever seen an open fire; but we had read of ancient savages making fires by rubbing sticks. We rubbed sticks till we were exhausted. Of course it was silly for we didn't even know the difference between green and dry wood. We therefore crowded together on the ground, shivering as much with terror as with cold. There was no sleep for us. The noises of the woods, from clicks and crackles to roars and yells, sent grip after grip of fear through our hearts. Sentier, these tales you read of people dying from pure terror are not true. If such a thing were possible, we would all have died the first quarter of the night. Yet, these Democratians spend night after night in the woods and enjoy it. We are just too much pampered by our machines.

"A party of them had camped, not half a mile from us, that night, just too far for us to see their fire. They wrap themselves in blankets and leave one person on guard, and sleep soundly all night. They found us in the morning, numb with cold and dumb with fear. The first I knew of them was a musical voice calling:

"'Quick, Jack!' with a little *Oh*-like intake of the breath. 'Someone in distress!'

"I looked up. Approaching was a girl in corduroy breeches and high-laced boots—antiquated, romantic. A knapsack. An old-fashioned rifle for shooting bullets. But there was a glow of health in her cheeks that made the chemical beauty of our girls seem ridiculous. To me, that moment, shivering in hungry, hopeless despair, she was the most beautiful, radiant being I had ever seen or imagined. She was the sister of Jack here. He was with her."

Quentin looked about the velvet draperies that concealed their prison walls, as though it were hard to believe that it all hung together somehow. He sank his face in his hands for an instant. Sentier was embarrassed. Sentier could sympathize with the love affair. Men of his day were experts in those. Quentin did not even look at Jack, and in a moment had thrown off the mood, and continued:

"They had us comfortable in a few minutes. Jack and his father came up very soon. Before our eyes they made a fire. Sentier, you ought to see a fire before you die. They boiled coffee and eggs. Did you ever eat an egg, Sentier? The delicious odors, the warmth of the fire, the beauty of the girl who was on an equal with the men in strength and efficiency, and had no simpering feminine wiles about her—I was sold on Democratia from then on.

"'Who are you, and whence are you?' was their first question.

"'Just on a pleasure cruise,' I put in quickly before any of the rest of our party could speak. 'Bound nowhere in particular. We liked this spot and wanted to look at it more closely, and got lost. We spent all night in the woods.'

"'Unarmed? Without fire?' The girl looked worlds of sympathy at us.

"'We're city folks, not used to being out,' I said.

"'So are we city folks—' Jack began, but his father silenced him with a look.

"They persuaded us to come to their camp, and promised to find our plane. After some sleep and rest I began to notice things. There were a dozen people in a tiny house of logs on the mountain. They were living there for a month. They had no heating system, no lighting system—depended on open fires. No kine-phone service. No tube delivery. Not even properly prepared food. They ate just animals and plants boiled over a fire. No transportation; they walked everywhere. Yet they were enjoying it. Doing it for pleasure! Can you imagine it?

"And can you imagine me enjoying it? I got interested early. I learned to build a fire. Too bad there's no place around here to build a fire. I learned to shoot a rifle. Much more thrilling than a shock-rod. At the end of the month I could walk ten miles and enjoy it. I could sleep out all night and make my own breakfast. Compared with these people, though, Sentier, I was helpless. Compared with them, all of us are helpless. Little helpless larvae, such as ants carry around.

"We depend for everything on machinery and on our Government. The Government gives us food and water and amusement and its machines work for us and take care of us. Without its care we would die in a few days. "These people haven't much government: a ridiculous meeting of so-called representatives once a year, which spends most of its time arguing and never gets anywhere. They have 'laws' which they obey when it's convenient and possible.

"But they don't need a government. We do. They can take care of themselves. With their own individual hands they can grapple with Nature, and wrest life and comfort from her trees and rocks and beasts. Jack here is only eighteen, but he could probably take you and break you up in short pieces. Don't grab your rod. He knows it won't get him anywhere. He could probably go several days without much food or sleep. Ever tried that, Sentier?

"We may have a wonderful civilization, Sentier, but as individuals, we're feeble sprouts. What's the good of all these millions of us, all alike? Humanity by mass production. What would be the loss if they all died today?

"We were taken to the largest of their cities, a primitive sort of place with individual buildings and individual cars running about. Jack's father was a high government official and had been vacationing in the mountains. He was a rugged and kindly man, very much concerned about the welfare of the people over whom his authority extended. He took us to his home and shared its comforts with us. Imagine that, Sentier! Taking a total stranger into your home, having him eat with you, sleep in your rooms!

"It wasn't long before I found myself in an uncomfortable pickle. These people were kind to us, doing all they could to make us feel at home. Friendly. Couldn't help loving them. And here I was spying. Preparing to betray their kindness to me. For, much as I liked their country and their ways, I knew that the Government Machine would not. I spent several weeks of torture.

"Furthermore, I was supposed to stay there a year. It was not plausible that even idle tourists would tarry for a year by the wayside. They would wonder, why didn't I go on?

"The father of Jack and Martha noted my worry and depression. He asked me about it, with blunt primitive directness.

"'There is something about your situation here that worries you,' he said. 'Tell me what it is, and I can help you.' See? None of the round-about diplomacy that we're used to. He got the whole story out of me.

"The deep lines in his face, with its little fringe of beard, made him look very wise and very kind. You've never seen a man with a beard, have you, Sentier? It adds dignity.

"'The only thing for you to do,' he said, 'is to stay and do your duty. We'll be friends, because we like you and know you can't help it. Go back when the time comes. If you don't, they will send others, who may be more dangerous to us than you are.'

324

"Then I was more at peace until the time approached to go. I kept my Secretary busy writing up notes, and the mechanics keeping the plane in condition. I went around doing my best to study the country. I learned about money and buying and political parties, about poor people and unemployment. I learned to drive one of their little cars. I actually held a 'job' and made my own living for a few weeks, though I think my employer was glad to get rid of me. But most of the time I was a 'guest,' an exception to the prevailing conditions in which everyone had to hammer out his living with his own hands or starve.

"I took long trips through their country in great steel carriages that run on rails. Martha accompanied me almost everywhere. She had been charming that first day in her rough hunting suit when she found us nearly dead; she was charming later in a thousand ways, in soft and long gowns, dancing to spirited music; in athletic white, vigorously playing a very active game called tennis; she knew her people and her country thoroughly, and was my guide and teacher in my studies.

"At our first meeting I was weak and helpless and half dead; she was sturdy and resourceful; I looked up to her on dizzy heights above me with a hopeless, sorrowful feeling. Ten months later, physically fit to look after her safety, I took her on a glacier-climb, paying all the expenses with 'money' I had 'earned' myself. There's a pride in earning money, Sentier; too bad you can't try it.

"We have practically eliminated wild animals from the rest of the world, but these people preserve them and limit their destruction for the sport of hunting them. It is a dangerous sport. Martha and I never suspected any danger, when we were climbing up the easy ice-slopes in a frolicking fashion. She was ahead, around a point of ice and out of sight, when I heard her screams.

"I hurried up. Two white bears had attacked her. One had her rifle in its mouth and was pawing and crunching at it. The other had her down and was rolling her back and forth with its front paws, and tearing playfully at her clothes with its teeth.

"Then they saw me. Both snarled. The one with the rifle dropped it and came at me. These creatures looked clumsy, but they can move.

The thing was on me before I could unsling my rifle, and I went down under it. As the beast pummeled me, I scrambled for the long hunting-knife which I had learned to wear at my belt as do all of these people out in the open. I plunged the knife into his ribs a dozen times before he finally dropped and slid down the icy slope. I was completely soaked in his blood.

"By this time Martha was also jabbing with her knife and was bloody from head to foot, but the bear was still going strong. She was cool enough, but concerned about her face. She held up her arm to protect it from the animal's long claws, and this interfered with her knife thrusts. I finished him with three jabs and he crashed down on her. When I dragged him off, she did not get up, but lay there moaning.

"She had a broken leg. I—a product of this effete civilization, pampered by the Government Machine, raised like a lily in a hothouse—I splinted her leg with the scabbards of the long hunting knives and hoisted her across my shoulders there on the slippery ice. I toiled back with her and it was night before I reached the car, and toward morning before I drove into a village and secured medical help. What would you do, Sentier—police are huskier than the average—with two bears and only a knife; and a girl you loved, with a broken leg, a hundred miles away from the nearest habitation? No buttons to push, no lever to set, no machinery to wait on you.

"I spent delightful weeks in Martha's company while she was confined with her fracture. Before they were over, she was pledged to be my wife. Why an able and beautiful girl like that should want to marry a clumsy and incompetent lubber like myself, I could not understand.

"'I don't want to go back to Washington,' I said.

"'Let us settle down right away, and forget about Civilization.'

"'I should like it, of course,' she smiled.

"'Let the old Government Machine find someone else to do its dirty work!' I exclaimed. 'I'm happy here. Never again could I be happy in those roaring hives back there!'

"We planned our home, and counted on a teaching position which had been offered me in one of their universities, and I was happy about my future with her, and with these delightful people. I hesitated about informing the Secretary and the Mechanic. They were not quite as much delighted with the country of Democratia as I was, and were eagerly looking forward to the end of the year, when they might go back to the brilliant lights and the gay entertainment of Broadway. It was difficult for me to force myself to tell them.

"Finally, when our preparations began to be outwardly apparent, Martha's father took us in to talk to him.

"'Do you think this wise?' he asked me. 'From what I gather, your Government Machine does not lose track of details, and does not forgive failures.'

"'How could it find me here?' I asked, but rather hesitatingly.

"'Another phase of the matter is this. You sympathize with us and our country. We would much rather have you make the report. Suppose they send another man, less friendly? What would happen to us?'

"So, I started back for Washington, with a heavy heart because I must leave behind a girl, who, in beauty, in force of character, in real ability, mental and physical, is worth, all the women in this feeble and degenerate civilization."

He had been talking with his head bowed toward his knees. When he ceased, there was silence. It was a queer silence, lacking things that ought to have been there. He looked up. Sentier was also bowed over. Slumped over, in fact. Jack stood behind him; and as Quentin looked up, Jack straightened up and shook his hands from the wrists as though to limber them up. As Quentin stared amazed, Jack gave Sentier a shove; the latter rolled down on the floor and flopped over on his back in a loose, sickening sort of way. His face was purple, his black tongue protruded, and there were black marks on his neck.

"Neat job," Jack said, "if you're really as surprised as you look. You went too far, reminding me of Sis and home."

Chapter III

Quentin looked down at the dead man, and up at Jack's stalwart figure.

"Democracy *versus* mechanocracy," he said. "That is the way it goes between individuals. Between the organized groups, it would come out exactly the opposite.

"The machine wins, though its subject people are weaklings. Wouldn't it be better for the race to destroy the machine?

"But *I* couldn't do it. Every fiber of my nature has been brought up to consider the Government Machine as a sacred mother—

"But, I'll bet Jack would have the nerve in a minute—"

"Come," whispered Jack shrilly, "let's get out!"

He was already stripping off the dead man's uniform. He held it up and surveyed it ruefully against his own strapping bulk.

"I'll put it on," Quentin said. "I can act the part where you cannot. It'll be your turn when the rough-house begins."

Quentin's clothes were put on the dead man, and the latter's keys were used to open the door. They walked past the sentry at the door, receiving his salute without the flutter of an eyelid, and marched down the hallway, Jack in front with the handcuffs on, but not locked. Quentin came behind him in the captain's uniform, bearing the shock-rod. They had no plan, except that Quentin suddenly thought of his secret airplane, and determined to get to it.

But how? It was out on Long Island. They were in the middle of a huge city, one solid structure honeycombed with mazes and labyrinths of streets and passages horizontal and vertical. The end of it was three or four miles away, three or four miles of endless, buzzing, swarming, whirling machinery and humanity between them and open country.

"Our best bet," Quentin said, "is to get down to the lowest level. There we ought to find some sort of a burrow to crawl out of. To the elevator."

They reached the elevator and pushed its button. Its door opened and they stepped in, setting the button on the "eight-below" level, the lowest of them all. The car started down.

A gong clanged and kept on clanging somewhere in the depths of the building. A loud speaker began to bellow hoarsely on the floor they were passing; its roar died down as they left the floor behind, but was taken up by another on the floor below.

"The guard has found Sentier," whispered Quentin, "and has turned in the alarm. Well, let's show 'em a scrap!"

A new voice began in the speaker. It was crisp and gave orders.

"—all doors," they heard as they shot past a floor.

"—shut off the Power and search all elevators—" on another,

"Hm!" said Quentin as the elevator slowed down and they saw through the bars a group of blue uniforms approaching. Jack was tense for a fight.

"Not yet!" Quentin warned him. "Remember we can't fight the organization."

"All right!" he shouted to the approaching policemen. "I've got one of them. One of you come along. And get the power back on quick and the elevator moving, so that I can hustle him back where he belongs."

The policemen saluted Quentin. One of them stepped in and glared at Jack. The elevator door closed. In a few moments the car shot upward again.

Quentin touched the policeman with the shock-rod, and as he lay limp, Jack put the handcuffs on him, tied his feet with a strap from the policeman's own puttees, and gagged him with a handkerchief. The policeman, unaccustomed to such rough handling, winced and shrank away, groaning. The elevator shot upward swiftly, passing floors by dozens and scores. The Euthanasia Chambers were left far below. On each floor were crowding people, clanging gongs, and bellowing speakers. Eventually they stopped. Outside was huge machinery, wheels, pulleys, motors. Above was the sky of wavy glass. Somewhere, far away below, were footsteps pounding up metal stairs. They were just under the roof, a thousand feet above the ground.

"Up on my shoulders!" said Jack, glancing up at the skylight.

Quentin unhooked the skylight, climbed out, and helped Jack up after him. All about them was a sea of roofs, miles and miles of them, flat dirty, with little cubicles and penthouses scattered by the hundreds and ventilators by the thousands. Above them on its tall flagpole waved the black streamer, which undoubtedly marked the location of the Euthanasia Chambers as a guide for aircraft. There were other flagpoles and other streamers, but no more black ones. They ran. They ran at random, not knowing whither.

They ran till their breath was all gone, and then sank down and lay flat. Jack still trembled at the sensation of having crossed a bridgeway between two buildings and glimpsed a street a thousand feet below, a faint stream of blended, moving masses. Just now there was no one in sight. The scene was no different than when they had started. Only the absence of the black streamer made him sure that they were in a different place.

"Bad fix," Quentin said. "We'll starve up here."

"Oh, no," Jack replied easily. "We'll depend on the sun for direction, and keep going till we find an end or edge. We'll find some way of getting to the ground and getting away."

"Well, you've got nerve, anyway. And it's better to die trying than to sit here."

Then they noted airplanes searching round and round above them. They crouched down in the shadows between the pipes and cubicles. The planes came lower and closer together.

"They got the planes out quick," Jack observed.

"*It* did, you mean. It's all automatic. The men are just tools. The whole city is an electrical brain, and is just a subsidiary of the Washington brain; a sort of inferior ganglion. The men could never think nor work that fast. The planes are now coming straight at us; evidently they have located us by some such methods as the refractograph, which by the refraction of light detects the column of carbon dioxide rising from our lungs, the telaud which can hear us whisper or our hearts beat, or the bolograph which locates us by the heat of our bodies."

A plane landed on a level place a hundred yards away. Another and another alighted beside it. Figures poured out and began to close in on the two fugitives. Ahead of them was the edge of the building, with a sheer vertical drop of a thousand feet. There was no bridgeway, no door.

"Ha!" Quentin pointed to a flagpole from which floated a long silver streamer. It was some sort of a commercial signal to aircraft. The halliards on which the flag hung extended down over the edge of the roof. "Those ropes run into a window below."

Figures in blue were running toward them. Jack slid down the rope first and disappeared. Quentin waited for the rope to loosen as Jack got off, uncertain as to whether it would hold their combined weight. But he found a policeman sliding down the rope after him. The policeman hung on tightly and moved gingerly; Quentin looked up and saw his face ashy pale as it looked down at him. For the two of them swung out in space over a canyon a thousand feet deep, at the bottom of which moved slow streams of men and machines. A blended murmur came up to the two tiny men dangling high up there on a rope.

The policeman was poking downward toward Quentin with his shock-rod. Other faces were looking down over the edge of the roof, tense and distorted. Jack shouted from below, some incoherent, encouraging thing. The policeman slid down faster to catch Quentin. Quentin jabbed viciously upwards with his shock-rod and felt it touch. The policeman went limp and seemed to float out into space. His blue body sprawled out and turned over and over as it fell. With deadly rapidity it grew smaller and contracted to a dot far down in the gloom below. Quentin felt himself drawn into the window and trembled as he sat down for an instant on the floor.

Jack was dragging him toward a door. He could see the flag halliards tightening as another man started down. Out in the corridor they found gongs ringing and speakers bellowing, but no people. On all sides there was a roar and clatter of machinery behind closed doors. They opened one and dashed into a huge room full of big machines in rows; steam sizzled and white linen flashed by. At the far end, from every machine in a long row came baskets piled high with clean laundry, and scudded along roller conveyors into openings in the wall. People were visible. The baskets of laundry disappearing into dark openings gave Quentin an idea.

"Come on!" shouted Quentin.

They ran across the room. Each seized one of the baskets, dumped the linen on the floor, set the basket back on the roller conveyor, and got into it.

The darkness of the pit closed upon them. Machinery clattered and steam hissed. They bent low, not knowing what was above them. They felt themselves sink rapidly and again tipped level; there were gears grinding as they rounded corners. There seemed no end of sinking down and down in the blackness.

Finally, after a clatter of paper there came a burst of light. They saw clothes dumped out of baskets, wrapped in paper, and shot into tubes, all by machinery. They leaped out on the floor. Again there were no people. No bawling speakers. No gongs. Only the open mouths of pneumatic tubes, an endless row of them, each marked with its destination. Quentin eagerly looked for *Brooklyn*. It took but a moment to find it.

"All aboard for Long Island!" he shouted in glee.

As a wrapped package came down the conveyor toward the Brooklyn tube, he rolled it off and they took its place. The lid popped shut on the tube, nearly rupturing their ear-drums, and they were plunged in darkness. After the first rush and swirl and roar, all was quiet for minutes.

Again there was a roar and a crash and a burst of daylight. The two fugitives jumped up and ran, knocking over several astonished people who were waiting for packages; their destination was an open door with daylight beyond. Out there was a row of trucks with laundry packages dropping into them from overhead chutes. They were automatic trucks such as are used for making deliveries beyond the pneumatic-tube zone.

They leaped into the foremost truck. Quentin set the switches on impulse for Bay Shore, because that was not where he wanted to go, and they both rolled back into the closed portion of the vehicle. The truck started slowly, gathered momentum, and automatically made its way out of the city.

After fifteen minutes of eternity, they looked out. The truck was moving swiftly along a country road. Twilight was gathering rapidly.

"We'd better jump out and let it go on," Quentin suggested. "It's clever and powerful."

"What is?" asked Jack, "the Police Department?"

"The Machine. The Government Machine in Washington and its subsidiary portion in New York. It's a big brain. The police are dumb tools."

They waited for the truck to slow up around a curve, and jumped out. They alighted on grass. Jack rolled over and jumped up. Quentin found his breath gone and his head dizzy. He crawled unsteadily into the shelter of some shrubbery. In a few minutes a half-dozen speed-cycles on the road and planes in the air whizzed by, in pursuit of the laundry car.

"See how quickly it works," Quentin said.

"It's uncanny to hear you talk about it!" Jack exclaimed. "It's inhuman!"

"Next it will be flares and spotlights," Quentin warned.

Quentin found walking difficult and felt a terrific headache. He must have gotten a crack on the head when he fell out of the truck. Jack supported him and they staggered on. Ten miles ahead was their destination, his little country bungalow with its secret cellar. This was familiar terrain for Quentin, but ten miles cross-country in the darkness was none the less difficult. Even crossing a road would be dangerous. As they stumbled across field and through brush and timber, Quentin felt himself growing weaker.

It was not long before the lights appeared. Ahead of them, to the right, the country was lighted as bright as day.

"They're headed wrong," Quentin chuckled as he staggered desperately along. "We're going to the left at right angles to them."

Quentin did not recollect the rest of the night very clearly. Jack's strong shoulders were a comfort without which he could not have gone a mile. His head cleared up now and then in flashes to answer Jack's questions, and again he would relapse into a half-comatose state in which he walked. The guiding of the way depended on him.

"No rest from the Machine," went round and round in his head. "On all sides of us, thousands, millions of tentacles are squirming to close in on us, day and night. Soon my buzzing brain will give out. Then the Machine will reach out and pick us up. The Machine ought to be destroyed—!

"But that is treason," leaped through his brain in a sudden shock. "How do I dare even think such treason? Because my head sings from the bump it got, I suppose. But suppose Jack thought that. That would not be treason. And Jack has physical courage to do things, even to destroy the Machine. It would be easy to do just that one square building. Wreck that, and the Government Machine is dead. Jack would dare it if I told him.

"But I can't make myself tell him. It is treason. Even to think it is treason. Why can't he see it himself? I keep giving him hints—"

Jack kept continuously interrupting him with questions.

"How can they make it so much like daylight over there?"

Quentin hoped in a dazed way that his explanation of the thousand-foot flare circles that eliminated shadows, was correct. Then again he trudged on in his sleep, till he was roused by Jack.

"How do we get across?"

He came wide awake for a moment. In front was a twenty-foot wall.

"The Long Island Transformer Depot. We'll have to go around. To the left. That was a bad crack on my head. I've got to rest."

Jack had to lift him and drag him a few feet before his legs got to swinging again. Then again came Jack's demand for a key.

"Got to move," Jack said. "The lights are starting this way."

"Here we are!" Quentin shouted as he came to again. He unlocked the door to the little bungalow. They found themselves in a small hallway from which steps led down to the spacious underground shop.

Jack gasped in amazement at it.

"I understood you to say," he exclaimed, "that you did this secretly and alone. Why, digging this cave would take years of time."

Quentin was nodding drowsily again.

"Power is cheap," he said. "See there."

There was a heap of cartridge-like things.

"I dug out this place with those. Screw a red one to a blue one and drop them. It is a slow explosion. No noise. But in a few moments everything, iron, rock, everything is a loose, fluffy powder. I swept it out. And now I've got to sleep. My head hurts."

Chapter IV

Quentin awoke to the humming of smooth, well-adjusted machinery. Bright sunlight shone full upon him. He lay and rested, and was conscious of a headache. There was a painful lump on his occiput. He studied the strange place about him.

Finally he realized that it was the cabin of his own secret plane. He sat up. Down below was blue water, and to the left a beautiful lacy shore and blue mountains. In front of him was Jack, peering ahead. As Jack heard a stir behind him, he sat up; his face lighted up to see Quentin awake.

"Where are we?" Quentin asked.

"I'm no geographer," Jack said, "but it must be the Mediterranean."

"See!" continued the boy. "We got away from 'em? Or from *It*, as you say." He grinned as though on a schoolboy lark.

Quentin shook his head gloomily.

"We're not out of it yet. Sooner or later it will get us — anywhere on this earth. My big hope is that I might see Martha first."

He sat, sunk in gloomy thoughts. Jack grinned happily. He seemed to be a creature that responded to the happy stimuli of the present, and forgot that there was a future.

"You need some breakfast, sir," he said. "Then you'll feel better."

Quentin ate and then lay down and slept again. After he awoke, he spent many hours searching the sky around him and the fleeting ground below. It was acute torture to feel that every moment a swarm of planes would swoop down on them. Every dot in the blue caused him to peer intently and with beating heart and clutching hands, until it was passed by safely. But it began to look hopeful as they passed over Asia Minor and into India, without any sign of pursuit or interference. He permitted pleasant thoughts of Martha to flow through his mind.

Above northern India he became alert. Eagerly he watched the Himalayas fall behind. The machine needed only an occasional touch for guidance. A shout from Jack called his attention to the green levels of Democratia. Slowly its woods and mountains separated themselves from the blue haze. Then they crossed its edge. They headed toward the capital.

Quentin's heart pounded. He was now confident that no matter what happened eventually, he would see Martha first. Up to the present time he had been racked with uncertainty. Her image rose up before his eyes, and his veins tingled and his breath came short with anticipation.

The radio of Quentin's plane could not tune in with the inferior ones of Democratia; none of his messages got through. Therefore, no one awaited them at the landing-field. But, after telephoning and driving in a car, they were eventually at the house of Jack's father, and Quentin and Martha were in each other's arms. And after that, the four of them were gravely discussing the future.

"There is no hope," Quentin said. "The Government considers that it owns the Earth. It has pronounced sentence and nothing on earth can prevent its being carried out."

"How do you suppose they will do it?" asked Quentin's host; "Explosives?"

"Hardly explosives," considered Quentin. "Gas probably. Gas bombs from planes. Electric charges and disease bacilli are possible, but the one is unnecessarily expensive and the other unnecessarily brutal. The Government Machine is inexorable; but it will do nothing unnecessary. It is hard for you to realize the absolutely perfect, impersonal logic of the Machine. My guess is gas, some swift, painless gas."

"Perhaps," Jack said, "they will shout us to death with those shriekers they had on all their floors."

"Now, Jack!" Martha protested, in tears. She clung to Quentin. "But it's just like you, being silly, even in the face of death."

"What I ought to do," Jack bantered, swelling up his biceps, "is to punch the face of death right in the nose." Jack loved his sister and was doing his best to cheer her up in his clumsy way.

Then they discussed whether or not an alarm ought to be spread among the people of Democratia. Quentin's host was in a responsible government position and had authority to decide.

"What would be the use?" Quentin asked. "No defense is possible. No escape is possible. There would only be panic and riots and needless suffering. It is most merciful to let it come as a complete surprise."

"We'll carry the burden, then."

Quentin and Martha spent most of the day clinging close together. There was no sleep for them nor for her father that night.

"Isn't it terrible!" Martha exclaimed, "to see that young animal, Jack, sleep soundly in spite of all this? Hasn't he any feelings? We may never see the morning light again."

But morning dawned bright and clear upon the smiling land. It was torture to the three people who anxiously scanned the sky. Jack went out to play golf and the rest of the nation went about its business.

In the middle of the forenoon four planes appeared in the southern sky. Shortly afterwards Jack came in, much interested in them, but showing no fear. He was certainly a primitive creature.

The planes came straight toward the city, and the three watchers prepared to die; and bade goodbye to each other and to Jack, who by this time had grown serious and looked worried.

Quentin was almost breathless when the planes settled hesitatingly on the landing-field. An emergency car hurried him and his companion out there. There, in a circle between the four planes, were a dozen people, most of whom Quentin recognized as prominent figures in New York life. But they looked pale and crushed; they looked about furtively and helplessly. Despair showed in their attitudes and in their silence. They livened up a little when they saw Quentin approaching. He looked at them in amazement and waited for them to speak.

"We've come to ask for help," one of them said. "Will you help us?"

Again Quentin could not find words.

"The world is in chaos," the man said. "Disorder. Starvation. Disease. People are dying by millions. Trampling, exposure, suicide—no one knows what to do."

"What in the world has happened?" Quentin managed to gasp.

"An explosion," the man answered. "The key parts of the Government Machine are totally destroyed. No one knows how to repair it. The world is disorganized."

Quentin stared blankly.

"We thought perhaps you had done it," the man continued. "We knew of your daring escape—"

Quentin silently shook his head. Then he got a sudden idea.

"Jack!" he said sharply, turning toward that young man. "You rascal—"

Jack sheepishly came out from behind his sister.

"What do you know about this?" Quentin demanded.

"Well," Jack stammered. "You were so positive that inhuman thing would catch us sooner or later—I didn't want to take any chances. It wanted to kill all of our people. And you were knocked out with a bump on your head—

"The red and blue cartridges looked interesting. I tried a pair out on a couple of police cycles that were snooping around outside the house. It wiped them out. "So I rolled you into the plane, blew the doors open, shoveled in the cartridges, and headed for Washington. I spent that trip screwing together as many as I could. Then I spilled a couple of hatfuls on the Government Building, and waited only long enough to see the corners begin to crumple. Then I lit out, straight up in the air. There were too many planes around—"

The rest was smothered in his sister's hug. His father had an arm about his shoulders. Quentin slapped him on the back.

The spokesman again approached Quentin. "Will you and these people help us?"

"We will," Martha's father said.

"We'll reorganize the world." said Quentin.

"As a democracy." Jack added.

"And you, Jack," Quentin said, "will do a whale of a big share of the job. We need guys like you."

The Finger of the Past

Waldo Swift, dapper young salesman of "*Palaeoscopes, Inc.,*" shifted his necktie infinitesimally into the position of utmost nicety, squared back his shoulders, and then picked up his little black case from beside the elevator door and stepped briskly and energetically toward Herodias Buffum's office. And indeed, the prospect upon whom he was about to call was regarded among salesmen as a tough nut to crack. He had been known to eject salesmen physically into the outer corridor. Therefore, Waldo Swift, in spite of the confidence he had in the appeal of the marvelous and astonishing invention he was "distributing," gathered together all the courage he had before he opened the door.

He found himself in the luxuriously furnished reception-room belonging to the executive offices of *The Radionic Remedies Company*, located on the 127th floor of *The Manufacturers' Building*. There were two other doors in addition to the one by which he had entered. Beyond one of them was the faint hum of typewriting machines, while the other, which bore the name of "Herodias Buffum, President," was slightly ajar. As Swift let his eyes rove about the room taking in first one elegant object and then another, he could not help hearing clearly the sounds that came from Buffum's office.

A distant door closed faintly, and a tinkling voice said:

"Good morning, sir!"

It was Miss Peacheline Fairchild, the stenographer, who glided efficiently into the room, even before Buffum had ceased jabbing the button on his desk.

"We've got a lot of work today," Buffum said deep down in his throat. "Starting on something new."

Miss Fairchild was already sitting with notebook ready and pencil poised. Buffum was walking about the room, hands clasped behind his back, his eyes on the ceiling.

"Whew!" he exclaimed. "A quarter of a million dollars to a country doctor for a prescription on a little card. What do you think of that, Miss Fairchild?"

"Yes sir," replied Miss Fairchild respectfully, with downcast eyes.

"Well," continued Buffum, "it was worth it. That little card is going to save our business. Did you know that *The Radionic Remedies* was just about on the rocks?"

By way of reply, Miss Fairchild gazed at him with large, sympathetic eyes. Buffum continued:

"The patent-medicine business is getting difficult. People don't fall for stuff like they used to. Our rejuvenation idea has gone stale in spite of our wonderful publicity department, and we're going into the hole. I've about worried myself nuts for a new idea."

Miss Fairchild was studying him carefully, trying to decide whether or not he was dictating, and whether or not she ought to be putting this all down. Finally she decided that it was not dictation, and nodded sympathetically. Buffum went on:

"Then comes along old Doc Cranbury with his prescription for a thought-stimulating tincture—God knows everybody needs it nowadays. Let's see: *Buffum's Brain Builder*! No. That's weak. Well, we'll get a name. The first thing is to get the whole organization to work on it. Take this, Miss Fairchild: Ahem! Ah-hrrr!—Wait. Let's have a look at the prescription first."

He started toward the wall, into which a heavy safe-door was let, when a mellow bell pealed softly. For just then, in the outer office, Waldo Swift had discovered the button marked: "Visitors Please Ring."

"Hell!" said Buffum. He turned to Miss Fairchild: "Bring him in and we'll have it over before we begin."

He eyed Swift's black case, as the latter entered the private office, while Swift's eye traveled about the still more luxuriously furnished room. It was certainly modern with its television screen, its photophonic beam projector, the huge keyboard for controlling the distant factory from the downtown office, the helicopter landing-stage outside the window sill. There were luxurious rugs and richly finished furniture; and amidst it, Buffum glowered at the square black case in Waldo Swift's hand.

"What the hell do you want?" he demanded.

Waldo Swift had a pleasant, cheery tone of voice. "This remarkable machine will astonish you. Tremendous value in your business, entertaining in your sure hours—"

"I can't be bothered now," growled Buffum.

"Just go right on working, sir," Waldo Swift said deferentially "I shall not interrupt."

He set his case on the floor, opened it, took out a complicated and delicate-looking piece of mechanism, and began setting it up.

"Just pay no attention to me for the moment," he said to Buffum. "As soon as I am ready I shall ask you to look at the screen for a couple of seconds."

But Buffum could not keep his eyes off the shiny, clicking little mechanism.

"What is the damned thing?" he asked.

Waldo Swift, working deftly with the apparatus, replied:

"This is the famous *Palaeoscope*. You can connect it with any person, scene, or object, and it will project a true and faithful animated picture of what happened to that person or at that place, at any past time that you may designate."

Buffum snorted.

"A bunch of boloney. You're wasting my time. I'm busy."

Swift never even noticed the discourtesy.

"I'm connecting it with your desk. What time shall we choose? Say this time yesterday. All right. Here goes!"

At first Buffum started suddenly, half rose out of his chair, and a few inarticulate gurgles escaped him. However, in an instant, Swift had moved a lever on the machine. It whirred and flickered, and on the screen appeared Buffum's desk, at which was seated Buffum together with an old, gray-whiskered man. The latter gravely handed over to Buffum a small card in exchange for an elaborately executed check. Buffum was then seen to walk over to the safe and elaborately put away and lock up in it the newly acquired card.

"That's far enough!" Buffum said sharply. He was evidently nervous. "Stop the thing."

Swift shut off the machine at once.

"Now," he said, "I shall be pleased to leave this model here with you for you to try out. I'll see you again this afternoon."

"I'll look it over," growled Buffum. "I might get one for the office-boy's Christmas present."

"After you've seen what it will do, sir," Swift said briskly, "you will want to order a hundred machines for your advertising department."

"Arrh!" snorted Buffum. "Quit blowing smoke-rings. You're wasting my time. I'm busy. All right, Miss Fairchild. Ready? Take this."

"Good day, sir," said Swift in the exit door. "I'll see you later."

"Hrrrumph! Damn nuisance," growled Buffum. "All right. Let's see, where was I? Oh, yes. We need the prescription of old Doc Cranbury's brain-tickler."

He got up out of his chair and walked to the safe again. Twirling the knobs, he swung open the door and reached in. His face became blank. He leaned in and searched frantically around. He became rigid. He tossed things back and forth in the safe.

"It's gone!" he screamed. "Help! Police! It's stolen!"

After a moment he quieted down, and walked about and groaned.

"I'm ruined!" he gasped, dropping into a chair. "The prescription is gone. The business is a wreck. Miss Fairchild, call the police."

Suddenly his eyes alighted on the *Palaeoscope* standing on a little table.

"Aha!" he cried. "If that pesticating contraption is any good, we'll find out what has become of that prescription. Never mind the police, Miss Fairchild."

Miss Fairchild dropped the telephone suddenly. She seemed unusually agitated. Buffum fumbled around the delicate mechanism for some time before he found the proper way to set and start it; but fortunately his hurried and clumsy efforts did it no harm. After several false starts it began to flicker and whirr smoothly and steadily. On the screen appeared a picture of the safe in the wall, darkened as though it were night. A young man entered by the door that led from the main office, twirled the knobs, and opened the doors of the safe. Buffum watched him in the picture in breathless fascination.

"Ho! ho!" he cried suddenly as the face of the young man on the screen turned fully around for a front view.

"So it's Oliver! My precious nephew! The police, Miss Fairchild."

Miss Fairchild scurried to the telephone and began dialing a number, while Buffum viciously jabbed the button on his desk, and then paced up and down the room snarling to himself. In a moment the door opened and a young man walked in. He seemed to be possessed of no particular personality nor distinctive appearance. He was just a nice young man, like thousands we see constantly on the street, neat, well-mannered, well-groomed, clever-looking.

"Now," said Buffum icily, standing and regarding the young man with a cold eye. "Hand over the prescription. I can prove that you've got it; so come on and quit acting innocent."

"Whassa big idea, guvnor?" the young man said calmly, evidently thoroughly accustomed to Buffum's eccentric outbursts. "Are you having a movie made?"

"Give me that prescription at once!" Buffum snarled angrily. "Or you go to jail. In fact, you'll probably go anyhow."

"Prescription for what?" asked Oliver with youthful sarcasm. "Keeping your temper and making your meaning clear? All right, I'll sit down and write you out a good one."

He took out his fountain-pen and began unscrewing the cap. Buffum became all the more enraged at this.

"Damn you, you're making me sore!" he shouted. "I can prove that you came in here last night, opened the safe, and took a prescription out. Now deny it."

Oliver shrugged his shoulders.

"I came in last night," he said, "and put away some important papers. But your twitter about a prescription leaves me cold."

The outer door slammed and there was a trample of feet in the reception-room. As the bell sounded, Miss Fairchild opened the door, and three policemen entered, looking around in bewilderment. Buffum stalked up to them.

"I charge this man," he shouted, swinging his arm toward Oliver, "with having opened my safe and taken a valuable document."

"Hm," said one of the policemen, with chevrons on his arm; "that's Mr. Mayflower, your nephew, isn't it?"

"What difference does that make?" roared Buffum. "Take him away and lock him up. I'll appear to charge him formally."

The policemen acceded deferentially to the demands of so powerful and wealthy a man as Buffum. Yet they were sorry for Oliver, and handled him as gently as possible. Oliver had a half-amused, half-cynical expression on his face, and said not a word. He only looked inquiringly at Miss Fairchild, and when he had gotten her eye, glanced toward Buffum and tapped his forehead. Miss Fairchild's face remained set and immovable; nothing could be read from it.

"The ungrateful whelp," Buffum continued to growl after the policemen had led Oliver out. "After I'd set him up in life! Miss Fairchild, we've got to get the prescription from him somehow, or the business is ruined. It can't be—a big firm like the *Radionic*—ruined! Miss Fairchild, we've got to get that prescription from him."

Miss Fairchild shrank into a corner and nodded dumbly; she wrung her hands as Buffum raved on.

"We'll have him searched at the station; then we'll go through his room. But I'm afraid. I'm afraid that the rapscallion has hidden that little card pretty thoroughly. Oh, what shall we do, Miss Fairchild? We can't let this business go on the rocks, and I've worried myself sick for months trying to think of something original. Oh, the young scoundrel! A quarter of a million dollars! I could choke him with my bare hands!"

Miss Fairchild shivered, probably at the thought of Oliver being choked with Buffum's bare hands. At this moment, the outer door was flung open as though some powerful force had burst it in, and a regal looking lady entered. Through a scornful lorgnette, and from behind the magnificence of a heap of furs, Mrs. Regina Mayflower regarded her brother sternly.

"Herodias!" she said in a voice such as one uses to call a child to account. "What's this I hear about Oliver?"

"The young rascal!" Buffum spluttered. "The scamp! Stole my prescription. Whole business depends on it. Won't give it back."

"Stole it!" Disdain, supreme disdain radiated from her words and from her whole attitude. The Mayflowers didn't steal, and she knew it.

"Sneaked in at night, and took it out of the safe," Buffum stormed.

"Yes?" Mrs. Mayflower intoned contemptuously.

"I can prove it," Buffum defended himself desperately.

"Ha! ha!" tinkled Mrs. Mayflower's laugh. "He can prove it!"

Buffum, still growling: "The scamp! The wretch!" He went to the *Palaeoscope*, took a good preliminary look at it, and began to fumble with it. In a moment it began to click, and suggestive shapes flickered across the screen, and disappeared tantalizingly. Buffum growled something to himself and continued to fumble with the apparatus. Mrs. Mayflower had noted something suspicious about the figures that had swiftly misted over the scene.

"Herodias!" she demanded. "What was that?"

"Hrrrrumph!" said Buffum. "What was what?"

"Put that picture on again!" ordered Mrs. Mayflower sternly. "What were you and that stenographer doing on that picture?"

Suddenly, as Buffum kept trying levers and buttons on the machine, the mechanism began to run smoothly, and the screen lit up brightly. Again it showed the safe, this time partly darkened, as though at twilight. Miss Peacheline Fairchild slipped stealthily into the room, her dim figure quite recognizable on the screen. She looked about her carefully, and then went to the safe, opened it, searched about; and took out a card that was plainly recognizable in the picture as Dr. Cranbury's prescription. This she put carefully into her handbag, closed the safe, and hurried out.

Buffum's mouth worked up and down in silence, like that of a fish out of the water. Then he began to splutter and choke with rage.

"You—you—you—" he turned to Miss Fairchild, but could get nothing more coherent out of himself. He seized the terrified girl by the arm and shook her. Finally, his wits and words came back.

"Regina! Quick!" he exclaimed. "Call back those policemen with Oliver. No! Not the telephone. The photophonic projector. You can pick them up as they go down the street."

Mrs. Mayflower responded with alacrity. She sent the powerful beam of light out of the window with the photophonic projector. Through the telescopic sights on the instrument she picked up the policemen leading Oliver, far down in the depths of the street. She swung it about until the spot of light enveloped them, and then spoke into the mouthpiece.

"Just a moment!" she cried. "Mr. Buffum wants you back up in his office. He now has evidence that Oliver did not take the prescription, and he has the real thief here."

She watched as the tiny group far down below swung about and started back. Then she shut off the instrument and swept haughtily back into the room. She disdained even to look at Miss Fairchild, but sat down in Buffum's luxurious armchair. Miss Fairchild fidgeted in an embarrassed way at a corner of the desk, while Buffum paced up and down.

"Where is it?" he spluttered when he had regained his composure a little. "Give it to me! I'll strangle you!"

Miss Fairchild, however, maintained a stubborn silence, and Buffum decided that it would be best to await the arrival of the police. It was not long before their steps were heard down the hall, and, together with Oliver, they entered. Oliver nodded and smiled as he glanced about the room, taking in the various elements of the scene and comprehending their significance. Then he bowed to his mother in playful deference.

"Officers!" said Buffum pompously, "I've found the real thief. I was mistaken about Mr. Mayflower. Release him and arrest this—this—this—young woman. I'll fix up all the formalities later. Now, Miss Fairchild, will you give up that prescription?"

Miss Fairchild only smiled at Buffum and shook her head. She went up to Buffum and whispered something in his ear. His face went blank; he opened his mouth as though to say something; then suddenly caught himself and stopped, and looked belligerently about the room. He clenched his fists and crooked his elbows.

"Now, Herodias!" demanded Mrs. Mayflower. "What is all of this? What did that hussy say to you? Tell me at once!"

"Damn foolishness!" muttered Buffum under his breath.

"Shall I tell?" asked Miss Fairchild, smiling archly at Buffum.

"You'd better!" said Mrs. Mayflower, "if you know what's good for you." Sternness filled the atmosphere about her.

"Give up that prescription!" repeated Buffum desperately.

Miss Fairchild stepped in front of him.

"You've promised me a new fur coat," she said, "and you've been putting me off—"

"What's that?" exclaimed Mrs. Mayflower horrified.

In the meanwhile, Oliver had been attracted by the fascinating complicatedness of the *Palaeoscope*, and was tinkering with its buttons and levers. Suddenly it began to flicker and then went on clicking steadily. The screen cleared, and on it appeared a picture of Buffum holding Miss Fairchild on his lap and chucking her under the chin. Mrs. Mayflower was petrified with astonishment, and Buffum was for the moment paralyzed. Miss Fairchild giggled hysterically.

Suddenly a crash resounded through the room, and the picture suddenly went out. Buffum had kicked the machine across the room. It lay in a far corner, a mangled wreck, and from it came little sparks and lights and clicks and whirrs, which finally died down to silence.

"Search her handbag!" Buffum commanded the policemen, following it up with a lot of incoherent growlings.

A policeman stepped over to reach for Miss Fairchild's handbag; but she was the quicker of the two. She opened her handbag, took out the prescription, and held it up so that Buffum could see it.

"Here it is!" she exclaimed.

Then she suddenly crumpled it up, put it in her mouth, chewed it up and swallowed it. She laughed out in triumph; but in the middle her laugh broke, and she burst into tears. Two policemen seized her, one from each side.

Buffum turned pale, and sank into a chair with a groan, his head down in his hands. He dropped there for a moment, and then got up and walked swiftly about, with incoherent growlings. He shook his fists and clutched his hands in the direction of Miss Fairchild.

Miss Fairchild broke away from the two policemen; ran up to Buffum, and threw her arms about his neck. Mrs. Mayflower shrieked and gasped.

"You used to be so nice to me!" Miss Fairchild wept on Buffum's shoulder. "I can't stand this."

Buffum kept backing away, while Miss Fairchild continued to cling to him. Everyone else in the room was tremendously embarrassed except Oliver. Suddenly, all eyes turned toward the window, whence a loud whirr proceeded. A little flivver helicopter slowly descended on the landing-stage. Out of it climbed the dapper Waldo Swift and stepped into the room through the window, carrying a little black case. He looked about him at the group in mild surprise, as though it were after all a part of his day's work.

"How do you do, ladies and gentlemen?" he said briskly.

Buffum turned on him angrily.

"This is all your fault!" he roared.

"Yes sir!" said Swift. "Anything is possible sir."

He looked over the occupants of the room, and turned to Oliver, who looked to him the most hopeful.

"The little lady here," volunteered Oliver, "er—ah—destroyed a very valuable document. The continued prosperity of this firm depends upon that document. The company is therefore ruined. Swallowed it, see?"

Swift smiled in sudden comprehension.

"Ah!" he said. "And you need the document. So very simple."

He looked about the room, noted the wreck of the *Palaeoscope* in the corner without the least quiver in his composure, and opened his black case. He took out an exact duplicate of the first machine, and for a few minutes was busied in setting it up.

"We'll set the time back to the same hour as before," he observed as he worked, "with you and the old doctor at the desk."

In a moment Buffum and Dr. Cranbury appeared on the screen, bending over the prescription. Swift manipulated things on the machine, and the view appeared to come closer and grow larger, until it became a close-up of the prescription only, with every letter clear and plain. Swift had out his notebook and was rapidly copying down

348

the prescription. As Buffum in the picture put the prescription into the safe, Swift shut off the machine. Then he tore the page out of his notebook on which the prescription was copied, and handed it to Buffum with a flourishing bow.

"There you are sir," he said. "Your prescription. This is just a trifling example of the service which the *Palaeoscope* can render you in your business and everyday life. May I put you down for a hundred machines?" he concluded, taking out his order book.

Buffum grasped eagerly at the copy of the prescription, and put it in his wallet with a sigh of relief.

"Make out an order for 500 machines," he said, 250 for our research department, and 250 for our publicity department. Come back in six weeks for another order."

He went over to his desk and bustled busily among a lot of papers; obviously to hide his confusion at the fact that Miss Fairchild was weeping convulsively in one corner. Oliver did the gentlemanly thing, and went over and patted her shoulder in sympathy. He bent over and spoke something low and soft in the effort to console her.

As soon as Buffum saw this, he leaped up and whirled around; he hurried over to Miss Fairchild, brushed Oliver aside, and motioned the policemen away.

"Now Miss—" he began; "now Peacheline, you go over to Kirsch and Baum's and pick you out any kind of a fur coat you want. And, would you like to—would you like to go to Peacock's and pick you out a ring, an engagement ring?"

By way of reply, she threw her arms about Buffum's neck and buried her face in his shoulder. In order to address Oliver, Buffum had to bury his neck and chin in her tousled hair.

"Oliver!" he said. "Ah-hrrr! You young scamp, from now on you are manager of the publicity department. Do you hear? And Regina, I can see business coming in again; so you may have that new airplane you've been wanting so long."

Millions for Defense

"It's about time you quit fooling around and got down to some real work. You've been tinkering long enough."

The coarse, red face of Jake Bloor spread into an unsympathetic leer and he grunted contemptuously.

"I promised your mother I'd put you through school," he continued. "Now I'm through with that, and a big bunch of boloney I call it."

That was the welcome that awaited John Stengel after graduation from college, upon his arrival at the only home he had, that of his uncle, who was a banker in the small country village of Centerville.

"Yes, sir," replied John, biting his lips.

His uncle screwed his lips into ugly rolls around his cigar, and then took it out and spat on the floor.

"This job I'm giving you in my bank," he went on, "is not a part of my promise to your mother. That comes out of the kindness of my heart."

That mind can and does triumph over matter was demonstrated again by the fact that John did not turn on his heel and walk out of the house, never to return. John Stengel, known to his fellow-students for four years as Steinmetz Stengel, stood five burly inches above his stocky uncle; his blue eyes blazed a resentment that was everywhere else concealed by his quiet and respectful bearing. The powerful arm that bent to run his big hand through his yellow hair could have knocked his corpulent uncle off his feet, but it dropped quietly at his side, and he again said:

"Yes, sir!"

For, graduation is a bewildering experience. The world is wide, and one is not sure just which way to turn. A fifteen-dollar a week job as a clerk in a country bank was nevertheless a discouraging job to the rosy aspirations that flowered at this time of the year, quite as brilliantly as did the roses; for behind him were four splendid years of distinguished achievement as a scientific student.

However, just now there seemed no way around it. The offer of this job from his uncle had come several weeks before. Jake Bloor had not presented it kindly nor gracefully; he had rubbed it in with patriarchal magnanimity, and with conspicuous contempt for John's scientific training, which he had permitted only because of his promise to his dead sister, when she had placed John in his hands. During the weeks between his uncle's offer and the date of graduation, John had thought hard and tried everything. Especially he had discussed the problem with his fellow-students and his instructors.

He had nothing else to fall back on. His parents had died when he was a child and left him nothing but the ill-natured promise of a grumpy uncle. He had tried in vain to get a position of any sort; but the country was in the grip of the most severe financial depression of the century. No positions were available anywhere. His failure to locate anything in the way of a livelihood, after several months of correspondence during his last year of school, was not surprising, with ten millions of unemployed in the nation. The bank-clerk job, even though it was offered largely as an insult to John's scientific training, seemed like a straw to a drowning man. It had occurred to John that Jake Bloor was prosperous even while other country banks were failing.

"Your uncle seems to be a good business man, and it will do you no harm to learn something about business," one of his student friends said to him.

"Keep up some scientific reading," the Dean of the Engineering Department said to him, "but by all means take the job. Keep your laboratory hand in practice somehow."

The Dean was much interested in John's future, and consulted with John at length about the matter.

"You will get there in the long run," the Dean said; "but do not permit yourself to become stagnant."

The suggestion of John's roommate, who was as brilliant and clever an engineer as John himself, seemed to offer the most promise of interest.

"These country banks simply invite robbery," Bates had said. "Perfectly simple to walk in and help yourself—"

"You mean that I ought to rig up some stuff to protect the shack in case of robbery? Good idea!" John was interested.

"Easy enough, wouldn't it be? And a good way to amuse yourself."

"And Hansie, dear," Dorothy had said to him, "I know you can do something great no matter where you go. This is only temporary, and we'll be patient, and some day we shall have that home together."

Dorothy was at the same time the Light of the World, and the hardest problem of John's life. They had decided that they could not live without each other; and yet here they were, finding it impossible to live together. But, as Dorothy held on to his arm, walking with him across the campus in the moonlight, and held her soft, brown head close to his and gazed at him with limpid, sympathetic eyes, John felt that he could and must accomplish anything in the world for this wonderful girl that a kind Providence had given him.

Centerville was certainly a drab and dismal place, after the glitter of life on the campus, whose great, picturesque buildings had thrilling things going on in them. Here there were half a dozen tiny business buildings strung out along two sides of the dusty highway, and a score or so of cottage residences scattered about, and beyond those, monotonous prairie in all directions.

There were two general stores; the one in the brick building was carelessly run and had a poor stock; the other was better arranged and more ambitious, but its wooden, gable-roofed shack looked almost ready to collapse in upon it. The garage was the busiest and most systematic-looking place in the neighborhood. Two "cafés" (in reality soft-drink parlors), one ragged and catering to coarsely dressed men, one somewhat cleaner and filled at noon with high-school students; a hardware store with dirty windows and a heap of nondescript junk within them covered with the undisturbed dust of years; a drug-store with its window full of patent-medicine and cosmetic posters mottled by fading, all gave John an indescribably dreary feeling of lostness and futility. The traffic that slipped down the highway all day, and the color and activity of the two filling stations, Standard Oil at one end and Conoco at the other, did but little to relieve him.

The bank itself made John think of the little toy banks that children play with; and when he first set eyes on it he was sure that it must have a slat in the top to drop nickels in. It was square, somewhat larger than a garage, with white-painted drop-siding and a flat roof. Within, it had iron bars across the windows, a single room divided in two by a counter with a rusty iron grill, a big iron safe set on wheels. The floor was unpainted and splintery; the ink in the bottle on the sloping-topped table at the door, was dry and caked, and the pad of deposit slips upon it was yellow and curled with age. Hardly anyone passed along the little street all day, and only rarely stepped into the bank itself. Between two and three in the afternoon there were a few merchants; Saturday evenings there might be three or four farmers in the bank all at once.

John smiled when he first saw the place. Providing there were anything to take, it would be the simplest and easiest of tasks for the modern bank-robber to clean the place out and get away. It certainly looked as though there might be something to take. His uncle Jake Bloor's huge, sprawling, white house brooded over the village like some coarse temple; and his big, throbbing cars glittered back and forth from the city, boasting insolently of money. It seemed especially insolent to John; because he knew there were countless unemployed who did not know where their next meal was coming from, and countless others who were ground almost flat to the earth by debts and losses at this particular time, while his uncle lorded it about without a care in the world nor a thought for others. It did not seem fair that this crude, heartless man, who had never done the world any material service, but had only selfishly pinched off for himself generous portions of the world's money which he had handled, should be rolling in safety and luxury, at a time when men who had invented and built and taught and organized were being faced with grim want. Things weren't right in the world.

353

John was young and human. We cannot blame him, therefore, for the fact that when he did eventually get to work to devise some scientific means for preventing a robbery of the bank, that his motive did not consist of any overwhelming loyalty to his uncle's bank. He did it merely because he took pleasure in the creation of something that would operate. The abstract idea in the mind, when the concrete working out of it does things that can be seen and felt—that is the thrill of the creative spirit. John loved his figures and his drawings; he loved the coils and the storage batteries, the clicking little gears and the quick little switches that tickled and made swift little movements of their own accord, as though they were living and intelligent things.

For many long, luxurious weeks he did nothing; it was a delight to be merely a sort of vegetable; to rest from the rush of the last weeks in school; to shed completely, if temporarily, the strain of looking into the future. His mind hibernated during that time, and lay fallow; for it required no effort to discharge his simple duties as clerk at the bank; and life in Centerville was an excellent anesthetic. His body made up what it had missed in exercise by long walks down the highway and along the railroad tracks. Long letters to and from Dorothy, punctuated the soothing monotony, and the thrill they gave him was all the excitement he wanted. They must have been good letters, as we might have judged could we have but seen him slip off into solitude on the first opportunity after their arrival, his face breaking out in delightful smiles—only no one saw him.

Finally, one day in the fall, after the heat of the summer was out of his bones, he began to get ambitious. First he put a coat of bronze paint on the rusty window-bars and on the grill-work of the counter.

"Looks like a new place in here," said old Larson the town constable, who was the first one to come in and see it.

John smiled.

"I believe my sixty cents' worth of paint will boost the confidence of the bank's depositors thousands of dollars," he bantered.

Jake Bloor guffawed when he came in and saw it.

"All right!" he sneered. "If you want to waste your pennies that way in this dump. But I think you're a damned fool!"

This was not very encouraging, thought John, for broaching the idea of installing some equipment for protection against robbery. He decided to say nothing about it for the present, and await a better chance.

A week dragged out its length after that, and John began to get restless. The autumn coolness was beginning to be stimulating and after his most excellent rest, John wanted to be up and doing something, using his hands and his brain. The matter of devising some protection against robbery in the bank was constantly on his mind. He turned over in his head various projects. He watched his uncle, constantly hoping for a chance to mention the matter.

Then one morning the city daily came in with two-column heads about the robbing of the bank at Athens, forty miles away. Three masked men had walked into the bank in the middle of the afternoon; one had forced the clerk to hold up his hands at the muzzle of a pistol, while the others had cleaned out the safe, gotten into a car, and disappeared. Eighty thousand dollars worth of cash and negotiable securities had vanished. No trace of any kind could be found of the robbers.

"I could rig up some stuff to prevent that sort of thing in your bank," John said, forcing his voice into a casual tone over his pancakes:

"Prevent what?" growled his uncle.

"Your bank being robbed, like the one at Athens," John said.

"Oh!" and a couple of grunts from the uncle.

"Doesn't it worry you? It might happen to us, you know." John was showing anxiety in his voice—whether for the fate of his uncle's bank or in his eagerness to be at some technical work, again, he could not tell.

"Oh, I suppose." And Jake Bloor went on reading.

"Do you mind if I fix up some apparatus to protect you?"

"All a bunch of humbug!" Jake Bloor exclaimed impatiently, gnawing at his cigar. "The swindlers are always after me with the stuff. They want to sell something, that's all."

"No. I don't mean for you to buy anything," John urged. "I'll make it myself."

His uncle roared derisively.

"That would cost more than ever!"

"It wouldn't cost you a cent!" John explained, holding down his anger with difficulty. After a moment's silence he regained his control.

"If you don't mind," he continued, "I'll fix it up for you at no expense to yourself."

"You're a damn fool!" Jake Bloor sneered; "But go ahead and have your fun. Only look out and don't do any damage. That's all I care about."

He got up and walked out of the house. In the door he stopped and snorted back at John:

"And don't kid yourself too much. Those fellahs are on to these tricks. Before you could kick off your alarm they would have you shot. Better take care of your hide."

John thought it over as he walked to the bank that morning.

"If he invites robbery, I ought to let him be robbed," he thought. "But, if he should be robbed, as it is probable that he will be, his bank being the richest as well as the most rickety for a long distance around, where would my job be? And, as four months writing of applications all over the country hasn't got me an answer, where would I be without a job? Seems that it is up to me to protect the bank whether he wants it or not."

Then his mind turned to the technical parts of the problem and began to run quickly about among them.

"I believe he is right, too," he thought, "about kicking off an alarm under the counter. That is an old dodge, and the robbers are probably ready for it. There must be a way around that."

For a solid month John was happy. He was the same old Steinmetz Stengel, whom his fellow-students gibed at, and at the same time loved so well, going about in an abstracted gaze, studying some complex problem in his head, or spending every spare moment of the day and many hours at night with the slide-rule and drawing-instruments, and with tools and materials, giving some astonishing child of his brain the outward concrete form that was necessary to make it a visible and functioning thing among men. Packages in corrugated paper and wooden boxes arrived for him at the little railway station; and there were a few automobile trips to the city.

When the thing was finished it differed vastly from the usual burglary protection equipment. Nevertheless it was quite simple. The keynote of it was a row of photo-electric cells just above his head, which received daylight from the window behind him, and permitted a steady flow of current from a storage battery, whose charge was maintained by a trickle charger from the lighting current. This storage-battery current held down a relay armature. Anything that cut off the light from the photo-electric cells would shut off the storage-battery current, release the relay, and set off the works.

When he had gotten it made thus far, he tried it out several times by raising his hands above his head while he stood at his window, as though he were facing a bank's customer.

"Hands up!" his imagination supplied the robber's command.

His hands went up; there was a click, and the three one-quarter-horse-power motors began to whirr.

The usual device in the country bank is a big alarm bell on the outside of the building. This had been a conspicuous failure in a number of recent robberies in the neighborhood. Those who were summoned by the alarm came too late or did not have nerve enough to interfere. In one case the accomplices on the outside had found it a convenient warning to help them get away, and in another they had held all the arrivals at bay, and made a good getaway with the booty. John discarded the idea of the alarm bell to awaken the village, and looked for an improvement on it.

A drum of tear-gas supplied the solution. One of the motors operated by the relay was so arranged as to shoot a blast of tear-gas right across the public side of the bank room, just where the hold-up men would be standing. A telephone-pair to the city fourteen miles away, rented at two dollars a month, comprised the next step; over these wires he arranged for an automatic signal in the sheriff's office, which would announce that the bank was being robbed, just as soon as the storage-battery current was cut off by the raised hands in front of the photo-electric cells.

A second motor set off by the relay, located in a box under the building, closed the outside door and shot an iron bar across it to keep it closed. John also reinforced this street door by screwing to it a latticework of iron straps and painting them neatly.

He felt highly thrilled the evening that he gave the apparatus its first trial. He tried it after dark, and therefore had to put a strong electric-light bulb into the street window to replace daylight, and instead of tear-gas he used a drum of compressed air. He rehearsed the whole scene in his mind: the door burst open by masked men, the pistol stuck in his face, and demand: "Hands up!" He put his hands up in as natural a manner as possible, and his delight knew no bounds to hear the relay click, so softly that no one not looking for it could possibly have caught it; he was even moderately startled at the sudden loud hiss of escaping air, and the street door slammed shut in a ghostly manner. He walked around in front of his window in the latticework on the counter, and felt the compressed air from the tank still blowing right across the place where the imagined robber was standing.

That ought to have been enough. It was amply sufficient to take care of any robbery that might have been staged. But John had a third motor at hand and some vague idea in his head. There was still something lacking, though he could not quite put his finger on the lack. For several days he was uneasy with the half-emerging thought that there was still something that he ought to add to this. But, try as he might, nothing further occurred to him. The arrangement, as he had it, seemed to be enough, and that was all he could think of.

He therefore demonstrated it to his uncle one evening. Jake Bloor said nothing, which was unusual for him. He was rarely silent. It may have meant that he was impressed; it may not. He did manage to keep the contemptuous look on his heavy red face. But he walked out without having said a word. The next morning he threw the newspaper sneeringly across the table at John, who was eating with his head bent down, thinking of Dorothy. John glanced at the captions, announcing that another bank had been robbed, and that the bank clerk, who had been in league with the robbers, had handed out the booty and was also under arrest.

"Good idea!" drawled Jake through his nose. "Combine that with your plan. Load up the robbers nicely and then turn on your tricks. With a gas mask you can take the swag off them and hide it before the police come—"

John heard no more. His mind was busy again. He saw the danger to himself. And, as never before, he observed the paltry meanness of his uncle's character. There was some deep subtlety in Jake Bloor's sarcastic persecution of the earnest, ambitious boy, which John could not comprehend. That Jake hated John seemed to be clear. But why? And why had he gotten him there apparently at his mercy for the purpose of getting him into trouble? The only thing that John had to go on was that his Uncle's old, patriarchal conception of the "honor" of the family had been hurt when John's mother had run off and married a poor but clever mechanic. That was in the eyes of all her relatives, a mortal sin, not even possible of explanation by her unoffending son.

But, John's mind ran more to mechanisms than to the tangled personal relationships of the family. A few days of hard thinking convinced him that there was only one way to protect himself, and that was to include himself in the field of the tear-gas. He would have to take his medicine at the same instant as did the rest of them. One October afternoon, out on one of his walks, he strode down the highway into the dusty sunset, and ahead of him a farmer was raising a tremendous dust in a field, getting together, with a horse hay rake, a lot of old weeds for burning. As the farmer moved his lever and pulled his lines, the row of curved steel tines beneath him poised and waited, and then pounced upon their prey, and John got an idea. He thought of a use for his third motor.

He was soon busy again in his improvised workshop, putting together two affairs that resembled big hay rakes, each as tall as a man; but the tines were of rigid steel, and when they closed toward each other, they could grip a man as tightly as a huge steel claw, and hold him immovable. He installed these, one on each side of his teller's window at the counter, with the motor under the floor so arranged that it could rotate them against each other and slip them past a catch which would lock them firmly together. When the photo-electric relay went off, anyone standing in front of the window would be raked in, clutched, and held in a steel fist, six feet tall. Yet, when these claws were turned back out of the way, painted with bronze paint, they mingled with the bronzed grillwork of the counter, and were hardly noticeable.

For some time Jake Bloor had been talking of taking a trip West for a several weeks' stay. There was no mention of the purpose of the trip, and it was discussed in a sort of secretive way, causing John to half suspect that his uncle might be bound on a bootlegging expedition. But he cast it out of his mind, considering that it was none of his business. He was too worried anyway, to think of that, by Jake's stern admonitions about bank affairs.

John was thoroughly frightened for Jake Bloor held him closely responsible for the veriest trifles as well as for the largest affairs, and yet had not properly inducted him into an adequate knowledge of the bank's affairs. It was an unfair position for John, and he felt like a blindfolded man walking a tightrope across a chasm; he was just trusting to luck that nothing went wrong before his uncle returned.

"Don't pass up any good loans," his uncle growled at the breakfast table on the day of his departure. "But, if I find any rotten paper in the vault when I get back, I'll wring your neck."

John said nothing, but was determined in his mind to loan nothing, and sit tight waiting for his uncle's return; for he could not tell good paper from bad. His business was engineering.

"I'll stop at the bank yet before I leave," Jake said, with an air of thrusting a disgusting morsel down an unwilling throat.

About the middle of the forenoon, the loneliest time of the day, John heard his uncle's car drive up in front of the bank. He could see suitcases strapped to the rear of it. Two men walked into the bank along with Jake, one of them carrying a large suitcase.

Jake Bloor drew a big pistol and leveled it at John with a sneer.

"Well, let's see how your plaything works," he said in a hard, ironic voice.

John protested vigorously.

"Tear gas is no fun—"

"Do you suppose I really want a dose of it?" his uncle roared. "Don't you dare put up your hands. Keep them on the table where I can see them. No kid tricks, either!"

His grim harshness now alarmed John.

"I'm more afraid of that big pistol than of the gas," John protested again. His voice stuck in his throat, and lights danced before his eyes; the whole business was such a shock that he could not puzzle it out, though his brain roared like a racing motor in the effort to make head or tail of it. "That thing might go off and hurt somebody."

"Damn right it might!" his uncle growled. "That's why you had better be careful and not play anything on me. Keep your pretty hands still, or I'll ruin them with a bullet. Now, turn around, march over to the vault, and bring me the tin boxes with the cash and the bonds.—Go on, damn it! I mean it!"

Jake snapped the hammer of the revolver, and John turned with considerable alacrity and went after the tin boxes of valuables in the safe. His face was pale and his hands trembled. The weakness of his ingenious plan was being shown up unmercifully. His uncle had no learning, but was diabolically clever in a practical way. John now expected to be the butt of his cruel sneering for weeks to come.

"I guess you win," he laughed nervously at Jake. "I give up. My apparatus was no good, and the laugh is on me."

Jake stamped violently on the floor.

"By, God I told you to get those boxes of bonds and cash. If you think I'm fooling, you're due to learn something in about ten seconds. This bank is through, do you know it?"

John reasoned rapidly. The only thing to do was to go ahead. If it was a joke, it would be interesting to see how far it would be carried. If it was not a joke, what else was there to do anyway? After all, life on nothing with no prospects was still considerably better than a bullet through his vitals.

"And don't touch anything, and keep your hands down low," Jake

361

reminded him with a thin ironic leer in his voice. "If you don't believe I'll shoot, just try something."

Like a magician on the stage, anxious to show that he has nothing up his sleeve, John avoided touching anything but essentials, and touched these clearly and gingerly. He handed over some $200,000 worth of negotiable valuables from the safe, truly a princely sum for such a tiny bank. The idea occurred to him when it was too late, that he ought to have had some sort of trip or switch or button in the safe itself. That is, if it were really too late. Perhaps this was just a good chance to discover the defects of his apparatus and elaborate upon it. If this were only a test, he was certainly learning rapidly. His head was already full of improvements, and he was willing to forgive the grimness of the joke for the help it afforded.

The two other men held John covered with pistols while Jake Bloor stowed away the tin boxes in the suitcase.

"Now," Jake said again in that offensive, thick-lipped sneer, "I suppose you have been wondering how I am going to get out of here and keep you from pulling something. Well, it's like taking candy from a baby."

He approached the window again.

"Keep your hands down on that desk!" he commanded.

Jake Bloor took out his pocket knife and went for the wire that was concealed on the outside of the cage.

"Lookout! Don't—" cried John in alarm.

"Ha! ha!" Jake thoroughly enjoyed his big laugh. "You thought I was too dumb to notice that this was your main feed wire from your battery under the floor, to your little light bulbs. Ha! ha! ho! ho! Your old uncle's not so dumb!"

"But—" John tried to protest again.

He was too late.

"Shut up" his uncle barked sharply, "and keep your hands down."

"O.K., joke or no joke," thought John. "It's on his head."

He shut his eyes tightly and took a deep breath.

Jake cut the wire and yanked out a big length of it, which he started to put in his pocket. But he did not get that far with it. John heard the faint, comforting little click. There was a harsh hiss of gas. The door slammed ponderously shut and its bar clanged to. In front of the teller's window there was a whirr and a clash. Loud screams rent the air.

John could not resist opening his eyes, in spite of his knowledge of what the gas would do to them. Just for an instant, before a searing pain cut fairly into them, he saw kicking, struggling, writhing, screaming figures rolling on the floor, and just in front of his teller's window, his uncle was squeezed flat in a cage of bronzed bars, unable to move but only to give general twitching. Then John got down slowly and lay on the floor, because of the stinging in his eyes, nose and throat.

A thousand swords burned into his eyes; he sneezed and coughed and felt so miserable that he could neither remain on the floor nor stand up; he kept squirming and writhing about.

He could hear the others groaning and writhing about and kicking the floor, and the loudest lamentations came from his uncle, hung up between the steel rakes. But no attempt that he could put forth was able to get his eyes open, which, in spite of his pain, he regretted. At that moment he would have given years off his life for a sight of Jake Bloor pinned up against the counter and gassed with tear gas, holding on to his suitcase full of money.

It seemed a hundred years of flashing, stabbing misery before relief came. Actually it was twenty minutes after the breaking of the wire when the sheriff from the city arrived with a car full of armed men. During this period, no one in Centerville had awakened to the fact that anything was wrong at the bank. John felt the breath of cool, fresh air, and strong hands lifting him. He was too dazed to pay attention to what was going on, and submitted when medicine was put down his throat. He was in bed for two days before he could get about properly.

On the morning of the third day his uncle came into the room. A burly man walked on each side of him. In fact, his uncle hardly walked; he was principally supported and pushed forward. Behind them came Dorothy; darting around in front of them, she had hold of John's hands.

"Johnny-on-the-spot!" she laughed, and kissed him in front of all the others, thereby embarrassing him tremendously.

But John had not missed the look of anxious concern on her face for an instant when she first came into the room, and before a quick glance told her that he was in good shape. He was grateful to Providence for her.

His uncle shuffled up to the bed.

"You're fired!" he attempted his quondam roar, rather anticlimactically. He looked very much used up.

"Tush! tush!" one of the big men said. "We can't fire that boy. We still need him." He was softly sarcastic about it.

John looked at them closely. They were certainly not the furtive creatures who had come into the bank that forenoon with Jake Bloor. In fact, he could see the edges of shiny badges peeping out from under their coats. It was only too obvious that Jake Bloor was under heavy arrest.

"But what I want to know," one of these big, official-looking men was saying, "is how you set off your stuff? This guy says he had you covered and that he cut your wires and pulled a section out of it."

John laughed heartily and long. "My uncle is clever," he said, when he could finally speak; "but he missed a slight, though important fact. That wire supplied a current from a storage battery, and as long as that current kept running, everything was peaceful. It was the *breaking* of the current, either by shutting off the light to the photoelectric cells by hands up, or merely by cutting the wire, that set off the relay and turned on the tricks."

"Oh-h-h!" said Jake Bloor faintly.

"I tried to tell you—" John began.

"Never mind," one of the big men said. "*We'll* tell him. But now we want you to come to the bank."

John dressed and went to the bank, where he again found his uncle and the two men. These two showed a persistent fondness for close proximity to his uncle; they would never permit him to move more than a few inches from their sight. There were also two smaller men going over the books.

"As I thought," said one of the latter. "Flat failure!"

One of the big men shook Jake.

"So you had the balloon punctured, and were ready to skip," he said quietly. "That won't sound good to the judge. Well, anyway, there's enough cash in your bag to pay off your depositors with—unless we have to divide it among those of the other banks he has robbed around here."

"Robbery and embezzlement both," said the other deputy. "That'll be about a hundred years at Leavenworth."

He turned to John.

"You will be required for a witness, so stay where we can reach you. I understand that the loss of this job is tough luck for you. Well, here's hoping you have no trouble finding another."

They all went out, bundling Jake Bloor with them. John and Dorothy were left alone in the bank.

With startling suddenness, the telephone rang shrilly. It was long-distance calling from the city.

"Are you the young man who devised the apparatus that caught the robbers in this bank? This is the Palisade Insurance Company, and we need somebody like you on our staff. Can you come into the office and discuss the details of your position? Thank you."

John and Dorothy looked into each other's eyes. That home of dreams was becoming a reality at last.

Mars Colonizes

"Men of the American Army," said the grizzled old General Hunt into the microphone, "we are on the eve of the last desperate effort to gain back our land from the invader. Also, in all other nations, armies are crouched to leap tonight. We must destroy the invader or die; and if we die, the human race dies with us. Our home, the Earth, will belong to the Martians."

The small bulb awakened yellow glimmers from the insignia on the General's tall, firm figure. It revealed also the mud walls of the adobe hut which served as headquarters. His young adjutant sat on the floor on a roll of blankets. On a rough bench near him waited a calm, elderly man in civilian clothes, holding in his hand a bunch of white cards covered with notes. Outside was night, and in that night were thousands of desperate men, so well hidden that even by day, a plane flying low over the country could not discover them. In mud huts, in iron huts covered with sand, in dugouts, in caves, for twenty miles east and twenty miles west, groups of men were huddled about radio speakers, listening. They were big, tanned men, splendidly developed physically; the finest specimens of manhood that the world had seen for ages. Rocks, dirt-colored canvas, baked mud huts, heaps of New Mexico mesquite and cactus covered stacks of weapons and ammunition and countless aeroplanes. Everything was ready for an attack flight on a few moments' notice.

The General's message to the men gathered in their hot hiding places continued.

For a while, Lieutenant Gary, the General's adjutant, was intent on his chief's words. Then a far away look came into his eyes. From his pocket he took the photograph of a beautiful girl and gazed at it

366

awhile. For a moment the general's voice was lost to him as the bright eyes from the photograph gazed into his own. What would the morrow bring forth? Would he ever see her again? The chances looked slim in the light of what he already knew of the story that was to be told over the radio. Yet he comforted himself with the knowledge that she had a little weapon and knew how to use it; and in case these cold fragile Martians won the day, he was calmly confident that she had the courage to account for several of them before she turned it against herself.

"We have two more hours," the general went on; "too short a time for sleep. The Staff has felt it wise, before we go over the top, for you young men to know better what we are fighting for. Once this was a happy land and we terrestrial humans owned it, lived on it, and prospered gloriously. In order that your hands may strike harder as the new day breaks tomorrow, I want you to learn the details of how the invaders took the Earth away from us, and how it comes about today that there are only a few handfuls of us left on the deserts.

"Dr. Wren, who has spent a lifetime studying the history of the Martian invasion, will talk to you until it is time for us to start, and will give you an account of how these invaders came to our Earth and took it away from us. Dr. Wren!"

The general's voice stopped. A rustle sounded in the countless speakers scattered over the deserts and prairies. Then began a clear voice, perfectly intelligible, never loud; one could picture its speaker as a calm and learned man, for it never hesitated; it was colored just enough to avoid monotony. It never rose to excitement, never left the matter-of-fact level.

Here is the story it told:

During the Golden Age, just before the Dark Epoch, there was a great deal of fanciful fiction written around the possible conquest of the Earth by Martians. It consisted largely of fantastic tales of weird, pseudo-human monsters wracking terrific ravages with machines, rays, and other destructive agencies, and sweeping aside mankind with an easy gesture. When the invasion and conquest really came, it was so different from what had been imagined, that it was not recognized for several generations. Yet, it was all so simple—as one looks back one sees that it was the only possible and probable thing—so simple that it requires no scientist to imagine it. It could all have been predicted by a person of good common sense.

Early one morning, four hundred years ago, Otto Hergenrader, the pilot of a transcontinental mail plane saw beneath him from the height of 4,000 feet, what appeared to be a splash in the Amargosa Desert in Nevada, which he was then crossing. It appeared so unusual that he looped around it and passed it again at the height of three hundred feet. It was indeed a splash; but a huge one, several hundred feet across. In the middle of its depression stood a dark object which looked like a huge projectile from a cannon, cylindrical, with a cone-shaped top, and black and rusty looking. About it slowly moved a number of smaller figures.

Hergenrader, on mail schedule, could not stop; but he radioed the news promptly as he flew on his way. The first man to land on the spot was Larry O'Brien, a reporter on *The Salt Lake City Tribune*, who caught the message in his plane, not a score of miles from the place. O'Brien's headlined article in the *Tribune* has become a historic document, though it was written in poor English and gave practically no information of any value. It described the tall, rusty-looking, shell-like mass, and the slow, pale people who came out of it. They spoke weakly, and showed him a diagram composed of black circles and dots on a white sheet. But he could make nothing of them, nor could anyone who read his article, which went on to describe the gathering of the nondescript throng about the object and its inhabitants. The arrival of troops by aeroplane and the roping off of the space from the crowd, the springing up of lunch-counters and pop-stands in the desert in a few hours, came in later paragraphs. By evening, a dozen scientific men from the Universities of four states were there. These required only a few minutes to deduce that a space vehicle from Mars had arrived. The names of these scientists and of the President who later entertained the Martians are moldering away in some hidden archives; but popular memory has preserved those of Hergenrader and O'Brien as the discoverers of the Martian vessel.

Within a few hours the scientific men had established a sort of rudimentary communication with the arrivals from Mars; and the mutual learning of each other's language began to progress rapidly. But the President did not wait for complete understanding by the spoken word before he set up a great banquet to welcome the planetary visitors to the Earth. It was held in Washington, the second day after their arrival. Speeches were made in both languages and sketchily interpreted by both sides, and great masses of newspaper reports of the occasion exist to this day.

The general public was astonished to learn the next morning that the Martians were people just like we are. They had faces and spoke and ate. They had no pear-shaped heads nor barrel chests. About the only differences were that they were much paler than we, and moved slowly and uncomfortably. Otherwise they were as human as any of us. Many special newspaper and magazine articles appeared to explain that ours was the only possible form that intelligent beings could assume, because the same natural laws operated throughout the solar system or the universe, and on Mars these laws have the same materials to work with. Intelligence requires a large brain; this brain requires a locomotor and a nutritional apparatus to support it; these mechanisms were all developed from the same primordial slime on Mars as on Earth and went through the same steps. While theoretically other evolutionary body forms are possible, they could not be stable; while they have existed transiently, they had to make room for the more stable forms.

When the Martians started off to their planet, with a roar of discharging blasts and a hurricane of sand, after a stay of two weeks of welcoming, feasting, oratory, and scientific conferences, they carried half a dozen Earth people with them. Just whose desire this was, is not known, but as the Martians had spoken inspiringly of vast, unimaginable wonders back on their planet, there were more volunteers for the trip than there could possibly be room for. They were eager to go, in spite of the warnings of the scientific men that they could not survive long on Mars. These travellers never returned, nor were they ever heard of again. The Martians could not be blamed, for they had

369

managed to convey to the scientific men of our race that two generations of selected individuals had been reared and trained for the expedition from Mars to Earth, under proper conditions, in order that they might survive the terrestrial environment.

Following the Martians' departure, we can imagine people all over the Earth alert for rusty cylinders in desert places, and watching the red planet through telescopes and wondering about future visits. We can deduce that their interest finally played out and was transferred to other matters, so that, for most of them before the Martians came again, it passed out of their memories and had been replaced by the sensational things with which their news agencies constantly supplied them. Eleven years later, when a huge meteor was seen to fall in the sand-hill region of western Nebraska, no one thought of Martians. Only when Dr. Condra arrived from the State University the next morning in search of the meteor, was the whole memory of the first visit revived.

Apparently Dr. Condra, of whom little other record remains, was a man eminently fitted to greet the visitors and pilot them around through prominent places and present them to representative personages. Their white faces and slow, rhythmic steps were soon seen in the high places of business and government, and even in society; and everywhere on the movie-screen and illustrated periodical page; and that was true not only on this continent but also in Europe.

Whereas, the first visitors remained two weeks, the second remained two months.

A situation developed which must have caused the Martians to consider our social and economic organization of the time a curious phenomenon. The Martians approached President Francisco of the United States, having ascertained him to be the highest personage in the nation on the soil of which they had first stepped, and offered him gifts, which consisted of some tons of rare metals, as tokens of appreciation of their fine reception and symbols of friendship. These metals such as tungsten, iridium, beryllium, etc., were expensive, and yet were in great demand in industry. Much public discussion followed in newspapers and magazines, most of which, still available today, looks very strange and illogical to us. The President could not accept the metals as a personal gift. He stated that he served his visitors only in his official capacity. Had he not taken this position, had he accepted the gifts personally, a storm of criticism would have flung him high and wide. Nor could anyone find any legal authority or precedent for his accepting the gift on behalf of any government or other public organization for the purpose of giving its benefits to all the people. The Martians insisted that the gift was to our people, and for such a thing no legal channels existed.

A brilliant thinker, whose name has now been forgotten, suggested that the benefit would best be transferred on to the people if the business concerns which needed the metals were permitted to purchase them at a low price. This idea was hailed with delight, and a lowering of prices was at once announced on fountain-pens, watches, electrical bulbs, radios, and similar commodities. The money was paid over to the Martians in various kinds of legal tender; and they accepted it with much interest and curiosity. Honorary citizenships were conferred upon them in this country, and titles of nobility, in other countries. Shortly afterward they took their departure.

There was another Martian visit three or four years later, with much better understanding between guests and hosts and more precious "gifts" of rare metals. The guests appeared publicly in most cities, and almost every person saw them personally before they left. Within the next fifteen years, rusty cylinders and white faced, slow-moving tourists were so common that they ceased to excite more than passing attention. Many people on Earth learned the Martian tongue, a difficult feat but an exhilarating exercise for the mind. The Martians learned about buying and selling, and a trade in rare metals sprang up between the two planets. People were glad to get low prices on the commodities requiring the rare metals, the manufacturers of these commodities made money; and the Martians who sold the metals made money. Soon several of the Martians who had acquired considerable terrestrial wealth were well known, and numerous honorary citizenships had been presented to Martian people.

Considerable worry promptly arose among economists in regard to the one-sided trade, all the money leaving terrestrial hands and getting into Martian hands. A number of books on that point are still preserved. But apparently the problem did not last long, for the Martians began to spend their money. That was logical, for it was of no use to them unless they did. Many people considered it odd that their first purchases should have consisted of real-estate.

The first transfer of property into Martian hands has been traced through the deed recording offices in New York and has been reconstructed from contemporary records. When two white-faced strangers stepped into the Metropolitan Real Estate offices one June morning late in the twentieth century, the manager had not the least idea that the deal he was consummating marked the beginning of a fearful era for the world. He only felt a keen delight in the speed with which the transaction was closed, and in the excellent price in cash which he received for "Le Soleil," his choicest and most modern apartment building facing Central Park. By this time, Martians appeared so frequently in almost all cities that they went about the streets without awaking more than a momentary glance of curiosity. So, it may be surmised that no one paid much attention when gradually, always plausibly, one tenant after another moved out of "Le Soleil" and one Martian after another moved in. This is also a deduction. No comments appear in historical sources upon the matter.

It was a good many years later, in the first decade of the twenty-first century, that the episode of Jonathan Heape called attention to what was really happening, and even then the general public failed to take it seriously. The following is from Jore's "Sources of the Martian Era."

Jonathan Heape was a retired farmer who enjoyed living in the city. He was a hard-headed son of the soil, who thought that the old-fashioned aeroplane was good enough, and refused to ride in the new-fangled passenger rockets. For some eleven years he and his wife had occupied one of a row of cottages in *Cote d'Or*, a new suburb of St. Louis. When a Martian approached him, offering first a generous and then a fabulous price for his cottage, Jonathan Heape first roared NO, and then told the Martian to go to hell and that he'd be damned if he'd sell his house, and finally shoved the Martian down the front steps. He stormed around vociferating against "the pesticatin' critters, worse than vermin!"

But Heape noted that for several blocks up and down the street on both sides of his house, the inhabitants of the houses had moved out and Martians had moved in; and soon no one was seen in the street except those white-faced people.

"We're the only white people left," said Jonathan six weeks later.

"They're whiter than you," his wife objected.

"I'll be damned if I move out!" Jonathan growled.

He found his obduracy uncomfortable. First, the sight of the "lumbering" Martians with their bleached faces taking possession of the street irritated him. Then there was the cold. The Martians had some method of refrigeration which kept the whole neighborhood at the low temperature which they seemed to prefer; and Heape had to keep his furnace going in mid-summer. Next was the twilight. How they managed to keep the whole neighborhood partly darkened all day, Heape could not imagine, but it annoyed him. Then the constant excitement that pervaded the formerly peaceful suburb, one big public occasion after another, that he never understood, going on all the time, made him indeed uncomfortable.

The Martians finally got at him legally. They incorporated the suburb and made certain "modern equipment" required in each home. The "modern equipment" was purely Martian in nature and totally incomprehensible to Heape. But he was stubborn enough and sufficiently well off to fight them when they went after him legally. He stood up in court, fiercely pushing away the hand of his lawyer who tried to hold him down, and made a crude but impassioned speech that has remained a classic ever since.

"The people of this country 'ud better look out!" he shouted. "If you don't wake up to what's comin' you'll all be pushed off the Earth, like I'm bein'. How many of their ships have landed on the Earth in the last forty years? I've counted 'em up. Six thousand! Surprises you, don't it? Surprised me. How many ships are there on Earth today?

Nary a one. These guys have moved in here to stay. Aha! Surprises you, don't it? How many of these clumsy, paper-faced vermin are there in Cote d'Or now? I've counted two hundred. And how many other towns are they buttin' into? Hell only knows. You people'd better look out. Honored visitors! Bah! Honorary citizenship! Plah!" He spat on the floor in their direction.

Everyone was sorry for the poor old man, embittered by the loss of the home to which his sclerosing tissues had become unalterably accustomed. But the law was so unequivocal on the point that the jury was forced to decide against him. He received a court order to "modernize" his house or move out. He went out of the courtroom storming that he'd see them new-fangled gadgets in hell before he'd move out.

The affair dragged along for several weeks more, and ended tragically. He refused to move. The sheriff came over to remonstrate with him in person, though the sheriff's sympathies were with Heape. Heape turned on the sheriff.

"Their money has bought you too!" he roared. "They bought the court—"

"You know that isn't true," the sheriff said sadly. "The judge and the jury were both sorry. They tried everything to stretch things for you. But the law was too clear; there was no hope."

Heape grew angrier, but the sheriff had his orders. He called on his deputies and began moving out furniture. A crowd of Martians gathered about outdoors and watched. Heape got out an old shot gun and loaded it deliberately in plain sight of everyone. Then he gave them ten to get out, and began counting.

"One—two—three." Both Earth men and Martians held their breath and remained motionless, everybody tense as a drumhead.

The deputies began to move more slowly, and to edge toward the door.

"Seven—eight—"

The sheriff slowly drew his pistol.

Suddenly Heape grew limp; his gun clattered to the floor and he crumpled on top of it. When they reached him he was dead. A post-mortem examination failed to clear up the question as to whether he had died from conventional heart failure, or whether the Martians had killed him by some secret, subtle method.

A glance at the newspaper files of the next hundred years shows such small struggles to have been numerous, but the public did not recognize their trend or significance. The isolated individual like Jonathan Heape recognized it because it hit him hard in his everyday life; but the general masses of people ignored it. As time went on, the conflicts increased in magnitude and violence.

For instance, in 2047, Rawlings, a garage owner, patented a device for exerting traction from an automobile motor directly upon the road, without the intervention of transmission and wheels. He had gotten the idea from the Martians, and had begun to wax wealthy in manufacturing his device. The Martians claimed it and sued him in the courts, but lost the case. They retired gracefully enough, apparently. But a year later Rawlings failed financially and committed suicide, because the Martians had put on the market a device much better and cheaper than his. This is one of the rare instances of an organized Martian group taking part in any kind of business dealings with the terrestrials. Usually they shunned business and remained aloof.

Other conflicts were more gruesome. Fights over women especially were common. The Earth women liked the Martians, who though weak, were good looking, and certainly had an effective way with the ladies. One of the earliest discoverable records comes from the "DENVER POST," because the scene created in the civic center of that city made a rare news scoop. A Mrs. Yardley, wife of a high school coach had become enamoured of a Martian, a rather no-account fellow among his own race. Yardley followed his wife one night and saw them meet. He stepped out and confronted them. The Martian carried the usual attitude of insolent superiority, and Yardley, infuriated, let go at the Martian with his fist.

The first blow split the Martian's head wide open, but Yardley hit him three more times before he fell, and broke several bones. It was a crowded hour and a throng gathered instantly. In this crowd were two

Martians, who immediately called the police and filed a complaint. Yardley was found guilty but given a light sentence.

On one occasion in El Reno, Oklahoma, a Martian was found taking a fifteen-year-old Terrestrial girl with him. A lynch mob gathered promptly, intending to hang him, but by the time they got to the chosen tree, only a few fragments of him were left in different people's hands. Through the agency of the Martians in the community, the "leaders" of the mob were tried and sentenced to the usual punishment.

In Boston, the Martians bought up several acres of land surrounding the Bunker Hill monument, though the site of the monument itself was beyond their reach. No one noticed what was happening until the venerated relic of the Revolutionary War was so completely surrounded by densely inhabited Martian territory, the people disliked to try to get through to visit the monument. Societies were organized for the purpose of reclaiming the monument. Whether any clear explanation was ever made to the Martians of the significance of the spot is not known, but lawsuits dragged on for years. On the day of the final unfavorable decision of the courts against the League of American Patriots, a mob gathered and marched through the Martian quarters. Many Martians who happened to be in its path were killed; buildings were fired, and there was a great deal of shooting and destruction. Suddenly the mob began to crumple. In a few short minutes, all of them were dead, blackened, scorched. This is the first record of the use by the Martians of the short-wave pistol.

Near the middle of the twenty-first century, the Martians sold the secret of this short-wave pistol to Terrestrial manufacturers. It must have been a paying proposition, for immense numbers of them were sold, and the Terrestrial manufacturers became quite wealthy. Whether or not the Martians ever considered that their weapons might be turned against them is a matter of conjecture; but this happened soon.

It was again a dispute over property, this time in Minnesota. A large tract of wooded land north of Minneapolis, originally a huge French estate, was purchased by Martians. The latter began to clear off the pine woods and to drain the lakes, and to turn the country into one of the painted deserts in which they preferred to live. The

Minnesota people were indignant at the butchering of their beloved landscape, and protested. The Martians insisted upon the right which their deeds to the property gave them. Then, a clever attorney found in the abstracts of title an ancient and forgotten provision that the land could not pass out of the hands of the family in any way as long as an heir was living, except into State hands for taxes. An heir was found and the courts began to grind. They ground for several years, by which time the Martians had built a great many huge, scattered buildings upon it. The courts decided against the Martians, and ordered the property sold back to the original owner.

The Martians refused. A sheriff was empowered to remove them forcibly, and granted the aid of the Minnesota National Guard. The vindictiveness with which the "removal" was carried out was striking. The troops were outnumbered by civilian helpers, armed with all sorts of weapons, ancient and modern, but short-wave pistols predominated. A few Martians escaped from the territory; most of them were "accidentally" killed. The buildings were all dynamited. When the troops and the mob left, water was flowing back into the lakes and the soil was all turned up, ready for pine trees to grow again.

Such examples as the above illustrate the individual isolated instances of how the Martian infiltration and the Terrestrial resistance came into conflict. But it was a hundred years before the masses of the people as a whole became conscious of what was going on. It was not until the end of the second century after the first landing of the Martians, that this conflict was carried into politics and legislation.

Paul Arnac, a Frenchman, was the first to make a public issue out of it. He introduced into the International Senate, a bill to restrict immigration of the Martians. His presentation speech sums up the situation fairly well as it existed at the time.

"Today," said M. Arnac, "there are Martian 'quarters' in all of our large cities. These 'quarters' are neat, orderly, modern, yes. But they are increasingly pushing out our own people.

"Gentlemen, you may not see it as clearly as I do, but our race is going to have to fight for its existence, and my bill is the first gun.

"I have the highest respect for the individual Martian gentlemen whom I know personally. I know Martians who teach in our schools; I know Martians who have reached high positions in the medical, legal, and engineering professions; I feel that we ought to consider ourselves complimented because they have chosen to throw their lot with us and live our life. Among my best and most respected friends are the two honorable Martain Members of this august Senate, who have so won the confidence of the Earth people as to be elected to one of the highest political honors that the Earth can give.

"But such Martians are exceptions. The masses of them do not mingle with us. They keep to themselves and look down upon us as children, with a patronizing attitude. Sometimes it seems that they are too busy—God knows with what—to have time for us. What is it all about, their activity? Their building, their machinery? I'm sure I do not know.

"They consider our money system a disgrace, though they condescend to use it in dealing with us. But if one of them gets rich and puts up a country estate or manufactures racing cars or yachts or planes, he is an outcast and considered a degenerate.

"If one of them marries a terrestrial partner, he is an outcast and a pariah to be spat upon and ground under the heel. He is not permitted to associate with or live among their better classes in their own sections. The children of these bi-racial unions are the worst outcasts of all, accepted by neither race. They already form a class by themselves which presents a terrible problem. They are physically unfit for labor and are not accepted among the intellectual classes; they sink into the utmost depths of degradation. I shudder to think of them. What shall we do with them?

"The loss of life in racial clashes, the moral degradation produced among our people by the Martian Screens, the havoc wrought among our youth who learn the habits of excitement and emotional indulgence from them—all these things have been terrible enough. They are going to be worse!"

Arnac's bill called for a complete barring of immigrants for twenty-five years, and then for admitting a thousand per year thereafter for fifty years, and then the question was to be reopened. There was much excited speaking. It is rather surprising to find in the records that only a limited number of Senators saw the handwriting on the wall; most were against the bill. One even fought it on the ground that the Martians had a much higher rate of sickness and death among them than we did, and required immigrants to keep up their numbers, calling attention to the increase of our own wealth and prosperity as a result of what the Martians had brought us; and to the new views of life and the expanded horizon for the intellect and the emotions that the Martians had taught us.

Arnac's bill was hopelessly defeated. Arnac himself spent the rest of his life collecting information and writing books upon the Martian problem. A small pamphlet which he published eight years after the defeat of his bill presents proof that forty members of that particular session of the Senate displayed a sudden and extensive increase in wealth quite promptly after the bill failed to pass the Senate.

However, the hostility and resentment against the Martians gradually spread among the Earth people, for many reasons. One of them was the Screen of Life. The Martians were after money. They wanted money in order to acquire property peacefully and legally. They sold for money many of the secrets of their higher civilization, for many of which we Earth people were not far enough advanced, either physically or mentally. It seems very silly to us of the present day that our ancestors should have been victims to such a silly thing as the Screen of Life. But remember that physical existence was comfortable in those days; food and clothing were not hard to get, and men were not as hard physically nor as upright as we today. Yet the mental aspect of life was difficult. People were under severe mental strain; far more mental strain than we, scattered thinly over the desert, can realize. In their cities was strenuous competition, every man against every other; not physically, but in a subtle economic sense, which was more unmerciful and terrifying than physical combat, and the struggle had no end in life, except for the rich.

It is not surprising, if we understand how harassed they were mentally, though comfortable physically, that they should grasp at opportunities for momentary forgetfulness. The Screen of Life afforded such an escape from the realities of the present moment, for which the Terrestrial people seemed to be willing to pay all they had. It was a little apparatus, which, if supplied with special batteries produced on an opalescent screen pictures out of the past, out of what purported to be the future, or out of pure fancy. The general trend of these pictures could be controlled by the operator, but to them, the apparatus itself added a glamour of emotional, sensational surprise that thrilled the beholder beyond measure. People with well-balanced minds were upset by these things; once seen they could not be forgotten. Only a portion of the Earth people who once became accustomed to gazing at the Screen of Life, could ever break their habit, a great many of them found its attraction so strong they could not give it up. They gave all they had for the machine and for the constant supply of batteries necessary to operate it; for the Terrestrials never mastered the secret of manufacturing either. Addicts would spend hours and days watching the Screen in a sort of half-conscious trance, totally oblivious and indifferent to what was going on. The habit was worse than any drink or drug habit that the human race has ever known; able business and professional men became degenerates who stared stuperously at Screens all day, and lost all they had. They were outcasts among their own people, and were despised by the Martians. But they cared nothing about their disgrace or their starving families; they clung to the oblivion of their Screens. All legal efforts to prohibit the manufacture or sale of these Screens failed because influential people were making too much money out of it.

During all of this period, although warnings ought to have been obvious, the masses were indifferent to the Martian encroachment. The average person does not like to be disturbed in the even tenor of his everyday life, unless by something sudden and startling; it was a long succession of small details.

Inter-racial fights, some of them extensive enough to be termed wars, were numerous. It is difficult to know which to call the first war, because the conflicts began as small affairs and increased gradually. But between 2099–2101 the Martians were driven completely out of

Australia by a terrific struggle that cost the lives of three millions of people and most of the Martians who lived there. For several years the Australians waited in armed and fortified terror for retaliation from the rest of the Martians on Earth. Nothing startling ever happened; but twenty-five years later there are records of Martians occupying portions of cities there.

In 2131, Castigli became famous as a humorist. So beloved were his witty remarks and his laughing sympathy with human follies and weaknesses among the masses of the people, that they were not satisfied to hear him on the radio and see him on the television screens; he had to appear personally before his devoted admirers. For three years he was kept busy traveling by aeroplane from Alaska to Buenos Aires. Off the stage, he was a timid, humble man; he never became wealthy. He was just a natural born troubadour of the twenty-second century, and audiences idolized him throughout the Western Hemisphere.

The Martians arrested him one day because he had landed in a Martian restricted area and caused disorder thereby gathering a crowd. Technically he was guilty. Not being able to pay a huge fine, he was thrown into prison. Had his admirers known, they would promptly have raised millions to pay his fine; but the matter was kept quiet. His free, roaming nature could not stand prison confinement and he committed suicide. Then the news came out.

In one night, the people of the Western continents rose against the Martians. They had learned by this time how brittle the Martian bodies were, and how easy it was to kill a Martian with a blow of a fist or a stick. Martian houses were broken into, and Martians were killed at meals and in bed. Martian deaths predominated at first. But by dawn the disturbers had everywhere been surrounded by organized groups of Martians. Many of them were brought into court and hundreds punished for all crimes, from disturbing the peace to first-degree murder. Both races suffered from this terrible blundering thing, which is merely a single example of how impossible it is for two differing races to live independently side by side; and the awful losses and sufferings that occur for no reason at all when they try to do so.

While the general trend of the story is a general crowding ahead of the Martians decade after decade, each generation of Martians gaining and Terrestrials losing, yet the Terrestrials in their struggles won some brilliant victories. If the Martians keep a history, they undoubtedly give in it a position of great honor to a military leader of theirs whom our literature calls Bare Head. This name was given to him by Terrestrials because his skin was able to develop sufficient pigment to enable him to go without a hat.

This is the story of Bare Head. The Martians were later getting into the southeastern States than elsewhere, because they did not like the heat and moisture. They also fared worse there because the Southerners did not take patiently to them. They did not win impartial decisions in the courts. About 2150 there was considerable distress there; uprisings were frequent and violent, and the whole section was put under military rule from Washington. Military camps were dotted through Alabama, Georgia, Florida, and South Carolina.

There was great indignation among the terrestrial population when quietly, gradually, with no one knowing how or when, a Martian army materialized in the midst of them, in the old Oglethorpe country. The Martian Army said nothing, did nothing—merely remained quietly on the spot while the civil and military authorities attempted to restore peace. But the Earth people became suspicious, and one morning the Martians found themselves surrounded by a dense ring of troops, artillery, aeroplanes and tanks. The Martians formed a circle, and old Bare Head could be seen through the field-glasses here and there among his men, who cheered him as he went by. For some two hours the two sides faced each other without a move or sound. Then suddenly an aeroplane appeared from the north, going like a bullet at five-hundred miles per hour. Within two minutes some kind of Martian ray had brought it down, but not before it had shot a rocket bomb into the middle of the Martian camp which blew out a huge, smoking crater.

For some time the superior weapons of the Martians told. Attack after attack of the Earth soldiers was repulsed, and thousands of them were slain in a few minutes as they attempted to close in. But after several repulses, the aeroplanes closed in above and the tanks below, and while old Bare Head rushed back and forth about his camp, the bombs rained in until nothing was left of the Martian post but a plowed and smoking field. Among the few Martian bodies recognizable was that of Bare Head.

At the end of the twenty-second century there arose the first of the line of Prophets. Just as in ancient Israel, these Prophets saw; and they preached and wrote and stormed. At this more modern age, their appeal was not so much to the emotions as to the intellect, by sound argument and scientific observation. The first of these great men whose name went down to posterity was Ansel Roosenhaas, who left behind him 147 books and 3,000 magazine articles, and who traveled and lectured constantly, trying to awaken the Terrestrial race.

"There are now ten exclusively Martian cities scattered over the earth," wrote Roosenhaas in 2197. "There, the Martians own all the real estate, having legally purchased it. Just as a restricted suburb is kept free from undesirable tenants, these Martians are excluding Terrestrials. They cannot legally forbid us from visiting their cities; but outside of casual visits, every other Terrestrial presence or activity is barred; and there are many quarters to which no Earth visitor penetrates.

"We must admit these cities are beautiful places, bright, airy, and soaring, in marked contrast to our own ponderous, dreary and, confused conglomerations. If we could only profit by them and incorporate into our own cities the openness and cleanliness, the harmony! But do we? No!

"Our people use these cities as resorts for emotional stimulation of the most dangerous type. The Martian food and drink seems like something from Heaven. They have become a goal for which our citizens neglect their business and their patriotic duty—for the sake of which they spend all their time and money in the Martian cities.

"I am positive that the Martians do not welcome our people in their cities. They do not like our intemperate way of partaking of their emotional indulgences. There is a great physiological difference between Earth men and Martians. The latter have a highly developed intellect, and their emotions are under such rigid control that they are hard to arouse. The Martian needs powerful stimuli to give his emotions sway and afford him enjoyment. (It is a curious fact that many of these visitors comment on the fact that there is a large proportion of hospitals in these cities).

"When the Earth people indulge in these stimuli: the food, the drink, the music, the Screens and the sex associations, their emotions blaze up in a fire that sweeps away all intellectual restraint. This, of course, is disastrous to the welfare of the individual, and ultimately to the welfare of the race. Once begun, our people find it impossible to stop the downward rush; they become slaves to their emotions. The only way to avoid destruction is to stay away from the initial stimulus that produces the emotional conflagration.

"Even the Martians succumb to their own emotional indulgences, and they have a relatively high proportion of illness among them, because their constitutions are less rugged than ours. The reason that the majority avoid illness is because they have sufficient self-control to know just how far to go and where to stop.

"The love relationship is specially disastrous to our people. Among Martians, love has become quite separated from reproduction, and is purely a social matter. The women of their better classes are so beautiful that a mere glance at them sweeps away the emotions of the Terrestrial beholder. The only ones among our own people who are able to see Martian women, and to behold them impersonally and retain their self-control are our artists and scientific men. The average man does foolish things when he comes near one of these lovely creatures from the other planet. Most frequently it is one-sided. These beautiful women scorn the Earth men, while the Martians are very hostile to any attention that is paid to their women.

"Marriage between Earth men and an inferior type of Martian women occurred from the earliest days of the infiltration, but received nothing but contempt from both races, and produced the class of half-breeds which now constitutes such a serious problem. Of course, there have been exceptions in these inter-racial matches, but they merely prove the rule. Such is that of Betty Benson, daughter of the Secretary of State a hundred years ago. She had an affair with an officer high up in some Martian company. She was a popular girl and the public took a great interest in the details of her life. All attempts to dissuade her from her Martian lover's side failed; she remained devoted to him. One day they appeared together at a huge public picnic, and gradually a mob gathered about them. There was considerable danger that her Martian lover might be injured by the carelessly wrought up mob; Martian bodies stood up very poorly under mob violence. Betty Benson put him behind her against a wall and protected him with her own body until the proper officials arrived to marry them on the spot.

"Usually, when Earth men of a high type do come into contact with the highly-cultured Martian women, inter-racial *affaires* result which are usually illegal. The reverse occurs, though somewhat less frequently; cultured earth women in liaison with high-class Martian men. For a hundred years there have been endless complications and scandals, and even fights and killings. By this time, the Martian love-technic has become pretty common knowledge among the leisure-class of Terrestrials; and our psychologists and sociologists consider it one of the greatest misfortunes that has ever occurred to us.

"Martian love-making is an intense, intoxicating storm of passionate indulgence of the emotions, a fire of beauty, poetry, and spirituality that the human heart has never before known in its history. But, it is one-sided. It affects the Martians only passingly. Their cold emotional organization is barely stirred. But it is too much for our own emotional structure. In Terrestrials it changes the whole life-tenor of an individual; it renders him unfit to do the work of the world. He can never forget it, and never be at peace again. It is gradually breaking up the best business, professional, and scientific elements of our race."

This is the end of Roosenhaas' remarks as I quote them; though I may add that the Martians became somewhat more emotional later. Possibly the greater percentage of oxygen in our atmosphere or the greater intensity of ultraviolet radiation that reaches us, speeded up their metabolism somewhat. But the harm to our people was done.

In spite of the storming of the Prophets, the early twenty-second century saw the Martians outnumbering the original Earth inhabitants. So gradually did the increase come that our people did not realize what was happening until long after they were in the minority. By that time nothing much could be done about it, and certainly nothing was done. For nearly a century, the Terrestrials lay dormant, in a sort of stupor. History records no great names, no great events. What people thought or did has been lost in the stream of time.

We can only know that when the twenty-third century began, the Martians owned most of the Earth, having acquired it peacefully and legally. As a general rule, the Earth people had voluntarily sold out their own birthright for some sort of indulgence. We know that by this time there were numerous Universities scattered over the Earth's surface, exclusively for Terrestrial students. The young people of the Earth's race went there and were educated at Martian expense in all the ancient learning and modern technology of the Martians: thought-reading, emotional control, associational focusing, atomic dynamics, space manipulation, transformation of matter. Some of them graduated and took their places in Martian civilization and became adopted among the Martian race. This was just the reverse of the situation two hundred years before, when we were adopting a sprinkling of Martian scientists, teachers, and professional men. The Terrestrial graduates were quite absorbed among the Martians and were lost to their own people.

The great majority of them went back to our own people; and before they reached maturity, forgot most of the things they had learned, or retained only the pernicious and undesirable portions of them. Only rare exceptions among the Terrestrial race had the constitution to live the high-strung life of the Martians. They did not like the Martian culture that they had learned. Again, among the records of these young people, we find records of comments upon the prevalence of illness among the Martians; a type of emaciation combined with feverish activity and staring eyes that was most gruesomely unpleasant to non-medical people.

During the twenty-third century there were developed over the Earth's surface several areas which were reserved as the exclusive right and property of the Earth people. The American Southwest (the Martians preferred colder regions), North Africa, much of the East Indies were exclusively Terrestrial and rarely visited by the Martians though they supported and maintained these regions. There was no denying the fact that the Martians were taking care of the Terrestrials in a patronizing sort of way, educating them, feeding them, paying them for anything on any kind of pretext—for land, royalties for discoveries on the land, etc., as though they felt guilty for having crowded us out of our home in the solar system. In these Terrestrial reservations, the Earth people were free to do as they wished, to cultivate the land, build cities in their own way, and to escape the intense emotional atmosphere which the Martians, unable to live the calm, deliberate Terrestrial life, had set up for themselves. These reservations were pleasant places, into which Terrestrial ideas of landscape beauty had mingled with Martian improvements in architecture and city planning. All the humans that remained on Earth at this time were well off.

What was the reason for the sudden renaissance of the twenty-fourth century? Why did the Earthly race suddenly stir, open its eyes, and awaken to its position and its danger?

"Shall we let this puny, half-sick race crowd us off the Earth?" was the slogan of the time, and it suggested the answer to both of the above questions.

For the Terrestrial race of this period was on a far different physical and mental plane from their ancestors of two centuries ago. They were tall and lithe and tan; their bodies were perfect and powerful. Their minds were keen, alert and intelligent. They were hardy and rarely sick. The transformation had been worked by the Martians, but in a most unexpected way.

The degenerating, softening influences that the Martians had shown us had proved too much for three-fourths of the human race. The laziness, the intoxication of the Screens, the fiery love play, the emasculating food and drink of the Martians had placed our people in an environment which only a relative few had survived.

A billion people had been eliminated from existence in the high-strung, Martianized world; and those that were left were the fittest, hardiest worthiest specimens that the human race had ever seen. They represented the best development of which the human mind and body were capable, and everything that Earthly development had given them was reinforced by the desirable things that the advanced culture of the Martians could teach. The force of necessity had taught them to co-operate, instead of fighting among themselves. This new race was capable of saving its home, where the old one could never have done it.

And thus we come down to the organization of the *Hoplites*. In 2389 was born the man who thirty-five years later brought together the nucleus of the force that tonight intends to dislodge the Martians from our planet, or destroy us all in the attempt. Celsius Modry spent a quiet and contemplative youth, and eventually became Professor of Geology in the Terrestrial University in the Texas Panhandle. It was on his long, lonely expeditions studying rocks among the mountains and deserts with a student or two, that he first evolved the idea of a disciplined organization of young men, modeled after the armies that the world had ceased to need for two hundred years.

Just as the ancient Greek Hoplite represented the best in equipment, as far as arms and armor were concerned, so our *Hoplite* of today represents the best mental and physical equipment that can be developed by intensive effort. For many years, Modry was content with developing his little organization at his own university. He drilled his young men physically until they were perfect specimens and their organization acted as a perfect unit; he developed them mentally until they were a fair match for the Martians. Yet outwardly, the ostensible purpose of the group was not military—not hostile to the Martians. On the surface, it was a health movement.

The idea spread like the wind. Group after group took it up. Modry abandoned his teaching work and dedicated his life to perfecting and training the various organizations. He worked out a standardized procedure so that a member of a distant group could come into any other group and feel perfectly at home whenever the work started. Most of the members for the first two generations worked enthusiastically and loved the movement because of the benefit it rendered them, and without the least idea that it had any strategic value. And long after Modry was dead, his name was remembered, and his work went on, improving and increasing.

Of course, in secret, Modry had been studying and seeking for a means of waging a successful offensive against the Martians. He died without success, but he left a worthy successor in Saoti Kuwato, who also spent his life trying to bring the work to a focus. It remained for our own General Hunt to define an objective, and prepare to act. He has, as you know, been preparing you and other *Hoplites* all over the world for the single leap that we are to make at the Martian vital centers tonight. During all these years of planning and drill, of accumulation of stores and weapons, General Hunt has lived in anxiety lest some word betray the hiding places or hint of our plans. But the system of Modry is perfect. Not a *Hoplite* has proved disloyal. Not a Martian has annoyed us.

Aeroplanes and bombs are ready; men and squadrons are drilled. In South Dakota lies the key city of the Martians. In other continents are other key cities. A sudden destruction of these will disorganize the Martian system long enough to permit us to attack and destroy the panicky remainder. Tomorrow, the Earth is ours, or we are no more!

The calm voice of Dr. Wren suddenly stopped. The men in the thousands of coverts remained for a while in tense silence. Lieutenant Gary tucked his photograph firmly in a pocket and tightened his heavy belt. The General stepped to the microphone and spoke in a level tone:

"Everyone slip out quietly to your stations now. Buglers remain behind at your receiving set. In ten minutes the bugle will sound here. It will be repeated by the bugler at each post, and it will be your signal to start. Once more I ask you: *shall we let this puny, half-sick race crowd us off the Earth?*"

It was excitement at the importance of his mission that caused Gary's heart to leap into his mouth when the bugler stepped up to the microphone. As the clear tones pealed forth, the Lieutenant followed the General to the aeroplane from which a covering of canvas and cactus had been removed; and in a moment they were whirring through the night. How cool and quiet after the day's heat it seemed. Did those peaceful stars know that in a few hours bombs would be crashing and blood would be flowing? It seemed to Lieutenant Gary that he and the General might have been in the air alone for all the sights and sounds that reached them, except for the navigator's constant whispering into his transmitter, and the twittering of the dials in front of him. But those dials gave the Lieutenant confidence in the thousands of planes that were spreading fanwise to form a circle about the Martian clot in South Dakota.

Lieutenant Gary would have welcomed action, excitement, trouble. But to sit hour after hour in a plane, expecting every moment to hear the crack of shots from Martians below, or to see some portion of the machinery melt as the result of some invisible ray, or to feel some unknown, unexpected, terrible blow from the science of the Martians, that was unnerving. His heart pounded hard and he could hardly sit in his seat.

According to the navigator, everything was going like clockwork. Not a plane had met with any trouble. All were in correct positions in the formation. When, after the lapse of hours, daybreak finally came, the planes were gathered in a huge circle around the Martian key city.

At the General's orders, they hovered, while a few scout planes crept ahead. A deep red light shone through the morning mists from some high spot in the city; it shone for a moment and went out. Again it came and went out. Monotonously this continued; even after the day had become bright, the deep red rays were plainly visible, going on and off. The scouts came back stating that there were no troops, no weapons visible; that one of the planes had purposely exposed itself to draw attention and nothing had happened.

"A trap of some sort," the general muttered. But he gave orders to close in swiftly and drop bombs.

Pinpoints appeared almost simultaneously from all quarters of the sky, and gradually came together until a huge circular cloud of them made a black halo over the city. Lieutenant Gary's eyes were on the ground. Not a Martian was visible anywhere.

The General hurriedly sent out an order to drop no bombs. A hundred planes were ordered to dash across the city and retreat in the opposite directions. Lieutenant Gary saw them streak across like bullets. But not a sign from the city, except the monotonous coming and going of the red light.

"I'm going over myself," the General said.

Lieutenant Gary eyed him in surprise. "They need you!" he exclaimed. "Suppose—please let me go."

"I can't understand it, and I'm going," the General replied. "Kamil Rey will make a good commander in my place if necessary. You may come with me if you wish."

He sent out a call for volunteers, and twenty planes followed him. At a slower speed they flew over the city and looked down. The red light, blinking on and off came from a tall tower. There were things moving. Some automatic conveyors kept up a monotonous procession. Several solar clocks rotated slowly. But nowhere was there a living being.

At a signal, the pilot dropped a small bomb in an open square. With a loud crash it scattered masonry far and wide, and all the planes fled as swiftly as they could gather acceleration. But in a moment they circled back. Not a soul appeared in response to the bomb.

"If it's a trap, they're good sports," General Hunt remarked. "It begins to look suspiciously as though perhaps something else—"

"What?" asked Lieutenant Gary.

"I can't imagine." The General mused abruptly: "We'll land and find out!"

As the signal went out, the twenty planes circled about, looking for a landing place. The General's plane landed in a large, open square near the center of the city. As the General was about to step out, the Lieutenant drew him back and stepped forth ahead of him, running into the open a dozen yards from the plane. He was expecting to drop instantly in his tracks, a charred corpse. But a minute went by and nothing happened, until the General clapped him on the shoulder.

"Good of you," he said, "but not necessary, apparently."

Everything was silent and motionless. They stared warily up the broad, empty street. The Lieutenant ran ahead as they passed each corner or doorway or any place where danger might lurk, until finally the General smiled and ceased to protest.

"I'll be able to tell the young lady that you're game, anyway," he said.

They were startled by a sudden movement and a clicking noise, but it was only some automatic machinery on a standing vehicle. Careful scrutiny showed it to be without occupants. Other groups of *Hoplites* were scattering in different directions. Ahead of them was a large building with a tall tower, in which the red light went on and off. It did not seem much brighter when they were right under it, than it had from the distance of ten miles. It went monotonously on and off. Just at their elbows was the door of a house

"I'm going in," Lieutenant Gary said, half-questioningly.

"Yes. We have to find out," the General stated.

They searched the broad rooms and found in one of them a dead Martian, woefully emaciated, with wide staring eyes. In another room, were two more, both dead, one on the floor at the foot of a chair, and one on a sofa.

They waited in front of the building of the tower until other groups arrived.

"Unquestionably the City Hall, or Administration Building," the General remarked. As the search parties came in one by one, they all reported the same—a silent city, with very few inhabitants, and those all dead.

Within the city administration building there was almost none. One was found crouched stiff on a stairway, another, reclining in seeming luxurious comfort on a chair in front of a desk. In one room were several bodies on a cremating apparatus; the cremating had not been done, and the bodies were in an unpleasant condition.

In a small room, high in the tower was the corpse of an operator still bent over a tremendously complex communication apparatus of some sort. The vast machinery was not all clear to the Terrestrials, but the microphone mouthpiece was plain, and the message in front of the operator left no possible doubt. In the simple script of the Martians, with which he was familiar, Lieutenant Gary could read the following:

"*We advise sending no more colonists to the Earth. The Martian race cannot survive on this planet. There is too much ultra-violet and too much oxygen. It increases our metabolism and burns our skins. The protective measures developed on Mars last one or two generations, but eventually prove futile. Not one family of colonists has ever lasted more than three generations: only the millions shipped over in space vessels have kept up our numbers. Our scientific men have worked hard to find something to protect us, but since colonists have ceased coming our numbers have melted away. In . . . . . (an untranslatable jumble of Martian characters standing for the city they were in), everyone is dead, and soon I shall be. I have left the distress signal on in the tower for three days but I get no reply from any of the other cities. I transmit the warning of the Scientific Council: 'Earth is not for Martians!'*"

The Oversight

John C. Hastings, senior medical student in the Nebraska State University Medical School at Omaha, looked out of the window of the Packard sedan he was driving down the road along the top of the bluff, and out in the middle of the Missouri River he saw a Roman galley, sweeping down midstream with three tiers of huge oars.

A pang of alarm shot through him. The study of medicine is a terrible grind; he had been working hard. In a recent psychiatry class they had touched upon hysterical delusions and illusions. Was his mind slipping? Or was this some sort of optical delusion? He had stolen away from Omaha with Celestine Newbury to enjoy the green and open freshness of the country like a couple of stifled city folks. Perhaps the nearest he had come to foolishness had been when the stars had looked like her eyes and he had pointed out Mars and talked of flying with her to visit that mysterious red planet.

"Do you see it too?" he gasped at Celestine.

She saw it, too, and heard the creak of oars and the thumping of a drum; there floated up to them a hoarse chant, rhythmic but not musical, broken into by rough voices that might have been cursing.

It was a clumsy vessel, built of heavy timbers, with a high-beaked prow. There was a short mast and a red-and-yellow sail that bulged in the breeze. The long oars looked tremendously heavy and unwieldy, and swung in long, slow strokes, swirling up the muddy water and throwing up a yellow bow-wave. The decks were crowded with men, from whom came the gleam of metal shields, swords, and helmets.

"Some advertising scheme I suppose," muttered John cynically.

"Or some traveling show, trying to be original," Celestine suggested.

But the thing looked too grim and clumsy for either of these things. There was a total lack of modern touch about it. Nor was there a word or sign of advertising anywhere on it. They stopped the car and watched. As it slowly drew nearer they could see that the men were coarse, rowdy specimens; and that the straining of human muscles at the oars was too real to be any kind of play.

Then there were shots below them. Someone at the foot of the bluff was blazing away steadily at the galley. On board the latter, a commotion arose. Men fell. Then voices out on the road in front of them became more pressing than either of these things.

"A young fellow and a girl," someone said; "big, fast car. Omaha license number. They'll do."

"Hey!" a voice hailed them.

In front, on the road, were a dozen men. Some were farmers, some were Indians. One or two might have been bank clerks or insurance salesmen. All were heavily armed, with shotguns, rifles, and pistols. They looked haggard and sullen.

"Take us to Rosalie, and then beat it for Omaha and tell them what you saw," one of the men ordered gruffly. "The newspapers and the commander at Fort Crook."

This was strange on a peaceful country road, but John could see no other course than to comply with their request. He turned the car back to Rosalie, the Indian Reservation town, and the men were crowded within it and hung all over the outside. Even the powerful Packard found it a heavy burden. In the direction of Rosalie, the strangest sight of all awaited them.

Before they saw the town, they found a huge wall stretching across the road. Beyond it rose blunt shapes, the tops of vast low buildings. What a tremendous amount of building! the thought struck John at once. For, they had driven this way just three days before, and there had been no sign of it; only the wide green fields and the slumbering little village.

The armed men became excited and furious when they saw the wall. They broke out into exclamations which were half imprecations and half explanatory.

"They put these things down on our land. Ruined our farms. God knows what's become of the town. Squeezed us out. Must be a good many dead. We have telephoned Lincoln and Washington, but they are slow. They can't wake up. Maybe they don't believe us." There were curses.

John could see great numbers of armed men gathering from all directions. There was no order or discipline about them, except the one uniting cause of their fury against this huge thing that had so suddenly arisen. Far in the distance, countless little groups were emerging from behind trees and around bends in the road or driving up in cars; and nearby there were hundreds more arriving with every conceivable firearm. The last man in the countryside must have been aroused.

The men climbed out of John's car and repeated their order that he drive to Omaha and tell what he saw.

A ragged skirmish line was closing in rapidly toward the big gray wall that stretched for a mile from north to south. Along the top of it, after the manner of sentries, paced little dark figures. John and Celestine were amazed to see that they, too, were Roman soldiers. The sunlight glinted from their armor; the plumes on their helmets stood out against the sky; their shield and short swords were picturesque, but, against the rifles below, out of place.

There came a shot, and another from the approaching attackers, and a figure on top of the wall toppled and fell sprawling to its foot and lay still on the ground. Hoarse shouts arose. A dense knot of Roman soldiers gathered on top of the wall. A fusillade of shots broke out from below, men running frantically to get within close range. The group on the wall melted away, many crashing down on the outside, and a heap remaining on top. The wall was completely deserted. The wind wafted a sulphurous odor to the nostrils of the two young people in the Packard.

Then followed a horrible spectacle. John, hardened to gruesome sights in the course of his medical work, came away from it trembling, wondering how Celestine would react.

A huge gate swung in the wall, and a massed army of Roman sol-

diers marched out. Bare thighs and bronze greaves, and strips of armor over their shoulders, plumed helmets, small, heavy shields; one
company with short swords, the next with long spears; one solid company after another poured out of the gates and marched forth against
their attackers.

The Farmers and Indians and other dispossessed citizens opened
fire on the massed troops with deadly effect. Soldiers fell by the hundreds; huge gaps appeared in the ranks; whole companies were wiped
out. But, with precise and steady discipline, others marched in their
places. Blood soaked the ground and smeared the trees and shrubbery. Piles of dead were heaped up in long windrows, with twitching, and crawling places in them. New ranks climbed over them and
marched into the blaze of lead, only to fall and be replaced by others.
The peaceful Nebraska prairie was strewn with thousands of armed
corpses.

Terror gripped the hearts of the couple in the Packard. The firing
began to halt. It became scattered here and there as ammunition became scarce. As the troops poured out in unlimited numbers, men in
overalls, sweaters, and collars and shirt sleeves began to retreat. The
grim ranks closed upon the nearest ones. Swords rose and fell, spears
thrust, clubbed rifles were borne down. There was more blood, and
the bodies of American citizens littered the ground that they themselves had owned and tried to defend.

John and Celestine, paralyzed by the spectacle, came to with a
jerk.

"It's time to move," John said.

He swung the car around just as, with a rattle and a roar, a score of
chariots dashed out of the great gates and the horses came galloping
down the road. The ranks of the infantry opened to permit pursuit of
the retreating skirmishers. The clumsy vehicles rattled and bumped
behind flying hoofs at a rapid clip, the men in them hanging on to
the reins and keeping their footing by a miracle. Gay cloaks streamed
backward in the wind, and gold gleamed on the horses' harness.

John bore down on the accelerator pedal, and the car leaped ahead
with a roar, a scattered string of chariots swinging in behind it. He

headed down the road and, once the Packard got a proper start, it left its pursuers ridiculously behind. Celestine shrieked and pointed ahead.

"Look!"

A group of Roman soldiers with drawn swords were formed on the road ahead, and more were swarming out of the shrubbery.

An officer waved a sword and shouted a sharp word.

"Stop, nothing!" John said through gritted teeth, remembering bloody overalls and sprawling limbs gripping battered rifles.

He put his full weight on the accelerator pedal and the huge machine throbbed and rumbled into life, a gleaming, roaring gray streak.

"Duck down below the windshield, dear," he said to Celestine. Never before had he used that word, though he had often felt like it.

The Roman soldiers quailed as they saw the big car hurtling toward them, but they had no time to retreat. The bumper struck the mass of men with a thud and a crash of metal. Dark spatters appeared on the windshield and things crunched sickeningly. The car swerved and swung dizzily, and John's forehead bumped against the glass ahead of him, but his hands hung to the wheel. The fenders crumpled and the wheels bumped over soft things. Just as he thought the car would overturn, he found himself flying smoothly down a clear road; in his windshield mirror a squirming mass on the road was becoming rapidly too small to see.

He laughed a hard laugh.

"They didn't know enough to jab a sword into a tire," he said grimly.

And there to their left, was the tiresome galley, sliding down the river. The countryside was green and peaceful; in a moment even the galley was out of sight. Except for the crumpled fenders and the leaking radiator it seemed that they had just awakened from an unpleasant dream and found that it had not been true.

They talked little on the way to Omaha; but they could not help talking some. Who were these men? Where did they come from? What did it mean, the piles of dead, the sickening river of blood?

They must hurry with the news, so that help would be sent to the stricken area.

The hum of the motor became a song that ate up miles. John worried about tires. A blowout before he reached the army post at Fort Crook might cost many lives. There was no time to waste.

Just as the roof-covered hills of Omaha appeared in the distance, two motorcycles dashed forward to meet the car and signaled a stop. The khaki-clad police riders eyed the bloody radiator and nodded their heads together.

"You've been there?" they asked. John nodded.

"You've been there?" he queried in return.

"The telephone and telegraph wires are hot."

"They need help—" John began.

"Are you good for a trip back there in a plane, to guide an observer?" the officer asked. "We'll see the lady home."

So John found himself dashing to the landing field on a motorcycle, and then in an Army plane, a telephone on his ears connected with the lieutenant in front of him. It was all a mad, dizzy, confused dream. He had never been up in a plane before, and the novelty and anxiety of it fought with his tense observation of the sliding landscape below. But there was the galley on the river, and three more following it in the distance. There was an army marching along the top of the bluffs down the river; a countless string of densely packed companies with horsemen and chariots swarming around. There were the huge flat buildings in the walled enclosure where Rosalie had stood. Out of the buildings and out of the enclosures, marched more and more massed troops, all heading toward Omaha.

Then they were back in the City Hall, he and the lieutenant, and facing them were the chief of police and an Army colonel. There was talk of the Governor and General Paul of the State Militia due to arrive from Lincoln any moment in an airplane; and the National Guard mobilizing all over the state, and trucks and caissons and field guns already en route from Ashland with skeletonized personnel. Secretaries dashed out with scribbled messages and in with yellow telegrams. A terrific war was brewing, and what was it all about?

The lieutenant stepped up to the colonel and saluted.

"If you please, sir, the galleys on the river—"

"Yes?" asked the worried colonel.

"They've got to be sunk."

"We have no bombs," the colonel answered. "We're just a toy army here, in the middle of the continent."

"No bombs!" The lieutenant was nonplussed for a moment, and hung his head in study. "Will you leave it to me, sir? Somehow—"

"Good fellow. Thank you," said the colonel, very much relieved. "Your orders are, then, to sink the galleys."

"Come!" The lieutenant said to John.

"Me?" gasped John.

"Don't you want to?" the lieutenant asked. "Men are scarce. I need help. You're the closest. And you've got a level head."

"Just give me a chance," John said eagerly.

The lieutenant spent fifteen minutes in a telephone booth. Then they dashed in a motorcycle to the city landing field where the plane lay. They made the short hop to the Army flying field. This all took time; but when they taxied towards the Army hangars, there stood men ready to load things into the plane. A stack of kegs labeled "Dynamite" and white lengths of fuse did not look very military, and their source was indicated by the departing delivery truck of a hardware firm. The men knocked the stoppers out of the kegs and wadded the fuses into the bungholes with paper.

"Bombs!" The lieutenant spread his hands in a proud gesture. "The Q.M.G. in Washington ought to see this. Maybe he'd trust us with real ones some day."

He turned to John.

"We'll use a cigarette-lighter down in the cockpit, and heave them over the side."

Out over the city they flew, and up the river. The trireme was steadily approaching, and the lieutenant flew his plane a hundred feet above the ship. They could see gaping mouths and goggling whites of eyes turned up at them. The decks were a mass of coarse-looking faces.

"Hate to do it," remarked the lieutenant, looking down on the decks packed with living men. "But, Lord, it seems to be the game, so light up!" he ordered sharply.

As John applied the cigarette-lighter and the fuse began to fizzle, the lieutenant circled about and again flew over the creeping galley.

"Now!" He shouted, and John rolled the keg over the side. It turned over and over endwise as it fell, and left a sputtering trail of smoke in the air.

It fell on the deck and knocked over several men. The lieutenant was putting height and distance between themselves and the galley as rapidly as possible, and rightly. In another moment there was a burst of flame and black smoke. Blotches of things flew out sidewards from it, and a dull roar came up to them. For a few minutes a mangled mass of wreckage continued the galley's course down the river. Then it slowed and drifted sidewise, and flames licked over it. Struggling figures stirred the water momentarily and sank. Not a swimmer was left; bronze armor does not float on muddy Missouri River water.

Above the second galley they were met by a flight of arrows, and the lieutenant hurriedly performed some dizzy gyrations with the plane to get out of bowshot, but not before several barbed shafts struck through the wings and thumped against the bottom. So they lit their fuse and passed low over the galley at full speed. There was less regret and more thrill as they rolled the keg with its sputtering tail over the side; the humming arrows made the game less one-sided. The high speed of the plane spoiled the aim, and the keg of dynamite plumped harmlessly into the water just ahead of the galley. The second time they figured a little more closely, and before very long, all four of the galleys were a mass of scattered, blackened wreckage.

John leaned back in the seat.

"Terrible way to squander human beings," he said.

The lieutenant's teeth were set.

"You haven't seen anything yet," he said to John. "We've got two more kegs of dynamite and no orders to the contrary. Let's go back to the front lines."

"Front lines!" exclaimed John.

The lieutenant smiled.

"You've studied medicine; I've studied war. It is two and a half hours since we left the meeting. The Roman—or whatever the blank they are—infantry has made ten miles south and west. Our troops from the Fort have easily made thirty or forty in their trucks, and started digging trenches and emplacing guns. That would mean that there must be fighting north and west of here. Isn't that so?"

"I hadn't thought of it," John admitted.

"Also by this time there must be two or three regiments of State militia on trucks and bound in this direction; and the artillery and machine-guns from Ashland ought to be ready any minute. We've got two more kegs. Are you game?"

As if in answer, a dull boom sounded from the northwest, followed by another; and in five minutes the banging was almost continuous.

John nodded his head. The lieutenant swung the plane around, and it was less than ten minutes before they saw the trenches of the Fort Crook troops spread below them; and from far into the north there poured column upon column of densely formed Roman troops, with the gleam of the afternoon sun upon the metal of their armor and swords. On the eastern end of the line the Roman infantry had reached the trenches and a sickening carnage was taking place. As they advanced steadily toward the trenches, the Roman troops were mowed down by the machine-guns of the Federal soldiers and the Omaha police, in swaths like meadow-grass laid flat by the blade of the scythe. During the period of a few minutes as they looked down they saw thousands of men fall; great heaps of twitching and bloody dead in armor and plumes were piled before the thin line of khaki.

"They don't need us much, but here goes!"

Far back over the enemy's lines, where the troops were massed the densest, they sailed, and dropped their black and smoking blasts and scattered several companies of bewildered soldiers. But others took their places and pressed steadily on.

"If we only had a few fighting planes and some ammunition for them—wouldn't we clean up the place!" gloated the lieutenant. "But there isn't a plane with a machine-gun on it in this division, and not an aerial bomb except some dummies for practice. The War Department isn't ever so very fast, and this certainly came suddenly. However, I'm sure they must be getting busy sending things over by now. Let's look westward."

The line was flung a dozen miles west of the Missouri River, and gradually was crawling still further west. The artillery from Ashland had stopped ten miles southwest of the place where fighting first began, and by now had set up their pieces and gotten the range with the aid of a commandeered, tri-motored passenger plane; they were banging shells at the rate of one every three seconds into the thickest of the troops. Even at the height of three thousand feet, the sight was horrible; there were red areas against the green of the landscape, and red areas on the piled up heaps that twitched and gleamed with spots of metal; the heaps piled up and grew into hills, between the gaping holes that the shells dug into the wheat fields.

"Ha! Look!"

The lieutenant pointed near the line at the middle.

"An artillery captain is looking for prisoners."

The barrage of one of the batteries was laying flat a wide area, but preserving a little circle intact in the middle of it. On this island, among a sea of smoky holes, stood a huddled group of Roman soldiers. One by one they fell, for flying fragments of high-explosive shell traveled far, and they did not know enough to fall flat on their faces. Then the barrage stopped and a platoon of men in khaki with rifles crept toward them.

The lieutenant looked like a man on the side-lines of a football game. He flew his plane low and gazed breathlessly at the combat below. For it was an exciting one.

The khaki-clad soldiers wanted prisoners alive. But the Roman soldiers understood nothing of the threat of the gun. Rifles and pistols were leveled, but served in no wise to stop them from making a fierce attack on the Americans with swords and spears. To save their own lives, the latter had to stop and shoot the Romans down.

All but a half a dozen armored men now lay flat on the ground. These gathered together for a moment's council, adjusted their shields, and balanced their swords and spears. They were preparing a charge.

403

The lieutenant on the ground obviously had orders to get live prisoners. He also knew his battle psychology well.

He formed his men in line; bayonets flashed out of scabbards and in a moment a serried line of them bristled forward on the ends of the rifles. The khaki-clad line started first. The men on the flanks ran as fast as they could go and dodged through shell-holes. The Romans started slowly toward the thin-looking center of the American line.

The aviation lieutenant rose in his seat and dropped the stick of the plane for a moment in his excitement. The plane veered and the fight below was lost to view for a moment. By the time he had swung the plane back, the circle of khaki had almost closed around the Romans. The latter stood back to back, spears straight out in front of them. It must have taken nerve to face that circle of advancing bayonets, outnumbering them six to one. They held, stolid as a rock wall, and John was almost beginning to think that they would fight to the death and kill a few American soldiers. But, just as the ring of bayonets was within a foot of the ends of their spears, they suddenly dropped their weapons on the ground, and held their hands in the age-old gesture, straight above their heads.

The men in khaki pushed them apart with their bayonets, and two to a prisoner, marched them back to the line; others stopping to pick up weapons. For the first time John noted that these men were all giants; even from the altered perspective of the airplane it was clear that they were six and a half to seven feet tall, and burly.

"We'll go back and report, then get a rest," the aviation lieutenant said, heading the plane toward the Army field. There he shook hands with John and arranged to meet in the morning for further work.

After a telephone conversation with Celestine, and a meal, John settled down in his room and turned on the radio. Program material had been crowded off all stations by the news of the war.

"The front lines are now fully equipped with portable searchlights and flares. But the Roman soldiers have quit coming. Apparently there will be no fighting during the night."

There followed a resume of happenings with which John was already familiar, and he shut the instrument off. Just as he was beginning to doze, his telephone rang. It was the pathologist at the Medical School.

"Hello, Hastings," he said. "You have been in on this from the start, and I thought you would be interested in our prisoners."

John hurried over to the hospital, where in one of the wards there was a squad of soldiers with fixed bayonets, and two of the giants on the beds. One had a shoulder wound and a thigh wound from high-explosive fragments. Both wounds were very slight.

"Mr. Hastings," said the pathologist, presenting him to a man bending over one of the prisoners, "Professor Haven is from Creighton University, and is the head of the Latin Department. He is trying to talk to these men."

Professor Haven shook his head.

"These men speak Latin but I don't," he sighed. "I've studied it a lifetime, but I can't *speak* it. And they speak a very impure, corrupted Latin. But, I'm making out, somehow."

He spoke slowly, in ponderous syllables to the prisoner. The man grumbled surlily. In the meantime, the pathologist called John away.

"One of the prisoners died," he said, "and we are doing a post-mortem. Just a slight flesh-wound; no reason under the sun why it shouldn't heal easily. He seemed to have no vitality, no staying power."

The post-mortem failed to make clear what had been the cause of death; the slight bullet wound in the shoulder could not have caused it. No other abnormality was found. They went back to the ward, and found another of the prisoners dead.

"Strange," the pathologist muttered. "They can't resist anything. And there is some odd quality about their tissues, both anatomical and physiological, that I can't put my finger on. But they're different."

"They're certainly stupid," the Latin professor said. "I have succeeded in making myself understood to this man. I asked him, who are they, what they wanted, why they were fighting us, where they come from. He does not know. '*Non scio, non scio, non scio!*' That's all I got out of either one of them, except that they are hungry and would prefer to lie on the floor rather than on the bed. They give me the impression of being feeble-minded."

"Good fighting machines," John remarked.

When he got back to his room, the radio was urging everybody to go to sleep and rest. There were guards detailed for necessary night work, and there was no danger. Freshness and strength would be needed tomorrow. But John was too excited following his strenuous day, and knew that sleep would be impossible. He kept on listening to the news from the radio, which was trying to solve the mystery of these Roman hordes.

"Who are they?" the announcer asked rhetorically. "Where are they from? What do they want?" His questions were asked but not answered. He reported that during the afternoon the entire world had been searched by cable and radio, and nowhere was there any trace of the departure of such vast numbers of men. Italy and Russia were especially suspected; but it was out of the question that such hundreds of thousands could have been transported without leaving some evidence. How had they reached the middle of the North American continent? No railroad knew anything about them; there had been no unusual number of airships observed in any direction. One was tempted to think that they came out of the ground. Someone proposed the idea, based on the popularity of Einstein's recent conceptions, that these men had somehow crossed the time dimension from Julius Caesar's time; a fold in the continuum might readily bring the period of the Roman Senate in contact with the period of radio and automobiles.

A few minutes later the announcer stated that he had received a dozen contemptuous and scornful messages about the idea from scientists and historians. If these troops had come from Caesar's time, their sudden disappearance would certainly have caused enough sensation to be recorded; and no such record existed. If they came from such a period, they must have disappeared from the sight of the people who lived then; otherwise one must assume that they went on existing in their own time as well as the present day. The idea was rent to bits. The announcer went on with rhetorical questions:

How many more men were there? What would happen tomorrow? At least there were comforting reports that in the morning the sky would be crowded with planes bearing tons of high-explosive bombs. It could not last long.

Suddenly John slapped his thigh. He went to the telephone and called up the aviation lieutenant.

"Hello!" he said. "Did I get you out of bed? Well, it looks as though neither one of us is so bright about war."

"Now what?" the lieutenant asked.

"Those last two kegs of dynamite you dropped on Caesar's army—"

"Yes?" the lieutenant asked.

"They ought to have been dumped on the buildings on the Indian Reservation, what?"

A faint oath came over the phone.

"Say, Hastings, I feel like resigning my commission and getting a job selling bananas. But, what do you say to correcting the oversight? At once?"

"I'm there. But wait. I'm getting positively brilliant tonight. Why not get the Latin prof to go with us and see what we can find out?"

"If I could slap you on the back by phone, I'd do it. I'm waiting for you with the ship. Hurry."

Professor Haven was delighted at the opportunity; the wizened little fellow seemed oblivious to the dangers of the undertaking. They put rifles in the plane, and two forty-fives apiece in their belts.

The walled enclosure was visible to the plane from a distance, because of a strange reddish glow that came up from it. The glow enabled the lieutenant to note that, a long, flat-roofed building offered a far better opportunity for a landing than did the ground, which was systematically spaced with guards. He shut off his motor several miles away, and managed his landing with marvelous skill and silence. Only the landing-wheels, bumping over the rough places on the roof, made any sound. They waited for thirty minutes in silence, and as no further sounds came from the camp, they crept out of the cockpit and stole along the roof.

The guards pacing about below seemed not to have noticed their landing. Ahead of them was a large, square affair like a chimney, with a red glow coming out of it. But, it was not a chimney, for no heat came from it. It might have been a ventilator; in fact as they approached they found that a strong current of air drew downward into it. They could lean over the edge and see a large, bright room immediately below them.

It was certainly no crude Roman room. It was a scientific laboratory, crowded with strange and delicate apparatus. Most of it was quite unfamiliar to John in use or nature, despite the fact that he was well posted on modern scientific matters, and could make intelligent guesses about scientific things or equipment even out of his own line. He could make nothing out of the things he saw below.

Just beneath them stood a huge Roman officer; the numerous gold insignia on his chest indicated high rank. He stood in front of a glass jar about four feet high, from which numerous cords led to a table full of intricate apparatus. Inside the jar there was something that looked like a piece of seaweed. It was hard, tough, leathery. In the bright light, it might have been a sort of a branching cactus. But it moved about within its jar. It gestured with one of its branches. It pointed at the Roman soldier, and nodded a large, head-like portion. A rapid rattle of words in a foreign tongue came up to them, and Haven, the Latin professor, craned his neck. John recognized a Latin word here and there, but could make out no meaning. Haven later translated what he had heard. The first words he distinguished were those of the big Roman general.

"We need fifty more legions of men by morning," he said apologetically.

"Why not?" a metallic voice replied. It continued monotonously, with scant intonation. "I'll start them at once and have them ready by daylight." There was a quick gesture of the leathery thing in the jar. Little groups of long, red thorns scattered over it.

The general went on.

"These people are good fighters. They may conquer us. We haven't a thousand soldiers left."

The metallic voice that replied conveyed no emotion, but the gesture of the cactus-like thing in the jar was eloquent of deprecation.

"To our science they are but a puff of wind," the droning voice said. "I can destroy them all by pressing a button. Do you think I have studied the Earth and its beast-like men for ages in vain? But, I want sport. I've been bored for too many centuries. So, to entertain me you shall have your five hundred companies of soldiers tomorrow morning. Now go. I must be alone."

The general saluted with an arm straight forward and upward, turned about, and walked out of the field of view, muttering something dubiously under his breath. For a long time, all was silent. Then the metallic voice spoke:

"Earth men, I perceive you up on the roof about the ventilator." The leathery thing in the jar stirred and the machinery on the table clicked.

The group on the roof started in alarm, but the wizened little Haven regained his composure first.

"Who and what are you?" he exclaimed.

"You ask as though you had a right to demand," the metallic voice droned. "But it pleases me to inform you, Earth men, that I am a being of the planet Mars. Tired of the monotony of life in our dull world, I decided to emigrate. I came peacefully."

"*Peacefully!*" exclaimed the lieutenant, but the metallic voice went on as though he had not spoken:

"I harmed no one until your people attacked my walled enclosure and destroyed my defenders. They have suffered. I am sorry. Let me alone, and I shall not molest you. I wish you no harm."

"But!" exclaimed Haven, "you cannot take possession of a hundred acres of land that belongs to other people, and lay waste to thousands more. That is their land. They will fight for it. How can they let you alone?"

"It is better for you not to bother me. The science of Mars is still millions of years ahead of yours—"

There arose a shouting and a clatter among the guards below. Their suspicions had been aroused by sounds on the roof. A trampling of feet toward the building increased in volume. The trio hurried to their plane, swung it about by the tail, and jumping in, took off with a roar, leaving a band of gaping legionnaires below, John eventually found himself in his bed at about three o'clock in the morning, and even then too exhausted to sleep. Questions kept running through his mind.

The creature's claim that it was a Martian made things more mysterious instead of less so. It was not possible to transport these hundreds of thousands of men from Mars. And the buildings and chariots and horses. It would have taken an enormous tonnage of vessels, whose arrival certainly would have been noticed. And to think that Mars was inhabited by Roman soldiers was a most preposterous and childish notion. And if the Martians were as far advanced in science as they claimed, why did they use the military methods of ancient Rome? Certainly there was still plenty about this that had not been explained.

John slept late and awoke exhausted by his previous day's unwonted stress. But the thundering of guns would let him sleep no longer. The radio told him that fighting was going on up around Sioux City and westward toward Fremont and Norfolk. Always the reports carried the same statements of the incredible slaughter of innumerable Roman soldiers by the modern engines of war against which their swords and shields meant nothing. It was an unbelievable nightmare, creepy, horrible destruction of life and a soaking of the earth with blood, and piling up of mounds of dead bodies scores of feet high on the green and peaceful prairies. The reports ended up with an optimistic note that airplanes with high-explosive bombs were due to arrive from the East at any moment.

Then his telephone rang. It was his dean calling him to a conference with the Commanding Officer of the area. The smiling aviation lieutenant was also present. They were discussing the advisability of destroying the Martian in his building, and thus stamping out the rest of the trouble.

"It might not necessarily stop all trouble, you know," the medical dean said; "those curious men are still loose in large numbers. I think that the creature, instead of being destroyed, ought to be captured and studied."

The dean's view finally prevailed, and it was decided to avoid destroying the spot on which the Martian stood. The adjutant was already busy directing. Army and Navy planes were now arriving in swarms from East and West. Arrangements were made to bomb all around the Martian's retreat, and then raid it with a small party when everything was clear.

Grimly, methodically, the Army and Navy fliers went about their tasks. They systematically covered the entire contested territory with high-explosive bombs. In three hours, a Nebraska county was a field plowed by a giant, in which persisted one little island, the long house in the walled enclosure, with its red-glowing chimney. Airplanes landed a platoon of the National Guard on the river, and these marched to the surviving building and searched it thoroughly. With them was John and his friend the aviation lieutenant, and also the dean and the Latin professor. They found nothing anywhere, except in the room below the ventilator, where the Martian was still sealed in his glass jar.

"Earth men!" the metallic voice said suddenly, and the leathery body jerked in surprise. "*Homines terrae!*"

Professor Haven spoke in Latin. He was imbued with the educated person's ideal of courtesy in the victor. "We regret to inform you that we have destroyed all of your men—"

"I have been watching you," the metallic voice said. Its tone conveyed no feeling, but the attitude of the branched body was weary. "I am surprised I must have missed something."

"Eh? What's that?"

"I must have missed something in my observations. After all, your fighting machines are very simple. I could have destroyed them in a breath, only, I did not know you had such things. I cannot understand why I did not find them before."

The men stood in silence, looking at the dry, hard looking thing, not knowing what to say. Finally the metallic speaking began again. John noted that the voice came from a metal diaphragm among the apparatus on the table, to which the cords led from the creature in the jar.

"I cannot understand it. When I planned to migrate to the Earth, I came here and remained many years, studying many men, their bodies, their language, their methods of fighting—fighting was something new to me, and I enjoyed it; we do not have fighting on Mars. I took all necessary observations so that I might prepare to live among them.

"Then I went back home and spent sufficient time in research to make everything perfect. Of course it took a long time. I devised a suit in which I could stand in your atmospheric pressure, heat, and moisture; methods of transporting the nuclei of my apparatus to the Earth and growing them into proper bulk when I arrived, so that I might carry only very little with me. I was especially interested in devising methods of growing human beings on suitable culture media. I developed men who were just a little larger and a little stronger than yours; yet not too much so, because I wanted to see good sport, though remaining sure of winning you over in the end—"

"Cultured these men!" Professor Haven exclaimed. He lagged a little in using his Latin words. "You mean you grow them like we grow bacteria in test-tubes?" He got his meaning across by many words and much effort.

"I grew these soldiers on culture media," the metallic voice answered, and a shriveled arm gestured in a circle. "With a forced supply of air for carbon, oxygen, and nitrogen, and water for hydrogen, I can grow a man in a few hours; or as many men at once as I have culture medium and containers for. They grow by simultaneous fission of all somatic cells."

"So they are not really human?" Haven seemed much relieved at the idea that the destruction might not have been that of human life.

"That depends on what you mean by human," the dried-up Martian said, by means of his machine. "To me, it means nothing."

"That accounts for the queer differences our pathologist found," the dean observed when the fact had been translated to him that these hordes of men were cultured in a laboratory.

"Now that you have me in your power," the Martian continued, "please explain to me how you kept all your destructive engines hidden when I was here on my preparatory observation trip."

The dean of the Medical School touched Haven on the shoulder. "Ask him how long ago he was here."

"It took me," the machine said, "just about a thousand years (our year is twice as long as yours) to work out my methods of transportation, maintenance, and culture, and to make a voice instrument with which to talk to these culture-soldiers."

The dean turned toward the Commanding Officer.

"Two thousand years ago," he said. "The Romans were just about at the height of their military glory. Explain that to him, and how the world and its people have changed since."

The queer, seaweed-like creature nodded in comprehension and settled itself down in its jar in resignation.

"That is the point I overlooked. For millions of years, the Martians, at the zenith of scientific knowledge, have remained stable. The idea of human change, of progress in civilization, had slipped my mind. Our race has forgotten it. Your race progressed, and left me behind."

A little discussion arose among them. All agreed that it would be most interesting and valuable to preserve the Martian carefully in some museum. A great deal of useful information could be obtained from him. Many benefits would accrue to humanity from his knowledge.

"Only," reminded the Commanding Officer, "how much power does he still have left for doing harm?"

The dean was interested, and bent close to the jar to have a better look. He put his hand on the glass.

There was a quick rush and a crash of furniture. The big Roman general leaped up from beneath a couch, where he had been concealed. With sword upraised he dashed at the dean.

"Look out!" shouted John.

The Roman general gave a hoarse cry. Fortunately it took a goodly number of seconds for him to cross the room. The Commanding Officer was tugging at his pistol holder. His automatic came out fairly quickly and banged twice. The Roman came rushing on almost to within a foot of the muzzle.

Then his sword dropped with a clatter on the floor; his helmet rolling several feet away. The case tipped. It toppled. It looked almost as though it would go over.

Then it settled back; but a crackling sound came from it. A crack appeared in the glass, and wound spirally around it. There was a sizzle of air going into the jar. Machinery clicked and sparks crackled.

The creature inside jerked convulsively, and then was still. In a few minutes it began to bloat, and a red mold spread rapidly over it.

Appendix I
The Future of Scientifiction

The outstanding characteristics of every period in human history have been reflected in the literature of that period. Fiction, especially, is more free to concern itself with the everyday life of the common man, than is any other form of literature. In ancient times the hero of the common man was the warrior and the orator, and the epic poem, which is the fictional type of the ancients, contains nothing but war and oratory — unless it be love, which is common to all ages. The fiction of the Middle Ages is distinguished by religion and chivalry; that of early modern times, when men broke out of their narrow corner in Europe and explored the world, is distinguished by adventure and romance. In recent fiction, what do we find as the preponderating element? Industrialism, politics, finance. What men do in real life, they do in books.

Science in fiction is not new. I saw an account of a trip to the moon by one Cyrano de Bergerac, written in the sixteenth century. There must be older examples. But, stories of that type, like Mrs. Shelley's *Frankenstein*, were few and far between; and certainly found a limited reading public.

Few men know or care anything about science. The average reader is not a student; he reads the familiar things that come easy.

It is only in recent years that Science has begun to invade the everyday life of the everyday man. Up to yesterday, science was a thing set apart; it dwelt in the sacred laboratories, which none but the initiated few might enter. Who wanted to write about it? Still less did anyone want to read about it? Today, science does for the common man in his daily life more marvelous miracles than the mightiest monarch of old could command. Did Solomon or Caesar ever ride as luxuriously as does your grocery clerk every Sunday in his Ford? Not only does the humblest of us have in his own home and under his hands such things as the radio, the electric washer, vacuum cleaner, refrigerator, the modern automobile; not only does he daily see such marvels as the airplane, the talking picture in colors, the wonders of surgery, of printing, of the phonograph, of telephony — but new things are constantly coming to remind him of the vast and thrilling possibilities of what is yet to happen.

The average man has ceased to wonder at the miraculous accomplishments of science; it is all a part of his everyday existence.

Not merely the material *impedimenta* of science, but the thought and method of science is becoming part of the life of the people of this nation. The lives and efforts of a constantly increasing percentage of them are becoming involved in science in one way or another. A hundred years ago the proportion of people that came into intimate contact with it was insignificant. Today, who shall say what proportion is constantly occupied in one way or another, directly in the service of our mistress? All the way from the men at the head of great research organizations and teaching in the high institutions of learning, on down to the humble repair man who "services" your radio or "finishes" your Kodak prints, science catches the many in her net. All these people live with science, and more or less *for* science. In one way or another they *think* science. Their number is great, and it is constantly and noticeably increasing.

Is it unreasonable, therefore, to predict that an increasingly large part of our country's population will want science served up in their fiction, rather than war or chivalry or exploration? Is it far-fetched to suppose that the fiction-writer's imagination, which, to please the reader, has heretofore exercised itself on the heights of Olympus and in the African jungles, with black magic and the Wild West, will soon for the same reason have to delve into the atom, press out past the confines of the solar system, and deal with intricate apparatus? If war comes next to love in the writings of men, when everyone is occupied with war, will not science come next to love when everybody lives by science and almost everybody works with science?

Scientific fiction as a fine art is truly new. Rarely does any fine art spring fully developed from the brow of its goddess. Years, decades of painful evolution will yet be necessary before Scientifiction can take its seat at the banquet, fully recognized by her sisters, Drama, Historical Romance, the Novel, etc. Scientifiction of today is not yet perfect; and those of us who write it recognize that fact better than anyone else. When we attempt to wed two such dissimilar personalities as Science and Literary Art, it is but natural that there should be a period of adjustment before conjugal life is perfect. But the point I make is, that progress is being made, *right now.*

Amazing Stories is a pioneer. Our Magazine is ineradicably down in history as the leader with the far-flung vision. A hundred or a thousand years in the future, men will point back to it as the originator of a new type of literary art. In the meanwhile, the art is spreading. Scientifiction is gradually creeping into general literature. Old writers are turning attention to it; new writers are developing. Above all, public interest is increasing.

There is a great, fallow development going on at the present moment. Some day the public will wake up to an intense, conscious interest in Scientifiction. Just as in the past in the realms of war, exploration, or mystery, so it will be in science: man will use fiction to express his pride in the deeds he has done, and his dreams of the things he wants to do and has not yet accomplished.

Appendix 2

Selected Letters

Amazing Stories, July 1928
Editor, *Amazing Stories:*

I note your various remarks in *Amazing Stories,* expressing the hope that the advertising in your pages will increase sufficiently to put the magazine on its feet financially. And, knowing that the amount of advertising depends directly on the extent of circulation, I am offering the following suggestion.

Your various letters of criticism from readers both *pro* and *contra,* are nevertheless from readers who are interested. Even to criticize a story unfavorably, a man must have displayed sufficient interest to read it through. You hear from readers of a scientific cast of mind; I have heard from members of "hoi polloi," the vast masses who like a good story, but are not particularly scientific.

Are you curious as to what they think of *Amazing Stories?*

After all, their money is good to you, and you can have it if you please them.

Their opinion, often crudely and inarticulately expressed, coincides with mine.

"Too dry," "too much mathematics," "too much stuff that doesn't mean anything," "too much theory," and so on, all mean that *the stories have a tendency to lack a modern literary quality.*

I don't care how much science you put in, if the stories conform to modern literary standards, the above criticisms will not occur. Let your stories have plot and unity of impression, and the general reader will like them, in spite of the science. He will buy your magazine by the millions.

I have tried to send you examples; yet I am not a literary star. "The Stone Cat," "The Riot at Sanderac," "A Little Here Below," and "The Puzzle Duel" are primarily literary; yet they contain all the science that a reader can take at one dose.

Which is the better purpose for your magazine, to provide light entertainment for the science people; or to carry the message of science to the vast masses who prefer to read fiction?

If I ever make any large success as a writer it will be to reflect the interaction of modern science and human nature—but that can't be done by handing out large suffocating doses of science.

Miles J. Breuer, M.D.
Lincoln, Neb.

Amazing Stories, April 1930
Editor, *Amazing Stories*:

Every now and then you publish a really first-class piece of *Scientifiction*; one that ranks with the good literature of the day and is worthy of living in some more permanent form than the covers of a magazine. This time I wish to congratulate you on "The Chamber of Life," by G. Peyton Wertenbaker.

Scientifiction, primarily, must entertain. In that way it differs from science, which may or may not entertain; for the principal function of a scientific article is something different from entertainment. But, in order that a short-story (by this term I mean the very specialized form of literature that has developed during the past fifty years) with a scientific foundation be entertaining, it has to fulfill some other stringent and difficult requirements. Some sort of a raving fancy, a wild, incoherent hodge-podge of machinery, or of stunts with rays or hypnotism or impossible apparatus, or some melodramatic adventure in the middle of South America or on Venus, among some caricatures of beings who express the inconsistencies of the author's psychology rather than any scientific principles — these things cannot possibly be entertaining to a person with an orderly mind, a scientific training and a taste for good literature. There are many such persons, and they deserve a good story now and then. Scientifiction can only entertain by sticking close enough to the orderliness of probability to resemble science at least superficially, and then by leading off the imagination of the reader on paths of exploration and speculation that actually do lead somewhere, without breaking his "imagi-nationary" neck.

Scientifiction has a definite mission in literature. To be successful, to receive the approbation of intelligent people, to *live* in the literary world, it must do one of three things: (1) It must express some new idea, some step forward in scientific imagination; it must look forward to what can be done, and probably will be done; (2) it must carry over scientific atmosphere and scientific information in a pal-atable form to the non-scientific reader. The busy man's best way of getting a whiff of geology is through a good geological scientifiction story; (3) or, it must display the interaction between human nature and scientific progress. After all, the most interesting things about science are not its own facts, but what it does to people.

Mr. Wertenbaker has remarkably fulfilled the third, but especially the first of these requirements. I think his "Chamber of Life" is a brilliant conception. It is a perfection and idealization of what we try to accomplish when we read a story or a book, or go to a movie. It is *entertainment* carried to its highest refinement. In a way, it is but a simple, logical conception, merely one step in reasoning ahead of the sound-and-color movie; but that is what all really great things are: simple. It is the great and simple things that moves us, not the vast, complex, labored efforts to soar and to cover the universe. Mr. Wertenbaker's idea certainly made a very powerful impression on my mind.

The other quality of excellence in his story is of course the workmanlike manner in which he put it together. I know nothing about him, and am quite curious to know if he is a professional writer. Correct short-story technic requires principally a proper knowledge of psychology; the psychology of the reader, and of the characters in the story. And Mr. Wertenbaker evidently has these, and has constructed a story that combines the two things that one does not see combined as often in scientifiction as one would like—a clever, original conception, and good story technic.

I hope you can get more stories like it, both from him and from others like him.

Miles J. Breuer
Lincoln, Nebraska.

Amazing Stories, January 1931
Editor, *Amazing Stories*:

Permit me to commend your November number. I am very much interested in your publication, and it gives genuine pleasure every time you get out some good things. I've never been an editor and don't know how it feels; but I rather imagine that in these days of quantity production and high pressure living and superficial achievements, an editor of a science-fiction magazine must be up against it sometimes if he really prefers literature to twaddle. I judge that by the stuff I read in the general run of science-fiction magazines. As far as my own reading goes, ninety percent of present-day science-fiction as a whole is on about the same plane as the general run of Wild West and low-brow detective tales. I can imagine the editor raising his hands to heaven and supplicating Providence to send him something with the least bit of literary flavor in it.

The November number was good; but two of the stories appealed to me especially as a student of the literary phases of science-fiction. One was Stanton A. Coblentz' "Missionaries From the Sky." Heretofore I have preferred Mr. Coblentz' (if there is a "doctor" or a "professor" before your name, please indulge my ignorance of that point) popular-scientific essays and books, to his fiction. Up-to-date he has not taken into consideration the fact that pure fantasy is not literature, and cannot appeal to the cultured reader. His stories have been largely untamed and unconfined soarings into the realms of scientific speculation, without the touch of realism that is demanded in modern literature, and with little interest in character and human motive. But, I like "The Missionaries From the Sky" partly because it is short. (Poe was right; many years ago he wrote that a long literary work cannot be a work of art, because attention and emotion cannot be sustained for a long time.) Partly because it gives us drama, conflict of human motives. And partly because it attains an atmosphere of realism, without which no science-fiction story can be anything else than a psychological document, interesting to the psychiatrist who is studying the mental state of the writer, but to no one else. Mr. Coblentz has the scientific background; I rejoice very much to see him also developing the literary touch. All I know about him is what I gather from reading his stories in this magazine, and all I say is based on such reading and on nothing else. Come again, Mr. Coblentz, with a *short* one, with real people and a convincing atmosphere.

The other is Jack Williamson's "The Cosmic Express." I have been intensely interested in Jack Williamson ever since I made his literary acquaintance. Though his first story showed chiefly promise of future possibilities, yet the promise was there. I have hoped that he would realize that real lovers of literature cannot possibly be interested in the play of rays on some distant asteroid, or the conflict of imaginary monsters that strained one's receptive imagination. I have hoped that he would understand that the only thing that the readers of the ages are interested in is *people*: what they are, but especially, what they do. I knew he would do it some day, and he has done it in "The Cosmic Express." In this story he has worked out one of the principal *raisons d'être* of science-fiction: the effect upon human nature and human action of mental progress, and the reaction of the one upon the other. Science is here, apparently to stay; human nature is here and always has been. What is going to be the result of the presence of this new thing, only come among us yesterday, scientific and industrial progress? Philosophers can tell us, perhaps. But how much better can the science-fiction writer tell us! And Mr. Williamson certainly caught the note this time. I was surely glad to see it, Mr. Williamson, and I hope you do it again.

Now I surmise that the readers of this magazine are thinking, that instead of wasting his time on long letters like this, Dr. Breuer ought to get to work and write a story of the type that he wants to see so badly. I agree; but it isn't so easy. The kind appreciation of my work that has appeared in these pages has done a great deal to encourage me and stimulate me to further effort; and I think any time that I spend in the praise of the work of other authors, will be well spent. Perhaps some of them will be urged to produce the *magnum opus* that we are always looking for.

Miles J. Breuer, M.D.
Lincoln, Neb.

Source Acknowledgments

These stories were originally published in *Amazing Stories* magazine: "The Man with the Strange Head," January 1927; "The Appendix and the Spectacles," December 1928; "The Gostak and the Doshes," March 1930; "On Board the Martian Liner," March 1931; "Mechanocracy," April 1932; "The Finger of the Past," November 1932; "Millions for Defense," March 1935.

"The Future of Scientifiction" and "Paradise and Iron" were originally published in *Amazing Stories Quarterly*, Summer 1929 and Summer 1930, respectively.

"A Problem in Communication" was originally published in *Astounding Stories*, September 1930.

"Mars Colonizes" was originally published in *Marvel Tales*, Summer 1935.

"The Oversight" was originally published in *Comet Stories*, December 1940.

Breuer's Science Fiction

This chronological bibliography of Breuer's works includes his stories and poems, as well as their subsequent reprintings, that do not appear in this volume.

"The Man Without an Appetite," *Bratrsky Vestnik*, c. 1916. Reprinted in: Groff Conklin, ed., *Great Science Fiction About Doctors* (New York: Collier Books, 1963). [*Note*: Julia Breuer sent this story to Conklin for the above anthology and indicated it first appeared in Czech in 1916, but it may have been an unpublished story from the *Amazing* era.]

"The Specter" (poem), *Weird Tales*, March 1927.

"The Stone Cat," *Amazing Stories*, September 1927.

"The Riot at Sanderac," *Amazing Stories*, December 1927.

"The Puzzle Duel," *Amazing Stories Quarterly*, Winter 1928.

"The Captured Cross-Section," *Amazing Stories*, February 1929. Reprinted in: *Avon Fantasy Reader #12* (New York: Avon Novels, 1950); Clifton Fadiman, ed., *Fantasia Mathematica* (New York: Simon and Schuster, 1958); Robert Silverberg, ed., *Other Dimensions* (New York: Hawthorn, 1973).

"Buried Treasure," *Amazing Stories*, April 1929.

"The Book of Worlds," *Amazing Stories*, July 1929. Reprinted in: *Avon Science Fiction Reader #2* (New York: Avon Novels, 1951); *Fantastic Stories*, April 1969; August Derleth, ed., *New Horizons: Yesterday's Portraits of Tomorrow* (Sauk City: Arkham House, 1999).

"Rays and Men," *Amazing Stories Quarterly*, Summer 1929.

"The Girl from Mars" (with Jack Williamson), *Science Fiction Series #1*, November 1929. Reprinted in: Jack Williamson, *The Early Wil-*

liamson (New York: Doubleday, 1975); Jack Williamson, *The Metal Man and Others: The Collected Stories of Jack Williamson, Volume One* (Royal Oak MI: Haffner, 1999).

"A Baby on Neptune" (with Clare Winger Harris), *Amazing Stories*, December 1929. Reprinted in: *Tales of Wonder* [Britain], Spring 1941, as "Child of Neptune"; Clare Winger Harris, *Away from the Here and Now* (Philadelphia: Dorrance, 1947); Donald Wollheim, ed., *Flight Into Space* (New York: Frederick Fell, 1950).

"The Fitzgerald Contraction," *Science Wonder Stories*, January 1930. Reprinted in: *Startling Stories*, January 1942.

"The Hungry Guinea Pig," *Amazing Stories*, January 1930. Reprinted in: Groff Conklin, ed., *Science Fiction Adventures in Dimension* (New York: Vanguard Press, 1953); *Amazing Stories*, October 1961; *Science Fiction Classics Annual*, 1970; David Hartwell and Kathryn Cramer, eds., *The Ascent of Wonder* (New York: TOR, 1994).

"Via Scientiae" (poem), *Amazing Stories*, May 1930.

"The Driving Power," *Amazing Stories*, July 1930. Reprinted in: *Tales of Wonder* [Britain], Autumn 1941, as "Lady of the Atoms."

"The Time Valve," *Wonder Stories*, July 1930.

"The Inferiority Complex," *Amazing*, September 1930.

"Sonnet to Science" (poem), *Amazing Stories*, December 1930.

The Birth of a New Republic (with Jack Williamson), *Amazing Stories Quarterly*, Winter 1931. Reprinted in: facsimile reprint by PDA Enterprises, 1981; Jack Williamson, *The Metal Man and Others: The Collected Stories of Jack Williamson Volume One* (Royal Oak MI: Haffner, 1999).

"The Time Flight," *Amazing Stories*, June 1931.

"The Demons of Rhadi-Mu," *Amazing Stories Quarterly*, Fall 1931.

"The Einstein See-Saw," *Astounding Stories*, April 1932. Reprinted in: *Avon Fantasy Reader #15* (New York: Avon Novels, 1951).

"The Perfect Planet," *Amazing Stories*, May 1932. Reprinted in: *Tales of Wonder* [Britain], Spring 1942, as "Breath of Utopia."

"The Strength of the Weak," *Amazing Stories*, December 1933.

"The Chemistry Murder Case," *Amazing Stories*, October 1935.

"Mr. Dimmitt Seeks Redress," *Amazing Stories*, August 1936. Reprinted in: *Amazing Stories*, October 1966.

"The Company or the Weather," *Amazing Stories*, June 1937.

"Mr. Bowen's Wife Reduces," *Amazing Stories*, February 1938. Reprinted in: *Amazing Stories*, September 1970.

"The Raid from Mars," *Amazing Stories*, March 1939. Reprinted in: *Space Adventures*, Winter 1970.

"The Disappearing Papers," *Future Fiction*, November 1939.

"The Sheriff of Thorium Gulch," *Amazing Stories*, August 1942.

In the Bison Frontiers of Imagination series